RED HAND

RED HAND

Shaun Clarke

Hodder & Stoughton

Copyright © 1998 by Shaun Clarke

First published in Great Britain in 1998
by Hodder and Stoughton
A division of Hodder Headline PLC

The right of Shaun Clarke to be identified as
the Author of the Work has been asserted by him in
accordance with the Copyright, Designs and Patents Act 1988.

10 9 8 7 6 5 4 3 2

British Library Cataloguing in Publication Data

A CIP catalogue record for this title
is available from the British Library

ISBN 0 340 70764 X

Typeset by Hewer Text Ltd, Edinburgh
Printed and bound in Great Britain by
Mackays of Chatham PLC, Chatham, Kent.

Hodder and Stoughton
A division of Hodder Headline PLC
338 Euston Road
London NW1 3BH

CHAPTER ONE

Billy Boy and his three musketeers, all with closely cropped hair under Nike baseball caps, open-necked shirts under bomber jackets, and blue jeans held high by braces to show off their badly smudged white trainers, met at the corner of their own street in West Belfast, just after noon. A cold wind was blowing, you could smell rain in the air, and the colour of the sky reminded Billy Boy of masticated chewing gum, which he used instead of smoking ciggies as he and his boyos swaggered along the pavement, pushing everyone else aside and receiving no argument.

This gratified them no end. To be feared was to feel grand. Thus, they were all grinning broadly as they hurried along to the Donegall Road, feeling right at home with the boarded-up doorways, broken windows, red-brick walls and garish Loyalist graffiti. They crossed the road as if they owned it, ignoring the swerving cars, giving the finger to the drivers who angrily hooted at them, performing like rap dancers when they reached the far side where the other pedestrians, observing them, kept a safe distance. Finally, they made their way down Roden Street to the back-alley garage of that senile old bastard, Jack Sinclair.

Jack was arse-up over the engine of a battered Ford Cortina, wearing his oil-smeared overalls, groping about in there, trying to fix something. Grinning, Billy Boy grabbed hold of Jack's bony hips and jerked him off his feet, forcing his head down until it was touching the lid of the air filter. Jack shrieked instinctively and kicked his legs frantically while the boyos cackled with mirth behind him.

'Ya fuckin' eejits!' Jack bellowed. 'Let me up!'

Ignoring him, Billy Boy said to the rake-thin, gaunt-cheeked Michael 'Head Case' Harrison, 'Go and turn the engine on an' let's give 'im a close shave with the fuckin' fan belt.'

'No!' Jack cried out in terror.

Laughing, Billy Boy slapped Jack on the shoulder and released him. He then grabbed him by the shoulders and spun him around until he was face front. Jack was beetroot-red with the sudden rush of blood to his head. His grey eyes, surrounded by crow's-feet, were wide with shock and anger.

'You fuckin' eejits,' he repeated.

'What's that?' Billy Boy said, cupping his hand over his right ear as if deaf. 'What did you call me?'

'Coulda fuckin' killed me,' Jack said, changing his tack to avoid angering Billy Boy.

'No great loss,' Billy Boy said, fearless as always in the presence of those who feared him. 'So where are the baseball bats, ya oul shite?'

'In the broom closet,' Jack said, wiping his sweaty face with an oily rag and leaving streaks of oil on his deeply lined, drink-flushed skin. 'But listen, Billy . . .'

Billy Boy cupped one hand over his ear again as his three musketeers went to the broom closet to collect the half-size baseball bats. 'What's that ya said?'

Though well over sixty, Jack was not remotely senile and certainly knew enough to fear the wrath of this bunch of hard lads. Nevertheless, feeling caught between two different kinds of fear – his fear of Billy Boy's wrath and his even greater fear of the Royal Ulster Constabulary – he said, 'Them baseball bats, Billy. Why do ya have to hide 'em *here*, like? I mean, I'm only an old man, not too many years left, an' if the firm get wind that those things are here, I'll have some quare explainin' to do.'

'Sure, we can't keep 'em in our homes, Jack. You know that. An' those bastards in the RUC aren't likely to suspect that a senile oul goat like you would be harbourin' offensive weapons, like. So shut up an' don't rile me.'

'All I'm sayin' is . . .'

Billy Boy cocked his hand over his ear again and asked, 'What was that, Jack?'

'Sure, I just want . . .'

'Some fuckin' peace an' quiet. Is that what ya want? I mean, we're out there in the streets, we're defendin' our community, an' all you can think about is yer own skin. Sure, yer as piss-weak as what comes out of your shrinkin' bladder an' that quare upsets me, Jack. Keep talkin' an' these fuckin' baseball bats'll be used on this thin excuse for a garage. Unholy mayhem an' destruction, ya shite-faced oul bastard, an' you'll have to close this dump up for good. Is that what ya want, like?'

'No, no, for God's sake . . .'

'Then button yer lip, Jack, before I get sick of yer yammerin' an' do yer head in.'

'Right, Billy Boy. Sorry.'

Leading his boyos back to the Donegall Road, baseball bat hidden under his bomber jacket, flick knife in the right-hand pocket, blood surging with anticipation, Billy Boy looked around him, at the dreary ruination of what had once been a pleasant road, and was reminded of the days, back in the late 1970s, when this area had been patrolled by the 'greens' (British Army troopers) in DPM clothing and fragmentation vests, armed to the teeth with sub-machine guns, assault rifles, pistols and CS hand grenades. Billy Boy had missed most of those days, but he had grown up on stories of how the Prods had fought the Provos, the RUC and the greens with every means at their disposal – assassination, sniping, bombing, kidnapping and torture – and he'd always deeply regretted having been born too late to take part in it. He could, on the other hand, just about recall himself at five years old, back in 1979, throwing stones at the Brits, screaming insults at them, and generally playing his small part in their harassment. God, he had loved it! Couldn't get enough of it. And now, with the greens gone, or at least greatly reduced in numbers, here he was, still in Belfast but in charge of his own gang, about to lay down the law and administer some punishment. It was compensation for all that he had missed when he was still a wee boy.

Turning off the main road, he led his three musketeers into a short, dead-end street that was lined with small terraced houses and had a high brick wall, covered with lurid Loyalist graffiti, raised at its far end. This often came in handy as no one with the need to do so (and many had such a need) could escape that way. Streets like this, while being a trap for those who lived in them, were a boon to those, like Billy Boy, who ruled them. They were as grim as they looked.

Billy Boy and his mates withdrew their baseball bats as they marched along the street, passing unemployed men in drab suits, heavily built housewives with scarves tied on their heads, and children playing on the pavement and road. Seeing Billy Boy and his motley crew, baseball bats now at the ready, the housewives scooped up their children or ordered them inside. Not wanting to bear witness to what was coming, the loitering men also hurried inside their homes, slamming the front doors behind them.

Billy Boy and his gang were trouble and everyone knew it.

They stopped at the home of Ralph Clarke, a local bookie who had been short-changing Billy Boy on his protection money by claiming to have earned less than he had done. When Billy Boy used the brass knocker, hammering noisily to announce his arrival, the door was opened by Mrs Clarke, a big middle-aged woman in a shabby flower-print dress, her greying dark hair in hair curlers. Before she could say a word, Billy Boy, a real expert, pressed his left hand over her face and pushed her roughly backwards down the hall, sending her tumbling onto the bottom of the stairs. Then, before she could scream a warning, he rushed into the small living room, followed by his boyos, all raising their baseball bats above their heads and bawling obscenities.

Still in his vest and pyjama bottoms, Ralph Clarke was seated on the sofa in the living room, flanked by his kids, one eight and one ten, watching a dumb quiz show on the telly. Before he could move, as his kids glanced up in fear, he was struck on the side of the head by Billy Boy's baseball bat, then grabbed by the hair and hauled down to the floor. Blood was already spurting from his head and the two kids were by now shrieking as Billy Boy and the others beat him senseless with their baseball bats, smashing him all to hell even as they laid into him with their trainers, kicking him this way and that.

'You cheatin' shite!' Billy Boy bawled, though he wasn't really angry, just doing his duty, like, not to mention having fun. 'Take that, you dumb, thievin' bastard!'

As the two kids howled and sobbed, huddling up on the sofa, their mother tried to rush into the room. Pushed back out by Tommy 'Bone Crusher' Reid (six foot, barrel-chested, dark-eyed and demented) she bounced off the hallway wall, fell back to the stairs again, and screamed like a stuck pig, adding to the general bedlam as Billy Boy and the others, still bawling obscene abuse, pummelled Clarke to a bloody pulp and continued kicking him around the floor. Then they demolished most of the living room with their baseball bats: smashing the TV set, sweeping bric-a-brac off the mantelpiece, pulverizing the cups and saucers on the table by the window, and tearing the curtains from the windows. Then they battered Clarke again, laying into him with their baseball bats, leaving him groaning incoherently on the floor in full view of his sobbing kids and hysterical wife.

Eventually satisfied, Billy Boy and his gang left the house, deliberately taking their time, ignoring the woman's shrieking and the sobbing of the kids, to saunter back along the street as if they owned it – which they did, in a sense.

'That should teach 'im, boss,' Dennis 'Big Boots' Welsh said, grinning moronically and walking bandy-legged on big feet that looked much bigger in their thick-soled white trainers.

'Ackay,' Billy Boy replied, feeling pleased with his morning's work and only regretting that his victim had been a fellow Prod instead of a Fenian. 'That little bastard won't cheat on us again. Now let's go for a belter.'

Returning to Jack Sinclair's garage, where Jack greeted them with fearful silence, they cleaned the blood off the baseball bats and stored them in Jack's closet. Then, exhilarated, all laughing and joking, they made their way back to the Donegall Road and on to a drinking club in another side street.

Like many of the establishments in this Loyalist area, the club was no more than a crudely constructed brick building with one door at the front, another leading into the narrow alleyway at the rear, and no windows at all. The walls looking onto the streets were decorated with large red-painted handprints, signifying the Red Hand of Ulster, and crude paintings of King William crossing the Boyne. Located strategically right next to the high brick wall that blocked off the end of the street, it too was covered in political graffiti, notably immense paintings of fearsome Loyalist paramilitaries wearing balaclavas and wielding a variety of weapons. The club looked grim from outside and was not much more inviting inside. The interior had walls of bare concrete, a dark linoleum-covered floor and naked light bulbs dimly illuminating its windowless gloom. It did, however, contain a DIY plywood bar, a stolen pool table, a couple of dart boards and an overhead TV set that constantly flickered silently, usually tuned to some sports programme, while rock music and Loyalist songs blared from overhead speakers. A pitiful attempt had been made to decorate the bare concrete walls with old newspaper cuttings about the Troubles and photos of previous martyrs to the cause, but these only lent a macabre air to the already tomb-like feel of the place. Fold-up tables and metal chairs stood in clusters on the floor; and the gloomy room, lacking ventilation, stank permanently of stale ale, cigarette smoke and sweat. The few women in the club looked every bit as rough as the men and, like the men, they drank heavily.

Ordering pints of Guinness, Billy Boy and his three musketeers exchanged greetings with the other denizens of this filthy dive, all hard men like themselves, though few were over twenty-five, then started boasting about what they had just done to that thieving wee bookie, Ralph Clarke. Billy Boy's vivid description of Clarke's sobbing kids, his hysterical wife and Clarke's bloody, broken condition when they had left him led to gales of laughter and encouraged a festive atmosphere along the bar.

Nevertheless, Billy Boy was intense and his mates, though trying to hide it, were growing nervous. They knew that Billy Boy was expecting news, either good or bad, and that if it were the latter Billy Boy was liable to go berserk and they would all be in trouble. For this reason, when another young man, Roy 'Joy Rider' Phillips, entered the club a few hours later and walked straight up to Billy Boy, his gaze hard and unblinking even in the smoky haze, all those around the bar fell silent, wondering what was coming.

'Well?' Billy Boy asked, trying to sound unconcerned, though his fierce blue eyes grew bright with anticipation. 'What's it to be?'

'You're almost in,' Joy Rider said.

When his mates all roared their approval, Billy Boy just nodded and looked smug, as if he had never doubted it for one second. Luckily, his boyos couldn't hear his heart pounding nor see his intense relief and excitement.

He was almost in. His day had come at last. There would be no turning back now.

Peace, my arse, he thought as he turned to the bar and ordered himself another pint of Guinness. *There'll be no peace once they've set* me *loose*.

He drank to that hopeful prospect.

CHAPTER TWO

Peter Moore had just finished his daily exercises, always extremely rigorous and performed without fail before breakfast, when his mobile telephone rang. Wearing only his boxer shorts and sweating profusely, having pushed himself to the limit as always, he dried himself with a towel as he removed the phone from the bedside cabinet and switched it on.

'Yes?' he asked.

'So what the hell have you been up to,' his wife Monica asked, 'that you're already breathing so heavily?'

Without thinking, Moore briefly closed his eyes, not wanting to face this so early in the morning. Opening them again almost instantly, he tried distracting himself by gazing down through the bedroom window of his small apartment, into the street where the trees were shedding their autumn leaves on cars parked tightly fender to fender. The street was located off Haverstock Hill in Belsize Park, London, and it still seemed new to him.

'Exercises,' he said.

'What kind?' Monica asked grimly.

'You know damned well that I exercise every morning, so stop making suggestive remarks.'

'Suggestive remarks with good cause. We've only been separated six weeks and I hear you're already playing the field.'

Moore sighed. 'Heard from whom?'

'Mutual friends. Is it true?'

'Some friends! No, it's not. So what do you want at this time in the morning?'

'It's after nine.'

'Just.'

'I was up three hours ago.'

'Bully for you.'

'I was up that early – as I always am these days – because I can't sleep at nights worrying about us.'

'Stop worrying, it's over.' Moore was breathing easier now, but he continued to wipe the sweat from his body as he gazed down on the street. He had the feeling he was being followed – he'd had the feeling for days – and was convinced that last night a man in a dark suit, possibly a pinstripe, hiding in blackness just outside the lamplight, had been observing his flat from across the road. Of course, he could be imagining the whole business, but it was best to be careful. It could be a private detective hired by Monica – he would not put it past her – but it could be more important than that. He had enemies everywhere . . .

'It's so easily over for you,' Monica said in her tight-lipped, carefully modulated, middle-class English way, 'because you've been through it so many times. How many times now, Pete?'

Pete sighed. 'Only twice,' he said.

'Twice *divorced*,' Monica corrected him. 'But more breakups than that. The two or three before me. Those other foolish creatures who lived with you for a long time, a couple of years or more, each imagining vainly that she'd be the one to finally pin you down. What fools we all are. And what a swine *you* are, Pete.'

Recalling those 'other foolish creatures', Laura and Jeanne, Madeleine and Rachel, Jacquie and . . . that other one, Pete felt a certain amount of guilt, but refused all the blame. He had treated all of them decently, or, at least, as best he could, but his lifestyle was the kind that few women could understand, let alone live with, and he couldn't help that. A man either gave in . . . to his women . . . or he gave up for good.

'It takes two to tango,' he said, 'and it takes two to dis-engage.'

'You're not to blame, right?'

'We were both to blame, Monica.'

'You're divorced twice and leave four or five others and it's never your fault?'

'I didn't leave them all. Some threw me out, remember?'

'I'd no choice . . . the way you live, Pete. No sane woman could stand it.'

'Well . . .'

'Disappearing for days on end, never saying where you'd gone, just leaving a note to say you'd be back in a few days and couldn't call in the meantime. Are we supposed to accept that?'

'I can't help . . .'

'Then all that exercising, day in and day out, getting into superb shape, only to suddenly start drinking like a fish and land up in trouble, sometimes in a police cell.'

'Not *too* often,' Pete said.

'Not to mention the other women – the phone calls and scented letters – and the endless demands from your other wives and the way you kowtow to them.'

'I have kids by two of them,' Pete reminded her, 'and that makes me responsible.'

'You really like it, don't you, Pete?' She wasn't listening to what he said. 'The more complicated the better. You have a low boredom threshold, so conflict kept you from being bored and you didn't care that it drove me to distraction and made me call my solicitor.' He knew that when she started using long sentences she was about to work herself up into a lather. He didn't need that this early in the day . . . 'And now, here you are, faced with divorce for the third time, with more legal aggravation, more debts, and you probably find it merely amusing. Is that decent, Pete?'

'I don't find it amusing,' Pete said, 'and I don't want this kind of conversation at this time in the morning. Why did you call?'

'I could call my solicitor again and stop the proceedings.'

Pete heard the slight tremble in her voice and prepared for the waterworks. 'No,' he said, 'I don't think so. It's too late for that.'

'It's never too late, Pete.'

'When I'm ordered out, I stay out. We've been separated for six weeks now, Monica, and I'm starting to like it.'

'You're a bastard, you know that?'

'I've already had all your insults.'

'You're going to end up a sad man.'

'We all end that way,' Pete said.

'You'll hear from my solicitor.'

'I already have,' Pete said.

'I'm going to take you for everything you've got.'

'That's not much,' Pete told her.

The line went dead and he switched his mobile off, then placed it back on the bedside cabinet. After dressing in an open-neck shirt, blue denims and sneakers, he glanced again down on the street, saw no one watching his flat, so went into his study to spend the rest of the morning working without actually going to the office. He was doing that a lot more these days. It was a sign of his increasing boredom. Monica had been right about that, at least: he did have a low boredom threshold and it was making him itch for another change, despite his many activities.

After switching on his computer, he picked up the phone and called his business partner, Stan Remington.

'Yes?' Stan said.

'It's me. Anything happening?'

'Obviously not enough to bring you into the office.'

'Not today, thanks.'

'Not even for lunch?'

'I'm having lunch with Mike Bentine.'

'That mad bastard! Pass on my regards.'

'I will.' The three of them had been buddies in the Special Air Service (SAS) until, four years ago, he and Stan had been RTU'd – returned to their original unit – and decided, when their time was up a few months later, not to stay in the service. Mike was still with the Regiment. 'So what's happening?'

'Not much,' Stan said. 'We've received a couple of overseas orders – the South African police – and an order for a CCTV system for a City bank. Nice little earners in both cases and they should keep us busy.'

'Good,' Pete said.

His main source of revenue came from the business he shared with Stan, selling audio and laser surveillance systems to banks, research establishments, security firms and wealthy individuals. However, most of his work in this line was handled by phone, fax or e-mail and did not require much personal customer contact. More interesting, as well as lucrative, was his part-time work as a private bodyguard to the rich and powerful. These jobs came along three or four times a year, usually involved overseas travel, generally lasted a week or so, and were the cause of Monica's complaint about his unexplained absences. But Pete desperately needed those jobs to stave off his boredom – that boredom he was suffering even now.

'We'll have lunch tomorrow,' he said.

'Yes, let's do that.'

'I'll come into the office at one.'

'Perfect,' Stan said.

Pete spent the rest of the morning at his desk, making calls to his various clients and responding to faxed letters and the daily stream of e-mail that came in from every corner of the globe. He kept waiting for Monica to ring him back and was grateful when she did not – since any further conversation between them could only lead to arguments. Nevertheless, he remained distracted and realized that he was starting to find this work almost unbearable. He wanted something new in his life. He needed something exciting.

About an hour before he was due to meet his former SAS buddy, 'Mad' Mike Bentine, he left his desk and went to look through the front window, down on the street below. Weak autumnal sunlight fell over the tightly packed cars and the trees that lined the pavements, but apart from a few passers-by there was no one of note down there. Nevertheless, he still had the distinct feeling that he was being watched.

Puzzled, he put on his jacket and left the apartment. Once outside, he glanced in both directions along the street, studying the parked cars and the few pedestrians, but he saw nothing that struck him as being odd. Satisfied, he made his way along the tree-lined street to Haverstock Hill, deliberately not looking behind him, then walked down to Belsize Park Underground station. There he caught a tube train to the West End.

In the train, which was crowded, he found himself studying the faces of those around him, many different ages and races, most weary, few smiling, trying to work out which one of them was watching him. He had no idea, but the feeling persisted that he was being observed.

Getting off at Leicester Square, he cut through Chinatown, packed, frenetic and colourful, then crossed Shaftesbury Avenue and entered Soho by way of Frith Street. He stopped near Old Compton Street, pretending to stare into a shop window, then glanced quickly left and right, hoping to see an odd movement, a hasty retreat, from one of the many people nearby, but again he saw nothing. Still convinced that he was being observed, he crossed Old Compton Street and continued walking, eventually entering a stylish restaurant named Soho Soho where he saw Mike Bentine already seated at a table with his back to the wall. Pete waved to him, then advanced to the table and took the chair facing him. Mike was nursing a whisky and smoking a cigarette. Though only thirty-five years old, with thick brown hair and slightly scarred, handsome features, he looked about fifty.

'Hi there,' he said, grinning through the smoke. 'As punctual as always.'

'And you're early, as always,' Pete replied.

'It's just my way of getting in an extra drink. So how are you, Pete?'

'Not bad.'

'And how's that mad bastard Stan Remington?'

'Stan's fine and sends his warmest regards.'

'And Monica?'

'I've heard from her lawyer.'

Mike grinned again. 'Another divorce, is it?'

'You make me sound like an American movie star, but I haven't married *that* often.'

'You've been married three times, lived with some others, had affairs in between, and in general led a pretty checkered life. You're not doing too badly, Pete.'

Looking back over his thirty-eight years, Pete realized that he *hadn't* done too badly, though he had often paid dearly for his pleasures. In fact, while many of his friends had expressed envy of his love life (the three marriages, live-in partners and many one-night stands), he wondered how all of that had come about and what it told him about his own nature.

It was not something good, he decided. In fact, he felt guilty about his many women and the four children of his first two marriages (he had visiting rights to the kids and spoiled them when he saw them), believing that they showed his weak character – a weakness based on his inability to commit to a lasting relationship. Right or wrong, he was a man who needed his freedom and could not settle down.

'Well, God's punishing me for my sins,' he told Mike. 'I'm in trouble again.'

'Trouble's your middle name. That's why you were RTU'd from the regiment. No doubt about it.' Mike and Pete had been in the

SAS at the same time, serving together in the Falklands War when they were both raw young men, then in the Gulf War in early 1991. Those, Pete knew, had been the best years of his life and now he often regretted his decision not to sign on again. He had made that decision for one reason only: the knowledge that, even if he had signed on again, he would not have been allowed back into the SAS. That knowledge, which wounded him deeply, had forced him back into Civvie Street, where he remained to this day. 'So what'll you have for an aperitif?' Mike asked him.

'Whisky's fine. On the rocks.'

Mike called the waiter and ordered two more Scotches. The waiter gave each of them a menu and went off for the drinks. Pete glanced around the restaurant and saw a lot of casually dressed young men and their attractive ladies. Most were talking excitedly, loudly, with a great deal of confidence.

'Christ, I feel old in here,' he said, turning back to Mike.

'Compared to this lot, we *are* old. London's become a city for the young – which is why I prefer it back in Hereford. The locals there actually make *me* feel young, so it's a good place to be.'

'I know what you mean,' Pete said.

They perused the menu at length, then ordered their meals and wine when the waiter returned with the whiskies.

'So how are things with the regiment?' Pete asked when the waiter, a suntanned and handsome young Italian, had left with the menus.

'Quiet,' Mike replied. '*Too* bloody quiet. There are no more wars to fight, old chum, which means that we can only retrain . . . over and over again. It's a real bloody bore.'

'But you're staying in?'

'Of course.' Mike shrugged. 'What else could I do after all these years? I'm in until I retire.'

'Still a DI?'

'More of a lecturer. I'm now with the CRW training wing. Since counter-revolutionary warfare is all we're likely to get involved with these days – if we even get that – I guess this new career choice is logical. All the real wars are over.'

'That's one of the reasons Stan and I left,' Pete said. 'After Iraq, there were no more wars to fight.'

'Bullshit. The pair of you left because you were RTU'd for

getting drunk and punching out a couple of officers. Both of you did that one too many times and were given the push.'

'From the regiment; not from the army.'

'After the SAS, who could stand being back with the greens?' Mike asked rhetorically, using 'greens' to describe the regular army.

'That's true. Not me, for sure.'

'You still miss the regiment?'

'Yes. I miss the excitement. That's why I hire myself out as a personal bodyguard. It's as near as I can get to the good old days, but it's still not enough.'

'You're drawn to trouble, that's your problem. You live and breathe for excitement. But you wouldn't get too much of that these days, even in the SAS.'

'I'm sometimes tempted to become a criminal,' Pete said, 'just to get that excitement back.'

'Let me know when you do it and I'll join you. But for now, let's just eat.'

Over the meal they reminisced about their fighting days with the regiment. Thus encouraged, Pete recalled vividly the only two wars he had experienced: the Falklands and Iraq. In 1982, only twenty-one at the time, he had fought with 22 SAS all the way from South Georgia to Port Stanley, East Falkland, surviving hunger, thirst, freezing cold, dreadful isolation, bombs, bullets, landmines and attacking aircraft, to gather vital intelligence, disrupt enemy communications and, when necessary, kill Argentine troops. Eventually, with his weary comrades – or, at least, those who had survived – he marched into Port Stanley and saw the British flag raised once again over Government House. He had thought at the time that this would be his only war, but approximately eight years later, in August 1990, after Iraqi tanks had rolled into Kuwait and put the world's oil reserves at risk, he had found himself, still with 22 SAS, enduring the fierce daytime heat, freezing night-time cold and torrential winter flash-floods of the desert as he took part in reconnaissance patrols, espionage and sabotage operations, and (even more dangerous, therefore even more exciting) daring hit-and-run raids in heavily armed 'Pink Panther' Land Rovers.

Alas, Operation Desert Storm lasted only a hundred days and after that there were no more wars to fight. War could certainly be hell but, right or wrong, some men loved it and Pete, being one of that breed, was bored mindless by peace. Back in Bradbury Lines, the SAS base in Hereford, he was assigned as a DI, or Drill Instructor, and grew more restless with each passing month. Though always a hard drinker, he now started drinking even more heavily, venting his frustrations in fist fights and other mischief until, when he and Stan Remington had had one too many drunken fights, the last time with some Army officers in a Hereford pub, they were thrown out of the SAS and returned to their original regiments. A few months later, when their second regular army terms were up, they left the service and went into business together.

'So how *is* the business?' Mike asked as he pushed his dessert plate aside and finished off the last of his wine.

'It's doing fine,' Pete said. 'It brings in the money and gives us something to do, but it isn't the same as fighting a war and that's what's getting to me. I'm edgy all the time – I want some action – and I don't know where to find it.'

Mike nodded his understanding. 'Yes, I know what you mean,' he said. 'The moralists tell us that war is hell, which it certainly can be. Unfortunately, for some, it's also seductive, though the moralists don't like to face that fact. You and me . . . we're the kind who tend to die a slow death when we're not being challenged or threatened. So no matter how hellish war supposedly is, those last two wars, in the Falklands and in Iraq, gave you and me the best days of our lives. That's a hard fact of life, pal.'

'Damned right,' Pete agreed.

When the bill had been paid and they were leaving the restaurant, Pete realized, with great discomfort if not actual shame, that almost certainly he had married three times and engaged in countless affairs, both long-term and short-lived, in a desperate, hopeless attempt to alleviate his chronic boredom by changing his life. Life, however, could not be changed that way and now, with this latest divorce, the piper was being paid.

After saying farewell to Mike and agreeing to meet him for another lunch next month (it was a monthly ritual) Pete walked towards Piccadilly Circus, intending to have another drink in his club in Victoria. However, the instant he started walking, his every instinct – instincts finely honed from years of dangerous surveillance work – again told him that he was being observed.

Though stopping and starting frequently – to gaze overtly into shop windows and covertly glance behind him – he saw no sign of a tail and started thinking that he might be imagining things. Determined to check whether or not his instincts remained sound, he continued walking: crossing Piccadilly Circus, going down Lower Regent Street to Waterloo Place, eventually taking the steps that led him to the Mall, then crossing the Mall and entering St James's Park. There, as he was circling around the sunlit pond, heading for Birdcage Walk, he glanced over his shoulder and saw a man in a pinstripe suit stepping out from the shifting shadows of an oak tree just ahead, his face pale and grave, his grey hair breeze-blown. The man raised his right hand in a gesture that was at once a silent greeting and a command to stop.

'Well, I'll be damned!' Pete whispered.

His instincts were still sound.

CHAPTER THREE

'And God bless you, too, my dear,' the Reverend William Dawson said, his voice histrionically resonant, bathed in oil, mellifluous, to the sweet-faced, grey-haired Protestant lady who, in her green overcoat, snow-white blouse and purple scarf, was trembling worshipfully before him. He squeezed her shoulder gently as she frantically shook his hand and then, to his embarrassment, turned it over to kiss the back of his wrist. Withdrawing his hand gently, he nodded surreptitiously to his grey-suited secretary Robert Lilly, adding, 'Always remember that I'm here to serve my congregation. Anytime, Mrs Reid.'

'God bless ya, Reverend Dawson! Ya do us proud! Sure, we love ya! God bless ya!'

Clearly overcome with emotion, Mrs Reid was still frantically intoning her blessings and declarations of love as Robert, bone-thin and white-faced, black hair plastered with haircream to his high forehead, expertly eased her out of the office and then stepped back inside. With a sigh, the large-framed Reverend went back around his desk and flopped back into his swivel chair. He clasped his hands together beneath his jowly, well-shaven chin and stared at Robert with eyes of the clearest blue. He sighed again, as if weary.

'Any more, Robert?'

'No more members of the church,' Robert informed him. 'Mrs Reid was the last one.'

'Thank God for that,' the Reverend said, leaning back in his chair and spreading his long athlete's legs under the desk, letting air in down there. Smiling at his secretary, he continued, 'No offence meant, Robert. As you well know, I respect the members of my congregation and, of course, my constituents, but there are times when their adulation becomes too much and makes me uncomfortable. Such adulation is seriously misplaced; it is the Lord they should worship.'

'Your humility is fitting, Reverend,' Robert said, 'and sets a good example to the rest of us.'

'I'm pleased to hear that,' the Reverend said, though in fact he had doubts about his own humility and could not help taking pleasure from the renowned adoration of his followers. In fact, he attended to the problems of his followers, both spiritual and material, in this spartan office in a modest side street in East Belfast, mere yards from his church, five mornings a week, with Saturday and Sunday given over to church services. While undeniably receiving satisfaction from this heavy responsibility, his constant exposure to human frailty and doubt, to the great and small problems of his tormented community, often wearied him and made him ashamed of his own limitations. Indeed, many a time, when he had finished his morning's work, his heart heavy with sadness at the sheer variety of the dismal problems brought to him, he had fallen to his knees, right here in this humble office, and begged the Lord to forgive him for his occasional uncharitable thoughts about those who came to him. He required forgiveness because sometimes they wearied him to the point of annoyance.

'So,' he said, 'what's next on the agenda? No doubt my day isn't finished yet.'

'I'm afraid not,' Robert confirmed.

'Well?'

Robert coughed into his clenched fist, then said, 'You have an appointment . . . an interview . . . with that reporter, Patricia Monaghan. She's waiting outside.'

Reverend Dawson frowned while running his fingers through his thatch of thick grey hair. 'Patricia Monaghan?'

'Yes, Reverend.'

'Isn't she . . . ?'

'Yes, Reverend, she's Catholic. A reporter for RTE Radio One in the so-called Republic of Ireland. She actually lives here in Belfast, in Stranmillis, but she works as a freelance.'

'I've heard of her,' the Reverend said, running his index finger down the bridge of his thin nose, then pursing lips that were oddly voluptuous in his otherwise hawklike patrician face. 'A strong-willed lady, I gather, and certainly not on our side. While not overtly supporting the Republicans, she's known for her sympathetic treatment of their cause. Why does she want to see me, of all people? She must know what I think.'

'She says she's collecting material for a radio programme about the uneasy peace and wants to include the Protestant point of view. As you're one of our most outspoken representatives, she thinks you should be featured.'

'I doubt that it's something that simple, but I suppose it's too late to say "no" now.'

'I think it would be a mistake, Reverend, to refuse to talk to her. She'd use the refusal to make it seem that you have something to hide.'

'Quite right. Show her in.'

The Reverend was pleasantly surprised when Patricia Monaghan was shown into his office and stopped in front of his desk. Having just spent the morning attending to the concerns of a great many Protestant women, most aged beyond their years by hardship, fear or grief, he was pleasantly surprised to note that Patricia Monaghan, though in her mid-thirties, was slim and long-legged in tight blue jeans, high-heeled boots, a revealing T-shirt tightly belted at the waist, and a short black leather jacket. Like most Belfast women, she had very pale skin, though in her case it was unlined, and her blonde hair framed delicate features and long-lashed bright green eyes.

'Well, Miss Monaghan,' he said, 'I must say this is quite a surprise. Most unexpected, indeed.'

'It's Mrs Monaghan,' she corrected him.

'So sorry. Please take a seat.'

'Thank you.'

The Reverend did not rise from his chair nor offer his hand. He merely indicated that she should take the chair at the other side of his desk. When she had done so, she removed a cassette recorder from her shoulder bag and set it up on his desk.

'Do you mind?' she asked as if it was an afterthought.

'No, of course not,' he said, convinced that no matter what he said, no matter what was recorded, she would edit the tape to suit herself – and not to his advantage. 'I gather that this interview is for a programme to be broadcast in the so-called Republic of Ireland.'

'It's the *legitimate* Republic of Ireland, Reverend Dawson, as you know full well.'

The Reverend smiled and clasped his hands beneath his chin to gaze steadily at her. 'I've heard that you're not easily intimidated and clearly it's true. So what's this programme about?'

'We're putting together an hour-long broadcast about the present uneasy peace and, for reasons of balance, we want to include the Protestant point of view. Naturally, as you're an ordained minister *and* a Member of Parliament – and, arguably, the most well-known Protestant minister in Northern Ireland – we think it's vital that your views should be included.'

'I'm hardly the most well-known Protestant minister in Northern Ireland,' the good Reverend corrected her. 'The Reverend Ian Paisley has that honour.'

'Not any more,' Patricia Monaghan informed him. 'With the recent success of Sinn Fein in local elections and the British government's increasing efforts to include them in the so-called peace process, Reverend Paisley is being marginalized as an out-of-date demagogue while you, Reverend Dawson, supposedly more reasonable, are coming forward as the new religious-political leader of the Protestant community.'

'I note your use of the word "supposedly",' the Reverend replied, 'and find it offensive. Do you mistrust me that much?'

'My personal views won't be included,' Mrs Monaghan replied, unperturbed. 'Can I turn the tape on?'

The Reverend ignored the question. 'From what I've read about you, Mrs Monaghan, and from your attitude this very moment, I take it that you still support the Republicans and strongly disapprove of the likes of me.'

'I don't actively support the Republicans, Reverend Dawson, though my general sympathies are certainly well known.'

'So how am I to believe that I'm going to be quoted accurately on your programme?'

'This isn't a newspaper interview, Reverend. You're being recorded and your own words will be heard.'

The Reverend smiled at her, then shook his head wearily. 'Come, come, Mrs Monaghan, I'm too experienced to accept that. No matter what I say, you can edit the tape in such a way that I'm made to seem as though I'm saying the very opposite to what I meant. You wouldn't do that, now, would you?'

He had said it in a jokey manner, to soften her up, but she was too smart to fall for it.

'That's not my reputation, though you'll hardly believe it, so either you give me the interview or you don't. It's your choice; not mine.'

'A good reply, Mrs Monaghan,' he responded, though he felt his teeth grinding. 'You may turn on the tape now.'

Studying her as she did just that, the Reverend realized that she was as tough as her reputation and that indeed he could not intimidate her. In truth, he respected her for this and was not bothered by it, though he knew that he would have to be careful while the tape was running. She was a Catholic and had Republican sympathies; that was all he needed to know.

'Reverend Dawson,' she said when she had turned on the recorder, 'you are at once an ordained minister of the so-called New Presbyterian Church and the head of the East Belfast Unionist Party. While both of these are, in a sense, breakaway groups, could you please explain how they came about?'

'May I just say, first of all, that I take exception to your use of the phrase "so-called" with regard to the New Presbyterian Church. While the New Presbyterian Church is, indeed, a breakaway group from the orthodox Presbyterian Church, it was formed and is run by properly ordained ministers, such as myself, and is therefore perfectly legitimate. As for the East Belfast Unionist Party, it was formed by myself as a protest against the recent betrayals of the Official Unionist Party – the largest political party in Northern Ireland – and, also, against the overt anti-Catholicism of the Reverend Ian Paisley's Free Presbyterian Church.'

'Another breakaway group from the orthodox Presbyterian Church,' Mrs Monaghan noted.

'Correct,' Reverend Dawson said.

'You've stated that you disapprove of the anti-Catholicism of the Democratic Unionist Party; yet, at the same time, you suggest that the Official Unionist Party is betraying the Protestant cause. How do you, a staunch Protestant and pro-British, reconcile these two seemingly disparate points of view?'

'It's true that I'm a staunch Protestant and openly pro-British

– certainly in the sense that I'm a British citizen and proud of it – but that doesn't mean that I approve of the kind of extreme anti-Catholicism being practised by the Reverend Ian Paisley and his Democratic Unionist Party. As for the Official Unionist Party, while I largely support its loyalty to Great Britain and Northern Ireland, I disapprove of its increasing tendency to support the inclusion of Sinn Fein in the ongoing peace negotiations.'

'So why do you believe Sinn Fein should be excluded? Is it because, as a Protestant, you still believe that the Catholics can't be trusted?'

'I refuse to be drawn into a blanket condemnation of all Catholics, most of whom, indeed, support neither Sinn Fein nor the IRA. I will say, however, that I *am* both a Christian and a Unionist. As a Christian, a Protestant, I naturally disapprove of the Church of Rome and do not wish to see Popery taking over the religious freedoms of my community. As a Unionist, I take the view that the composition of Great Britain – England, Scotland, Wales and Northern Ireland – has existed for hundreds of years and therefore represents a stability that neither I nor most of my constituents wish to see changed. Unfortunately, while the majority of Catholics think the same way, a fanatical minority, both here and in the Republic of Ireland, thinks differently and wishes to impose its heretical beliefs on the Protestant majority.'

'By fanatical minority, you clearly mean Sinn Fein.'

'Correct.'

'Yet Sinn Fein has repeatedly won seats in local elections, which proves that they have *some* support in the community. Do you not therefore feel that they have a legitimate right to be included in future peace talks?'

'I'm not interested in whether or not Sinn Fein has *some* support,' Reverend Dawson said, speaking clearly and with conviction, 'because, as both a minister of the church and a politician, I'm obliged to take a stand against what they represent – which is, of course, violent insurrection.'

'Surely, with this argument, you're confusing Sinn Fein with the IRA. The former is the *political* wing of the latter and, as such, isn't involved in violence.'

'Nonsense! Sinn Fein is the political *front* for the IRA and, as such, when it cannot win by reason and argument, it quietly supports the latter's violent, often barbaric activities.'

'But violent, barbaric activities aren't the sole province of the IRA. Can you justify the atrocities of Protestant groups such as the UVF?'

'Violence begets violence and the bestial behaviour of certain Loyalists only lends strength to my argument. So long as Sinn Fein acts as a front – I repeat: a *front* – for the IRA, it must be viewed as supporting violence as part of an ongoing plan to destroy Northern Ireland – *Protestant* Ireland – and replace it with a so-called united Ireland – so-called in the sense that few citizens, north or south, want it. It would, after all, be a united Ireland beset with all the evils of communism and Popery. I am a Christian and a Unionist, Mrs Monaghan, so I say this with feeling.'

Reverend Dawson could see that his words were incensing the Catholic reporter, but her growing rage only made those words seem much grander to him. Sitting back in his chair, he took his hands from beneath his chin and let them rest, slightly apart, on the desk in front of him. The very attractive Patricia Monaghan stared steadily at him, her green eyes uncommonly bright, though displaying no warmth.

'You insist that you're not anti-Catholic,' she said eventually, her voice soft, controlled and even slightly seductive, 'yet everything you've said so far indicates that you don't trust the Catholics at all.'

'I am a Protestant, Mrs Monaghan, and the word itself describes what we are – in short: *we protest*.'

'Which means?'

'We take our pride in protesting against anything we don't believe in. So, we protest against Catholicism – though that doesn't mean we wish to suppress it as the Church of Rome would surely suppress us if it were given the chance.'

Mrs Monaghan, gravely lovely, stared thoughtfully at him as if trying to read his mind, then smiled slightly and asked her next, more dangerous question.

'Can I change the subject slightly, Reverend, by asking what you think of recent reports that certain UDA splinter groups have been assassinating prominent Catholics in the hope of encouraging an

IRA backlash that would, if it occurred, destroy the fragile peace process?'

'Why would they wish to do that?' the Reverend asked, though he had, without thinking, straightened up in his chair and was feeling distinctly uneasy.

'Right now, the British government, desperate for a resolution of the problem in the North, is backing away from its traditional commitment to the Loyalists. It's widely believed that an IRA backlash would bring the British army back here and compel the British government to turn away from the Republicans and support the Loyalists once more. This, in turn, would give back to the Loyalists the autonomy they had previously in the Six Counties.'

Aware that this very attractive, albeit steely woman, who could not herself be intimidated, was trying to intimidate *him*, the Reverend, not frightened but certainly cautious, took his time in replying.

'I can neither confirm nor deny that what you say is true, since Belfast is always awash in rumours. I *will* say, however, that anything is possible and that such reasoning may indeed be motivating certain splinter groups right now. But what, pray, has this question got to do with me, my church, or, indeed, my personal politics?'

Even as he asked the question, the Reverend leaned forward in his chair to look directly and, he hoped, honestly into the lovely green eyes of Mrs Monaghan. She, as he noted, leaned forward as well, casting her shadow on her still running portable cassette recorder, to let him see the steel in those green eyes that he had thought were so lovely.

A steel trap, he thought.

'Leaked intelligence reports indicate,' Mrs Monaghan said, still speaking quietly, though no longer sounding seductive, 'that one of the groups responsible for those assassinations is known as Red Hand – obviously an abbreviation of the Red Hand of Ulster – and that it's controlled by the Loyalist paramilitary group, the Ulster Defenders.'

'So?' Reverend Dawson asked, thinking, *A steel trap, indeed. Be very careful with this one.*

'Well, Reverend, it's certainly a well-known fact that the Ulster

Defenders group is fanatically anti-Catholic, as opposed to being merely anti-Republican, and was, in its early days, a Protestant youth movement funded by your East Belfast Unionist Party. Do you have any comment?'

Realizing that this woman was indeed intimidating him, the good Reverend leaned even farther forward, cupped his chin in his hands again, and tried to hide his concern behind a smile that had little warmth in it. His blue eyes, he knew, could be like laser beams and he tried to make them so now.

'I understand what you're driving at,' he said, 'but I'm afraid you're quite wrong. While it's true that in the early days of the East Belfast Unionist Party – indeed, shortly after our formation – we funded a Protestant youth movement called the Ulster Defenders, it's equally true that the youth movement was not then involved with any kind of violent activity – it was *politically* motivated: canvassing and so forth. When, a few years later, it was taken under the wing of the UDA and turned into a paramilitary group, we washed our hands of it. So neither the East Belfast Unionist Party, nor myself as an individual, have anything whatsoever to do with the present-day Ulster Defenders – nor with its Red Hand splinter group. Those are the facts, Mrs Monaghan.'

But the beautiful – and beautifully deadly – Mrs Monaghan was not about to let him off so lightly. 'I can find no record,' she said, 'of a public denunciation of the Ulster Defenders by the East Belfast Unionist Party. Was such ever made?'

The Reverend took a deep breath, then let it out again in an embarrassingly audible, drawn-out sigh. 'No,' he said after that lengthy, tingling pause. 'No public denunciation was ever made.'

'Why not?'

'A human mistake, Mrs Monaghan. Because we were embarrassed that a youth movement funded by our party and, therefore, allied to our church, had been turned into a particularly vicious Loyalist paramilitary group. A mistake, I repeat . . . an all too human error . . . but that's *all* it was.'

'So are you willing to confirm now, for the record, that neither the New Presbyterian Church, the East Belfast Unionist Party, nor yourself personally, has anything to do with either the Ulster Defenders or the Red Hand splinter group?'

'I can confirm it absolutely,' the Reverend said.

'Thank you, Reverend Dawson.'

Mrs Patricia Monaghan turned off her cassette recorder, placed it back in her shoulder bag, then stood up and, without another word, walked out of the office. When she had gone, Reverend Dawson called Robert Lilly into the office and stared thoughtfully at him.

'That woman could be trouble,' he said eventually. 'Let's keep a watch on her.'

'Yes, Reverend,' Lilly replied. 'I think that might be wise.'

'These damned Catholics!' the Reverend muttered under his breath before kneeling in prayer.

He had some sins to atone for.

CHAPTER FOUR

When they picked Billy Boy up, just after ten in the evening, his knees were practically knocking – though he wasn't about to let them see that. They had told him to be outside his local club at ten and he was there just as they'd demanded when they pulled up to the kerb in what looked like an ordinary Ford Cortina, though it was, as he realized when he clambered into the back, lined with reinforced, bulletproof steel plates. There were three of them in the car – two up front and one beside him – all about his age, and though they didn't say a word, they all turned to stare at him with eyes that resembled the kind of holes he made when he pissed into the snow on a winter's night, which he often did after having a good blinder. Black holes in the off-white snow: that's what their eyes looked like. When he saw those eyes, he knew these guys were the hardest of the hard men and that there was no possibility of going back now. Well, he could be as hard as they were and, he told himself as the car turned into the Donegall Road, he probably was already.

You can't fucking scare me, he thought, *'cause I'm already even harder than you. Better fuckin' believe it.*

His knees stopped knocking after that, though some nervousness remained because, even though they were no longer staring at him, the ignorant bastards still hadn't said a word to him.

'So where we goin', like?' Billy Boy asked as the car continued along the Donegall Road, passing shop windows covered with protective metal shutters, brick walls covered with Loyalist graffiti and the usual gangs of young hoodlums who gathered nightly at the end of the lamplit side streets to smoke, drink beer from cans and perhaps deal in crack or Ecstasy with the growing number of drug pushers.

'Shut yer mouth,' the kid beside him said – and that was *all* he said.

Billy Boy shut his mouth, knowing what was good for him, and contented himself with staring out the window as the car turned into Sandy Row and headed along a road lined on both sides with shops of all kinds, including bookies. It was a shabby-looking place, with waste ground between ruined buildings where shadowy figures lurked, though it looked perfectly normal to Billy Boy, except for the fact that it had no pubs. This, he had learned from his Dad, was because during the real Troubles, Sandy Row was where the Loyalist hard men had congregated and the pubs, natural targets for the Provos, had gradually been closed down and replaced with well protected drinking clubs. The pubs had never reopened.

This, however, was not a problem in the Shankill Road, the Loyalist heartland. Billy Boy always experienced an odd feeling of loss when he visited the Shankill, either by day or by night, because he had heard so many stories of the Good Old Days, before his time, when the Troubles had been at their height, RUC checkpoints had blocked off many side streets, and the roads were patrolled constantly by heavily armed British soldiers. Billy Boy always regretted that he'd missed that particular time, when men his age had fought the British troops with automatic weapons, pistols, home-made petrol bombs and even bricks. But the Brits had long since gone and the check-points had been removed, leaving only a pretty normal, if decidedly seedy, working-class road packed with shops, pubs, cafés, chippies, bookies, video shops and second-hand-furniture shops. As usual, gangs of men, either young or elderly though invariably segregated by age group, stood at the street corners or outside the pubs and bookies, bathed in pools of yellow lamplight, smoking, drinking and having a good bit of crack – conversation, not drugs. In fact, the Shankill Road looked just like the Falls, the Republican heartland, which was located mere minutes away from it. This ensured plenty of aggro on both sides and helped keep up the tension.

Turning off onto one of the many seedy side streets, the Ford moved between rows of shabby terraced houses, many still bricked up, and eventually stopped at the far end, facing a closed garage, near a brick wall covered with a large painting of two men wearing black balaclavas and preparing to fire their semi-automatic weapons over a coffin decorated with the Red Hand of Ulster and inscribed: *UVF – UDA: In Memory of Fallen Comrades.*

Billy Boy studied that poster with pride, though he didn't move from his seat until the piss-hole-eyed kid beside him slipped out first and then beckoned for him to follow. The other two stayed in the car, keeping an eye on the quiet lamplit street, while the kid who had been sitting beside Billy Boy led him up to the dicker – a teenager used as a lookout – who was standing by the closed doors of the garage. The dicker had a shaven head and was wearing off-white Nike basketball boots and a navy-blue tracksuit under a shabby red-and-white ski jacket. The kid who had been sitting beside Billy Boy was wearing exactly the same, except for the colours. He nodded at the dicker, who then opened the door of the garage, letting a pool of bright light pour out onto the dark pavement, then nodded in turn for him and Billy Boy to enter.

Following the first kid in, he found himself facing a long rectangular wooden table, darkly varnished and badly scratched, that had been placed across the floor of the garage and was surrounded by the paraphernalia of the workshop, including piles of old and new tyres, heavy-duty jacks, cans of oil and shelves stacked with tools. Seated behind the table were three of the hardest young men of the Shankill: Alf Green, Joe Douglas and Jack Peel. Though none was more than thirty, they all looked a lot older, each having at least one scar on his face and all with a brutalized appearance and eyes devoid of warmth. Standing beside them, at the left-hand side of the table, was Roy 'Joy Rider' Phillips, the humourless young hard case who had brought Billy Boy this invitation for a talk and, hopefully, initiation, a few days ago. Joy Rider was packing a pistol that bulged under his jacket.

'Have ya come?' Alf Green, the leader of the pack, said to Billy Boy, greeting him with that oddity of Belfast speech.

'Ackay, Alf,' Billy Boy replied from where he still stood about three feet from the table. 'Here I am, all right.'

'You still want to join us?' Green asked, nodding towards Joy Rider to indicate that he had passed on Billy Boy's request.

'Sure ya know I do, Alf. All of ya – ya all know that. I've bin makin' it clear as day for fuckin' months, so you can't have no doubts, like. I want in real bad.'

There was silence as the three hard men studied Billy Boy,

considering his words, trying to take his measure. Then Joe Douglas, Green's second-in-command, started tapping the blunt end of a pencil against the table and said, 'So why do you want to join us when you've got your own gang?'

'Because m'own gang's just a bunch of tearaways, but you lads are the best. I mean, I'm not recognized – I'm just viewed as a fuckin' hoodlum – but you lot have the backing of the Ulster Defenders an' that means ya get all the real jobs. Also, yer dead set against the peace process, that lickin' of Sinn Fein's boots, an' you'll do anything, no limit, to derail it. I'm all for that, like.'

Another lengthy silence was broken when Jack Peel, an old schoolmate of Billy Boy's, once as soft as a tub of lard but now lean, hard and well known for his brutality, raised his gelid gaze from the table to meet Billy Boy's eyes. 'We've a wee bit of a problem with you,' he said.

Trust him to raise a problem, Billy Boy thought. *I might have known that bastard would try to shaft me. Well, his day will come.*

'Oh?' he said, looking innocent. 'What problem?'

'You've the reputation of bein' a loose cannon, a cowboy, someone way out on his own, not willin' to take orders and, even worse, someone who takes unnecessary risks, thereby puttin' those around him at risk as well. You're also known to be ambitious – you want too much too quickly – and reportedly you've no idea of teamwork unless you're in charge. That's our problem with you.'

Billy Boy felt like strangling him. Peel had been a soft touch when at school and Billy Boy had bullied him mercilessly until they both left at fifteen. But Peel had changed since then, having joined a gang early on, a Loyalist paramilitary unit financed by criminal activities, and taken part in torture and execution on a grand scale. Now here he was, the third in line in this chain of butchers, studying Billy Boy with his icy unblinking gaze and recalling, no doubt, how he'd been bullied by Billy Boy when they were younger. He'd had no love for Billy Boy then and wouldn't have any now. He wouldn't want him around.

'Sure we've all got reputations we don't deserve,' Billy Boy said, 'and a lot of what's said comes from envy. I can work in a team if I have to, but so far I've just bin runnin' with my own boyos and I nat'rally take charge. If I get in, if I get to work for you, I'll do

what I'm told. As for bein' a loose cannon, a cowboy . . . whatever
. . . Ya gotta remember that I didn't have much experience when
I formed m'own gang. I made mistakes – sure, we all do – but
I learned pretty quick, like. With you lads behind me, and me
doing real work, not shit, I'll not be the loose cannon you think
I am; I'll be part of the team. Sure ya can take that as read.'

The three men behind the table glanced at each other, trying
to read each other's minds, then Alf Green returned his steady
gaze to the front and asked, 'Do you know our operating policy,
Billy Boy?'

'Ackay – to kill Catholics.'

'What Catholics?'

'Any Catholics who might cause us trouble.'

'No, Billy Boy, that policy's dead and buried. Our new policy,
recently agreed and already put into practice, is to kill Catholics at
random, irrespective of who they are, no matter how unimportant
or seemingly harmless, so long as they happen to be found in a
place where it's easy to pick 'em up for execution. Would you do
that, Billy Boy?'

'Ackay, sure I would.'

'Have you ever killed anyone, Billy Boy?' Joe Douglas asked
him.

'Sure ya know I have.'

'We certainly know that you've killed a few, both Catholic and
Protestant,' that bastard Peel interjected, 'but they were all done
in the heat of the moment, the victims usually beaten to death with
baseball bats when you were in the company of lads helpin' you out.
Those were punishment beatings of petty criminals who'd cheated
you. None of them were carried out for sectarian reasons or done
coolly, with premeditation. Have you ever killed someone in cold
blood? I don't think so, Billy Boy.'

It was true, Billy Boy realized, thinking back on his own recent
past, that he'd killed a few here and there without actually setting
out to do so. All of them had died, accidentally, as it were, in the
heat of the moment from the batterings they'd received from him
and his mates using their baseball bats. Billy Boy knew, however,
just how excited those batterings had made him; recalled vividly
the almost sexual heat that had flooded him when he heard the
victims' bones breaking, heard their screams of pain, saw their

blood drenching their clothes. He also knew that he felt no guilt at all over the ones who had died; in fact, their dying had given him an extra charge and made him feel ten feet tall. Kill Catholics? No way he couldn't do it. He hated the Taigs with a passion, didn't trust them an inch, and didn't want them taking over Ulster, so he'd kill the bastards all right.

'All right,' he said, 'I'll admit I haven't done that, but I hate the Taigs – sure ya know damned well I do – an' I can kill 'em in cold blood.'

'Really?' Peel asked.

'Yeah, really,' Billy Boy said with conviction. 'Just let me prove it.'

'We will,' Alf Green said. Turning his head slightly, he nodded at Joy Rider who instantly left his position beside the table and went to a doorway at the back of the dimly lit garage. The door was open and light was pouring out, briefly silhouetting Joy Rider as he shouted to someone inside. He then stepped aside as two other men emerged, dragging something between them. As they advanced to where Billy Boy was standing in front of the table, he saw that the men were actually holding up another man who had a rag stuffed into his mouth to prevent him from speaking or screaming. His shirt had been removed and his naked body was badly battered, with some ribs clearly broken. His body was also covered with a gruesome combination of cigarette burns and bloody, criss-crossing lines where he had been cut repeatedly, probably slowly, with a knife. When the two guards reached Billy Boy, one of them turned to the tortured, shivering man, snarled, 'Get down on yer fuckin' knees,' then punched him on the back of the neck with his clenched fist. Still gagged, the nameless man made no sound as he dropped onto his knees, kneeling just beside Billy Boy, his shivering shadow stretching along a pool of dim light to touch Billy Boy's feet.

'We found him walking home from a pub in Whiterock,' Alf Green explained in a quiet monotone. 'We didn't know who he was and we didn't give a shit; we only knew that he was a piece of Catholic filth – and that's all we *needed* to know. Under torture, he revealed that he's called Patrick Boyle, has a wife and three young kids, works as a binman and has never been involved in politics in his life. Does this make him an innocent Catholic? No. In our view, there are *no* innocent Catholics, so he has to be put down. Now prove you can do it while he's looking you right in the eyes and begging for mercy.'

Green nodded at Joy Rider who violently jerked the rag out of the kneeling man's mouth. The man gasped for air and burst into tears. Green nodded again at Joy Rider who withdrew his Czech 75 pistol from under his jacket and silently handed it to Billy Boy.

'Do you know how to cock it?' Joy Rider asked sarcastically.

'Ackay,' Billy Boy said.

'Then cock it and put this bastard's lights out,' Joy Rider said.

Showing no hesitation, Billy Boy cocked the pistol and aimed it at the head of Patrick Boyle. Still on his knees, a shivering, bloody, burnt mess, Boyle looked up at Billy Boy with brown eyes brightened by shock and dreadful fear.

'Please don't!' he sobbed. 'For Christ's sake, what've I done? I mean, I've never been involved in anything in my life, so why me of all people? I've a wife and children, for Jesus' sake. God Almighty, for Christ's sake, please don't do this! Oh, God help me, *please don't!*'

Billy Boy shot the whimpering shite. One clean shot through his temple, gun barrel pressed tightly against it, just above the left ear. Boyle's head exploded as he jerked sideways and hit the floor like a sack of potatoes. He kicked and twitched for a few seconds after that, but went still soon enough. Billy Boy, feeling a cold, dry excitement, handed the pistol back to Joy Rider, then returned his gaze to the men behind the table.

'So,' he asked, 'am I in or am I out?'

'You're in,' Alf Green said.

Without even bothering to remove the body of the unfortunate Patrick Boyle – the dickers would clean that mess up later – they inducted Billy Boy into their grand fraternity. The process was surprisingly simple. Alf Green slid a Bible and a revolver across the table and asked Billy Boy if he was willing to swear an oath. Billy Boy, who had sworn a lot in his life, said that he would. Alf Green then placed the revolver on top of the Bible and asked Billy Boy to place his hand on the gun. Billy Boy did so. Alf Green then quoted an interminable fancy-worded oath which, as Billy Boy translated it, simply meant that he would be loyal for the rest of his life to the organization, to God and to Ulster . . . in that order. Billy Boy, who had never kept a promise in his life, solemnly repeated the oath.

'You're now a member of Red Hand,' Alf Green said.

It was as simple as that.

CHAPTER FIVE

Pete now knew for sure that he had, indeed, been under observation and that the man stepping out onto the path from the shivering shadows of an oak tree, his right hand upraised, his grey hair breeze-blown, was his friend Daniel Edmondson of MI5. Pete slowed down, but kept walking until he was right in front of Edmondson. When he stopped, Edmondson, slim and dandy in his pinstripe suit with shirt and old school tie, lowered his right hand and held it out to be shaken. The two men shook hands.

'I had the feeling I was being followed,' Pete said, 'though it never entered my head that it might be you.'

'So who did you think it was?' Edmondson asked, turning away and indicating that Pete should walk on with him.

'I wasn't sure,' Pete said, falling in beside Edmondson as the latter started strolling around the pond. 'People who sell surveillance equipment make enemies, so I thought it might relate to my work. I also thought it might be a detective, placed on my tail by my wife, who's presently suing me for divorce. I didn't think of you. I surely didn't. I mean, it's been a long time.'

'It doesn't seem so,' said Edmondson.

In fact, he and Pete had first met in 1997 when the latter, then already hiring himself out as a personal bodyguard, had been approached by the former to act as such for an American VIP paying a propaganda visit to Belfast. Edmondson, however, being with MI5 and never one to miss a good opportunity, had asked Pete to keep his eyes and ears open for any intelligence he could pick up while in the Province, this being more important, as he had carefully informed Pete, than guarding a relatively unimportant Yank politician. Pete had complied with his request, enjoyed his often dangerous intelligence gathering when not actually minding the American visitor, and brought back valuable information.

Edmondson had been pleased, and he and Pete had met occasionally after that, though they had not actually worked together again during the past two years. Obviously this was about to change and Pete was intrigued.

'So why have you been observing me?' he asked.

'I wanted to talk to you.'

'But why observe me first?'

'I didn't want to use the telephone,' Edmondson said, 'and, as I'm often under observation myself, I was waiting for the right moment to approach you. I didn't want it to be anywhere we could be overheard; then you came into this park. That suited me fine.'

'How long have you been following me?'

'Only since last night. Nothing too mysterious about it. I followed you from your office, hoping to talk where it was suitable, but there were too many people around when you walked from the tube station to your flat. I hung around a bit, hoping you'd come out again, and when you didn't, I left it. Naturally, I was back, bright and early, this morning. I waited outside all morning, then followed you into town, to that restaurant in Soho – Soho Soho, was it not? How amusing! And then followed you from there to here. So how are you, Peter?'

'Not bad.'

'Does that mean not too good?'

'Not really. I'm fine. The business is going well and I still do the other work occasionally—'

'As a bodyguard,' Edmondson interjected.

'Yes . . . So apart from the fact that I'm about to be divorced, I have no complaints.'

'Really?'

'What does that mean?'

Edmondson led him up to the path around the pond, removed a paper bag of breadcrumbs from his coat pocket and threw crumbs to the swans as he walked. In his pinstripe suit with shirt and tie, moving casually through sunlight and shadow, autumn leaves falling about him and rustling around his feet, he looked the picture of worldly, jaded elegance.

'Another divorce,' he said eventually, evenly. 'You have quite a record there.'

'That's what a friend said yesterday, so don't you start as well.'

Edmondson smiled. 'It has a bearing, Peter. It can't *always* have been the fault of the ladies. Some of the blame must be yours.'

'I won't deny that. I've accepted that I'm not cut out for married life, no matter how good the woman.'

'You're a restless individual.'

'Yes, I guess so.'

'That's why I approached you a couple of years back when I'd learnt about you through one of my associates.'

'What associate?'

Edmondson smiled again. 'You asked me that at the time, Peter, and I said I couldn't tell you. That proviso remains.'

'So what was it about what you were told that made you approach me? That always puzzled me.'

'Your SAS record, naturally. That was certainly a starting line. Even though you were RTU'd, you were an exceptional soldier and we quite *liked* the reasons for your RTU – those, and your general record of insubordination and risk-taking, convinced us that you were a man easily bored and constantly, almost obsessively, in need of challenges. We therefore weren't surprised when, reviewing your file—'

'You have a file on me?'

'Of course . . . We weren't surprised when we learnt that when you left the army you not only created a highly successful business, selling government-approved high-tech surveillance equipment, but also acted as a freelance bodyguard. This man, we realized, was truly *easily* bored and therefore would be easily seduced into dangerous activities. You proved the point when you so readily accepted the challenge of intelligence gathering in Belfast . . . and I believe you're going to prove the point again.'

'Oh, really?'

'Yes, really.'

Pete did not ask the question. He knew that Edmondson would get around to telling him what he wanted in his own good time and in his own particular way. As they continued walking around the pond, with Edmondson throwing crumbs to the swans, acting like a normal man just out for a stroll, Pete glanced across the park and saw, beyond the line of trees, the architectural splendours of the

Mall and, rising above them, the Victorian and Georgian buildings
of the West End. Born in Belfast to working-class parents, he had
grown up romanticizing this city, which he only knew at the time
through movies and TV. Loathing Belfast, with its religious and
political antagonisms, he had, like so many before him, been glad
to leave – though, in his case, leaving as a child with his parents –
and had eventually ended up in London, the romantic city of his
boyhood daydreams. Once in London, he had fallen in love with it
and taken advantage of it until, after enlisting in the British Army,
he had been taken away from it. Now, looking at it, feeling himself
to be a Londoner rather than an Ulsterman, he was struck by how
majestic it was when compared to his home town. He was a long
way from home now.

'So what have *you* been up to lately?' he asked of Edmondson.

The MI5 man shrugged and grinned. 'The usual,' he said.
'Investigating our own kind. Bad enough that we have to deal with
terrorism, both in the Province and overseas; now we're faced with
a mounting wave of corruption among our own security forces.'

'That always existed,' Pete said. 'No big surprise there.'

'No, but what's constantly surprising is the broadening scale of
the corruption and the calibre of the people involved. Right now,
for instance, I'm looking into the possibility that half a million
pounds from Scotland Yard's undercover account has been stolen
by three or four detectives who were supposed to be using it to stop
the American Mafia from selling weapons to Irish terrorist gangs.
The Mafia were preparing to ship a three-and-a-half-million cache
of stolen arms and explosives from the US via Africa to Northern
Ireland and the stolen money was supposed to have been used to
trap them. Posing as representatives of Irish terrorists, the detectives
involved secretly recorded their meetings with the Mafia gangsters
at hotels in London and Houston, Texas, but unfortunately, as
they were doing that, they somehow managed to mislay half of the
money being used as bait. Whether or not they were responsible, I
still can't say, but it's typical of the kind of thing I'm having to deal
with more and more these days. It's pretty damned depressing.'

'More so than dealing with Northern Ireland?'

'It's on a par, I'd say.'

'Things are still bad over there, I note,' Pete said, convinced
that this was where the conversation would eventually lead him.

'Dear Lord, there's no end to it.' Edmondson shook his head wearily. 'For a while there we thought that it was really dying down; that our only problem was convincing the IRA to lay down their arms. Of course, nothing in Ulster is that simple. A few weeks back, just as we were about to gain the trust of Sinn Fein, we learnt that a network of Protestant spies in and around Belfast has been carrying out extensive surveillance on leading Catholic *and* Protestant figures, including judges, RUC officers, military commanders, intelligence officers, highly placed paramilitary men on both sides of the divide, and even prominent members of the church, both Catholic and Protestant. These particular spies, we believe, include teachers, insurance officials and other white-collar workers. We also believe that they've been using information in personnel files that they had access to as part of their work, including material from the files of organizations such as BUPA and BT. The information gathered has been stored in most of the hard-line Protestant areas of Belfast and it's being passed on to the most powerful Loyalist paramilitary groups in the city.'

'Shit!' Pete exclaimed.

'Nor does it end there,' Edmondson told him. 'These people, whoever they are, are into computer hacking.'

'In what way?'

'We have evidence that a government-sponsored scheme for problem youngsters is being used as a starting point for Loyalist paramilitary computer hackers to penetrate the bank records of selected targets. We found this out by decoding encrypted terrorist computer files seized by the RUC, but most of the intelligence seized was on floppy discs and that leads us to the uneasy conclusion that the information may have been copied and could still be available. As you rightly sussed, an awful lot of people, both Catholic and Protestant, are being targeted by Protestant paramilitaries. We need to know why.'

'Well,' Pete said, helplessly intrigued already and sensing what was coming, 'they're obviously targeting those being watched as possible figures for blackmail or assassination. But why are the targets from both sides of the divide?'

'That's the million-dollar question,' Edmondson said, 'and we think we might have the answer.'

They continued walking, passing others doing the same, while the breeze shook the branches above their heads and sent down a gentle fall of autumn leaves. Edmondson continued throwing crumbs to the swans as he talked, sounding calm and pragmatic.

'Nothing in Ulster is ever simple,' he said, paraphrasing slightly something he had said a few minutes before. 'Lord knows, it took us long enough to get Sinn Fein to the negotiating table and, of course, just as they're about to sit down and negotiate, certain Loyalists have decided that they don't want it.'

'Certain Loyalists have always been against it,' Pete said. 'That's why they're called Loyalists.'

Edmondson was not amused. 'It's been a long, hard slog to get Sinn Fein to the negotiating table without offending our Unionist voters. Unfortunately, it's our belief that just as we're about to get them to sit down together – to actually create a workable peace plan approved by both sides – certain Loyalists, intent on maintaining the status quo and resentful of what they view as our *surrender* to Sinn Fein – have embarked on a campaign of disruption. Their immediate plan, we believe, is to assassinate leading Catholics and thus compel the IRA to break their ceasefire. Should that fail – should the IRA see sense and fail to respond with their own brand of violence – the Protestant paramilitaries will start assassinating their own kind – or, to be more precise, those leading Unionists who've openly expressed their support for the peace process. Either way, they intend to destroy the peace process and force the British government to send the security forces back into the Province, thus returning the status quo to the Loyalists. This, we believe, is why these Protestants, whoever they may be, are targeting not only Catholics but also their own kind. We simply can't let it happen.'

'Which is where I come in.'

Edmondson smiled. 'Where else?' He stopped walking in order to more fully appreciate the beauty of the swans in the pond, gleaming white in reflected, silvery sunlight as they glided sublimely through outspreading fans of rippling water. He threw them some more crumbs, checked the paper bag, grimaced with disappointment to see that it was nearly empty, then sighed and walked on. 'You're going to your club, I take it?' he said.

'Yes,' Pete replied. 'Christ, you probably know when I take a shit. Why me, of all people?'

'Why not? COBR,' Edmondson continued, referring to the Cabinet Office Briefing Room and pronouncing the word as *Cobra*, 'thought you were ideal for the job when I read them your background. Born and bred in Belfast, but left at an early age, living in Birkenhead, then went off to London and joined the Army. As a background, that's perfect for us. As for your experience . . . the SAS, the Falklands and Iraq, then that little business for me and a few other intelligence jobs here and there . . . You could *melt* into Belfast, dear Peter – sorry, I know you prefer Pete – and that's what we want. So *melt*, Pete! Do this for us.'

'What makes you think I'd even want to? That's a dangerous job.'

'That's exactly why you might want to do it. It's a *very* dangerous job.'

'It's true that I can be thrilled by a challenge, but I'm not into suicide.'

'Come, come, Peter – Lord, I can't call you Pete – let's not be melodramatic. It's not suicidal, it's just dangerous, and we both know you thrive on that. Indeed, that's why you're always in trouble, Peter . . . That dreadfully low boredom threshold.'

'I'm not in trouble now,' Pete said, 'and I'm not ready to die.'

'You're not in trouble?'

'No.'

'Of course you are.' Edmondson crumpled up his empty paper bag, dropped it conscientiously into a waste-paper basket, then turned away from the pond and headed, considerately, towards Birdcage Walk and the general direction of Pete's club. His smile was charming, though treacherous. 'For a start,' he said, 'you're in trouble with your wife. This will be your third divorce, the previous two cost you a packet, and from what I gather Monica's out for blood and will almost certainly get it.'

'How do you know that?' Pete asked.

The question clearly amused Edmondson, making him smile again. 'High-powered solicitors – and Monica's is one such – move in circles that always curve back to us. Don't ask, Peter . . . *We know*.'

'And the rest of it?'

'The selling of high-tech surveillance equipment is like the selling of armaments: it's legitimate but it needs a lot of permissions and faces many hurdles. Like many arms dealers, Peter, you've jumped many of those hurdles – or, rather, skirted around them – and gentlemen in certain quarters are asking questions that could land you in trouble. We could help you there, Peter.'

'Thanks a million,' Pete said. 'Is there anything else?'

'Alas, yes . . . This personal bodyguard business. Admiring as I do your low boredom threshold and need for fresh challenges, I have to tell you that some of the gentlemen you've protected in the past few years are involved in politically, sometimes legally, dubious activities, which makes anyone involved with them, however briefly, equally suspect.'

'That's bullshit,' Pete said.

'I have to tell you, Peter, that I was in fact *reminded* of you – which is why we're now speaking – by an MI5 report about a certain Third World dictator for whom you did – in all innocence, I am sure – act as a personal bodyguard. Since that dictator is now high on our list of suspect persons, you, too, having been closely associated with him, are on a list of those marked for observation and, possibly, censure. By censure – as I'm sure you appreciate – I mean investigation of every aspect of your life, with particular emphasis on your business dealings. These would include the sale of surveillance equipment and so forth, sometimes, alas, without the proper permissions . . . and, of course, your general finances, including money held overseas in what you might have optimistically imagined were tax-free holdings. So please believe me, Peter, when I say that this offer I'm making . . .'

'To go to Belfast.'

'Correct . . . Apart from giving you a fresh challenge and being profitable to you, this offer could save you an awful lot of heartbreak. So please consider it carefully.'

Pete considered it as they walked on and he realized, without too much effort, that Edmondson, always charming, forever ruthless, knew what he was talking about. Almost certainly Monica *would* pursue him for all she could get. Given his ongoing alimony payments to his other former wives, not to mention child support for his four children, this would not be all that much, though clearly it would leave him pretty broke. As for his surveillance equipment business, while he had always tried to walk the straight

and narrow with regard to the law, the fact could not be avoided
that anyone involved in such sales could easily be found guilty
of *some* infraction or other by civil servants determined to find
them so for their own purposes. Should that happen in this case,
Pete's business would collapse overnight, leaving him with only
the occasional bodyguard work. That, however, would not last
very long if, as was being suggested, MI5 or, indeed, any other
branch of the civil service, decided to make things difficult for
him. So, all in all, he was pretty well boxed in and would only
get out when he had done as Edmondson was requesting.

Besides, he *was* bored out of his mind and also had the need to
get away from London until such time as Monica, inexhaustible
when worked up over something, had gained satisfaction through
her solicitor. So, given no choice on the one hand and, on the
other, actually being keen to go, he decided to comply.

'What the hell?' he said. 'What can I lose apart from my life?'

'Don't be morbid. Think positive.'

'Tell me how,' Pete said. 'You have me, lock, stock and barrel.
But what is it, precisely, that you want me to do and how, exactly,
am I to do it?'

Smiling, Edmondson led him out of the park, into Birdcage
Walk, and then proceeded towards Pete's private-members' club,
obviously knowing exactly where it was located.

'Really simple, dear Peter, though absolutely dangerous. I mean,
why should I lie to a trusting friend?'

'Don't bullshit. Just tell me.'

They had reached the outer limit of the park and were turning
into Birdcage Walk. Edmondson, taking the lead once more, led
Pete unerringly to his club while saying, 'What we want you to do
is find out exactly who these Protestants are: the ones who want
to disrupt – in fact, destroy – the ongoing peace process. Once
you find them, you must terminate their activities, no matter how
extreme the measures required.'

'What does that mean?'

'I'm sure you understand English, Peter.'

'So I can be as extreme as necessary, but I have to make the
decisions myself and can't expect help if a decision I make happens
to be wrong.'

'You're so clever, Peter.'

'And if I'm caught I can expect no help either.'

'I'm afraid you don't exist, Peter.'

'Wonderful,' Pete said. 'You warm my heart. So what's the game plan?'

'There isn't one,' Edmondson replied as he led Pete, unerringly, into the street where his club was located. 'You simply do it as best you can. You take on a new identity – though obviously one that is Belfast-based, since that's where you were born – but an identity that suggests you were overseas for years – Australia sounds good to me – and have just returned home after that long absence.'

'That may not be easy.'

'Easy as pie,' Edmondson said, since it wasn't *his* head on the chopping block. 'You're a fully trained television technician, are you not?'

'I was,' Pete replied.

'And did you not, through the SAS, further that training with instruction in telecommunications at the Hereford and Royal Signals establishments at Catterick and Blandford?'

'Yes, I did,' Pete admitted.

'So what better than returning to Belfast, after many years in Australia, as a trained television engineer determined to set himself up in business in his home town? TV engineers get invited everywhere – into the homes of the rich and the poor, the powerful and the socially disenfranchised, the Protestant and the Catholic – so you'd certainly meet a wide variety of people and, given the Ulsterman's love for crack, be practically drowned in local information. How's that for a start?'

'I do all this by myself? Without help?'

'You were born and bred there,' Edmondson replied without the slightest trace of cynicism, 'and for that very reason, we believe you can do this better *without* our help. So, are you definitely in, Peter?'

'Do I really have a choice?'

'Of course,' Edmondson replied, stopping at the door of Pete's club with barely a glance at the door number, which he clearly knew well. 'It's not a matter of blackmail. It's just that you can either continue to be bored, suffer the slings and arrows of undignified divorce proceedings, and perhaps – and I only say *perhaps* – find yourself faced with charges relating to the illegal sale of weapons

– for high-tech surveillance items are now so viewed – or possibly contentious liaisons with foreign despots . . . Yes, Peter, all that . . . Or, instead, you can defeat your boredom and avoid a lot of soul-destroying unpleasantness – not to mention receiving all the financial benefits offered by a grateful British government – by simply spending a few months in Belfast, sniffing the wind on a daily basis, and, once having sniffed out the rot, doing the necessary, no matter how distasteful it may be. I sound sardonic, but I'm serious about this. So of course, for your own sake, you must go, as I'm sure you will.'

Pete stared up at the door number and brass nameplate of his private-members' club. Then he looked into Edmondson's pale blue eyes.

'Are you a member of this club?' he asked.

'No, of course not,' Edmondson said.

'Have you ever been here before?' Pete asked.

'No, of course not,' Edmondson repeated.

'But you know that I'm a member and you know the address,' Pete said, 'which means you know everything about me. Yes, I'll go to Belfast. Now do you want to come in?'

'Not really,' Edmondson responded drily. 'I never drink until I've had my dinner.'

'Then fuck off,' Pete said without malice. 'I'll call you from Belfast.'

'I knew I could depend on you,' Edmondson said. Then he grinned and walked off.

Pete entered his club for a drink, thinking of the file they had on him and wondering what was in it. Not that it really mattered any more; they had files on everyone these days. He had a drink and made plans.

CHAPTER SIX

The curtains were still closed at eleven in the morning when Patricia Monaghan opened her eyes and blinked a few times, staring up at the ceiling. Then she remembered where she was and turned her head to gaze across the room.

Sean was still sleeping, half propped up on the bed, the right side of his face scorched, the arm on the same side wrapped in bandages and stained with dried blood. He was unshaven and breathing heavily, clearly in pain, but she knew that no matter how long it took, he would, in the end, be okay. The doctor had told her so.

Sighing, rolling off the sofa where she had been sleeping so as not to disturb him, she tiptoed into the bathroom, attended to her ablutions, then, feeling more refreshed, returned to the main area of the shabby one-room apartment being used as a Republican safe house.

Not wanting to raise the blind and let sunlight in, not wanting to waken Sean unnecessarily, she just pulled the edge of the blind aside and glanced down on the street of terraced houses below.

The street was quiet and drab in dim autumnal sunlight. It was a street in a housing executive estate in Ballymurphy. A couple of dickers, both armed, though their weapons were hidden under their ski jackets, were standing guard at the garden gate directly below.

Sean would be moved on tonight, to another safe house across the border. There he would receive proper medical attention and otherwise be well looked after until his wounds were properly healed. Only the burn marks on his face would not be healed, at least not completely. He had been scarred for life.

'Pat? Is that you?'

She heard his voice clearly, though it seemed weak and lacking in timbre. As she released the blind and turned around to face him, he tried to sit up higher, though clearly he was having difficulty in doing so.

'Yes,' she said, 'it's me.' She walked to the bed, kissed him on the forehead, then rearranged the pillows behind him to let him sit up more comfortably. Just raising himself to settle back against the pillows cost him a great deal of effort.

'I can't see you properly in this darkness,' he said, still sounding weak. 'Raise the blind and let the light in.'

'Right,' Patricia said. She raised the blind, letting in the grey, depressing autumn light, and glanced down at the street. The two dickers were still there, smoking fags, talking quietly, occasionally scratching their close-cropped heads as they kept their eyes peeled. Patricia returned to the bed and smiled down at Sean, receiving a weak grin in return. Though unshaven and with that ugly burn mark covering most of his right cheek, he was still an unusually handsome man. His brown eyes had always made him seem romantic and he looked that way still.

'How do you feel?' Patricia asked him.

'Well, I've felt a lot better in my time,' he replied, 'though I guess I should count my blessings that I'm still alive. Just how good or bad am I?'

'You're not bad at all.'

'Don't you be lying to me, now. I'd rather have the truth, Pat.'

'The truth is you'll never look as handsome as you did, but that arm will be okay in time.'

'So I sacrificed my good looks for the cause. Any more damage?'

'No. I swear to God, Sean. You're badly battered and bruised – and your face, of course, is scarred – so you probably feel a lot worse than you really are. You'll be okay eventually, though.'

Sean nodded, then touched his fingers tentatively to the badly burned, wrinkled skin on his right cheek. 'How bad is the scarring?'

'Not bad,' Patricia said. Reaching into her shoulder bag, which was lying on the table beside the bed, she withdrew a small hand mirror and held it up in front of him. He studied his burnt cheek and winced, then smiled ruefully, bravely.

'Not *too* bad,' he said.

In fact, most of the right side of his face had been scorched by the flames and was now a badly wrinkled vivid pink. 'The doctor said that most of it would heal in time,' Patricia told him, 'though you'll always have a small bit of scarring over the cheekbone.'

'How much?'

'From the cheekbone to the ear, up to the side of the eye, and down as far as the chinbone.'

'That's a lot.'

'Well, you won't be the pretty boy you were, but you'll be all right, Sean. It'll make you look a bit like a pirate and might attract the ladies.'

'And you?'

'If I could kiss that cheek, I promise you I would, but right now it would hurt too much.'

'Me or you?'

'It'd hurt you so much you'd probably come flying off that bed, squealing like a scalded cat.'

She smiled when she said it because she didn't want him to know just how shocked she had been when she first saw him after the bombing. He had been such a handsome man, so gentle-looking, almost poetic, his features not hardened by what he did in 'the war' or 'the struggle' (as the Provies would have it). But that livid scar on his right cheek, which she had said was not much – a pitiful white lie – had actually given him a sinister, frightening appearance that made him seem like someone entirely different. Now he looked even harder than the hardest of the Provies he had controlled – and that knowledge broke her heart.

'It hurts now,' Sean said with not the slightest trace of self-pity, just stating a bald fact. 'It hurts fucking non-stop.'

'The doc'll give you more morphine when he comes back, before we move you on.'

Sean sighed and sank back against the pillows, closing his eyes. 'I feel like shit, sure I do.'

'There's no help for that,' Patricia told him. 'You'll just have to bear it.'

'Don't worry, I will.' He opened his eyes again and this time they were livelier, more thoughtful, brightened with concentration. 'So does anyone know who did it yet?' he asked.

'I certainly don't. The Prods didn't phone in to claim responsibility for it and your own kind are keeping their mouths shut, so it's still an open-and-shut case.'

'It was the Prods,' Sean said, glancing down at his heavily bandaged arm, no doubt feeling the pain of his scorched cheek and probably still trying to recollect that nightmarish split-second when, outside his home in the lower Falls, he had turned the ignition key in his car and set off the bomb. Lucky for him, the explosive, a home-made Semtex job, had been badly put together and also placed too far back under his car to do him permanent damage. 'Who else would have done it?' he added. 'The only question is: *What* Prods?'

'I'm sure you have your suspicions.'

'I've a pretty good idea. Some Prod bastards who want the peace even less than we do and think that, by killing a few like me, they'll encourage the Provies to retaliate. That's the only excuse *those* bastards need to call an end to the ceasefire.'

'Some ceasefire,' Patricia said.

'I know you're cynical,' Sean said. 'But at least the present ceasefire, if not always successful, is a step on the way to something lasting. And if it lasts, Sinn Fein will be respectable and certain Prods don't want that.'

'Certain *Catholics* don't want it, either,' Patricia said, 'and that's the whole problem. Bigotry and mutual suspicion are all both sides know. Your kind just don't trust the Prods, Sean, and their kind don't trust you.'

Sean sighed. 'I guess you're right there. Not me personally, but my kind. For myself, despite what you sometimes say when you're angry, I'm all for giving the peace initiative a chance and letting Sinn Fein at least try their best by talkin' to the Brits and the Loyalists around a big table. And because of that – because I've stated it publicly – certain Loyalists have tried to use me as the bait – to use me as *dead* bait – to hook the Provies and tug them in so hard they'll break the ceasefire. That way, the Loyalists could retaliate and force the Brits to back them to the hilt all over again.'

'The Loyalists who'd do that at this point,' Patricia said, 'would have to be pretty well placed. They'd have to be more than some hooligan splinter group from a filthy back street in Sandy Row.'

'Not true,' Sean said. 'I've heard stories that point in the direction of certain Loyalist splinter groups. I mean, take the Red Hand—'

'A bunch of cowboys,' Patricia interjected deliberately, wanting to keep Sean talking.

'They were once,' Sean responded. 'But now, from what we've heard, they're being controlled by those fanatical anti-Catholics, the so-called Ulster Defenders.'

'Another bunch of self-styled paramilitaries, not particularly well placed.'

'*Deliberately* not well placed – or, at least, not highly profiled – because they're backed by the East Belfast Unionist Party. That *is* well placed, it has a high profile, and it's widely known to view the peace initiative as a betrayal of its damnable Orange State. So my bet is that the bastards who bombed my car were at least *supported* by the Ulster Defenders.'

'Which gets us back to the East Belfast Unionist Party.'

'Right,' Sean said. 'You've got it.'

'But according to the Reverend William Dawson,' Patricia said, 'whom I interviewed only a few weeks ago, the East Belfast Unionist Party severed all connection with the Ulster Defenders a long time ago.'

'Believe that and you'll believe anything,' Sean said. 'That Reverend Jehovah Dawson has more sides than a prism and he dazzles even the likes of you. You have to turn a little sideways and squint to see *him* in perspective. Sure you should know better, Pat.'

Patricia smiled and shrugged. 'Maybe.'

Sean studied her thoughtfully for a moment, then said, 'How long have I been here?'

'About two weeks.'

'Sure it seems like a bad dream. Two eternal weeks of going in and out of consciousness, dreaming about what happened, never seeing it clearly, and waking up to find you in the room, either sitting there on the sofa or reading or whatever, and not knowing if you're part of the dream or are actually real. I only knew you were real when you touched me – stroked my brow or wrist – before I slipped back into sleep. Two weeks like forever in a dream and the smell of you everywhere.'

'You smelt me?'

'I imagined I could. Your perfume, your newly-washed hair, the smell of your cunt. Oh, yes, I smelt that, all right – or, at least, thought I did. And you know the worst of it all?'

'No,' Patricia said. 'Tell me.'

'It's the yearning for you, the need to be touched by you, to fuck you, but not being able to do anything about it. Sure that hurt me more than the rest of it, and in fact it still does.'

Smiling, she pulled up a chair and sat on it with her knees touching the bed. She was wearing a short skirt and it shifted back over her knees to reveal her smooth thighs. She had long, shapely legs and Sean had always liked to run his hands over them as he worked himself up. Right now, he couldn't move his right hand, but she was seated on the left side of the bed, so she took that hand and gently pulled it down until the fingers, calloused and manly, were resting on her thigh.

'Have a squeeze of that,' she said.

He squeezed her thigh, then smiled and closed his pain-filled yearning brown eyes. He ran his hand up and down, stroking and squeezing her smooth skin as she slipped her own hand under the bedsheet and groped about until she find out how he was. When she found, as she had suspected, that he was becoming erect, she smiled more broadly and slipped her fingers around him.

'Ah, God!' he murmured. 'Christ! Sure that should cure all the rest of it. Ah, Jesus, don't stop!'

She had no intention of stopping. She liked the feel of his heat and hardness, his belly's rise and fall, his helplessness in her grip, his abject surrender to her as she worked her ways on him. God, she loved him, she did, and would do anything to please him, taking pleasure from his surrender, knowing full well that he had always loved her and knowing how rare that was. Oh, people claimed to love each other, particularly the married ones, but she knew from her own childhood and from later observation that love between married couples was more rare than most would admit. The Irish were hypocrites, Prods and Catholics alike, and they never spoke the truth, the plain, unvarnished truth, when it came to matters of sex. In fact, she was convinced, a lot of them, the men in particular, took to drink to deaden the desires they refused to acknowledge.

Not Sean, though. He'd always been straight that way. He'd always loved her with a passion, making her feel that she was needed, and she'd responded with every fibre of her being and had no shame about it. Now, as she gazed upon him, his ecstatic face, his heaving loins, feeling his heat and his hardness, she had no shame about leaning down over him and taking him into her mouth. He tasted good, sure he did, filling her up, making her head swim, and when he came, when he shuddered and cried out, she drank him up as if drinking from a fresh well in the Blackrock Mountains on a sky-blue, sunscorched, eternal day.

She swallowed him, taking his essence into herself, and then straightened up again. He had somehow made his way down the bed, maybe to make it easier for her, and now he was practically flat on his back, though with his head still propped up on the pillows. He had lovely thick curly brown hair that matched the brown of his eyes, but now his hair was a mess. She smiled and ran her fingers through it, using her hand as a comb.

'There,' she said, 'you didn't think you could do it, but I've just proved you wrong. That must mean that apart from the breakings and the bruising, apart from that burn on your face, you're as healthy as rain.'

'It means I'm going to recover,' he responded, 'and you've just made me want to.'

'Well, that's good,' she said. Then she sighed, stood up, and prepared to leave. 'I have to go now. I'm on a job this afternoon. But some of the lads will be in to see you soon, to make sure you're not lonely. They'll be taking you over the border tonight and you'll be there a long time.'

'Too long. Sure I'll go crazy not seeing you. That's the worst of it, Pat.'

'They'll keep you busy,' she said. 'That arm's going to need special treatment. You're also in for a couple of skin grafts, whether you like it or not. I'm not saying it'll be pleasant, but no matter how long it takes, they'll keep you distracted. Then, when it's finished, you can come back, though maybe under an alias.'

'Will you be coming to see me?'

'I will, but not often. It's too risky to do it too frequently, but I'll try making it now and then. Expect me, but don't expect me too soon. That's all I can say for now.'

'All right, Pat. Kiss me goodbye.'

She leaned down to kiss him full on the lips and then straightened up again. Her heart was beating and she was filled with the pain of loss, though she wouldn't lay that upon him. She wanted to make it as easy for him as possible, so she made a joke out of it.

'I'll have a grand time without you,' she said. 'At least I'll know you're safe, not out doing God knows what, and also well out of the reach of other women. I'll be content, knowing that.'

'They have nurses in that safe house.'

'*Male* nurses – and you're not the kind for that.'

Smiling to display more happiness than she felt, she walked to the door. She was just about to open it when he said, 'You still have your doubts, don't you?'

She was holding the door handle, but she didn't actually turn it. 'Yes,' she said, 'I still have my doubts. You won't wipe those out easily.'

She started to turn the handle, but his voice stopped her again. 'Even with those doubts, would you be willing to do anything I asked?'

'No,' she said. 'Never.'

'What if it wasn't too extreme?'

'What's "extreme" mean?'

'Your personal involvement in violence. If I didn't ask for that, but only asked for general help, would you be willing to offer it?'

'What's "general help" mean?'

'Maybe something you wouldn't particularly like doing, but something that'd be invaluable to us. Maybe something involving men.'

'You'd ask that of me?'

'I might not have a choice.'

'I love you, but sometimes you're a bastard. Do you really love me, Sean?'

'Sure you know that.' There was silence for a moment, a *long* moment, and Sean finally broke it. 'Well, would you do it?'

'I'd rather not.'

'But you would.'

She wanted to say 'No' but she couldn't. She simply loved him too much. 'Yes, Sean,' she said.

'Do you love me enough to do *anything* for me, Pat?'

'Anything but violence.'

'How far would you go, other than that?'

'God, Sean, don't . . .'

'How far?'

She held her tears back as she turned the door handle and opened the door a few inches. Then she stood there for a moment, unable to move, mesmerized by his voice, chained by her love for him, imprisoned by the very freedom he had given her and shamed by that knowledge.

'As far as you want me to,' she whispered.

'That's all I need to know,' Sean said.

When Patricia left the room, closing the door quietly behind her, she felt more bruised and bloody than Sean had looked. But she had made her commitment.

There could be no turning back now.

CHAPTER SEVEN

Sitting in the stolen transit van beside Joy Rider, who was driving, with Bone Crusher Reid, Big Boots Welsh and Head Case Harrison in the rear, Billy Boy was feeling pretty high. He was feeling his way particularly because he'd had a fair bit of crack – the drug, not Belfast conversation – and more generally because for the past couple of weeks with the Red Hand Loyalist splinter group he'd had the time of his life, going out just about every evening to administer punishment beatings with baseball bats, kneecappings with pistols or power drills, assassinations on doorsteps and in living rooms, the presence of the victims' distraught families notwithstanding, and the picking up stray of Catholics for lengthy torture and ultimate execution. These jobs were, Billy Boy knew, being used to test him and so far he hadn't failed one test. However, he was high, also, because he'd persuaded the Red Hand leaders to let him keep his own small gang on the condition that they did nothing without prior permission. Thus, this evening, under the temporary leadership of Joy Rider, they were going out to prove their mettle by picking up another stray Catholic and putting out his lights. Billy Boy was in heaven.

'So how's your old man, then?' Joy Rider asked as he drove along the Ormeau Road, looking for a Catholic wandering alone in this dark, dangerous hour.

'Okay, like,' Billy Boy said, thinking of his grim little two-up, two-down terraced house just off the Donegall Road and not being comforted by the thought of it. 'Sure he still gets pissed as a newt every night and gives me Mum her hammerin's, but apart from that he's doin' okay and keeps out of m'hair.'

'I haven't seen 'im for a year or two,' Joy Rider said, 'but when I used to go to your place, I liked him. I mean, he's the one who got me into the Orange Lodge, so I'm sort of grateful for that. Still a member, is he?'

'Ackay. Still has his bowler hat, white gloves and orange sash. His mates address 'im as a District Worshipful Master an' he likes that a lot.'

'Sure he always took it serious,' Joy Rider said, sounding respectful while his sneaky, slightly deranged eyes flitted repeatedly left and right, taking in both sides of the road, scanning the lamplit, desolate pavements. 'That's why I look up to him.'

'He takes it serious all right. He was one of those who went to Portadown in '97 to lend his support to the Orangemen who marched on the church in Dumcree – you know? The march that caused all them fuckin' riots.'

'Course I know,' Joy Rider said. 'I was one of those riotin'. Throwin' petrol bombs at the so-called security forces.'

'Fuckin' ace,' Billy Boy said.

'A right palaver that was,' Joy Rider said, visibly swelling with pride. 'One mate of mine got hit by a plastic bullet an' the poor bastard's still in a coma. Another got hit by a round that went right through his fuckin' arm to puncture a lung an' a blood vessel. Another few inches an' he might've bin dead, but even now, two years after the event, he can't even hold his baseball bat to administer punishment. Because of that, we had to drop 'im from Red Hand. Broke his heart, sure it did.'

'The poor wee bastard,' Billy Boy said sympathetically. 'I bet he hates those fuckin' Taigs even more now for all the anguish they've caused 'im. I mean, those Catholics, they cause us nothin' but trouble and fuckin' strife. We should ship the whole lot of 'em across the border an' not let 'em back. Who the fuck needs 'em here?'

'Don't ask me,' Joy Rider said.

Billy Boy was feeling pretty close to Joy Rider these days, given what they had shared together this past couple of weeks. In fact, Joy Rider had been elected by Alf Green to 'break in' Billy Boy and his gang to the Red Hand way of doing things, which mainly meant stealing cars that could be dumped or set on fire after being used for illegal purposes; collecting the revenue from various protection rackets; administering punishments to Protestant miscreants, such as wildcat drug dealers, burglars, sex offenders, touts and other traitors; and, of course, abducting, torturing and murdering Catholics, either for some specific reason or simply because they *were* Catholics. Joy Rider had supervised all of these activities with an admirable lack of formality; and Billy Boy, who normally hated to take orders from anyone, had in this case been able to do so without too much aggro. That said a lot for Joy Rider. Also, Joy Rider had already, at his tender age, been in the Maze – and that made him special.

'So what was it like in the Maze, then?' Bone Crusher asked from the back of the van, as if reading Billy Boy's thoughts.

'Fuckin' cool,' Joy Rider replied. 'They treated us with kid gloves. We were on H-block 3, the Provos were on H-block 7, and they kept us well apart for our mutual good, but other than that left us alone. Talk about fuckin' soft! Sure they'd give us anything we wanted, let us bring anything in, just so long as we didn't give 'em trouble or threaten to riot. Sure, we got everything, didn't we? Fuckin' TVs and computers and washin' machines and ciggies and booze and even intimate visits from our wimmen. Thing is, ya see, that it was a programme of appeasement, 'cause they knew that if we didn't get what we wanted, we'd fuckin' riot and slit a few throats. We were prisoners of war, weren't we? That's how we viewed ourselves. So they had to give us that kind of status or invite fuckin' mayhem.'

'The Provos as well?' Big Boots asked from the back of the van, where he was sitting opposite Bone Crusher and Head Case.

'Ackay – and those bastards really abused it. Claimed they had stiff backs and were given wooden boards that they used, along with chair legs, to reinforce an escape tunnel they were diggin'. Asked for washin' machines, got 'em, an' used parts of 'em to construct a generator to power the lights in their fuckin' tunnel. Asked for computers, got 'em, an' used the wirin' from them to channel the electricity for the lights. Dug the tunnel with tools from the prison workshop. Used the baseplates from toasters as spades. Pulled the rubble out in a volleyball net nicked from the gym ... Security? Don't fuckin' joke me! By the time that tunnel was discovered, it was two and a half feet square, seven feet deep, and only ninety feet away from the perimeter fence of the fuckin' prison. If they'd asked for a fuckin' machine-gun, they'd have probably gotten it – 'cause those fuckin' guards would do anything to keep their peace with the so-called political prisoners.'

'The fuckin' eejits,' Head Case said, looking envious that he hadn't been there himself.

'Eejits wasn't the word for 'em. Those Prod wardens were so soft, they didn't do a thing when the prisoners on both sides refused to talk to them on the wing, demandin' the governor or someone on his level instead. Practically every demand the prisoners made was met, so we had it made in there.'

'If *I'd* been there,' Head Case said, 'I'd have built a tunnel to H-block 7 and beaten the shite out of a couple of them fuckin' Provos. Damned right I would.'

'If you'd bin there, you'd have bin shittin' your pants every time a Provo glared at you,' Joy Rider said. 'But if you want to beat the shite out of a Catholic, you can do it right now. There's just what we want, lads.'

They were now cruising along the lower Ormeau Road, a small Catholic enclave that was relatively safe for the Prods to drive past because it bled into the university area where Protestant and Catholic students mixed. Nevertheless, it was not a particularly safe place for a Catholic to walk alone at night (no area of Belfast would be considered safe by a Catholic) and the man they now saw making his way along the pavement, moving unsteadily between moonlit darkness and yellow lamplight, was only unconcerned because clearly he'd had too much to drink. It was just before midnight and right now no one else was in sight.

'Fuckin' perfect,' Joy Rider said. 'Get ready to grab 'im, lads.'

He swerved to the side, raced alongside the pavement and braked to a screeching halt right beside the pedestrian. Before the unlucky man even knew what was happening, the three lads had jumped out of the back of the van and hared across the pavement to nab him. Bone Crusher struck him with his half-size baseball bat, a single sharp blow to the side of the head, and as the man jerked to the side and started stumbling to his knees, Head Case and Big Boots grabbed him under the shoulders and dragged him to the van. After heaving him up and throwing him face down on the floor, they followed him in and were in turn followed by Bone Crusher who slammed the doors shut even as Joy Rider gunned the engine and the van roared off again.

'Got 'im!' Big Boots bawled as if he'd caught a rabbit for supper. Then he kicked the groaning man in the ribs and took the seat just above him.

'Fuckin' Catholic turd,' Head Case said as he too gave the groaning man a kick. 'Your fuckin' time's up, son.'

'Search him,' Joy Rider said from up front as he drove at a perfectly legal speed through the bright lights of the busy city centre, heading for the M2 motorway.

Instantly, Big Boots leaned over to grab the groaning man by the hair and jerk his lowered head around, forcing him to roll onto his back. Just for fun, Big Boots thumped him on the mouth with his clenched fist, loosening some of his front teeth and drawing blood; then, after letting the man's head fall back onto the floor, which it struck with a sickening thud, he ripped the two sides of his victim's jacket apart, making the buttons pop, and emptied out the two inside pockets, producing a wallet, a comb, a couple of bookie tickets and a membership card for a video club. Throwing the other stuff to the floor, he searched through the wallet. It contained nothing other than a few tatty fivers, a couple of telephone cards, a plastic discount card from a local supermarket, and a tattered black-and-white photo of a man and woman posing in front of a backyard wall, both wearing clothing thirty years out of date. There was neither a driving licence nor a credit card – in short, nothing that could properly identify the owner.

'Fuck,' Big Boots said, 'this poor bastard hardly exists. He doesn't have *anything*. All *this* shit is *worthless*.'

'Probably on the dole,' Head Case said.

'Just like us,' Bone Crusher added.

Big Boots threw the man's meagre possessions on the floor of the shaking, rattling van, then reached down to grab him by the hair and bang his head up and down a few more times. The man cried out in pain and started sobbing once Big Boots had let his head fall back again, striking the floor with that dreadful thud.

'What's yer name?' Big Boots asked.

'For the love of God, mister, I'm not—'

Big Boots grabbed the man's right hand, which had been waving frantically, pleadingly, in the air. He pressed it down onto the floor of the van and then stamped brutally on it with his booted foot.

The man's scream drowned the sound of cracking bones, then he started sobbing again.

'Just answer the fuckin' question,' Big Boots said. 'What's your fuckin' name, shite-hole?'

'Patrick Green,' the man sobbed while spitting blood from his lips and wiping the tears from his bloodshot, dazed eyes.

'Patrick fuckin' Green?' Bone Crusher asked, then gave the Catholic a good thump on the side of his ribcage with his half-size baseball bat, thus making him scream in agony once more. 'What kinda fuckin' name's that? Half Catholic, half Prod! Are ya havin' us on, like?'

When the sobbing man did not reply, Bone Crusher gave him another thump with his baseball bat and the man, after screaming again, sobbed frantically, 'I'm a Protestant! Swear to God, mister! Really, I am! My Mom's a Prod but she married an Englishman an' he liked the name Patrick. It's as simple as that, like. Believe me, mister, that's the truth! Please, mister . . . Jesus Christ, oh my God . . . Please, mister, believe me!'

'You lyin' shite!' Head Case said. 'We found ya walkin' down the Lower Ormeau Road, so don't say yer a Prod!'

And he kicked the man in the ribs, breaking a few, to get his point across. The man screamed and kept talking.

'I don't live there,' he sobbed. 'I just happened to be walkin' there. I don't even know how I happened to be there. I was too drunk to know, like.'

'Fuckin' great,' Head Case said.

'Ack, dear God, please believe me! I just went out for a booze-up with some of m'mates – all Prods, swear to God! – in a pub in Stranmillis and I got so drunk I can't even remember leavin'. I musta wandered across the King's Bridge and then down the Embankment and eventually ended up where ya found me. Swear to God, Mister, that's all I can tell you. Please God, mister, don't hurt me more!'

'We're gonna hurt ya till ya can't fuckin' believe it,' Head Case said, 'an' all that lyin' palaver won't help ya. Say yer prayers while ya can.'

'Jesus, mister! Please don't!'

Bone Crusher smashed the man full in the face with his baseball bat, smashing the teeth previously loosened, and the man screamed and went into some kind of spasm, then shivered convulsively as he threw up on the floor of the van.

'Ah, shit!' Big Boots exclaimed, moving his booted feet away from the sickening mess.

'Kill the fuck!' Head Case shouted while also keeping his boots clear of the mess.

'No!' Joy Rider shouted back over his shoulder. 'Don't touch him no more. I want that bastard alive when we get to Carrickfergus to answer some questions more intelligent than that shite of yours. So just let the cunt lie there.'

'Ackay, that's right,' Billy Boy said, now high on the almost relentless violence of the past fortnight and no longer able to envisage a future without it. 'Sure we're bound to get somethin' out of the lyin' shite when we let him know what real pain is. They all talk in the end.'

'Don't they ever?' Joy Rider said.

Later even Billy Boy would be loath to think about it and no description would be adequate to the occasion. Suffice to say that they were all enraged that the little shite should lie to them; that they were even more enraged because they were high on crack; that, being high on crack, they were showing off to each other; and that no matter what the little shite said, they would not let up on him. In fact, the questions became irrelevant, since they knew him to be lying. So even before Joy Rider braked to a halt, they had decided their victim's fate and, in so doing, also decided that the torture should be punishment instead of a means to an end.

They worked him over in a dark field located high above the sea between Carrickfergus and Larne, in the moonlight of midnight, in a chill wind that howled like a banshee, in the dipped headlights of another car that had been waiting there for them; and they ensured, by shoving a rag into his mouth, that his screaming would not be heard. They taped the rag into position, winding the tape around his head, pulling it tight, suffocating him, and when they saw the vomit seeping out around it, they knew that the end was near. Seeing that, they saw no joy in further tormenting the Catholic shite, and so they placed his shivering body in the driver's seat of the stolen van, taped his wrists to the steering wheel, released the handbrake, and let the vehicle roll down the grassy slope until, with the gagged man still inside it, it went over the cliff edge.

It smashed into the sea-washed rocks far below and then burst into flames.

'Good riddance to bad rubbish,' Billy Boy said, then he turned to Joy Rider and boldly asked, 'Have we passed another test?'

'I knew that fucker,' Joy Rider replied, 'and he *was* a Protestant – none too bright, I'll admit – from Sandy Row, probably trying to make his way back to there via Shaftesbury Square. He was telling the truth, you fuckin' eejit, and ya should've checked what he was sayin' and properly ascertained—'

'What?' Billy Boy interjected.

'Ascertained . . . made sure of . . . his identity before ya put his fuckin' lights out.'

Billy Boy took a deep breath and let it out carefully. 'My mistake,' he responded with all the sincerity he could muster, which was not much at all. 'It won't happen again . . . So what's this master plan we're bein' prepared for when our lords and masters, the Ulster Defenders, finally decide that we're worthy?'

'You'll be told that when yer worthy.'

'When's that?' Billy Boy asked.

'When you learn to tell the fuckin' difference between a Catholic an' a Prod who just happens to be in the wrong place at the wrong time.'

'Sure ya set us up,' Billy Boy said.

'Ackay,' Joy Rider responded.

'Was that poor fucker we've just done in an old friend or just a passin' acquaintance?'

'What's the difference?' Joy Rider said.

Real hard men, Billy Boy thought. *Harder than I'd imagined. I'd better watch myself here . . .*

After walking back with the others to the car that was waiting for them beneath the moonlit trees, he let himself be driven away from the boiling black smoke pouring up from the van still burning far below to be dispersed in the eerily howling wind above the monstrously roaring sea.

Billy Boy had often dreamt about the sea, though he had never been in it. Now, as he watched it receding, white-flecked, stippled by moonlight, he felt that it was calling out to him by invading his mind. He saw the Prod being burned up in the car and drowning at the same time.

You fuckin' eejit, Billy Boy thought, defying the sea's now distant, roaring by pretending he didn't give a damn. *That fucker Joy Rider set you up, so you'll have to watch yourself there. You'll have to watch yourself everywhere.*

Billy Boy was only twenty-four years old, but already he felt like a wise old man. It was good to be smart, like.

CHAPTER EIGHT

The Reverend William Dawson put in a good morning in his modest office in East Belfast, doing the Lord's work, listening to the concerns of certain members of his congregation whilst also, as a Unionist MP, dealing with the problems, religious and otherwise, of his constituents. Shown in by the rake-thin, gaunt-faced, pinstripe-suited Robert Lilly, they entered one by one, some nervous, others wide-eyed with awe, to unburden themselves to him and beg for his advice.

Though a certain number of them were male, they were mostly females and surprisingly, though the middle-aged and elderly predominated, a good proportion of them were younger, including some troubled adolescents. The latter were often touching in their naivety, being concerned, in the midst of a city torn by civil strife, with such mundane matters of the youthful heart as first love, rejection, guilt caused by sinful thoughts (by no means a purely Catholic hang-up) and also, alas, unwanted pregnancies. While the majority of the girls in such cases came to seek advice because, in this strict Protestant society, they were frightened to tell their parents or wanted to know the Reverend's views on the possibility of abortion (he always expressed his disapproval, thus displaying at any rate one prejudice he held in common with his Catholic adversaries), the young men tended to come for a wider variety of reasons, most of which were to do with problems relating to their involvement in illegal or paramilitary activities.

The fastest-growing problem was, of course, drug addiction – mainly crack and Ecstasy. But a longer-standing, ongoing difficulty was the dilemma of young men who had joined Loyalist paramilitary groups for romantic reasons and then found themselves being forced to engage in purely criminal activities, including protection rackets and armed robbery. Many of these young men came to

Reverend Dawson to unburden themselves of guilt and try to find
a way out of their dilemma. Others came to see him because they
had deliberately or accidentally crossed a particular paramilitary
group and so needed protection from the punishment squads.
Where the young men either wanted to disengage from the
organization they had regrettably joined or needed to go into
hiding after 'offending' the paramilitaries, the Reverend boldly
contacted the group involved, told them that he was taking the
offender into his personal care, and then passed the young man on
to one or other of the growing number of government-sponsored
schemes for problem youngsters, some of which were under his
own supervision. The Reverend was often praised for his bravery
in doing this, but he always modestly brushed such praise aside.

'I am merely doing the Lord's work,' he would say, 'and the
Lord will protect me.'

However, the majority of those who came to see him were
middle-aged or elderly women who had lived through the Troubles
and had in some way or another been marked by them. A veritable
cross-section of the society, these women came in tears and torment
to the Reverend for spiritual and, occasionally, material assistance.
A broader gallery of unfortunates he could not have hoped to
find and they did, between them, paint a bleakly comprehensive
picture of just what was going on at ground level in this divided
society.

They came to him to say, 'Lord have mercy on his soul, but
they shot him down in our own livin' room, right before my eyes
and in front of my two teenage girls. Now I don't have a husband
and my children don't have a father and I don't know how we're
goin' to survive. God help me, what do I do, Reverend?'

They came to him to say, 'Sure I knew somethin' was up when
them two hard men came to see him, barging into my house
without a by-your-leave an' just sittin' there waitin'. Thank God
he wasn't in, 'cause I'm sure they'd have taken him right then,
but when I told him about them – about how they came to find
him and waited there for hours before leavin' – he got this scared
look on his face an' then shut his mouth tight. He disappeared the
next day, Reverend. That was three weeks ago. He just went off
to work and he never came home and now I don't know if he fled
an' is still alive or if they picked him up and killed him an' buried

him somewhere. My only child, Reverend, only sixteen years old and I haven't heard a word an' I'm sick with worry. Can ya help me, Reverend? *Please* help me.'

They came to him to say, 'I can't take it no more, Reverend. We're on the Valium night an' day. They keep callin' up – they never say who they are – to tell me that my daughter's a whore who fornicates with the Fenians. Sure she's only fifteen, Reverend, an' still a virgin, I'm sure, but she's in love with this wee Catholic lad from the lower Falls – we live in the Shankill – an' that's all there is to it. It's just an adolescent romance, no harm in it to be sure, yet they call me to say they're gonna pick my daughter up an' tar-an'-feather her for bein' a Fenian's whore. Now I keep the front door barred and I won't let her go out an' she sobs all the time an' keeps threatenin' to kill herself and we're practically livin' off the Valium. What can we do, Reverend?'

They came to him to say, 'He was allus a decent man, Reverend, a kind an' thoughtful man, a good father to our children and always stood up for the Catholics, but then our eldest lad was shot, cut down by a Provo death squad – a completely random killing; he just happened to be in the wrong place at the wrong time, walkin' home from a party – and when that happened, well, he . . . my husband, I mean . . . he turned bitter and started talkin' about the Catholics as if all of 'em were animals. Then he started goin' out a lot late at night an' I guessed what was happenin'. He denied it, of course, sayin' I was just imaginin' it, but when the RUC came knockin' on our door, I knew I was right. They got him shortly after that – the security forces came at midnight, knockin' the front door down with sledgehammers and draggin' him out of bed like he was just a sack of spuds – and now he's in H-block 3 with the other Loyalist paramilt'ries an I'm gettin' anonymous phone calls all the time. They say as soon as he gets out we'll get the bastard an' you'll get your pension. I pray, Reverend, but now I've got ulcers an' I can't sleep at nights. Is this lack of faith, Reverend?'

They came to him to say, 'I can't pray any more. I try but I just can't. I still want to believe – like I used to believe, Reverend – but when I close my eyes and try to feel His presence, I can't feel it no more. It's because He took my child – no, Reverend, don't try stoppin' me! He's the Almighty, after all, ordaining all that is, so those bombers were merely the instruments of His divine will

. . . Six years old, she was, a little angel, always happy, an' she sits there in that restaurant with all the other innocents, mostly wimmen like her granny – both of 'em just sittin' there, havin' a nice day out – an' then the bomb, the instrument of His will, blows her arms and legs off . . . So I left the Church, Reverend. I didn't want to be a hypocrite. I've lost my faith, which means I've lost the will to live an' I can't rectify it. That's all I've got to say, Reverend.'

They came to him to say, 'Please help me, Reverend,' or 'Speak out against them, Reverend,' or 'God bless ya, Reverend, you're a bulwark against those Popish schemers,' or 'Bless ya, Reverend, sure we know you're our defender,' or 'I want to die, Reverend.' They came one after the other, in their sorrow, grief and fear, to lay their great burdens upon him in the hope of relief.

'They trust me so much,' he said to his secretary when the last shattered soul had left his office that particular day, 'and yet I fear that I fail them. I am all too human, dear Robert, and my failings torment me.'

'You take on too much,' Robert replied, 'and it's bound to exhaust you.'

'Yes,' the Reverend sighed with what he realized instantly was a little touch of self-dramatizing martyrdom, 'I suppose so . . . But let's get out of here, Robert,' he added, determined to pay for his sins with more Christian work, 'and see what's happening elsewhere. Let's do our daily rounds.'

Leaving the office, they took the sky-blue Honda Accord parked in the Rosetta Road in the Protestant area of Cregagh. Not a man to give himself airs and graces, Reverend Dawson sat up front beside Robert who was driving. As they drove towards the centre of the city, along the Ormeau Road (where, in fact, the Reverend had his very nice red-brick home, inhabited by his wife and three teenage children, all members of his congregation) he glanced out of the window at the oak trees shedding their leaves on the wintry grey, wet, rainswept pavements. He thought, as he had done so often, of how attractive most of Belfast was, despite the image presented by television which invariably concentrated on the bricked-up houses and ruins of the small areas devastated by the Troubles of the past and not yet rebuilt. In fact, Belfast was truly a green and pleasant city, divided by rivers and loughs, dominated by its ring of soaring mountains. What a pity, then, that the Troubles – the Catholics' so-called 'War' or 'Struggle' – had blighted so much of it for so long. If only that problem could be resolved, this place would be perfect.

'Remember what this city was like when we were growing up?' the Reverend asked of Robert as he gazed distractedly out of the car, now crossing the winding River Lagan to enter West Belfast. 'It was very different then, wasn't it?'

'Ackay,' Robert replied, removing his left hand from the steering wheel to pat down a dangling lock of his well oiled black hair. Robert still used Brylcreem, the Reverend recalled, and that dated him perfectly. 'Sure it was all a lot nicer then. They were grand days indeed.'

Failing to cast his mind back over the whole of his sixty-six years to 1933, the year of his birth, when thirty per cent of Belfast's workforce was unemployed and the poor, Catholic and Protestant alike, were forced to march on the Lisburn Road workhouses to demand a minimum wage, the Reverend dwelt instead on a post-war Belfast of cobbled streets, gospel halls, mission halls, churches, greyhound racing tracks, and pubs known as 'porter houses' or 'gin palaces'. The only son of a fiery fundamentalist gospel preacher, the Reverend had been taken from an early age to the mission halls where he was seduced by magic-lantern shows about the jungles of Africa and South America, where Irish missionaries had gone to preach the gospel to the pagan natives. More pertinently, he had been informed in the mission halls of how, in the incomprehensibly distant year of AD 590, St Columbanus, along with twelve brother monks, had left Bangor Abbey to carry the gospel to distant shores. Others followed and Ireland soon became known worldwide as 'the Isle of Saints and Scholars'. Inspired by that knowledge, Reverend Dawson had followed in his father's footsteps and became a fundamentalist preacher, haranguing those emerging from the porter houses and gin palaces for destroying themselves with the 'demon brew' and beseeching them to come to the Lord – though only if they were Protestants, of course. Now, when he looked back on those days, the Reverend, not immune to nostalgia's roseate glow, longed for the simplicity of the past before Ulster, a Protestant country, had been torn asunder by the Popish evils of its Catholic minority. Thus, while he was not as virulently anti-Catholic as, say, the Reverend Ian Paisley, he was beginning to long helplessly for an Ulster in which there were no Catholics at all. This was a sad fact of life.

He longed even more for this when, during his busy afternoon, accompanied by his faithful secretary Robert Lilly, always reverential and obedient, he visited the hospitals where, alongside the sick and the elderly, he attended to those kneecapped, badly beaten or shot by the paramilitaries; when he dropped in on various of his constituents to listen to sad tales of husbands and sons forced to flee from home because of threats from the paramilitaries or given over to the drugs sold by them, or taken to drink because of shattered nerves; when he called in on RUC stations and police cells to counsel those who had found themselves in trouble after being involved, often involuntarily, in the illegal activities of the Loyalist splinter gangs who now ruled their localities through violent intimidation and forced those they were 'protecting' into doing their bidding. Though the Reverend supported the Loyalists, both in word and in deed, and was convinced of the necessity for paramilitary defence, he often felt uneasy about his own, often secret, involvement in the conflict and wished that he could be free of it all and concentrate solely on his church.

He felt this especially when he made his last visit of the day to a housing executive building located on the outskirts of Belfast, in a Protestant industrial estate near the town of Antrim. There, many of the young men he had rescued either from drink, drug addiction or the clutches of paramilitaries they had somehow offended were productively engaged on a computer-training course which would, hopefully, help them to find work when they were deemed fit to return to their own homes or when, in the case of those who had fled from paramilitary punishment threats, it was finally deemed safe for them to do so. Though this scheme was government-sponsored, it had been initiated by Reverend Dawson and supervised by the efficient Robert Lilly. Now, when he saw how well the youngsters were doing, the Reverend, not exactly computer-literate himself, was very impressed.

'But just what *are* they doing?' he asked Robert as they both stood behind a row of seated teenagers, studying the brightly coloured graphs, columns and lists on the glowing, humming computer screens.

'They're learning about the Internet and e-mail, CD-ROMs and so forth,' Robert replied, 'by accessing all kinds of information through them and processing that information in a wide variety of ways. Nowadays, through computers, you can reach banks, insurance companies, universities, all kinds of libraries, and even places like the White House, the Pentagon, and the Vatican. You can make contact with other computer operators worldwide and build up an impressive network of contacts in just about every field imaginable. So we're hoping that when these lads learn to do that, they'll have no trouble in finding work once they leave here.'

'I'm impressed,' the Reverend said. 'And if we can persuade some of them to work for us, that would be even better.'

'Some are deeply grateful to us,' Robert responded, 'and have already told me that they'd like to show their gratitude by working for us, either in the church or in the constituency, when they're free to do so. Indeed, some have come to the Lord since they've been here and that's made it all worthwhile.'

'Absolutely,' the Reverend said.

After leaving the building, they drove back though Belfast, coming off the M2 motorway and slipping into the dense peak-hour traffic of the late afternoon. It was dark already, but the lights of the city burned bright through slanting sheets of rain.

'Have we heard any more about the redoubtable Mrs Patricia Monaghan's radio programme?' the Reverend asked as Robert drove past Ormeau Avenue, where the Belfast branch of the British Broadcasting Corporation was located. Patricia Monaghan did not work for the BBC, but she was, after all, a reporter for a radio station in the Republic, so the proximity of the BBC had probably reminded him of his uncomfortable interview with her.

'Not about the programme itself,' Robert replied as he followed a long line of traffic through the slanting, silvery rain, creeping towards Shaftesbury Square. 'That programme probably won't be aired for months and probably hasn't even been completed yet. I say this because I can tell you for a fact that Mrs Monaghan hasn't yet finished with us.'

'What does that mean?'

'She's been watching us, Reverend. Following us around. Checking where we go and who we speak to. She's even been taking photos of us with a long-distance lens. So, no, she certainly hasn't finished with us.'

'She's following us and we're following her.'

'That's right, Reverend.'

'We'd better continue doing so. Clearly, as I suspected, that woman is up to some mischief.'

'She's after an exposé,' Robert said, 'and obviously willing to work hard to get it.'

'God protect us from the Catholics,' the Reverend said.

'Amen to that.'

The Reverend had many enemies and was used to being spied upon; nevertheless, the thought of being observed by Patricia Monaghan made him distinctly uneasy. He was therefore made even more uneasy, perhaps thinking of his own sins with regard to the present conflict, of all those whom he had helped and who could now be used against him, when he returned to his office and the telephone rang even before he had taken his coat off.

Robert picked the phone up, listened intently, then frowned. He placed the phone back on its stand and raised his darkly evasive gaze.

'There's a new man in the Shankill,' he said, 'and he's been asking questions.'

'Check him out,' the Reverend said.

CHAPTER NINE

Waking in his tiny two-up, two-down house in a street off the Shankill Road, Pete Moore, the 'new man' in the Shankill, was reminded by the presence of the naked woman sleeping beside him that this was Monday morning and that he had spent yet another Sunday evening drinking heavily in a Loyalist pub. He had been here for three months now, working as a self-employed television-and-video repairman, and he had made a point of socializing a lot to ingratiate himself with his Protestant neighbours and, in particular, with the local hard men. Presenting himself as a widower whose Australian wife had died five years ago in Melbourne, he had made a point of picking up a variety of unattached Protestant women in the drinking clubs, not only to appease his sexual needs but also to gain a reputation as a man who played as hard as he worked. This, he knew, would make him an item of curiosity to the hard men, arousing their reluctant admiration for him and making them view him as someone whose interests were not strongly political but self-interested and hedonistic. They would, therefore, be less inclined to suspect him of having returned to Belfast for ulterior motives. He was also aware of the fact that when this particular woman, Ann Chalmers, was seen by the neighbours leaving his house at this early hour of a Monday morning, they would gossip about him and his wicked bachelor ways. Not used to this kind of brazen promiscuity in Protestant Belfast, they would think him a basically decent Protestant lad who had lived too long with foreigners and been corrupted by their alien mores, but otherwise had nothing to hide.

Pete Thompson, he thought as he came out of sleep. *You're no longer Pete Moore; you're Pete Thompson. Say it like a prayer every morning and you should be okay.*

Though born and bred in Belfast, he'd had to change his identity
in order to cover up his past connections with the SAS. He had done
this by paying a brief visit to Belfast a few weeks before actually
moving there and trawling through the death columns of editions
of the *Belfast Telegraph* published in the year of his own birth.
Aware that his easiest mistake would be in responding to his own
first name if so addressed, forgetting his false name, he searched
for details of a long-deceased person with the first name of 'Peter'.
Eventually, he came across details of a boy, Peter Thompson, who
had died shortly after birth, a few months after he himself had
been born. He jotted down the dead boy's date and place of birth,
the date of his death and the names of his parents, including his
mother's maiden name. Armed with these details, he paid a visit to
the local registry office where the boy's birth certificate had been
issued, identified himself as Peter Thompson, said that he had lost
his birth certificate and requested a duplicate copy. When asked
for the relevant details, he was able to give them and then simply
paid his fee and walked out with a new birth certificate in the
name of Peter Thompson. Once in possession of this vital item,
he had returned to London, filled in the form for a new passport
under the name of Peter Thompson, a Belfast-born British citizen,
boldly forged the required referee's signature, putting him down as
a doctor who had known Peter Thompson for ten years, and then
submitted the application, confident in the knowledge that only
one per cent of all fraudulent referees were rumbled. A passport
in the name of Peter Thompson arrived in due course.

In possession of his new birth certificate and passport, he then
needed an employment record that could not easily be investigated.
As he intended posing as a TV repairman who had emigrated
to Australia in 1984 and returned to his home town after the
untimely death of his Australian wife, he asked an old friend,
Athol Wilkerson, a former intelligence officer with the Australian
SAS, to trawl through the Aussie equivalent of Companies House
in London and come up with a curriculum vitae based on his
supposed employment with a television-and-video maintenance
company that had gone into liquidation four years ago. His
friend had not failed him and now he was in possession of
a new identity, new birth certificate and passport, and a new
curriculum vitae that showed his employment record in Australia

and could not be checked, since the company named was no longer in business.

Thus, when Ann Chalmers yawned beside him and murmured, 'God, what time is it, Pete?' Pete Moore, though now masquerading as Pete Thompson, had no cause to be confused and responded naturally.

'Nine o'clock,' he said, yawning deliberately, staring sleepily at his wristwatch.

'Oh, Christ, is it?' Ann responded in panic, jerking upright, letting the sheet slip off her naked body to expose breasts still firm. 'God, I'm gonna be late for work, sure I am! Why didn't ya waken me?'

'Just woke up myself,' Pete responded. 'Late night we had last night in that pub in the Shankill. They locked the doors after closing time and we stayed until three in the morning. A good time was had by all.'

'I'll bet,' Ann said, slipping out of bed still naked and frantically picking her clothes up off the floor as she made her way, bent over, to the bathroom. 'Jesus Christ, why did I drink so much? Sure I feel bloody awful. I'm gonna be late for work, I can tell ya, an' it's all your damned fault.'

Pete grinned. 'You don't start work till nine-thirty and the store's only ten minutes away.'

'So make me a cup of Java, then,' Ann said as she disappeared into the bathroom and slammed the door shut.

Still grinning, Pete slid off the bed, put on a dressing gown and prepared a quick breakfast of tea and buttered toast, which is all that Ann ever had in the mornings. She was, in fact, only the latest in a number of unattached women whom he had picked up in the pubs of the Shankill, but she was one of the most attractive and talkative of them all. As Pete was an unattached stranger – and, even better, one who had lived overseas; in other words, a well-heeled novelty – picking up the women had been relatively easy and he'd only had to be careful that he didn't do it with a woman attached to one of the men who frequented the same pub. Ann was unattached in the sense that her husband, an RUC sergeant, had been shot to death by an IRA active service unit when on his way home from work about five years ago. Childless, she regularly went to the same pub where she had previously gone with her husband for the simple reason that she still had friends of both sexes there. Pete, she had insisted, was the first man she'd been involved with since her husband's death and the men she knew in the pub were only old friends of her late husband. In fact, most of those men were either Loyalist paramilitaries or RUC officers supporting them on the sly, either for sectarian reasons or for personal gain. As most of them had gradually come to accept Pete for what he said he was – a hometown lad returned, matured and tragically widowed, after many years in Australia – they were an invaluable source of information to him – as were the women, particularly the talkative Ann.

The woman concerned interrupted his thoughts by emerging from the bathroom where she had hurriedly washed herself in the sink. Now wearing a figure-hugging tweed jacket and skirt, an old-fashioned style but attractive, her long legs in high heels, and with her blonde hair combed and clipped up in a bun above her big blue eyes and smooth forehead, she looked like a respectable working woman – which indeed she was when she wasn't sinning with Pete. Grinning, shaking her head from side to side, she sat facing him across the small kitchen-diner table and started in on her tea and buttered toast.

'What's the time?' she asked him.

He glanced again at his wristwatch. 'Nine-fifteen,' he told her. 'That's five minutes to finish your breakfast and ten more to get to work. You'll walk in just on time.'

'Good,' she said. 'That oul bag I work for is a bugger for punctuality. I'd rather work for a bloody Catholic than for her, but sure what can ya do?'

'Have you *ever* worked for a Catholic?' Pete asked.

'Course not! No Taig would give me a job if I applied, but then I'd never apply in the first place.'

'Why not?'

'I wouldn't wanna work with one of them Virgin Marys starin' at me all day long. Fuckin' voodoo, they are.'

'Rubbish!' Pete exclaimed.

'Don't you rubbish me, Pete! Sure you've bin out of this country for most of yer life an' you've forgotten just what the Taigs are like. They fill their houses with all them Catholic statues and pictures, their Virgin Marys and Sacred Hearts of Jesus, those wee lights they turn on to illuminate them when they pray, and they carry on with their fuckin' rosary beads like they're practising witchcraft – which they probably are! Thanks, but no, thanks. I'm not religious, but I have a healthy fear of what the Catholics get up to. Besides, all Catholics are filthy.'

'What?'

'They say you can tell a Catholic by his smell because Catholics rarely wash or take a bath. I mean, in the days when we had coal, they'd keep it in the bloody bath instead of the coal hole. And even now, from what I've heard, half the Taigs in those housing executive homes that they get easier than we do use the bath for their rubbish. Not like you, Pete. I mean, your bathroom's so neat and tidy, I can't believe you don't have a live-in woman here. So where did you learn to be that tidy?'

I learnt it in the Army, dear, Pete thought, *though I can't tell you that.*

'At home in Donegall Avenue,' he lied. 'We only lived in a tiny two-up, two-down near the Windsor Football Grounds, but my mother was fanatical about cleanliness and neatness, so we were strictly disciplined in that regard – and some things you just don't forget.'

'You'll make a man a wonderful wife some day,' Ann teased him. Realizing, however, that his tidy bathroom could turn out to be a mistake, Pete decided to keep it untidy in the future. 'Anyway,' Ann continued, 'I've had my wee slice of toast and cup of tea, so I'm off to work now.' Pushing her chair back, she hurried to the hallway, pulled her shoulder bag off the coat-hanger, then turned back to face him. 'So when will I next see you?' she asked hopefully.

'Friday evening?'

'That's grand.' Smiling, she hurried back to the table, kissed him full on the lips, then straightened up and rushed out of the house, closing the front door firmly behind her.

When she had gone, Pete carried on with his own breakfast in a more leisurely manner while he finished reading a wide variety of yesterday's newspapers, the Sunday ones, both English and Irish. He read the latter with particular care because they told him a lot more about what was going on in Belfast and helped him to define just where most of the paramilitary activity on both sides was taking place. Also, when it came to reports of what was indisputably an increasing number of illegal acts by Loyalist paramilitary gangs, the same names kept cropping up. Now, after a month of studying the papers, including the dailies, he had the names of the gangs that mattered most.

This was a help only insofar as it told him which gangs were into crime for personal profit and which were most likely to carry out Loyalist assassinations for the cause. Bearing in mind that he was trying to trace a Loyalist group that was using computer technology to build up dossiers on potential assassination victims – albeit choosing, unusually, figures from both sides of the divide – he had decided that the best way to trace the brains behind the operation was to start at the bottom and work his way up; in other words, with the gangs likely to do the actual dirty work when that time came. Those gangs, he had decided, would not be the splinter groups presently running wild with baseball bats and CD gas canisters, causing mayhem in their own communities, but the more disciplined gangs of seasoned paramilitaries backed by the larger, long-standing Loyalist groups such as the UDA, the UVF (supposedly outlawed but still functioning with brutal efficiency) and the more recent but increasingly powerful Ulster Defenders.

From what he had learned during his three months of trawling the Shankill, mostly by frequenting the pubs used by the hard men, it was clear to him that neither of the major paramilitary groups, no matter how strong or influential otherwise, was in a position to obtain the kind of computerized details discovered by the RUC's Special Branch and passed on to MI5's Daniel Edmondson. He had, therefore, finally come to the frustrating conclusion that his trawling of Loyalist pubs was leading him nowhere and that he had to go somewhere else for his information. He was doing that this morning.

Shortly after ten o'clock, when he had finished scanning the newspapers, he dressed in a roll-neck pullover, corduroy trousers, suede boots and a thick windcheater jacket, then left the house and entered the freezing October wind that blew along this narrow street of terraced houses. As he walked along the pavement, glancing at the small two-up, two-down houses without gardens, he thought how normal it looked, how seedily respectable, and how normal had seemed most of the men he had met during the past months, both in the pubs and in the houses to which he had gone to repair TV and video sets. While some of them were hard, talking that way and looking the part, others were quietly spoken, almost diffident. Yet these, too, Pete knew from their reputations, were also men who had repeatedly tortured and killed.

At first, whether visibly hard or superficially mild, they had treated him with suspicion, but gradually, as word spread about his hard drinking, womanizing and great skill as a TV and video repairman, he was accepted as a Prod who had been away from home so long he hardly knew – and cared even less – what went on between the various factions in Belfast. He was therefore widely viewed as a politically naive newcomer who was entertaining to talk to, particularly good at his work, and harmless. Gradually, after three months, he had blended into the background and found it relatively easy to pick up information. The Belfast people, he soon learned, even the hard men of the paramilitaries, were surprisingly lax about secrecy and often too boastful for their own good, so he had picked up a great deal of information through casual conversations with individuals in their own homes or during drunken blarney sessions in the Shankill Road pubs. He had learned a lot in a short time.

The street he was walking along led into the Shankill Road, which was as busy as always. From there he took a bus, preferring its anonymity, to the centre of the city, disembarking near Royal Avenue. He deliberately walked from there to the City Hall, went around it and only hailed a taxi when he was passing the trendy restaurants, wine bars and pubs of Dublin Road. As this particular taxi did not specifically work the Shankill Road area, he felt safe enough in asking the driver to drop him off at the main gates of Queen's University. Just to be sure, however, he waited for the taxi to pull away into the traffic before walking on to a pub located a short way up the Malone Road. Entering the pub, which was practically empty at this time in the morning, he found his old friend, Sergeant Major Walter Bannerman, waiting for him, seated at a round, darkly varnished table. Formerly a Field Intelligence NCO, or Finco, with 14th Intelligence Company, which had supervised many covert operations against the IRA, he was now doing similar work at the British Army's Northern

Ireland headquarters in Lisburn. Tall, pink-faced, white-haired and roughly handsome in a well-pressed grey suit with shirt and tie, he raised his right hand languidly in welcome, then pointed to the glass of Guinness that was already sitting on the table, facing his own.

'I knew you'd be as punctual as always,' he said, 'so I thought it safe to order. It's only a half, so you can drink it quickly and we can get out of here before the lunchtime crowds arrive. So, Pete, cheers! Good to see you again.'

'Cheers.' Pete raised his glass in a toast, sipped some of the Guinness, then glanced around him at the gleaming oak tables, soft-backed chairs and sofas, art nouvea lamps and potted plants in the large, shadowy pub. 'It looks kind of Victorian,' he said, 'but it's too new to be genuine.'

'It *was* genuine,' Bannerman said with a wry smile. 'A real old Victorian pub. But it was bombed out a few years back, so they rebuilt it as close as possible to the original. Of course, most of the original fittings were irreplaceable, so they had to mock them up. Not a bad job, really.'

'No, not bad at all.' Pete turned back to Bannerman. 'Now about this business . . .'

But Bannerman raised his right hand to silence him. 'No, Pete. We'll talk about your business in my office in HQ Lisburn. Not only because it's safer but also, given what you've already told me, I think you'll be needing a weapon – if not for now, then for the near future when, or if, you get close to what it is you're after.'

'That may be true, but I can't be seen going into your HQ. That building must be under constant observation, even if from afar.'

Smiling, Bannerman nodded his agreement. 'Of course it is,' he said. 'Which is exactly why I decided to meet you here. We'll leave by the back door – the owner's an old friend of mine – and clamber into a nice little transit van just like the one you use for your TV business. You can't be seen in the back of that van, so we'll enter HQ in it, have our little chat, make sure you get a weapon, then you'll leave HQ the same way and get dropped off somewhere else. Now drink up and let's go.'

They finished their glasses of Guinness, then, at a nod from Bannerman, they left the table and went into the Gents. It had a back door leading into the street behind the building. The back door was unlocked. Opening it, Bannerman led Pete out into the street, which was lined with terraced houses and packed with cars. One of the vehicles was a transit van that had no windows. It looked just like the van Pete normally used for his work. He and Bannerman clambered into the back, then Bannerman closed the doors behind them and the driver, hearing the sound of the closing doors, turned the ignition on and pulled away from the kerb.

The journey to Lisburn only took about fifteen minutes. During that time neither passenger said a word. When the van eventually stopped, Bannerman led Pete out into a large underground car park that was filled with vehicles of all kinds, including troop trucks and armoured cars. An elevator carried them up out of the car park and deposited them in a corridor lined with offices, one of which was Bannerman's. He led Pete into the office and closed the door behind him.

'Take a pew,' he said, then walked around his desk to sit behind it and clasp his hands under his chin. The walls of the office, Pete noted, were practically bare, though a computer was resting on the desk, surrounded by an immense pile of diskettes. Clearly most intelligence gathering these days was done with minimal paperwork. 'So,' Bannerman said. 'Fire away.'

Pete told him what he had learned from MI5's Daniel Edmondson and explained exactly why he was in Belfast. Bannerman listened without interruption, then, when Pete fell silent, he offered a slight smile.

'Of course we know about this,' he said. 'We work closely, after all, with the RUC Special Branch and they brought the diskettes to us in the first place . . .' He waved his right hand to indicate the software piled up around his desk . . . 'So we felt obliged to copy them and pass the copies on to MI5. They told us that as a result of our findings, they were going to send someone in undercover – someone with no official connection to the security forces – and now they've done so and it turns out to be you. I'm really not surprised, Pete.'

'Why not?'

'Because I was one of the ones who recommended you – or, to be more accurate, supported the choice when your name was placed before me.'

'And why did you do that?'

'Because given your relative inexperience in undercover work of this kind, you turned out to be a natural when, with our backing, you did that little job for Edmondson a few years back. Also, I have a few well-placed friends in the SAS and, when you came here on Edmondson's behalf, I checked you out through those old friends. They all confirmed that though you were known as a bit of a bad boy – which was why you were thrown out of the SAS – you were still considered to be an exceptional soldier and a real loss to the regiment. So for those reasons I supported Edmondson when he chose you for the task.'

'Thanks a million,' Pete said sardonically. 'So what do you think about my appraisal of the situation?'

Bannerman nodded judiciously, his fine-boned fingers still clasped beneath his chin. 'I think you're right,' he said. 'We've looked into this ourselves and it's not our belief that even the most organized of the Loyalist paramilitary groups could gather in the kind of intelligence we found on the diskettes. They *could*, of course, carry out the assassinations of any targets chosen through that intelligence, be they Catholic or Protestant, but the information was almost certainly gathered by Loyalists somewhat removed from – and almost certainly more respectable than – the paramilitaries themselves.'

'More respectable . . .' Pete mused. 'That's a good point. Do you mean civil servants?'

'Some civil servants, certainly . . . but not all. Our analysis of the data found on the various diskettes suggests that the information has been picked up by computer hackers with friends in a wide variety of helpful places. These would include government offices – meaning, as stated, civil servants with access to important data on the movements of judges, military commanders and RUC officers; schools and universities – meaning teachers who can unobtrusively collect useful information on the parents of their pupils; insurance companies – meaning white-collar workers who can cull intelligence on a wide variety of so-called ordinary citizens, including paramilitary activists on both sides of the divide; and, finally, religious organizations – meaning clerical assistants who can fish for confidential information on prominent members of the Church, both Catholic and Protestant. So that's where the intelligence is coming from . . . from respectable sources.'

'But so far you haven't any clues?'

'No, Pete, we haven't – which is why you're here. I can only help you by saying that we're absolutely convinced that this rather broad band of sources has to be under the control of a single person or group. And you are, of course, correct in assuming that the only way you'll find that respectable source, which will surely be well hidden, is to work your way upwards from the ground where the cannon fodder, as it were, will be more visible.'

'The cannon fodder being the paramilitary splinter groups.'

'Exactly. If mass assassinations are planned, those groups will be tasked with the killings because they're dispensable. Most of the dumb sods don't know that, but they'll be given the task. So find out who's behind them and you'll have found the person or group behind the whole damned business.'

'Who do *you* think is behind it?'

'Someone we can't touch.'

'Who?'

'Because we can't touch him, I can't tell you his name.'

'Okay, don't tell me his name. Is he a civil servant?'

'While it *is* our belief that certain civil servants are involved in the gathering of intelligence, it is *not* our belief that a mere civil servant could have access to such a wide diversity of information.'

'A schoolteacher or university lecturer?'

'Ditto. Good for picking up information on the parents of their pupils, but wouldn't have a hope of accessing information not relating to the educational system. So such a person could only work as part of the intelligence-gathering system – he could not be in control of it.'

'An insurance company employee?'

Bannerman shook his head from side to side. 'A better choice than the former, but still not good enough. He would certainly have access to a good deal of information on a wide variety of citizens, but most of the information would relate purely to background details – age, state of health, married status, number of children, financial situation, address, et cetera – while providing little in the way of intelligence relating to general activities or movements. So, again, a valuable contributor to the system, but not someone able to control it.'

'Which leaves us with only religion.'

'You said it – not me.'

Pete grinned. 'I still don't want any names, but are you willing to tell me if any particular religious bodies on the Loyalist side are related to the paramilitaries or have – or have had – any association with them in any way?'

Bannerman shook his head wearily, as if he couldn't believe Pete's naivety. 'All of them did at one stage and some still do,' he confirmed. 'But that's all I can tell you.'

'No more?'

'Absolutely not.'

'That's not a hell of a lot.'

'It's an awful lot more than you think.'

'I'll think about that,' Pete said. Grinning, he pushed his chair back and stood up, preparing to leave. Bannerman, however, waved his left hand, indicating that Pete should wait, then he opened the right-hand door of his desk and withdrew a pistol. He walked around the desk, saying, 'If you get as close as I think you're going to get, you might well need this.'

He stopped in front of Pete and handed him the pistol. Pete had been expecting a Browning 9 mm High Power Handgun – the renowned SAS 9-Milly – but this weapon was unfamiliar to him.

'It's the new Five-seveN pistol,' Bannerman explained, 'made by FN Herstal in Belgium. For counter-insurgency work here in the province, we're now using this instead of the old Nine-Milly.'

'Why?'

'Because according to the MoD, terrorists in the province are now wearing the kind of lightweight body armour that makes the Nine-Milly virtually useless. As you doubtless know the Nine-Milly fires bullets weighing nearly seven and a half grams at a speed of three hundred and fifty metres per second. The Five-seveN, on the other hand, fires bullets weighing only just over two grams, at a muzzle velocity of six hundred and fifty metres per second – nearly twice as fast as the Nine-Milly.'

'Those are 5.7 mm cartridges – the same ammunition used in a sub-machine gun.'

'Correct. It's a scaled-down rifle round and the bullets can punch holes in brick walls or pass through tree trunks. It can, in fact, punch through forty-eight layers of laminated Kevlar armour at two hundred metres and, even better, it holds four times as many bullets as the .44 Magnum.'

'That's potent,' Pete said.

'Damned right. In fact, it's been considered by Scotland Yard's SO19 Firearms Unit to be too potent for normal police duties; so it's only being used by them for anti-terrorist and hostage rescue operations. We're using it as a back-up in the event of the jamming of our HP-5 sub-machine guns, which, as you know, happens all too bloody often. But we're also using it because it can be drawn from underarm holsters and fired rapidly from a double-handed crouch position – more so than with the Nine-Milly because its streamlined shape makes it less likely to catch in clothing when being drawn, so less likely to be fired accidentally. Finally, it's extremely light and produces about sixty per cent less recoil than what you've been used to.'

'Ammunition?'

'You'll leave here in overalls and carrying a metal toolbox – just like the one you already use – to enable you to get out of the transit van in a highly visible area without anyone taking any notice of you. We'll drop you off in the centre of town, near a Shankill Road bus stop, and you can just hop on a bus like any other worker and make your way back to your own place, looking just as you always do. The toolbox, however, will contain the pistol, its cleaning kit and enough bullets to let you reload half a dozen times. Even you, no matter what trouble you get into, won't need that much.'

Bannerman turned away from Peter to open a six-foot-high closet at the side of his desk. He withdrew a set of overalls from the closet and handed them to Pete. They looked exactly like the overalls that Pete normally wore when he went about his business, fixing television sets and video players in the Shankill Road area. Pete put the overalls on over his corduroy trousers and roll-neck pullover, then put his heavy windcheater jacket back on over the overalls. As he was doing this, Bannerman withdrew a metal toolbox from the bottom of the closet, placed it on the desk and opened it to let Pete see the pistol's cleaning kit and enough bullets to fill half-a-dozen clips. He then placed the Five-seveN pistol in the toolbox, closed the box and handed it to Pete.

'Let's go,' he said.

Bannerman led Pete out of the office, back along the corridor and then down into the large basement car park, where the transit van was still parked. A man wearing overalls similar to Pete's was sitting in the driver's seat. Bannerman did not introduce him.

'This man will drive you,' he said instead, 'and I want you to sit in the front, not the back, just like any other working man with his partner. When you get out, you'll be taken for just another working man being dropped off by his partner at a convenient bus stop. Please don't speak to him, Pete, and don't contact me again about this matter. From this point on, you're on your own.'

'Understood,' Pete said.

Bannerman smiled and held out his hand. 'Good luck,' he said.

They shook hands, then Pete heaved his metal toolbox up onto the seat and clambered in to sit beside the driver. Bannerman was already walking away, disappearing in the shadows of the vast underground car park, when the transit van roared into life and moved out into the wintry grey light of the Belfast afternoon.

About twenty minutes later, Pete was clambering down from the transit van, waving goodbye to the driver as if they were good buddies, and taking his place in the queue for the bus that would take him up the Shankill. Ten minutes after that, he was sitting at the table in his own kitchen, still wearing the overalls, checking the Five-seveN pistol, and wondering which particular religious person or group was connected, either openly or covertly, with the worst of the Loyalist paramilitaries.

He would have to talk to the hard men.

CHAPTER TEN

The meeting took place in the Romper Room of a Loyalist drinking club located near the corner of the Shankill Road and Peter's Hill. The club was protected with tall mesh-wire fences, heavy steel doors and scanning cameras. The RUC, though they knew what went on in there, rarely asked questions; nor did they demand that the illegal wire fences be removed. Inside, the club was like most of the others, which meant it contained a bar, a lot of chairs and tables, a dart board, an overhead TV set that was rarely turned off though the sound was often turned down, and, of course, the Romper Room out back.

As Billy Boy entered the Romper Room for his latest meeting with the heads of Red Hand, he was fully aware that the so-called Romper Rooms of the paramilitary drinking clubs, obscenely named after a perfectly innocent Ulster Television children's programme, had originated in the early 1970s as places where abducted Catholics were humiliated, hideously tortured and then killed in front of an audience that invariably was drunk and often took part in the battering, burning, slicing and general tormenting of the unfortunate victim. The 'romperings' had died out a few years later, though Catholics and Prods alike continued to die in other ways, but the Red Hand paramilitaries had recently reintroduced them. They had, indeed, as part of their new campaign to strike terror into the hearts of the Catholic community, conducted quite a few recent 'romperings' in this very room.

As he closed the door behind him and faced the three top dogs of Red Hand, Billy Boy glanced about him at the bare pine-board walls, and noted that they were still stained with patches of dried blood where various Fenians had, in his presence and sometimes with his assistance, been gutted and even crucified to the walls with daggers stabbed through their hands. Even now, Billy Boy

head job – execute him – and this caused him to experience a
small stab of panic, his thoughts racing ratlike through a maze
of the things he might possibly have done wrong or, just as likely,
have been *reported* to have done by someone out to get him for
personal reasons.

'What more could I want?' he asked cautiously.

'We still have that wee problem,' Jack Peel said, 'of your reported
ambitions to be somethin' bigger than ya are. We were wonderin'
if you'd really settled for what you've got an' will continue to be
a good team worker for as long as yer in the Red Hand.'

'Like I say, I think I've proved m'self an' you've no need to
worry. I mean, the work you lads have given me . . . well, it's
great and I'm in my element, like. But why do ya ask?'

'Because something really big's coming down,' Joe Douglas
said, now drumming a pencil rhythmically, annoyingly, on the
table, 'an' we need men who can work in a team an' do what
they're told without question.'

'Well, I'm yer man,' Billy Boy said, now forgetting his resentment
of them and becoming excited at the very mention of that mysterious
'something big' that was being whispered about up and down the
Shankill. 'Something big . . . ? What's that mean, like?'

'You'll learn in due course,' that icy little bastard Jack Peel
said, 'but first you have to do a bit more to let us know where
we stand with you. Are you willin' to do that?'

'Of course,' Billy Boy said with conviction, while thinking, *Some
day I'll get you, ya little shite. Sure ya can count on it, mate . . .*
'Sure ya can count on me, lads.'

'We have a job for you,' Alf Green said. Then he leaned across
the table to push the rifle close to the edge on Billy Boy's side.
'Pick it up,' he said.

Relieved that he wasn't going to get a head job, Billy Boy picked
the rifle up off the table, but still failed to actually recognize it. After
weighing it and balancing it between his two hands, he judged it to
be about five feet long and thirty pounds in weight. He'd never
seen it before.

'What is it?' he asked.

'A Barrett Light .50 rifle,' Alf Green informed him. 'The so-called
sniper's supergun presently being used by the Provo death squads.
It's usually fired from a tripod and can fire a bullet half an inch

in diameter at a speed of two thousand miles an hour. The bullets can pierce concrete and are even effective against helicopters. A direct hit to the torso would mean almost certain death – and, even better, you don't have to be an expert to shoot it.'

'I'm a fuckin' good shot,' Billy Boy said, feeling insulted.

'You may be a fuckin' good shot,' that antagonistic sod Jack Peel said, 'but that rifle can be used to kill victims up to a mile away, which is something you can't normally do, fuckin' good shot or not.'

'From a mile away?' Billy Boy said, then gave a low whistle of admiration. 'Fuck, boys, that's a long way away. I mean, I stand corrected, like.'

No one was amused. Not one of the bastards smiled.

'Jack's correct,' Joe Douglas said. 'Once that so-called sniper's supergun is mounted on a tripod and the sights are correctly zeroed, you can hardly miss – even if you're as blind as a fuckin' bat.'

'Which is exactly why it's been used recently,' Jack Peel said, 'for the killing of British soldiers and RUC officers in south Armagh and Fermanagh, as well as right here in Belfast.'

Billy Boy studied the rifle in his hands with a great deal of interest, aware of the silence in this room which had so often resounded to rock music and the screaming of the damned. Eventually, when even he, now so used to the screaming and so easily excited by it, could no longer bear the silence, he raised his eyes to stare boldly at each of the men behind the table.

'So what's the job?' he asked steadily.

Alf Green leaned his elbows on the table, rested his chin on his clasped hands and said, 'We want you to put out someone's lights and we want it done this evening.'

'No problem. Who is it?'

'A man called William Leek.'

Even Billy Boy knew who William Leek was and he couldn't hide his feeling of shock. 'Councillor Willie Leek?'

'That's correct.'

'But Willie Leek's a *Protestant*,' Billy Boy said disbelievingly. 'I mean, he's one of *us*, like.'

'True,' Green replied, 'but we have reasons for wanting to dispose of him . . . and we want you to do it with that particular rifle.'

'But why him?' Billy Boy asked, confused. 'I mean, we've got all those fuckin' Taigs out there and you want to top *him*! I mean, why . . . ?'

'Are you refusing to take orders?' Joe Douglas asked tersely.

'Ack, no, but I . . .'

'I thought you said you'd do exactly as you're told,' Billy Boy's old enemy Jack Peel said, his eyes as sharp as ice picks. 'Without question, like.'

'Yeah, well, I will . . . But all I'm sayin' is . . .'

'If you want out, just say so,' Peel said, enjoying himself by backing Billy Boy into a corner and watching him sweat. 'But if you back out, yer out altogether an' that leaves you nowhere.'

'I'll do it!' Billy Boy exclaimed, realizing that he didn't have a choice, not caring who his victim was, and only concerned with why these three bastards would want to top one of their own kind instead of a Taig. 'I just wondered why him of all people.'

'Don't,' Alf Green said. 'Don't bother yer head with that. Just take it that we want Councillor Leek dead and that we want it done with a weapon believed to be used solely by the Provos. Is that enough for you?'

'Ackay,' Billy Boy said, determined to prove his mettle and get rewarded with an invitation to join up for 'the big one'. 'Sure that's enough for me, Alf. So what's the routine, like?'

They told him the routine and, when they were finished, he walked out with the so-called sniper's supergun, a young man with a mission.

CHAPTER ELEVEN

Councillor William 'Willie' Leek's BMW had swerved off the side of the road and smashed through a wire fence before crashing into a telegraph post. Even from where Patricia was standing, just outside the police barrier, she could see that the windscreen had been smashed to smithereens, though whether from the crash or from gunshots she couldn't say. The sun was going down, casting its dying light on the scene and that light, added to the arc lights that had been raised around the BMW, produced an eerie chiaroscuro effect that made the wrecking crew, the police and the paramedics look oddly inhuman. Aircraft were constantly taking off and landing from the nearby airport.

Councillor Leek was still in the car, slumped to the side beside the empty driver's seat, his head partly out of the smashed side window. From this distance, Patricia could not see exactly where he had been hit. This, she realized, might have been a blessing as it meant that she could not see the bloody mess inside the crashed vehicle.

Pressed against the barricade and hemmed in on both sides by other journalists and press photographers, facing a solid line of sombre-faced RUC police constables, she spoke into her tape recorder, describing what she *could* see as she surveyed the whole scene. Right now the wrecking crew, two men wearing blue coveralls, were using a crowbar to force open the jammed door on the dead councillor's side while the paramedics, wearing white smocks and trousers, waited patiently behind them, holding a stretcher. The ambulance was parked by the side of the moonlit road, out of the range of the arc lights; it was surrounded by four police cars, all with roof lights rotating and flashing. The whole area had been cordoned off with barricades and solid lines of helmeted police constables. Other policemen, standing outside the

barricades in both directions, were detouring the traffic trying to
get to and from the nearby airport.

The man in charge, Chief Inspector Bill Spencer of the RUC
CID, obviously called out from home and wearing a gaberdine
over an open-necked shirt and floppy black jeans, was running
his fingers through windblown grey hair and looking thoughtfully
in all directions around him. A constable was standing close beside
him, taking notes as he talked.

'My, my!' someone said just behind Patricia as he pushed up
beside her. 'Our representative from the Republic of Ireland is
present. How are you, Patricia?'

Switching off her tape recorder, she looked to the side and saw
the broad grin of the *Belfast Telegraph* reporter Frank Cooney. He
was a big man with a shock of silvery hair and a floridly handsome,
cynical face. Cooney's cynicism was redeemed, in Patricia's eyes, by
his mischievous charm and what she had often sensed was buried
sadness. That look of veiled sadness was, she knew, often caused
by the Troubles, by some personal tragedy relating to sectarianism,
but you never asked about that in this city; you just let it lie. As for
Cooney, though he was a Prod working for a Unionist paper, he
had always been extremely helpful to her on a professional level.
She respected him for that.

'I'm fine,' she said. 'I'm just frustrated that I can't get in closer,
check out that scene for myself, and have a few words with Chief
Inspector Spencer.'

'You won't get beyond this barricade until the dead man's been
removed from his vehicle and driven away in that ambulance. Only
then will the crafty, keep-it-close-to-the-chest Spencer give us a few
minutes of his valuable time.'

'Sure I know that,' Patricia said. 'Thanks for the call, by the
way. How did you find out so quickly?'

Cooney rolled his eyes to indicate the other reporters and press
photographers bunched up around them. The former were calling
noisily to Chief Inspector Spencer to lower the barricade and
let them in (he ignored them); while the latter were jumping
frantically up and down, cameras raised on high, flashguns
popping, attempting to take photos above the heads of the
police constables lining the barricade.

'How did *this* lot find out so quickly?' Cooney said. Then he grinned and answered his own question. 'We all received a phone call from a man who passed by the scene of the crime and phoned the police at the request of Leek's wounded driver. That man, though he performed his duty, was clearly no fool. Once he'd phoned the RUC, he then phoned every newspaper in town, plus Ulster Television and BBC Radio, selling the story for a fee. Each of us thought we were getting an exclusive and so here we all are.'

'So you gave me a call even when you thought you had an exclusive? That was good of you, Frank.'

Cooney shrugged. 'I'd nothing to lose. These bastards . . .' He nodded left and right to indicate the other journalists. '. . . work for the competition, whereas you're a *radio* reporter whose work is only broadcast in the South. So I'd nothing to lose and one day you might return the favour.'

'I'll keep it in mind,' Patricia said. Looking to the front again, she saw, in the eerie chiaroscuro created by the combination of moonlit darkness and silvery arc lights, that Chief Inspector Spencer had finished dictating notes and was now supervising the transfer of Councillor Leek's body from the crashed BMW to the ambulance. Covered in a white sheet, Leek was carried to the ambulance on a stretcher held by two white-jacketed paramedics. As the ambulance doors were being closed, a couple of police constables, given orders by Chief Inspector Spencer, took up guard positions in front of the crashed BMW.

'He's going to let us take photos of the car,' Cooney said to Patricia, 'but not of the victim.'

'Bad taste,' Patricia said.

'And inflammatory,' Cooney added. 'A photo like that could have the Loyalists up in arms and lead to a whole new war with the Provos. Spencer's got his head screwed on . . . And talk of the devil, here he comes.'

True enough, Chief Inspector Spencer was approaching the barricade, his ruddy, weathered face showing no great deal of enthusiasm at the prospect of speaking to the press. Nevertheless, he stopped at the other side of the barricade between two of the police constables and, almost overshadowed by them, spoke to the reporters.

'A few words for the hard-working press,' he said, gaining a few laughs.

'Is the dead man really Councillor Leek?' a reporter asked disbelievingly when the laughter had died down.

'Yes,' Spencer said. 'Councillor Leek was shot in the head by a sniper while en route from the airport to Belfast, travelling in his own vehicle. A single shot killed him instantly. His driver was badly wounded in the arm, but he'll recover eventually.'

'When did the incident happen, Chief Inspector?' another reporter asked.

'We believe the incident occurred about one hour, forty minutes ago, at seven thirty-five p.m. approximately.'

'What about Councillor Leek's killer?' a woman's voice called out.

'We've combed the surrounding area in all directions, but so far we've found no trace of the sniper. We will, of course, continue with our investigations.' Spencer ostentatiously checked his wristwatch and then looked up again. 'That's all I've got to say for the moment, but I'm open to questions.'

'Exactly how did Councillor Leek die?' a male reporter asked. 'I mean, how was the assassination carried out?'

'According to the driver's recollection,' Spencer said, 'which is of course pretty vague due to shock and the speed of the execution itself, there was no sound of a shot. So—'

'You mean, he can't *remember* the sound of a shot?' another reporter interjected impatiently.

'No.'

'So what *does* he remember?'

'The driver's main recollection is of the windscreen exploding and Councillor Leek's head suddenly snapping sideways, almost hitting his – the driver's – left shoulder. The driver wasn't really aware of what was happening until the blood from the Councillor's head wound splashed over him. Still not too sure of what was happening – or not believing it, more likely – the driver lost control of the BMW and swerved off the road, going through the wire fence and crashing into that telegraph pole. The crash threw the driver forward, but he was saved by his safety belt. When the car stopped, the driver saw the wound in the councillor's head – obviously a very visible, mortal wound – and panicked and jumped out of the car. Only then did he realize that he, too, had been hit – wounded in his left shoulder. However, he managed to stagger back to the road and hail a passing car. He, Councillor Leek's driver, despite his wounded arm, stayed at the scene of the incident while the passing motorist went on to call the police from the next public phone box. We duly arrived at the scene of the incident and found the councillor dead. That's all I can say for now.'

'How was the driver wounded?' Patricia asked.

'A single bullet in his left shoulder.'

'So at least two shots were fired,' Cooney said.

'No,' Spencer said. 'Only one. It would seem that the bullet, fired from a point south-east of the car, smashed the windscreen, passed all the way through Councillor Leek's head and then struck the driver's left shoulder.'

Cooney, who had covered many similar assassinations and knew just what he was doing, glanced back over his shoulder, at the low-lying grassy hills at the far side of the road. Turning slightly to the side, he pointed in that direction and said, 'If the sniper fired from south-east, he could only have done so from an elevated vantage point on those hills way over there.'

'You should have been a detective,' Spencer said sardonically. 'That's exactly what we deduced.'

'That's a long way away,' another reporter noted.

'Almost a mile,' Spencer said. 'Which probably explains why the driver didn't hear the sound of the shot.'

'What kind of sniper could make that shot?' someone else asked sceptically.

'It's not the sniper,' Spencer replied. 'It's the kind of weapon used. I wouldn't normally tell you this, but I want it reported this time. The bullet used was half an inch in diameter. Even after smashing the councillor's head to pieces, it made an awful mess of the driver's arm. In short, it was fired at tremendously high velocity and that, plus its half-inch diameter, suggests that it was fired by a Barrett Light .50 rifle. That weapon, usually mounted on a tripod, is renowned for its accuracy.'

'It's also known as the sniper's supergun,' Cooney said, 'and used almost exclusively by the Provo death squads.'

'Correct,' Spencer replied. 'So as far as the RUC is concerned – and you can quote me again – this is clearly another assassination of a prominent Protestant by a Provo death squad or sniper.

I'm afraid that's all I can say for now. Are there any final questions?'

'Yeah!' a photographer called out. 'Can we pass through the barricade, Chief Inspector? Can we photograph the car?'

Spencer nodded. 'You've got ten minutes to take all the photos you want before the BMW's towed away.' He nodded at the two police constables manning the barricade, indicating that they should raise it. As the barricade went up, the constables lined along it hurriedly dispersed and clambered into the Black Marias parked a few metres away. While this was going on, Spencer raised his right hand and waved at the police constable standing by the front of the ambulance. The constable waved back, then angled his head up to speak to the ambulance driver. Instantly, the ambulance roared into life and drove slowly up to the raised barricade. As it inched its way through the massed journalists and photographers, they scattered and hurried towards the BMW, still being guarded by two police constables. A few of the more enthusiastic photographers took shots of the ambulance as it passed through. Spencer watched the ambulance departing, then he clambered into the back of his police car and was driven away. Patricia and Cooney, neither of whom had a camera, remained where they were.

'My photographer's one of that lot,' Cooney explained, nodding in the direction of the photographers and reporters now swarming around the crashed BMW like wolves around a fresh carcass. 'He'll take the photos direct to the *Telegraph* while I write up my article at home and send it through by e-mail. So I'd better get home right quick and get on with the article.'

'I'm a *radio* reporter,' Patricia reminded him, 'so I don't need ghoulish photos.'

'Then let's go,' Cooney said.

Grinning at each other, they proceeded to walk back to their separate cars, parked about fifty metres along the road in the moonlit darkness.

'From what I know of him,' Patricia said as they walked, passing under the overhanging beech trees and kicking up the dead leaves, 'Councillor Leek was a popular figure with the Prods.'

'With certain Prods,' Cooney corrected her. 'With the majority of Prods, probably . . . But like anyone with a high public profile, he had his enemies.'

'Who would they have been?'

'The Catholics, for a start. Leek was a staunch Unionist, a Grand Master of the Orange Lodge, and an outspoken supporter of British rule.'

'Sounds like a perfect Protestant to *me*,' Patricia said tartly.

Cooney chuckled and shook his head ruefully. 'Well, he may sound like a perfect Protestant to a wee Catholic girl like yourself, but he *did* have enemies amongst his own kind.'

'Such as?'

Cooney stopped briefly to light a cigarette. He puffed a cloud of smoke, shrugged his shoulders, then walked on again. 'People like Paisley and the Reverend William Dawson.'

'Why would they resent him?'

'Because despite his Loyalist credentials, Leek had started to express his belief that the only way to gain peace in Northern Ireland was to listen to Catholic grievances and invite Sinn Fein to the peace talks, with or without arms decommissioning. He thought that was impracticable anyway. In fact, Leek was one of the Prods personally responsible for getting members of Sinn Fein onto the City Council and ensuring that they were included in all major policy decisions regarding the city. While that gained him the respect of many Catholics, it certainly turned a lot of his own kind against him.'

Now it was Patricia who stopped walking, forcing Cooney to stop as well. He stared at her through the cigarette smoke drifting out of his nostrils. His gaze was shrewd and amused.

'Are you suggesting,' Patricia said, 'that this particular assassination may *not* have been the work of the Provies?'

'I'm not suggesting anything,' Cooney responded, then started walking again, thus compelling her to do the same. 'I'm merely saying that certain Republicans would *not* want Leek dead whereas his death would be welcomed by certain Loyalists of the more fanatical kind. Of course, over the past few months the Provos *have* been using that sniper supergun to knock off the odd Prod and not all of them would respect Leek as some do – so they might well have done it . . .'

'But?'

'I just think it's odd that of all the prominent Prods available, many vehemently anti-Catholic, the Provos should mark someone like Leek for assassination – one of the few Prods to openly stick up for them where it mattered the most.'

They had reached the many reporters' cars parked under the overhanging trees at the side of this back road across the mountains. Moonlight fell on the bonnets of the cars and made them gleam dully. The mild breeze was fiercely cold. Patricia and Cooney stopped by the latter's Vauxhall Cavalier to face each other again.

'Ignoring my Republican sympathies for the moment,' Patricia said, 'let's assume that the Provies *didn't* carry out this particular assassination and that it was, in fact, carried out by the Loyalists. Do you think that Leek's overtures to Sinn Fein would have been enough to warrant his death?'

Cooney inhaled on his cigarette and exhaled a stream of smoke through pursed lips, forming a smoke ring that was soon dispersed by the chilling breeze. 'Ignoring my *Loyalist* sympathies for the moment,' he said, 'let's accept that certain Loyalists don't want peace because they view it as a betrayal by the British government. In a similar vein, they'd view any Protestant supporting the inclusion of Sinn Fein in the peace talks as a traitor to the Loyalist cause. Councillor Leek could have been viewed in just that light and marked for assassination accordingly. I'm not saying the Loyalists did it, you understand. I'm just saying they *might* have.'

'What kind of Loyalists would even consider it?' Patricia asked.

Cooney checked his wristwatch, frowned, then opened the door of his car and slipped into the driver's seat. After putting the key into the ignition, he looked back up at her. 'A fanatical group,' he said. 'A group like Red Hand. Those bastards have based themselves on the old Red Hand Commandos of the early 1970s, but they're even more fanatical and barbaric. A group like that would certainly view Leek as a traitor and happily do what's been done. Goodnight, Patricia.'

He slammed the door of his car, turned on the ignition, then drove off with headlights blazing, turning back the way he had come and soon disappearing in the darkness. Taking her own car, Patricia drove in the same direction, heading back to Belfast, thinking of what Cooney had said and recalling, as the lights of the city centre came into view, that the Red Hand paramilitaries came under the wing of a larger group, the

Ulster Defenders, which had strong links with the East Belfast Unionist Party.

The MP heading that party was one of the two men mentioned by Cooney as strongly disapproving of Councillor Leek. That MP was the Reverend William Dawson of the New Presbyterian Church.

CHAPTER TWELVE

All the talk that evening in the Loyalist pubs of the Shankill was about the assassination of the generally loved and admired Councillor William Leek. According to what was shown on the constantly switched-on TV sets of the city and relayed in the newspapers, Councillor Leek, known affectionately as 'Willie' to his constituents, had been shot and killed by a Provo sniper early that evening when travelling in his BMW from Belfast International Airport, taking the back road over the desolate Black Mountain. According to legend he had always deliberately taken that route because he liked to avoid the city centre and instead reach his home in the Lisburn Road by travelling through the outlying working-class areas of West Belfast. He had done this, so it was said, because he was originally from the Donegall Road area and liked to be reminded of it, even if it meant passing around Ballymurphy, Turf Lodge and Andersonstown – all hardline Republican areas – before reaching the relative safety of the A1 and the Lisburn Road.

'The thing about Willie,' Joe Reid said to Pete as they stood elbow-to-elbow in a noisy, smoky Loyalist hole in the upper Shankill Road, 'is that he never forgot his roots and also – ya know? – he'd great affection for the whole of West Belfast, including all them fuckin' Taig areas.' Joe was six foot one, all chest and beer belly, balding and harelipped, a Loyalist paramilitary who'd been in and out of the Crumlin Road jail so many times that he was thinking about buying shares in it. 'I mean, he came from the Donegall Road and like a lot of kids from there he used to get to the mountains by walkin' up the Whiterock Road, right between Ballymurphy and Turf Lodge, which meant bravin' the Fenians on both sides. Of course, we all did that in those days. It wasn't so bad then. We might occasionally get picked on by a gang of

wee Fenians – they'd call us Prod counts and take our sweeties
and marbles, maybe muss us up a bit, but mostly they did us no
real harm and so we used that road often. So, Willie, you see,
he used that road as well, knew the whole area like, and so he
always took the back road over the mountains so he could come
home through his old haunts – sorta touchin' his roots, like.'

'Sounds like a nice guy,' Pete said, sipping some Guinness and
wiping his lips with the sleeve of his jacket, just like his new
friends did.

'He *was* a nice guy.' Joe nodded vigorously, affirmatively. 'A
real decent man. Regular churchgoer – Reverend Dawson's New
Presbyterian Church – and a lifelong member of the Orange Lodge
– a Grand Master, no less.'

'Married?' Pete asked.

Joe shook his bald head from side to side. 'He never married –
no shame in that – and, you know, it has to be said, he looked
after his mother like she was royalty, like the Queen of England.
Close as this they were.' Joe held up his crossed fingers, which
were thick, gnarled and, according to lax conversation, had lethally
tightened around the neck of more than one unfortunate Catholic
in recent Romper Room sessions. 'An' he treated his friends, his
constituents, his relatives, just like he treated his mother. A real
decent wee man, he was.'

Drinking his Guinness, Pete glanced around the crowded pub
and saw a lot of faces that were gradually becoming familiar to
him. The pub was a dilapidated watering hole of the kind common
to the Shankill: almost certainly not redecorated since it opened
fifty years ago, its walls covered in flowered wallpaper now stained
a dirty yellow with years of cigarette smoke, the mirrors cracked
and scratched, some of the stuffed seats torn, the floor filthy with
cigarette butts, crumpled potato-crisp packets, cigarette packets,
ash and spilt booze that had never been mopped up and was
now dried-out and smelly. Loyalist posters hung from the ceiling
between naked light bulbs, just above the heads of these Loyalist
boozers, male and female.

Surveying the large room, looking casual but missing nothing,
Pete saw various paramilitary hard men, most of whom he now
knew personally, their equally hard-faced women, some of whom
he had met through their husbands or boyfriends, and off-duty

RUC officers wearing plain clothes and clearly out for an evening of pleasure and illicit business combined. The relationships between the Law and the Lawless in this town, Pete had learned, were intricate, tenuous, corrupt and always potentially dangerous. The old war between Catholics and Protestants was now a war between gangsters who came in all shapes and sizes, in many disguises. All the rest was bullshit.

'He had faith, you know,' Brian Dogherty said, still on the topic of the late Councillor Leek, 'that nothin' would happen to him, that the Fenians in those estates, even if they recognized him, wouldn't touch him 'cause they had respect for him.' Brian, four foot eight, all muscle and bristling energy, peaked cap on the head, his grey suit like a used dishcloth, choked and coughed, exhaling clouds of ciggie smoke, then went on with his rant. 'And in fact, they *did* respect him – at least most of 'em did – but then those shites, those Provo cunts, they probably topped him for that very reason. I mean, those bastards are animals, they're as ignorant as fuckin' pigs; they wouldn't recognize a good man if he came down off a cross with bleedin' hands. As for wee Willie Leek, well, I mean what can ya say? He went out of his way to accommodate those Fenian bastards, to bring Sinn Fein to the table, to give the Taigs more rights, and they *still* turned around an' fuckin' topped him an' that just about says it all. Those Catholics, they're all a bunch of murderous bastards and the Provos are worst of all.'

'It might not have been the Provos,' Pete said. 'It might have been someone else.'

'Someone else? Who?'

'Maybe someone on our side. I mean, Leek had certain sympathies for the Catholics, got some onto the City Council, and openly supported the inclusion of Sinn Fein in the ongoing peace talks – so there must have been Prods who had it in for him.'

'Ack, not that many,' Joe Reid said, puffing a cloud of cigarette smoke as he spoke, lisping slightly because of his harelip. 'Sure what kind of Loyalist would want to kill wee Willie just because he wasn't a fanatical anti-Catholic? I mean, the Fenians, particularly the Republicans, don't want to believe it, but a lot of us Prods would be willin' to meet them halfway – that's what Willie was tryin' to do – but they're not willin' to meet *us* halfway, which is why they shot Willie. I mean, they didn't want him making any offers that they'd have to refuse.'

'Why would they refuse?' Pete asked, encouraging these two Loyalist paramilitaries to talk, having seen just how careless their kind could be when swilling down the booze. In fact, half of the sectarian executions in Belfast, Pete was convinced, came about because of drunken conversations just like this one. Many an innocent man had died because of a spiteful falsehood uttered under the influence of drink. Likewise, many a guilty man had died because his formerly secret activities had been exposed by a careless drunken remark. Certainly the paramilitaries, despite their paranoia and obsession with conspiracies, both real and imagined, were remarkably lax about confidentiality when they came together in what they erroneously believed were 'secure' pubs like this one. They talked too loudly and too much, which was to Pete's advantage.

'Because they don't want to believe,' Joe replied, talking loud enough for the whole pub to hear, 'that we Loyalists are sometimes willin' to compromise – not all of us, I grant you, but some. So if someone like Willie Leek, God rest his soul, put out an invitation to talks, the Republicans, who really don't want peace, would have looked bad . . .'

'Intransigent,' Brian Dogherty clarified.

'Ackay, intransigent . . . The Republicans would have looked intransigent if they'd refused. I mean, it would have made for a Loyalist propaganda victory – so naturally, to avoid havin' to refuse, the Provos got rid of Willie instead.'

Impressed once more by the fact that sectarianism in Belfast was alive and well and hopelessly intransigent on both sides, Pete had another sip of his beer and saw, over the raised rim of his glass, three hard men entering the pub. He had seen them in here before and now knew their names: Alf Green, Joe Douglas and Jack Peel. They usually came in together and always, when they entered, there was a brief, almost palpable change in the atmosphere, an undercurrent of fear, that lasted for the time it took the three men to cross the room and sit at a table clearly reserved for them. When they made that brief journey, as Pete had also noted, they seemed to exude an invisible force that made the drinkers packed closely together part like the Red Sea to let them through. The noisy conversation in the large room did not abate, yet the change in atmosphere was definitely there, only abating when the three men were seated around their table near the back door.

Clever, Pete thought when he saw where the three men were sitting, nodding grimly for the barman to serve them. *If anything unpleasant comes through the front door, they can flee through the back. Those bastards know what they're doing.*

Pete had learned during his early days in this troubled city not to ask direct questions about anyone. Instead, he had simply let conversations go where they might and had picked up his information that way. Thus, without having had to ask a direct question, he had learnt that the three men now waiting patiently to be served and trading a bit of crack with other customers were members of the rapidly growing Loyalist paramilitary group, the Ulster Defenders. So far, he had not ascertained precisely what their positions in that group were but, judging by the ripples they caused when they came in, they were men to be treated with respect, which in this town meant men to be feared.

Though Pete had often wanted to ask about them, he had been wise enough not to do so. Now, however, as if reading his mind, Brian Dogherty, small, broad and restless, leaned sideways and raised his head to whisper conspiratorially, though loud enough to make himself heard over the din, 'Now if there *were* Loyalists wantin' to get rid of the likes of Willie Leek, them boyos over there would be the ones to do it. I mean, that lot, they'd do *anyone*.'

Turning slightly sideways, Pete saw that Dogherty was nodding in the direction of the three men sitting by the back door. They were now being served personally by a visibly obsequious barman and as usual not one of them offered him money. It was drinks on the house again.

'Those guys?' Pete said innocently. 'Aren't they members of the Ulster Defenders?'

'Ackay,' Dogherty said. He had another swig of Guinness, loudly smacked his lips, then wiped them dry with the sleeve of his filthy coat.

'The Ulster Defenders are almost legitimate,' Pete said deliberately. 'I mean, they're like the UDA. I can't imagine them sanctioning anything like the killing of Councillor Leek.'

'Legitimate my arse,' Dogherty responded, blinking rheumy, bloodshot eyes and trying unsuccessfully to focus on the glass he was raising unsteadily to his face. 'They're legitimate like Sinn Fein's legitimate an' we all know what that means – a legal front for an illegal organization known as the IRA.'

'The Ulster Defenders are like that?'

'Ackay. Didn't ya know that? Sure they're backed by a perfectly legitimate Unionist party an' they use that to give themselves a voice in Westminster and with the media. But they're an umbrella, like. A quare *big* umbrella! An' that umbrella's keepin' the rain off a lot of highly active splinter groups – like the one run by those three bastards yonder.'

Pete turned his head slightly to gaze again at Alf Green, Joe Douglas and Jack Peel. They were drinking their beers and trading crack with friends, but none of them seemed truly relaxed and they rarely smiled. Those talking to them, though often grinning, sometimes laughing, did so artificially, as if not too sure of how to respond. There was a lot of fear there.

'What splinter group?' Pete asked casually, turning back to Dogherty.

'The Red Hand,' Dogherty said. 'The hardest of 'em all. To them the only good Taig is a dead Taig an' any Prod who even *knows* a fuckin' Taig is suspicious in their eyes. Not that I'm saying they'd a hand in Leek's death – that was the Provos for sure – but if *any* Prod would even consider killing someone like Leek, those three would be the lads to do the job without blinkin' an eyelid.'

Pete looked at the three men drinking their beer by the back door and realized why he had thought they were something special . . . and certainly dangerous. Turning back to his drunken friends, he said, 'Well, you just never know . . . I mean, in Belfast anything's possible.' He deliberately shook his head from side to side, as if bemused by his own thoughts. 'You just never know.'

'I'll tell ya one thing,' Joe Reid said, leaning towards Pete, looming over him, his harelip curled in a crooked grin as he, too, spoke in a supposedly conspiratorial tone of voice that carried clearly to both sides of the packed bar at least. 'Ya ask me, a lot of them disappearances of the past few weeks are the work of Red Hand.'

'Ya think so?' Dogherty asked, practically breaking his neck to stare up at his big mate. 'Sure what makes ya think that?'

Big Joe tapped his broken beetroot nose and gave them the wink. 'Them Loyalist disappearances weren't due to the Provos,' he said. 'For a start, the Provos have never claimed responsibility for 'em and they would have done if they'd bin the ones responsible. For another thing, none of them that disappeared left any kind of note behind, which they would have done if they'd intended committin' suicide. So, ya know, we're all wonderin' like.'

'They might not have left a note,' Pete reminded him, 'if they were fleeing from one of our own punishment squads. They wouldn't want to risk having their families knowing their whereabouts and maybe having that information forced out of them.'

'Naw,' Dogherty said, scratching his noise and gazing into his glass of Guinness as if into a crystal ball, his body as broad as it was tall, practically quivering with restless, murderous energy. 'They may have gone undercover but they're not fleein' from our own kind; there's too many of them disappeared these past few weeks for them to be running from *our* punishment squads. It has to be somethin' else . . . somethin' real big, like.'

'So how many have actually disappeared?' Pete asked.

'About a hundred,' Big Joe said.

'*What?*'

'Ya heard me right, boyo.'

The front door of the pub opened and Pete saw Ann entering, slim and sexy in skintight denims, open-necked shirt unbuttoned to just above the rise of her breasts, a shiny black overcoat and high-heeled black boots. Her long blonde hair, usually pinned up in a bun for work, was hanging to her shoulders, neatly framing her big, searching blue eyes. Holding a smouldering cigarette in her hand, she glanced left and right, squinting through the dense tobacco smoke, looking for him.

'So why do you think the Red Hand are involved in those disappearances?' Pete asked, still shocked at the sheer number involved and wanting to finish this particular conversation before Ann reached the bar.

Big Joe tapped his beetroot nose again and gave him the wink. 'Them bastards are up to somethin',' he said. 'The word's out on the street. The whisperin' has it that just about everyone who disappeared did so shortly after havin' a meetin' with those three over yonder. When asked what the meetings were about, none of the men ever said. But none of 'em, so it's said, showed the slightest concern an' a lot of 'em were visibly excited – so no way were they threatened with a head job. Those men, wherever they are, went there of their own accord and at the behest of those three over there. I'll say no more than that.'

Standing on tiptoes to glance over the bobbing heads of the many men standing between her and the bar, Ann finally saw Pete, waved and started towards him, wending and pushing her way determinedly through the tightly packed, noisily conversing, laughing drinkers.

'If it's big, it may be bigger than Red Hand,' Pete suggested, as if just playing around with ideas, which in a real sense he was. 'Maybe something organized by that umbrella group . . .' He paused as if he couldn't quite recall the name. 'What did you call it?'

'The Ulster Defenders,' Dogherty said. 'Though, God knows, it could be somethin' even bigger than them – or maybe somethin' behind them.'

'Who's behind 'em?' Big Joe asked.

'The East Belfast Unionist Party.'

'They're too respectable to have anything to do with the paramilitaries,' Big Joe said. 'I mean, they're backed by the church.'

Finally managing to push her way up to the bar, Ann leaned forward to place her hands on Pete's shoulders and kiss him chastely on the cheek. 'Evenin',' she said, flashing her warm, mischievous smile, first at him, then at Big Joe and wee Dogherty, both of whom smiled right back. Pete turned to Big Joe.

'What church?' he asked.

'The New Presbyterian Church,' Dogherty told him. 'Another breakaway church. It's headed by the best preacher we've got in this town . . . the Reverend William Dawson.'

'That fuckin' old phoney,' Ann said. 'I'll have a gin and tonic.'

'Coming up,' Pete replied, grateful to have some distraction from the thoughts that were spinning wildly in his head and sucking him into a black hole. Beyond that lay the nightmare.

CHAPTER THIRTEEN

They hadn't told him so, but something in the attitude of Alf Green and his two honchos at their last meeting had convinced Billy Boy that this was the last test and that when it was done, if it was completed successfully, he would be invited to join them for 'the big one': that mysterious forthcoming operation that was being discussed in loud, melodramatic whispers up and down the Shankill. Billy Boy was therefore feeling pretty excited when he clambered out of the Ford Cortina driven by Head Case Harrison, hurried across the pavement and entered the house of a Loyalist friend, Phil Blackie, who had helpfully absented himself for the day. Bone Crusher Reid and Big Boots Welsh were already at the house, the former standing just outside the front door to keep unexpected visitors away, the latter making his way up the stairs, carrying what Billy Boy would need for what could be a lengthy observation of the 'killing zone'.

Carrying the Barrett Light .50 rifle, its tripod and ammunition in a canvas travelling bag, Billy Boy followed Big Boots up the stairs and heard Head Case coming up just behind him. When he reached the landing at the top of the stairs, he found Big Boots, dressed as usual in a bomber jacket, blue jeans, smudged white trainers and Nike baseball cap, standing on a chair and grunting breathlessly as he pushed open the trapdoor to the loft. When the trapdoor had fallen back into the loft, thudding dully onto the rafters and sending down a fine fall of dust, Big Boots gripped the edge of the opening, took a deep breath, then hauled himself up into the loft. Once there, he dropped to his knees and reached down to receive the canvas bag handed up to him by Billy Boy. When Big Boots had taken the bag off his hands, Billy Boy pushed the chair away and, instead of using it, placed his foot (his trainers were wrapped in heavy socks) in a stirrup formed by Head Case's clasped hands. Head Case heaved him up until he could wriggle his way into the loft, coming to rest beside Big Boots.

Taking the canvas bag from his mate, Billy Boy 'mouse-holed' his way along the loft area above the terraced houses all the way to the far end of the street, until he reached the cramped space in the roof of a house overlooking the killing zone. In this case, the killing zone was a garage and spare-parts shop, located at the end of this street just off the Crumlin Road, not far from the infamous jail. The business was owned and run by Ken Bruce, a Loyalist councillor on the Belfast County Council, which also included members of Sinn Fein.

Billy Boy wasted no time in checking out his killing site. Knowing that right now, at the other end of the terrace-long loft, Head Case would be handing up the rest of the kit to Big Boots, Billy Boy examined the roof carefully until he found the slate nail that had been removed a few days before by Big Boots and replaced with a rubber band that allowed the slate to be raised and lowered, thus providing a small 'window' for observation and, when required, a firing port for the barrel of the Barrett Light .50 rifle.

Raising the slate, he glanced down on the street and saw a light shower of snow falling obliquely on the frosted road and pavement opposite. From what he could see of the street, it was practically deserted – not many out in this vile weather – apart from the odd customer either driving into Ken Bruce's garage or entering his spare-parts shop by the door at the side of the plate-glass window. Bruce lived with his family above the shop, but right now he was doing his political work at the Belfast City Council and probably would not return until the early evening. Though a member of that mixed-denomination council, he was strongly anti-Catholic and also aware of the fact that he was on an IRA death list. For that reason, he always travelled these days with two bodyguards.

The poor fucker, Billy Boy thought. *He mistrusts the Fenians, thinks the Provos are out to get him, and instead he's going to be killed by his own kind. He'll turn in his fucking grave when he finds out. He'll stop believing in God.*

Billy Boy had no idea why Red Hand wanted to kill one of their own kind and he didn't give a damn. His one thought was that when he killed Councillor Bruce, he would be initiated into what he now thought of as 'the mystery' or 'the big one'. He had no idea of what that was, either, but he desperately wanted to find out and, if he killed the good councillor, he would almost certainly find out at last.

Hearing the approaching muffled footsteps of Big Boots, who had just mouse-holed his way along the loft and was now approaching the killing site, Billy Boy dropped the slate back into position and turned to face him. Big Boots was making his way gingerly from one joist to another, being particularly careful not to step on the thin plaster between the joists that formed the ceilings of the bedrooms of the terraced houses below, and he was carrying another canvas bag in his free hand. Settling onto his knees beside Billy Boy, he placed the bag gently down between two joists and whispered, with a big, cheesy grin, 'Well, if ya fuck up an' they catch ya, you'll not have far to travel to get into the Crumlin Road jail.'

'Don't talk unless ya have to,' Billy Boy rejoindered, 'and even then, keep yer fuckin' voice down. We don't want that family in the house below to hear us up here. I mean, they're not in the picture, like.'

The family in the house directly below had no idea that an assassin had chosen their loft as an ideal site for the shooting of the man who lived and worked directly opposite. In fact, they would not know a thing about it until the first shots rang out, by which time it would be too late for them to do anything about it either way. Billy Boy would be out of here and gone before the male of the household – in the unlikely event that he was foolish enough to do so – could make his way up into the loft to find out what was happening. Billy Boy would be out of the loft and out of the street before the RUC or the British troops arrived on the scene. A piece of piss, really.

Still kneeling on the rafters, Big Boots opened his canvas bag and began withdrawing from it the variety of items they would need for a vigil that could, if for some reason Councillor Bruce did not return that evening, be much longer than Billy Boy had anticipated. The items included extra layers of socks, two thick sweaters and two pairs of gloves to help them combat the cold; high-calorie rations consisting of biscuits, cheese, chocolate and boiled sweets; two vacuum flasks, one containing hot coffee, the other hot tea; a couple of plastic bottles containing water for drinking and hygiene, such as the washing of their hands after they'd wiped their arses; and a pack of plastic bags that could hold their excrement, then be sealed and set aside after use. This last was not strictly for the purposes of hygiene – not high on Billy Boy's list of priorities at any time – but because the smell of piss and shit could filter through the ceiling and alert the people living below of the presence of someone in their loft.

As Big Boots was laying these various items neatly around him between the dust-covered, cobwebbed joists, Billy Boy prepared his killing site. First he raised the loose tile and fixed it to the upright position with sellotape, thus opening the small window that gave him a good view of the killing zone. Next, he very quietly opened the tripod and positioned it gently on the floor, bracing the steel legs between two joists. Finally, he checked his beloved 'sniper's supergun', ensured that it was still clean and well oiled, then loaded the magazine and attached the weapon to the tripod, with the barrel turned away from the window, which he needed for the purpose of observation. This done, he sat sideways on a joist, his feet placed on the neighbouring joist, and commenced his long wait for the arrival of Councillor Bruce. Big Boots, with nothing else to do, sat on his arse a few yards away, just waiting for the signal from Billy Boy that would tell him the councillor had arrived and that he had to pack up the kit, race back to the trapdoor, and prepare to help Billy Boy escape.

It was a long, cold wait. Billy Boy and Big Boots were already wearing thick socks over their trainers to keep the noise down in the loft, but within an hour they had to don their second pullovers and also put their spare socks over the first set to prevent their feet from freezing. They were keeping one of the bottles of water for an emergency – should the councillor change his plans and arrive home hours, or even a day or so, later – but the dust and cold in the loft forced them to drink the tea and coffee at regular intervals; this in turn compelled them to piss into the plastic bags in full view of each other.

An hour later, Big Boots, who had the habits of a baby, decided he had to shit and did it into a plastic bag, in full view of the grinning Billy Boy, by balancing precariously on two joists, his arse just above the dusty, cobwebbed loft floor, the bag held awkwardly to his arsehole with one hand, the other gripping a joist for balance. When he had finished, he wiped his arse with some tissue handkerchiefs, shoved the dirty tissues into the plastic bag, then sealed the bag and set it on the floor, a good metre away. Fastidious to the end, he soaked some tissues with water from one of the plastic bottles, wiped his hands clean, then likewise placed the tissues on the floor beside the plastic bags.

When they left, they would leave these items here, to rot eventually and stink out the house below.

Sitting at the small window formed by the raised slate, Billy Boy carefully observed the street below. The snow was still falling obliquely on the frosted road and pavements, sweeping across the now brightly lit plate-glass window of Councillor Bruce's spare-parts store. It was already growing dark and the street lights had come on. Bored, Billy Boy passed the time by recalling his assassination of Councillor William 'Willie' Leek.

Billy Boy had enjoyed it. Briefed by Red Hand of the councillor's movements, knowing that at a certain time in the early evening he would be arriving at Belfast International Airport from London and taking the back road from the airport over the Black Mountain, Billy Boy had picked a spot, located about twenty minutes' drive from the airport, where, apart from being a particularly desolate area, there were low hills that rose up south-east of the road. The subsequent job was a pushover.

He had waited there for half an hour or so, positioned behind the tripod-mounted Barrett Light .50 rifle, until the councillor's car came into view around a bend in the road. Though the sun was sinking, it was still bright enough for the councillor's car not to be using its headlights and Billy Boy had a clear view of the councillor sitting up front beside his driver. Taking careful aim, Billy Boy had fired a single shot. He saw the windscreen exploding and the car swerving violently across the road. It was smashing through the wire fence at the side of the road and crashing into a telegraph pole before Billy Boy could get off a second shot. He did, however, see that the councillor had slumped to the side of the car, with his head half out of the broken window.

Warned by his advisers at Red Hand not to hang around for a second longer than necessary, Bill Boy had packed up the supergun and its tripod, placing them back into the canvas travelling bag, and was hurrying back to his Ford Cortina, parked in the shadows at the bottom of the hill, when he saw the councillor's driver falling out of the car and rolling a few feet over the ground, clutching his bloody left shoulder. The man had then risen unsteadily to his feet to stare at the crashed car – and at the dead councillor – in a dazed, disbelieving manner. Not interested in the driver, not wanting to hang around, Billy Boy had returned to his own car and driven off at normal speed, confident that it would be some time before anyone passed the assassination scene and reported the incident. About thirty minutes later, Billy Boy was back in Belfast, feeling pleased with himself.

In fact, as he now recalled, he had been even more pleased when, later that evening, news of the assassination had been broadcast on the radio and on TV. Billy Boy had got a real buzz standing in the pub with his mates and watching the TV footage of the assassination site, now a busy scene with police cordons, wrecking crews, squad cars, a single ambulance, reporters and press photographers. Shortly after, there were blurry, close-up images of the crashed car, but by that time the councillor's body had been removed to avoid shocking the public.

Ackay, Billy Boy had really enjoyed seeing that TV footage in the presence of his mates, though unfortunately he hadn't been able to tell them that he was the assassin. That was his only real disappointment. Otherwise, he'd felt grand.

Recalling that evening, Billy Boy became excited all over again and looked forward to the arrival home of Loyalist Councillor Ken Bruce. His excitement was useful as it helped to distract him from the deepening cold in the dark, unheated loft, but eventually, after three hours had passed, he started to feel as cold and miserable as Big Boots looked, shivering over there on the joists a few metres away.

Luckily, the councillor's car, a silvery-grey Volvo, came into view a few minutes later, at 7.05 p.m. It braked to a halt at the kerb, directly in front of the plate-glass window of the spare-parts shop. This was helpful to Billy Boy, as the light beaming out of the broad window and onto the frosty, snowswept pavement clearly illuminated the councillor's vehicle.

Instantly, Billy Boy swung the barrel of his tripod-mounted weapon around until it was facing the small window formed by the raising of the slate. Big Boots saw him do this and clambered instantly to his feet to start back along the loft to the trapdoor in the house at the far end of the street. Billy Boy looked down through the sights of his sniper's supergun and saw the councillor's two bodyguards emerging from the back of the Volvo to take up watch positions on the pavement on either side of the vehicle. Wearing heavy overcoats that hid their weapons, they were framed and sharply silhouetted in the light from the brightly lit shop window.

Billy Boy released the safety catch on his weapon. Councillor Bruce's driver remained behind the steering wheel, preparing to drive off, as the councillor himself emerged from the offside front of the vehicle. A silvery-haired, portly man, he was, like his bodyguards, wearing a heavy overcoat that made him seem fatter than he was. He was just about to turn around and close the car door behind him when Billy Boy fired two shots in quick succession, the first aimed at the councillor's body, the second at his head.

The first shot punched the councillor backwards against the car and the second took off half of his head and made him jerk to the side. As he fell against the open door, the car roared away with a squealing of brakes, letting the councillor fall to the ground and exposing the two bodyguards at the shop window, both with pistols in their hands, both glancing wildly in all directions. Still framed and silhouetted in the bright light of the plate-glass window, they made perfect targets and Billy Boy fired at each of them in turn.

One man was virtually picked off his feet and smashed backwards, limbs asprawl, through the plate-glass window, showering the pavement and the other man with shards of flying glass as the latter spun around in a semicircle, quivered as if whiplashed, then fell solidly to his knees. Unable to resist it, Billy Boy fired two more shots at him, one at his body, the other at his head, and he was punched back, almost bent over his own feet, then twisted sideways and flopped across the pavement with his head gushing blood.

'Fucking ace!' Billy Boy said.

Without further ado, but with the sounds of female screaming emanating from the house directly below and from the far side of the street, he packed up the rifle and tripod, placed them back in the canvas bag, then made his way with all due speed, given the awkwardness of having to hop from one joist to the other, along the loft to the trapdoor over the house at the very far end. Looking down through the trapdoor, he saw Big Boots looking up, waiting for him. Billy Boy handed Big Boots the canvas bag and the latter took it and then pushed a chair under the trapdoor. As Big Boots hurried down the stairs, taking both canvas bags with him, Billy Boy inched himself through the trapdoor, stood on the chair, pulled the trapdoor shut behind him (to make it more difficult for the security forces to find out what house had been used as an entry point) and then followed Big Boots down the stairs and out of the house.

Bone Crusher was still standing guard outside the front door of the house. Head Case had already turned the car around and was parked in the same place, but facing the Crumlin Road exit, mere metres away. Glancing to his left, Billy Boy saw that a crowd had already gathered at the far end of the street, around the two dead bodies outside the spare-parts shop – the councillor on the road and the bodyguard on the pavement – and around the smashed window of the shop itself, into which the other bodyguard had fallen. It was quite a long street and the people down there, not thinking to look in this direction, were pointing to the upstairs of the house facing the dead councillor's premises. Confident that the sound of the gunshots would not have been heard at this end of the street – which was also the noisy end because of the dense traffic in the Crumlin Road – and that their departure from the street would not even be noticed, Billy Boy jumped into the front of the car beside Head Case, who was driving. After closing the front door of the escape house, Bone Crusher clambered into the rear of the car beside Big Boots, who had the canvas bags on the floor at his feet, and Billy Boy then told Head Case to take off. Head Case did as he was told and, mere seconds later, the car was turning into the Crumlin Road and heading back to the Shankill.

Less than ten minutes later, Billy Boy was in the toilet of the Red Hand drinking club in the Shankill, washing out his ears with cotton wool, then washing his arms and hands, to remove any traces of cordite or lead residue left by the discharge of his weapon. Later, when he got home, he would have a proper bath and then burn his clothing, trainers and gloves to ensure that the police could find no traces of cordite on them either. Now, however, feeling flushed with excitement, he left the toilet and returned to the main room of the club, where the three top dogs of Red Hand – Alf Green, Joe Douglas and Jack Peel – were still sitting around a table, drinking pints of Guinness and waiting for the news on TV.

After telling them about the success of his mission, Billy Boy had expected them to congratulate him, but that untrustworthy wee shite Jack Peel had merely said, 'Let's wait and see if he's dead or not', that surly bastard Joe Douglas had merely taken the canvas bag off him and stored the weapon in a cupboard, and Alf Green, without a smile or even a word of thanks, had told him to wash himself in the toilet and come back out for the news. Now the three of them were sitting there, as humourless as always, drinking and looking up at the TV, waiting for the news to start.

Well, fuck you, Billy Boy thought.

The news, however, was good. It included a dramatic flash item about the assassination of Councillor Ken Bruce and his two bodyguards. It showed the scene of the crime and confirmed that all three men were dead. The assailants, according to the news, were unknown.

When the news flash ended, Jack Peel turned the TV off and then he and the other two bastards turned to face Billy Boy. The latter had never known what to expect, but certainly he had not even remotely imagined the statement that was now being made to him by the unsmiling Alf Green.

'We want you to disappear.'

CHAPTER FOURTEEN

As Pete walked along the cliff path, high above the eerie lunar landscape of the Giant's Causeway with its bizarre rock formations and amphitheatres of stone columns, swept by light gusts of snow and whipped by a fierce, freezing wind that made the sea roar and explode far below, he wondered why Frank Cooney had decided to meet him in this spectacular – and spectacularly desolate – location.

Making his way along the winding, windblown path, glancing down at the stepping stones formed by a mass of basalt columns packed tightly together and lined with bizarre rock formations, he thought of the Red Hand paramilitary group, of the other Loyalist paramilitaries who were disappearing inexplicably on a daily basis, and of the Reverend William Dawson and his breakaway church and Unionist Party. His every instinct told him that they were somehow tied together and, in turn, tied to the problem that had brought him here in the first place . . . to locate the Loyalists hacking into local computerized systems in order to compile a mass of data, much of it confidential, on prominent citizens, both Catholic and Protestant, who were almost certainly being earmarked for assassination. But as, on the surface, the elements he had put together seemed to have little in common, he was starting to feel that his instincts were betraying him and that he was fooling himself.

Shivering even in his thick overcoat and scarf, he kept following the narrow, grassy path, wiping flakes of snow from his watery eyes, leaning into the fierce wind and staring beyond the Grand Causeway, through a curtain of falling snow, to the tall, bizarrely shaped rock formations known as the Chimney Tops soaring high at the far side of the Amphitheatre. As he turned another bend in the path, heading for the first viewing point, Weir's Snout, he saw Frank

Cooney standing in the fenced-in viewing point, being pounded by the wind, his greying hair flapping wildly, gazing out to sea as the snow fell about him. He turned his head when Pete approached him and then offered a slight, sardonic smile. He had a handsome face flushed with years of drinking, but his eyes were alert.

'Frank Cooney?' Pete said.

'Correct. And you're Pete Moore, I take it.'

Pete nodded. 'That's right.' He glanced about him, at the angry sea and the windswept fields, the snow sweeping fiercely across them, then turned back to Cooney. 'Why the hell did you want to meet me here? This place is like Siberia.'

'No sea in Siberia,' Cooney replied. 'As for this place . . .' He shrugged. 'I used to meet a good friend here – he was in your kind of business, SAS and so forth – and we tended to come here to discuss matters, far from the maddening crowd.'

'And from prying eyes and ears.'

'That first and foremost,' Cooney agreed.

Pete knew from information received from Daniel Edmondson that Frank Cooney was a Belfast journalist for the Unionist *Belfast Telegraph*, that his only daughter had been killed in the crossfire of an aborted IRA robbery, and that, despite this tragic fact, he was renowned for his objectivity regarding both sides of the divide. According to the MI5 dossier, Cooney believed that the paramilitaries of both sides had been heavily engaged in organized crime for years and were gradually hardening into brutal criminal gangs that had no interest in any kind of peace. Because of this belief, Cooney had often assisted British intelligence with invaluable information about the paramilitaries, both Catholic and Protestant. Doubtless, then, the 'friend' he had mentioned had been here undercover on behalf of the Brits.

'So what happened to your friend?' Pete asked to break the lingering silence.

'He came here to do a job, completed it and then disappeared.'

'Back to England?'

'No. He disappeared off the face of the earth and never returned.' Cooney waved his hand airily to take in the surrounding fields and the land far beyond them. 'I suspect he's buried somewhere out there. Another unmarked grave on the green hills of Ulster.

Another ghost set loose to haunt us. We're a haunted race, Mr Moore.'

'Call me Pete.'

'How can I help you, Pete?'

Without waiting for a reply, Cooney turned away and started walking along the narrow path. Pete hurried to catch up with him and fell in beside him. They walked together along the edge of the cliff, the sea on one side of them, empty grazing fields on the right, tufts of brown grass thrusting out of the deepening snow with veils of more snow drifting over them. Cooney had been recommended personally by Daniel Edmondson of MI5, so Pete, knowing that he could trust him, told him exactly why he was here and what he had surmised so far. Still walking, Cooney listened thoughtfully, not speaking until Pete had finished.

'So you think,' Cooney said when Pete fell silent, 'that because I move around a lot, have friends on both sides of the divide, and have helped British intelligence before, that I can tell you who these computer hackers are. Well, I'm sorry. I can't.'

'I didn't think you'd necessarily know,' Pete corrected him. 'I just thought that with your knowledge of what goes on here, you might be able to make some connections for me.'

'Try me,' Cooney said.

Pete shivered, now feeling the biting cold, and yearned to be indoors, away from the blasting wind and sweeping snow and the sea's demonic roaring. 'There's a lot of talk in the Shankill about some really big – *unusually* big – Loyalist operation in the offing. At the same time, a large number of paramilitaries are inexplicably disappearing.'

'Yes, I've heard about that,' Cooney said.

'Well,' Pete continued, 'according to some of my new paramilitary friends in the Shankill, just about everyone who disappeared did so after having a confidential meeting with the heads of Red Hand. None of them emerged from those meetings showing any kind of misgivings and, indeed, most of them seemed thrilled by what they'd been told . . . then they disappeared. So they weren't running from the threat of punishment or even execution; they were disappearing voluntarily and, clearly, were keen to go.'

'So everyone's now relating those disappearances to a really big operation that's coming up in the future?'

'Yes,' Pete said. 'And somehow, for some reason I can't quite figure, I keep thinking that all that data being collected is related to this mysterious "something big" that's being discussed in noisy whispers up and down the Shankill.'

'Something big sounds to me like a big hit list,' Cooney said, 'and for that they'd need an awful lot of data on an awful lot of targets. I suspect that's the connection you were trying to make in the back of your head.'

'So if that's what we have here, who do you think is likely to be behind it?'

Cooney shrugged. 'Who knows?'

They continued walking along the windblown path, above the dark, savagely pounding, raging sea, through the thickening, blinding snow, leaning into the howling wind.

'What do you know about the Reverend William Dawson?' Pete asked eventually.

'Why do you ask?'

'Because I learnt a few days back that the Red Hand paramilitaries are an offshoot of the Ulster Defenders who are, reportedly, backed by the East Belfast Unionist Party. That party's headed by the Reverend William Dawson.'

'So you think there's a link between Reverend Dawson and the Red Hand group which, according to what you've told me, almost certainly had something to do with the recent disappearances of so many other paramilitaries.'

'Yes,' Pete said. 'Which means that Reverend Dawson, or his East Belfast Unionist Party or, even, his breakaway New Presbyterian Church, could *also* have something to do with the disappearances.'

'It's possible,' Cooney said eventually, after a thoughtful pause.

'It's more than a possibility,' Pete insisted, thinking of his conversation a few weeks back with Sergeant Major Walter Bannerman, at the British Army's Northern Ireland HQ in Lisburn. 'I was recently talking to a friend who's presently working for British intelligence right here in the Province, trying to deduce who'd be in the most likely position to collect the kind of information that was found on those mysterious diskettes, and he whittled it down to the likelihood of a respectable Protestant religious organization . . . or individual. At least . . .'

'Yes?' Cooney prodded when Pete paused, confused by what he had just recollected.

'Well . . . He *seemed* to have whittled it down. It was only when I left his office that I realized he'd given me no real reason for suggesting a religious organization. He'd given me good, solid reasons for why the other possibilities wouldn't have worked and, by so doing, left me with that sole remaining possibility. However, as I say, it was only when I left his office that I realized he hadn't given me the slightest reason for why a religious organization would have been in a better position to collect such information from such a wide variety of secular data banks . . .'

'So he deliberately planted the idea of a religious organization in your head?' Cooney interjected.

'Right,' Pete said.

'Did he offer any suggestions?'

'No . . . But one thing I remember clearly . . . When I accused him of not giving me a hell of a lot of information, he replied, "It's an awful lot more than you think".'

'In other words, he was telling you off the record to concentrate on a religious organization, or individual, as the most likely controller of all those unknown Loyalist computer hackers.'

'Yes, I think so . . . And since the Reverend William Dawson, through his breakaway political party, has a connection to the Ulster Defenders, thus to Red Hand, it *is* possible that he knows what's going on and may, indeed, be behind it.'

'You're supposing, I take it, that there has to be a link between the inexplicable disappearances of so many Loyalist paramilitaries, the mysterious big operation that's being planned right now – almost certainly the assassinations of targets on an exceptionally long hit list – and the collection of data on an unusually large number of potential targets, both Catholic and Protestant.'

'You've got it,' Pete said. 'So what about the Reverend William Dawson? Just who, or what, is he?'

'Let's turn back,' Cooney said.

They started back the way they had come, towards the outthrusting Weir's Snout. The waves were breaking over the rocks far below and exploding into immense clouds of spray that was brighter than the winter's grey light, illuminating its stormy gloom with showering diamonds. The snow continued to fall.

'The Reverend William Dawson,' Cooney said quietly, distractedly, almost as if talking to himself. 'An interesting question mark. Presently favoured by the Brits – and, indeed, by many Belfast Prods – over the more notorious Reverend Ian Paisley. When you're talking Paisley, of course, you're talking something else again – someone the media used to love before they grew tired of him. You're talking fire and brimstone, hell's fires, damn all the Popish heretics. You're talking Elmer Gantry, a deep-south American fundamentalism. Sure the man tantalized and tormented us for years, but now his time is past.'

'I agree with you,' Pete said.

Cooney nodded, smiling slightly, his head lowered to keep the swirling snow from getting into his eyes, to avoid the harsh, cutting wind. 'Now the Reverend William Dawson, well, he's something else again. Oh, he's good in the pulpit, he can spit fire and brimstone too, but he's basically a modernist, well educated, sophisticated – degrees in economics and political theory as well as in theology – and he knows all the tricks of propaganda, religious and otherwise. A religious bureaucrat, you might say, in control, the velvet glove, and he knows how to tread the fine line between his own openly expressed Unionist views and those of the Catholic minority. An adroit politician, in other words, and the Brits, among others, love him for it. Now Paisley is widely viewed as a demagogic anachronism and Dawson, widely seen as more conservative or pragmatic, is the up-and-coming religious politician for the Prods.'

'You mean he's clever,' Pete said.

Cooney sighed. 'Yes, that's just what I mean.'

They had reached Aird Snout and Pete heard the sea smashing over the rocks of the Giant's Causeway, rushing, roaring, exploding and then subsiding, sucked back into cataracts of howling wind and the darkness of winter light. On the horizon, holding sea and sky together, a ribbon of black clouds expanded. Snow flakes continued to speckle the sullen sky.

'But could Dawson be connected in any way,' Pete asked, 'to the kind of paramilitary operation we're envisaging? Is there any connection between him and, say, Red Hand?'

'Yes, definitely,' Cooney said, as if surprised by Pete's naivety. 'Certainly, at least with regard to your second question, there's no doubt about it at all. While no *direct* connection can be made between Reverend Dawson and the Red Hand paramilitaries, the latter insists that it's a splinter, or breakaway, group from the Ulster Defenders – and that particular group was, in its early days, a Protestant youth movement funded by the Reverend Dawson's East Belfast Unionist Party ... So the connection, however tenuous, *is* there.'

'But is Red Hand actually a splinter group or is it still under the control of the Ulster Defenders?'

'The three leaders of Red Hand – Alf Green, Joe Douglas and Jack Peel – were instrumental in the formation of the Ulster Defenders and still take part in its most important meetings. So no question, they're still involved with it – and on a pretty high level.'

'Which gets me back to the Reverend William Dawson.'

'I would say so,' said Cooney.

They had reached Weir's Snout and again were overlooking the Giant's Causeway. In the warmer months of the year, they would have seen, far below, tourists milling like ants on the huge stepping stones and bizarre lava-rock formations, but now, in the dead of winter, there were no tourists about and Pete felt that he was on another planet, its sole inhabitants being himself and Cooney. There were more black clouds gathering on the horizon and the snow was still falling.

'Any way I can find out about Dawson's less publicized activities?' Pete asked.

Cooney sighed and shook his head, as if disbelieving his own words. 'You're not going to believe this,' he said. 'But please bear in mind that this is Ulster where nothing really makes sense.'

'Just tell me,' Pete said.

'Let me write this down for you,' Cooney responded. He stopped walking, removed his notebook and pen from his coat pocket, then began to scribble while saying, 'This particular woman, though a Catholic with Republican sympathies, is *not* an activist and is, I believe, one of the most objective reporters in the Province, albeit working for a radio station in the Republic. We're friends and I trust her judgement. Don't tell her I sent you and don't tell her what you're doing – she *is* a Catholic, after all – but if you can get her to talk – and I'm sure you can – she might be able to tell you more than I can.'

'How come?' Pete asked.

'She's presently obsessed with the Reverend William Dawson. She's been researching his background, interviewed him as well, and is still, as far as I can gather, hot on his trail. Not being a Protestant, therefore not on his side, she might know more, and be more forthcoming, about his private life than even his most intimate acquaintances. This is her name and the pub she frequents two or three times a week.'

Cooney tore the page out of his notebook and passed it to Pete. After studying the name, which meant nothing to him, Pete put it into his wallet.

'What makes you think I can get her to talk?' Pete said.

'I respect this woman, so please treat my words with care. Her husband, a history teacher in a Catholic school in West Belfast, was killed some time ago, blown up in his car outside his own house. Since then, this fine woman has been drinking too much and having too many casual affairs – she's trying to deaden the pain of it and, in my view, going about it the wrong way – but . . .' Cooney shrugged. 'There you have it . . . She likes men – she's always been frank about that – so I'm sure that you, with your reputation as a ladies' man, can get to know her and then maybe – just maybe – get her to talk.'

Pete felt oddly embarrassed and amused at once. 'Has that bastard Edmondson been talking to you?' he said.

Cooney grinned. 'Well, naturally if he wants me to talk to you, he's going to tell me about you.'

'What else did he say?'

'He said you were a wildcat operator, but that you'd keep your lips sealed.'

'He's right.'

'I'm relieved.'

They walked on to the Visitors' Centre, which was closed at this time of the year. For this reason, the car park was empty except for their own two vehicles. The lawns, normally green, were white with snow, though the wind blew it restlessly.

The two men shook hands and turned away to their respective

cars. Pete remained standing there, deep in thought, as Cooney slipped behind the wheel and turned on the ignition. Then, just before Cooney drove off, he changed his mind and waved Pete over to him. Pete walked to Cooney's car and leaned down to listen to what he was saying.

'Apropos those Loyalist paramilitaries who disappeared,' he said. 'I've heard that Catholic paramilitaries are disappearing as well, but the Provos are being more quiet about it. When you speak to my friend, a bright lady, you might care to check it out.'

He waved his hand and drove off.

Pete stood there, unable to move, shivering again as he watched Cooney's Vauxhall Cavalier turn into the main road and race away, soon disappearing in the rapidly descending darkness beyond the thickening snowfall.

The snow was falling all over Northern Ireland and, Pete realized glumly, on the graves of the undiscovered dead. It was that thought, as well as the cold, that made had him shiver.

CHAPTER FIFTEEN

Entering the East Belfast offices of the Reverend William Dawson, Patricia was again struck by how spartan they were. This was, she was pretty sure, a deliberate ploy of the good Reverend's, a display of his Christian modesty and lack of pretension. She was not taken in by it.

When she entered the outer office, she found Dawson's secretary Robert Lilly seated behind his mahogany desk beside a humming computer, reading a pile of letters and placing them either in the tray to his right or in the one to his left. He glanced up when she came in and did not seem pleased to see her. Studying his gaunt white face and darkly evasive gaze, that thinning jet-black hair plastered down on his high forehead with what might have been Brylcreem, she realized that she found him repulsive, though also oddly frightening. In his threadbare grey suit, nondescript shirt and striped tie, he still seemed bone-thin, almost unnaturally so, and she found herself thinking crazily of him masturbating in the torment of his bachelor's celibacy, his Christian self-denial or, perhaps, sneaking out at nights to commit rape or find himself a whore. This was, of course, an outrageous thought, perhaps springing out of her secret shame at her own recent activities; nonetheless, it lodged darkly in her mind as a faint possibility.

'Ah,' Lilly said coldly, 'Mrs Monaghan. Back to see us again.' He checked his wristwatch. 'And punctual as always. We *do* appreciate this as the Reverend's time is, as you can imagine, extremely valuable.'

'Of course,' Patricia replied, wanting to slap his face. 'So is the Reverend in?'

'When Reverend Dawson makes an appointment, he keeps it. I'll tell him you're here.'

'Should I take a seat?'

'No, don't bother. I'm sure he'll see you immediately.' Lilly pressed a button on his intercom and spoke to Reverend Dawson, telling him that Mrs Monaghan had arrived. 'Send her in,' Reverend Dawson's voice, distorted and metallic, said over the intercom. Lilly nodded, switched the intercom off, and returned his darkly evasive gaze to Patricia. 'Go right in,' he said.

Seeing that Lilly was not about to rise and open the door for her, Patricia walked around his desk, opened the door for herself and stepped into the Reverend's small, humble office. He was seated behind his desk, which was littered with paperwork, mostly letters, and as Patricia closed the door behind her, he fixed his steady blue gaze upon her.

'Well, now, Mrs Monaghan,' he said, sounding perfectly pleasant, though his slight smile lacked warmth. 'I must say I was surprised to hear that you wanted to speak with me again. I had assumed that your radio programme would have been completed and aired by now.'

'I'm sure that if the programme had been aired, you'd have known about it and taped it.'

The Reverend chuckled and nodded, then indicated the chair facing his desk with an airy wave of his hand. 'How right you are,' he said. 'But please, take a seat.'

Patricia sat in the chair and studied the Reverend carefully, noting his bright blue eyes and his matinée-idol good looks, not diminished by his head of thick grey hair, the lines on his healthy, pink-skinned face or the jowls under his cleanly shaven strong chin. He seemed like one of those famous actors who, though past their prime, could turn the charm on and off at will and still attract the ladies.

No wonder his congregation is mostly female, Patricia thought. *They probably melt in the pews.*

'So what do you want to know this time?' he said. 'What surprise is in store for me?'

In fact, Patricia hardly knew what to ask him, since she hadn't really come here for that. She was here because her good friend, Frank Cooney, a man with eyes in the back of his head, had recently informed her that twice in the past fortnight he had seen a couple of Dawson's men, members of his East Belfast Unionist Party, parked outside the Europa Hotel when she, Patricia, was in the bar. Those men could, of course, have been there for any number of reasons, but since Patricia had been observing Dawson for the past couple of months, Cooney believed that Dawson's men were now observing her.

What kind of Reverend would put a tail on a reporter who had conducted a radio interview with him?

Patricia hadn't come here to ask Dawson that question – she didn't think she would have the nerve and Cooney might have got it wrong – but she wanted to talk with him, about anything, really, simply to sound him out more and possibly learn what made him tick. Now, when she saw his slightly mocking smile and ice-bright gaze, she wasn't too sure if she would be able to do that. This Reverend Dawson was no fool.

'No surprise,' she replied after hesitating too long. 'I just wanted to clear up some questions raised by our last interview.'

'Such as?'

'Given that some of your statements about the religious divide in Ulster are seemingly contradictory, I'd like to try clarifying your attitude with regard to it. Although, unlike the Reverend Ian Paisley, you appear on the surface not to be fanatically anti-Catholic, you still take little notice of what many feel are genuine Catholic grievances.'

'Such as?' the Reverend asked again.

'Well, the major Catholic grievance is that this is an Orange State, a privileged state for the Protestants, and the Catholics are discriminated against when it comes to employment, housing, and power sharing. So what do you say to that?'

'You don't have your tape recorder,' the Reverend observed.

Blushing, realizing that she had forgotten to bring the tape recorder and that he was smart enough to be suspicious of that fact, Patricia recovered quickly enough to withdraw a notebook and pen from her shoulder bag, saying, 'I didn't think it was necessary as this isn't really an interview. It's really just a matter of a few questions to fill in a few gaps.'

'Very good,' Reverend Dawson said with a bleak smile. 'Are you ready?'

'Yes, Reverend.'

Dawson leaned back in his chair and clasped his hands behind his head. 'I may not be as fervently anti-Catholic as the Reverend

Ian Paisley, but I *will* admit openly that I sometimes get weary of complaining Catholics and those – usually not Belfast residents – who accept the complaints without question. In fact, relatively speaking, most of this Protestant versus Catholic business is nonsense. The Catholics *were* a persecuted minority, but that's all in the past. Indeed, I would go so far as to say that in many instances, particularly with regard to employment and housing executive homes, the Catholics are now favoured over the Protestants, even if only for the purposes of propaganda – to win hearts and minds, as it were.'

'That's a phrase first used by the SAS,' Patricia said before she could stop herself, 'when they were in Malaysia and Borneo, using a hearts-and-minds campaign to get the natives on their side and turn them against the other side.'

The Reverend studied her coolly, then decided to smile again. 'Yes, of course, I probably read it somewhere . . . and the SAS were, as I recall, very successful in their hearts-and-minds campaign.'

'So I gather,' Patricia said dryly.

'Well, I can assure you,' the good Reverend said, 'that my little slip of the tongue in no way indicates that I am, or ever have been, a secret supporter of the SAS. What I *can* say with confidence, however, is that in a desperate attempt to win hearts and minds both here and internationally – to allay the criticism that they're favouring the Protestants over the Catholics – the British government is pouring money into the Catholic communities and also favouring them over the Protestants when it comes to employment and housing.'

'You really believe that?' Patricia asked, trying to hide the anger she felt rising.

'Absolutely,' the Reverend said. 'The evidence is there for all to see. Protestants are being forced to wait in the queue while Catholics, generally deemed to have more pressing needs, are favoured with housing executive homes. Catholics are also being favoured with financial grants and opportunities for setting themselves up in business. Indeed, even Mackies' foundry, one of the biggest sources of employment in this city and formerly staunchly Protestant, is now owned by Catholics. As for power sharing with the Catholics, why, even the City Council, which admittedly still has a Unionist majority, at least has Sinn Fein members. Similarly, Sinn Fein councillors are constantly involved with colleagues from the Official and Democratic Unionists in every major renewal project in this city.'

'Yes, but . . .'

'Just think about it, Mrs Monaghan,' the Reverend continued, determined not to let her stop him. 'In London, where all this yammerin' goes on about how the Catholics here have no voice, they don't even have a Greater London Council any more. Here, on the other hand, we have a citywide assembly in which councillors, Catholics and Protestants alike, can have a say in the running of their own government. Your British ministers laugh at our twenty-six district councils, but they represent the only places in Britain where both sides of the community share political responsibility in a proper constitutional context. Why, we might soon even have a nationalist mayor! So I really fail to see how the so-called Orange State can be criticized for discrimination against the Catholics.'

'One of the reasons, surely, is that the Loyalists, despite what you say with regard to improvements in the social status of Catholics, still violently mistrust the Catholics and block every attempt at a reasonable peace settlement.'

'We react that way,' the Reverend said, unconsciously sounding like the representative voice of the Protestant majority, *his* people, 'because experience has shown us that if you concede one point to Sinn Fein, they will treat that concession as an act of weakness and instantly make even greater demands. We react that way, also, because we know that Sinn Fein still believes in the ballot box *and* the Armalite – something proven yet again, if I may say so, by the barbaric killing of two highly regarded Loyalist councillors: William Leek and Ken Bruce. We, on the other hand, believe in the ballot box *without* the Armalite – and that's where the difference between us lies.'

'You believe in the ballot box,' Patricia ventured, 'because the Protestants are in the majority, which means you can't lose.'

This time the Reverend's smile was genuine. He seemed to be enjoying himself. 'Democracy rules,' he said.

With that comment, Patricia knew that she had come to a dead end and would not be given much more time. Why she was bothering in the first place, she really didn't know, since in the end, when what would be done had been done, it wouldn't make a damned bit of difference. The very thought of it made her feel dirty and that didn't help matters.

'I've just about finished, Reverend,' she said, 'but can I conclude by asking why you, a man of God as well as an MP, encourage Protestant fears of oppression by the Catholics should the latter ever be given equality in Ulster?'

'I categorically deny that I encourage such fears. On the other hand, as a Protestant, I naturally warn my congregation of the evils of Popish ideology. The Catholic church, I should point out, is not as tolerant as the Protestant church and it would, if given half the chance, impose various unacceptable restrictions on the Ulster Protestants.'

'Nonsense!' Patricia said.

'No, Mrs Monaghan, it's not nonsense. May I just point out to you that here, in Ulster, a Catholic can marry a Protestant without changing his or her religion, but the same privilege is not granted to a Protestant, who must change his or her religion if they wish to marry a Catholic.'

'I think that's really . . .'

But the good Reverend raised his right hand to silence her, as if he were back in the pulpit, about to launch into one of his fire-and-brimstone sermons. 'May I also point out that Catholic Ireland – the so-called Republic of Ireland – is the most repressive country in Europe, constantly banning books, plays, films and even television broadcasts that the rest of us, in Ulster and in Europe, can freely watch. Finally – though I could certainly produce many other examples – may I just remind you that a great many Protestant women would find it deeply offensive to be told by the Pope that it's a sin for them to use contraception. These are but a few of the fears that most Protestants would have should the Catholics ever gain control of Ulster.'

'Fears aren't necessarily realities,' Patricia said.

'Nevertheless, a great many people, Protestants, have those fears and that makes them real enough to them.'

Convinced that the good Reverend exploited such fears, albeit with more subtlety than was displayed by Ian Paisley, Patricia put her notebook and pen back into her bag and stood up to leave.

'Thank you for your time, Reverend Dawson. You've really been most helpful and I don't think we'll have to meet again.'

'You mean, you'd rather that we *didn't* meet again, but I can understand that.' The Reverend smiled at her and spread his hands forgivingly in the air. 'Alas, we're on opposite sides of the divide and can do little about it.'

'Goodbye, Reverend Dawson.'

Patricia turned away to leave, but before she reached the door, Reverend Dawson called out her name. She turned back to face him and saw that he was no longer smiling.

'You haven't asked me a single question that will add to what you already have,' he said. 'So why did you *really* come to see me?'

Taken by surprise, the words popped out of Patricia's throat before she could swallow them. 'I want to know why you're having me followed.'

Reverend Dawson was silent for some time, his steely blue gaze steady upon her, unblinking, searching. Eventually, after what seemed like an eternity, he spread his hands on the desk and said, 'Because *you*'ve been following *me*, Mrs Monaghan.'

Shocked that he knew this, Patricia burned up with guilt, then rallied herself and came out with what she hoped was a commonsense response.

'Yes,' she said, 'that's true enough. I'm a reporter, after all. I spend a long time preparing my programmes and I do my research; and if that means tracking the movements of a subject, then that's what I do. I wanted to know where you went, who you talked to on a daily basis, and since I sensed that you wouldn't tell me what I wanted to know, I used sneaky tactics. That's what reporters *do*, Reverend.'

'Absolutely,' the Reverend said, seemingly understanding and unoffended, though Patricia had doubts about that. 'So when you were following me, Mrs Monaghan, in the line of duty, as it were, did I go anywhere or do anything that struck you as being unusual?'

'Well . . .'

'Come, come, don't be shy. My bark's worse than my bite.'

Patricia wasn't too sure of that, but now she had little choice but to spit it out.

'I saw you talking to members of the Ulster Defenders.'

'So?'

'When we last talked, you insisted that you no longer had any connection with that particular paramilitary group.'

The Reverend stared steadily at her for a moment, then offered a melodramatic sigh. 'And where, pray, did you see me talking to these gentlemen?'

'Outside your church,' Patricia said.

The Reverend smiled indulgently and shook his head from side to side, as if disbelieving his own ears. 'Was this after a church service?' he asked.

'Yes.'

'Mrs Monaghan, please . . . A great many people attend my church and it is not my function to cast out the sinner. Indeed, as you surely must know, it is the sinner that the Church should most welcome. Regardless of the sins they may commit as paramilitaries, some of those men have deeply rooted religious beliefs and attend church regularly – my church and others. If you saw me talking to them outside my church, that would be perfectly normal as I always step outside after the service to speak to those members of the congregation who wish to have words with me. So the fact that you saw me speaking to those men means nothing at all. Certainly, it can't be taken as a sign that I am in any way still connected to their organization.'

Discretion being the better part of valour, Patricia decided not to tell him that on another occasion she had seen his secretary, Robert Lilly, actually entering the Shankill Road headquarters of the Ulster Defenders. She had waited outside, checking the time he spent in there, and he only emerged two hours later . . . in the company of three well-known Loyalist paramilitaries: Alf Green, Joe Douglas and Jack Peel – widely rumoured to be the three heads of Red Hand.

'All right,' she said. 'I'll take your word for that. So let's assume that you've nothing to hide—'

'Which I have not.'

'—why were you, a Christian minister, so concerned about being observed by me that you had me placed under observation at the same time? I am, after all, only a reporter doing my job.'

'You *may* just be a reporter doing your job, but you're also a Catholic, sympathetic to the Republicans, and that gives me cause for concern. Please bear in mind, Mrs Monaghan, that I am not only a Protestant minister, but also a notably outspoken Unionist MP. As such, I naturally have enemies in the Catholic community, particularly amongst the nationalists and Republicans. Therefore, if I'm being observed, I like to know why. I am *not* a gangster with bodyguards and spies, but I have to be careful.'

'And that's all there is to it, Reverend Dawson?'

'Yes, that's all,' the Reverend said with conviction. 'Now please stop following me. I'm sure you have enough for your radio programme without spying upon me.'

Patricia nodded. 'Okay.'

'It stops immediately?'

'Yes.'

'Then we stop following you.' The Reverend pushed his chair back, stood up, and came around the desk to stop just in front of her. He held out his hand. 'Good day, Mrs Monaghan.' They shook hands.

'Goodbye, Reverend Dawson.'

The Reverend politely held the door open for her as she left his office. In the outer office, Robert Lilly, still seated behind his desk beside his humming computer, glanced at her with his darkly evasive gaze.

'So how did it go?' he asked.

'Fine,' Patricia said.

'You'll be makin' tracks, then,' Lilly said.

'I'm off and running,' she told him.

Revolted by the sight of him, but also slightly unnerved, she hurried gratefully out of the building, flagged down a taxi, and told the driver to take her to a named pub in the Shankill Road. It was just before five in the evening, but darkness had already descended, the street lights were on, and the snow, which had been falling for a month now, since just before the New Year, was turning to muddy sludge. Depressed by the sight of it and still feeling oddly troubled by her visit to Reverend Dawson and his revolting male secretary, she lit a cigarette, inhaled with relief, then sat back in the seat to smoke and gaze distractedly out of the window.

The Christmas decorations were being removed from shop windows and the city was gradually returning to normal, which secretly pleased her. She disliked Christmas and was always glad when it was over. The forced conviviality had always made her feel lonesome, even when she was not spending the time alone. This year, however, she had not spent Christmas in Belfast. Instead, she had gone south to visit Sean where he was recuperating in a private country house used as a combination of medical centre and safe house for IRA men either wounded or on the run. The ground floor of the grand house was still used by its owner, a wealthy retired Republican solicitor with many useful connections in the legal world and, of course, in the Garda. The upstairs of the house was, however, secretly given over to the Provies who were never seen downstairs when innocent people came to visit the solicitor.

Patricia had missed Sean desperately, but when she saw him in an upstairs room of that house, clearly recovering from his wounds but with his formerly handsome face scarred for life, she realized that he had changed, was more bitterly anti-Unionist, and wanted to use her in ways that she felt were degrading. Nevertheless, she had not been able to refuse him (she had never been able to do so) and thus, once back in Belfast, she had done, and was still doing, what he wanted. Now, trembling in the back of the taxi as it turned into the Shankill Road, bright and busy as always with a lot of the shops still open, she knew that she would continue to do what had to be done, even while it was filling her with shame and a growing fear for her future.

When the taxi pulled up in front of the pub she used most often, she tipped the driver extravagantly, perhaps to pay for her sins, and then took a deep breath and went inside. As usual, even at this early hour of the evening, the pub was busy, though most of the men, either Republican supporters or actual Provos, were ganged up around the bar, leaving the tables free. A lot of them knew Patricia well and waved at her when she entered, then went back to their noisy conversations. Patricia ordered a large Bushmill's on the rocks, exchanged pleasantries with the men beside her while waiting for the drink, then, when she had received it and paid for it, took a seat at a table near the wall, facing the front door. She nursed the Bushmill's while smoking too many cigarettes and thinking of the Reverend William Dawson, of what was being planned, and of her own sordid part in the whole business. When her drink was finished, she bought herself another double and settled in for the evening.

A couple of hours later, the pub was even more packed and all of the tables had been taken. Still smoking too much and starting to feel drunk, though no less depressed, Patricia glanced across the room and saw a stranger sitting at another table, his gaze fixed steadily upon her. He was a well-built man, almost certainly under forty, with brown eyes, auburn hair and a roughly handsome, good-humoured, lived-in face. When Patricia returned his gaze, he glanced to the side and waved at some of the men along the bar. They grinned and waved back.

Clearly, then, though new to this particular pub, the stranger was known to some of the men in it. A total stranger, or someone not Catholic, would not dare to enter here otherwise.

Who is he? she wondered.

As if reading her mind, the stranger returned his gaze to the front and stared at her again. It was, she realized, a deliberate stare, so she raised her glass and smiled at him. He returned the gesture, then pushed his chair back and stood up to cross the room and join her.

Why not? Patricia thought.

CHAPTER SIXTEEN

Shortly after Patricia Monaghan left his office, Reverend Dawson called Robert Lilly in to see him. When Robert entered, slipping like a ghost around the door, closing it quietly behind him and offering a wan smile, the Reverend realized that there was something about his secretary that had always vaguely disturbed him. He was, of course, a good Christian and an excellent assistant, discreet and supremely efficient, but for all that, there was something about him that deeply depressed Reverend Dawson. Robert was too reticent, too closed up and dried out, an old man in the body of a young man, already fading away. Single and unworldly, still living with his parents in a housing executive house out in Cregagh, he appeared to spend every waking minute either working here or taking part in church activities. The Reverend could hardly fault him – indeed, he could not – but he sometimes wished that Robert could be a little more lively and brighten the gloom that seemed to travel with him.

Feeling guilty about these negative thoughts, Reverend Dawson invited Robert to have a late-afternoon drink.

'A little whisky will do us both good,' he said. 'It's been a wearisome day. Sit down, Robert. Let's talk.'

Robert sat in the chair at the other side of the desk as the Reverend withdrew two glasses and a bottle of whisky from his desk drawer. However, before the Reverend could start pouring, Robert raised his right hand. 'No, thank you,' he said, almost whispering. 'I rarely drink at all, Reverend, and certainly not before tea.'

Unexpectedly annoyed, but trying not to show it, the Reverend said, 'I trust you don't mind if I do.'

'Of course not,' Robert said.

The Reverend poured himself a generous whisky. He had a sip, settled into his chair and gazed silently at Robert, who smiled wanly back while managing not to look directly at him.

'So what did she want?' Robert asked eventually, to break the Reverend's distracted silence.

'Patricia Monaghan?'

'Yes.'

'She asked me a lot of irrelevant questions, then confessed that she wanted to know why we were having her followed.'

'How did she find that out?'

'That's what *I'd* like to know.'

'There are eyes and ears everywhere,' Robert said, disassociating himself and the Reverend from the other snoopers in this city of vile secrets. 'So did she have anything to say for herself about what she'd observed?'

'Not much. She saw me talking to our friends from the Ulster Defenders and took it as a sign that I was still connected to the organization. Naturally I pointed out that even so-called terrorists sometimes attend church and that I'm there to speak to the sinners as well as the saved. That dampened her ardour, I think.'

Robert was not amused. 'Had she anything else to report?' he asked.

'No, thank the Lord.'

'Do you think she meant it?'

'What?'

'That she saw nothing else.'

'Yes, I think she meant it.'

Robert's darkly evasive gaze wandered restlessly about the room, then settled back on the desk below his nose, rather than on the Reverend's impassive face. 'Nevertheless,' he said, 'she saw you talking to those men. That's not good. Who knows what she'll get from it? She could still use it to connect you to the Ulster Defenders and cause you no end of embarrassment.'

The Reverend sighed. 'I suppose so.'

'I think we should keep our eyes on her to ensure that she keeps her word and stops spying upon us.'

'I told her we'd stop that,' the Reverend reminded him.

'A white lie is necessary occasionally,' Robert responded with surprising boldness. 'Please, Reverend, trust me in this. That

Catholic woman, as you rightly said yourself, could still be dangerous to us.'

'Perhaps,' the Reverend said. 'But please try to be more discreet about it.'

'I will,' Robert promised.

A fine state we've come to, the Reverend thought. *The things that decent Christians have to do just to survive in this city. May the Good Lord forgive us all.*

'So how are our troubled teenagers coming along?' he asked, feeling uneasy and wanting to change the conversation.

'Fine,' Robert replied.

'Still making great advances in their computer studies?'

'Yes, Reverend. They're now very advanced. We didn't waste our time when we set up that training establishment. Most of the teenagers are too busy to feel as troubled as they were and some have been totally turned around by the work. As for those who financed it, most have visited the establishment, seen what the boys are doing, and expressed their admiration and gratitude, so it's certainly been worthwhile.'

'Sure I'm delighted to hear that,' the Reverend said, letting the whisky release a little of the Ulster brogue that he'd deliberately dropped when undergoing his theological studies in England a good many years back. He had another sip of whisky, licked his lips and then said, 'So what about the new man in the Shankill? Does he seem straightforward?'

'We're still not sure,' Robert responded. He withdrew a piece of paper from the side pocket of his coat, unfolded it and kept glancing at it as he spoke. 'Name of Peter Thompson. Born in Belfast in 1961. Brought up in the Donegall Road . . .'

'A Protestant, then.'

'Of course. Left Belfast in 1971, when he was ten, to go and live in Birkenhead with his parents, eventually leaving school at fifteen to train as an electrical engineer, specializing in television and video. Emigrated to Australia, on his own, in 1984, when he was twenty-three years old, and worked for a television and video maintenance company in Melbourne, Victoria. Eventually, he married, though no children were produced. He returned to England for brief visits on two separate occasions, for the separate funerals of his parents, then returned for good about four years ago, shortly after the unexpected death of his Australian wife. He spent most of those four years working as an independent TV and video repair man in London, then came back to Belfast in October last year, moving into the Shankill. Working again as an independent TV and video repair man, he's reportedly very good, very personable, and has succeeded in building up a nice little business, based on word of mouth.'

'A churchgoer?'

'Hardly. In fact, he seems to be a bit of a drinker and womanizer, spending most of his free time in the pubs of the Shankill and being seen with a wide variety of unattached women. The general feeling on the street is that although he's come home, he's been away too long, lost his roots, and picked up the more liberal mores of the Aussies. In other words, he's widely viewed as someone who works and plays hard and seems to take nothing else too seriously. He's not religious and appears to be apolitical.'

'He's straightforward, then.'

'No,' Robert said, surprising the Reverend. 'We have our doubts about that.'

'Oh? Why?'

'For his first few months in the Shankill, when he was setting himself up in business, he certainly *appeared* to be straightforward, interested in nothing other than drink and women. But recently, these past few weeks, he's been trawling the Shankill pubs and asking questions.'

The Reverend placed his glass back on the desk and straightened up in his chair. 'What kind of questions?'

'About the Ulster Defenders and Red Hand . . . and about you, Reverend.'

Reverend Dawson was silent, deep in thought, for a long time, then he picked up his glass, polished off his drink, placed the glass back on the desk and stared grimly at Robert.

'Pursue him,' he said.

CHAPTER SEVENTEEN

P ete couldn't believe his luck. Turning off the Shankill, he drove along a dismal side street, glancing left and right, looking for the right number, still not believing that he had received a phone call from the wife of Joe Douglas, one of the three heads of Red Hand, asking him to come around to her home and fix her jammed video. Now, when he was about halfway down the street – terraced houses on both sides, the doorsteps scrubbed and clean – he saw without looking for it the place where Joe Douglas lived. He could tell because a bunch of louts, all wearing ski jackets, thick-soled trainers and Nike baseball caps, were loitering on the pavement and in the road in front of a particular house. Known as 'dickers' – the same nickname as the teenage males who had kept a lookout against the security forces during the Troubles – their presence here indicated that this was the house of a leading hard man. It could only be Douglas's home.

As Pete pulled up to the kerb in front of the house, the dickers studied him carefully. Pete's name – 'Pete Thompson' – and address and phone number, including his mobile number, were painted on the side of his small van. He saw the dickers scanning the details with squinting eyes, some silently mouthing the words as they read.

The mutant generation, Pete thought. *Probably joined the paramilitaries before they left school and can still barely read or write. Educated in kneecapping and bank robbery and the firing of weapons. No doubt where their future lies.*

Pete clambered out of the van and said to the nearest dicker, 'Is this where Joe Douglas lives?'

'You're Thompson, the TV man?'

'Right.'

'Joe's expectin' you.'

Douglas's front door was open and while the dicker went to

announce Pete's arrival by shouting through the hallway door, Pete opened the back of the van and pulled out his tool box. The box had a false bottom. In the bottom, carefully wrapped in padding to muffle its metallic rattling, was his Five-seveN pistol and its rounds of 5.7 mm cartridges. He hadn't brought the weapon for the purpose of eliminating Douglas. It was just a precaution. Approaching Douglas's front door, he received a nod of consent from the tough young dicker.

'Go right in,' the dicker said.

Pete opened the hallway door and stepped into the small, tidy living room. He was greeted by a heavy-set woman with red hair tumbling to her shoulders, framing bright green eyes in a face that remained quite attractive but was lined by a lifetime of anxiety. Large-breasted and long-legged, she was wearing a respectable cashmere sweater and skirt. Her feet were in flat shoes.

'Have ya come then?' she said by way of greeting.

'Yeah . . . Pete Thompson . . . The video?'

Mrs Douglas nodded towards the twenty-three-inch TV set in the corner, with a video player on the shelf beneath it. The TV set was turned on. Pete had noticed that TV sets were *always* turned on in Belfast homes, often with the sound turned off. He still thought it was strange.

'Don't know what's wrong with it,' Mrs Douglas said flatly while lighting a cigarette and puffing a thin stream of smoke from unpainted lips. 'Ya can play a tape, like, but ya can't rewind the bugger an' when ya try to pull the video-cassette out, the tape gets caught up inside. I've already torn a coupla tapes from the video rental shop an' they're screamin' blue murder.'

'Let's have a look at it,' Pete said.

In fact, he was feeling crushed with disappointment not to find Joe Douglas at home, but he tried not to show it. He would fix the video player temporarily, but do it in such a way that the same fault, a loose roller, would gradually reappear about a week from now. With luck, he'd be called back for a second visit and Douglas might be here then.

'Would ya like a cuppa tea?' Mrs Douglas asked.

'Yeah, that'd be great,' he said, speaking like a local.

With the cigarette dangling from between her lips, leaving her hands free to work, Mrs Douglas disappeared into the small kitchen just off the living room. Glancing around the room, Pete saw the usual cheap prints and ornaments supplemented by photographs of the local Orange Lodge – Joe Douglas was in the group, wearing his suit and orange sash – as well as a framed, garishly coloured local Orange Lodge banner and a truly dreadful painting of the Queen. A real Loyalist household. An open fire was burning in the tiled grate and the room was extremely warm.

Kneeling on the floor, Pete pulled the video player off its shelf, laid it on the carpet, opened his tool kit and went to work as slowly as possible, hoping that Joe Douglas might eventually arrive. In fact, even as he was thinking this, he heard a hoarse male voice in the kitchen, a man conversing with Mrs Douglas, then Joe Douglas himself emerged, wearing only his pants and a white vest, his feet in badly frayed bedroom slippers. Pete noticed this last, in particular, because it was now after five in the evening and Douglas looked like he'd just got out of bed. He also noticed that Douglas, a muscular man turning to fat and giving in to a beer belly, had Loyalist tattoos on both arms: one a crude depiction of William of Orange, the other a Lambeg drum inscribed with the classic motto: *No Surrender*! Douglas was nearly bald and this, combined with the three or four tiny scars on his face – reportedly made by shrapnel fragments from an otherwise failed IRA bomb attack on him – made him look as brutal as his reputation would have him. Like his wife, he had a cigarette dangling from his lips and when he slumped into one of the two armchairs near the open fire, he exhaled a cloud of blue smoke. His eyes, which were heavy-lidded and seemed dead, focused on Pete.

'You that fella that's bin to Australia?' he asked, his voice hoarse and flat.

'Yeah, that's right,' Pete said, glancing up and grinning before going back to his work again.

'You come strongly recommended,' Douglas said.

'I pick up all my work by word of mouth,' Pete replied. 'Who recommended me to you?'

'Sammy West out in Bloomfield. Old friend of mine.'

'Oh, yeah,' Pete said. 'I think I know who you mean. Did his TV a couple of weeks back. It's clapped out but he won't give it up for nostalgic reasons, so I've been there a few times.'

'That sounds like Sammy, all right.'

In fact, Pete recalled Sammy West clearly. A tight-fisted bastard who lived with his mother in a two-up, two-down and was a member of a local Loyalist gang. He wouldn't get a new TV only because he was too tight to spend the money. Each time Pete had visited him, he'd blubbered on about the evils of the Taigs and the glories of Loyalist paramilitary history. He'd bored Pete almost mindless.

Mrs Douglas emerged from the kitchen, carrying two mugs of tea. She handed one to her husband, placed the other on the floor beside Pete, then said to her husband, 'I'm just goin' up the road for a bit of crack with Madge. I'll be back in an hour or so to make tea.'

'Okay,' her husband replied, obviously not a man given to many words. His wife nodded and walked out. He sipped some tea, had a drag on his cigarette and exhaled another cloud of smoke. 'So what was it like, then?'

'Pardon?'

'Australia. I've often thought of emigratin' there, but it just never happened, like. What was it like?'

'Terrific,' Pete said. 'A really good country. Lots of work around, good money, and a fantastic climate. The Aussies work hard and play hard, so a good time was had by all.'

'I hear you work hard an' play hard as well.'

'What else is there to life?'

Douglas stared thoughtfully at him for a moment, his grey eyes as cold as stones, then he sipped some tea and had another drag on his cigarette. He blew a couple of smoke rings.

'Plenty,' he said abruptly. 'A lot more than work and play. So what d'ya think of the situation here? Does it ever enter yer head, like?'

'Well,' Pete said carefully while sipping at his tea and ostensibly concentrating on the dismantled video player, 'it certainly didn't while I was in Australia and I only really started thinking about it when I went back to London four years ago. Even then, though, I have to confess, it just seemed like a problem in another world – one I'd left behind long ago. I mean, I was only a kid when I left here, so it didn't impinge on me.'

'But now you're back here,' Douglas said, talking as if he was just passing the time – being sociable, like.

'Yeah, well,' Pete responded, trying to sound as casual as possible, though he knew he had to be very careful, 'it's pretty hard to get away from it here, so, you know, I guess I think more about it than I did before. I mean, when you get something like those two recent assassinations – the local councillors; I forget their names—'

'Leek and Bruce.'

'Yeah, right . . . Well, when you read about things like that, or see it on the telly, it certainly makes you think, doesn't it? I mean, what's the excuse for it?'

'Those fuckin' Provos don't need an excuse,' Douglas replied. 'An' they did it for sure.'

'You think so?'

'Who else?' Douglas said. He had a sip of tea, wiped his lips with the back of his hand, then eased his arse slightly off the chair and released a soft fart. 'We're tryin' to meet 'em halfway an' they *still* go out and commit these atrocities. Sure ya can't trust a Catholic.'

Pete nodded as if agreeing, while continuing to fiddle about inside the video player, taking his time. 'I guess not,' he said. 'And now I hear a lot of Loyalist paramilitaries are disappearing – probably shot by the Provos as well. Looks like they're out for a new war.'

'Ackay, sure that's certain. That's what it's all about. They're doin' it to make us retaliate and give 'em an excuse to go all out. Cunnin' bastards, they are.'

Aware that the paramilitaries who had disappeared had gone willingly after having had a chat with the heads of Red Hand, including Douglas here, Pete realized that Douglas was being disingenuous and giving nothing away. He knew damned well that the missing paramilitaries were not dead and that the Provos had nothing to do with their disappearances, but he wasn't about to say that. Pete glanced at him and saw him slumped in his chair, the flames from the open fire casting fingers of flickering shadow and light over his humourless scarred face.

'What's wrong with the video player?' he asked.

'Loose roller, I think.'

'Can it be fixed?'

'I think so.'

Douglas had another sip of tea, inhaled on his cigarette, and created a drifting veil across his face with the smoke he exhaled.

'Closed-circuit television. Used routinely these days and per-fectly legal.'

A glimmer of light was now showing in Douglas's dead eyes, revealing muted excitement. He threw his smouldering cigarette butt into the flames of the fire, then looked up again. 'Sounds like ya could be invaluable to us without soilin' yer lily-white hands.'

'I don't want to get involved in any violence. I'm no good at that sort of thing and I've no experience at all.'

'Sure ya won't have to soil yer hands,' Douglas repeated, though he could hardly keep the contempt out of his voice – contempt for this soft man. Nevertheless, he leaned forward in his chair to say, 'Know anything about computers, boyo?'

'A little. It depends on what you mean.'

'Maintenance of hardware and sortin' out problems with the software.'

'Yeah,' Pete said, trying to hide his excitement by looking slightly confused. 'I guess I could do that.'

Douglas nodded. 'So meet us next Friday evening in that pub and we'll have a proper discussion.'

'I'm not sure . . .' Pete responded, hesitating deliberately as if, being a soft man, he was nervous.

'Ack, for Chrissakes, boyo . . .' Douglas waved one hand impatiently. 'Ya'll only be doing us a few wee favours in line with yer everyday work. Sure there's no danger at all. Yer lily-white hands'll stay clean. Now will ya do it or not?'

'I'll see you next Friday,' Pete said.

'Good man. That's the ticket. What do I owe ya for that wee repair job?'

'I'll send a bill,' Pete said.

'Don't make it too big,' Douglas told him.

'I won't. See you Friday.'

'Good day to ya.'

'See you.'

Pete left the house. The dickers were still lounging about outside, monumentally bored, probably itching for some action, some poor Catholic they could abuse, and they looked even more threatening in the lamplit darkness, their hard eyes fixed upon him. Ignoring them, growing excited by what he had just heard – a confirmation that Red Hand was using computers for *some* kind of job – he drove off in his van, heading for the pub recommended by Frank Cooney.

He did not have to drive long. Turning at the end of the street into the Shankill Road, he just had to drive down in the direction of the city for a couple of minutes. Parking illegally on the road (there was nowhere else to park and the van might get wrecked or stolen in a dark side street), he locked the vehicle and then entered the pub.

It was not a pub that he had been in before, but it seemed cosier than most of those along the Shankill. Quickly scanning the smoky, crowded room, he saw an attractive blonde woman sitting alone at a table, smoking and drinking with an air of deep solitude. He knew instantly, from the description given to him by Frank Cooney, that she had to be the woman he was after.

He went straight to the bar and ordered himself a pint of Guinness. Even though he had never been in here before, he knew some of the men along the bar, all paramilitary hard men, and engaged some of them in bantering conversation until his pint had arrived. Carrying the drink, he left the bar and took an empty table that placed him almost directly facing the blonde woman.

He studied her as he drank, not looking directly at her at first, and wondered why a woman who looked like that would feel the need to deaden her grief over a dead husband by fooling around with a lot of men. Still . . . that could help him.

He studied her obliquely for a long time and then finally, when he felt that he was ready, he stared directly at her. When she boldly returned his gaze, he deliberately turned away and waved to some of the hoodlums along the bar. When he turned back, the woman was still staring at him and that gave him his confidence.

She raised her glass and smiled at him. He returned the gesture, then pushed his chair back and stood up to cross the room and join her.

Some of the men standing along the bar were watching his progress with big, knowing grins on their faces. He knew what they were thinking and it was exactly what he had wanted them to think.

That playboy's at it again, they were thinking. *His brains must be between his legs.*

As long as they thought that, he was safe and right now he felt fine. He stopped at the blonde woman's table and raised his glass and smiled down at her.

'Do you mind if I join you?' he said.

'Why not?' she replied.

CHAPTER EIGHTEEN

Billy Boy had disappeared and now he felt like something else – a fucking extraterrestrial – as he weaved through the gloomy, smoke-filled forest, hearing his own breathing amplified in his S6 respirator mask, blinking repeatedly to see through the misted-up eyepieces of his black ballistic helmet, trying to hold his weapon in his skintight aviator's gloves, which deadened feeling, and feeling weighed down by his heavy CRW Bristol body armour with its anti-high-velocity-sound ceramic plates. He was further weighed down with his MX5 stun grenades, which bounced rhythmically against his hip as he advanced, and by the Browning 9 mm High Power handgun holstered on the other hip. In fact, he felt as heavy as a fucking elephant and, worse, claustrophobic.

Holding his Ingram 9 mm sub-machine gun at the ready, he concentrated on avoiding the hidden wires which, if tripped, would explode another CS gas canister and make his team's progress more difficult. The smoke in the forest, he knew, was actually CS gas, and already two members of his team had been seen to rip their masks off hysterically, instantly choke on the gas in the forest, and then either run back in the opposite direction or fall, stumbling and vomiting, to the forest floor.

Not me, Billy Boy thought determinedly. *I'm going the whole fucking route.*

Glancing around him, he saw the remaining members of his assault team and realized why he was beginning to feel like an extraterrestrial. In their heavy body armour, ballistic helmets, respirator masks and gloves, with their stolen Davies Communication CT100E headsets and microphones attached to the masks and helmets, they did indeed look like immense, goggle-eyed, misshapen aliens, the more so because they were moving ghostlike through the smoke created by the exploding CS grenades.

Billy Boy thought it was great, but he definitely felt claustrophobic. He didn't mind the polluted air of Belfast, but this was something else again. Though the respirators kept him and the others in the assault team from talking directly to each other, they could still communicate, albeit with eerie distortion, through their headsets and microphones. Billy Boy felt that he was on another planet and that was eerie as well.

Nevertheless, he kept advancing, weaving through the trees, trying to avoid the trip wires, and eventually he burst out of the forest and saw the big house. Known as the 'Killing House', it was a sprawling country mansion in the mountains of Mourne, miles from anywhere, with only a narrow, overgrown track leading up to it, just about wide enough for a car, few of which ever came this way. Between the forest and the house was a broad field, hemmed in on all sides by chestnut trees, exposed in the afternoon's misty light. It was a dangerous field to cross.

'Let's go,' Billy Boy said, speaking into his respirator and raising his left hand to give the signal to advance. As he stepped forward, so did the others, advancing at the half crouch, weaving left to right to avoid the potential gunfire of the enemy. That gunfire, like the CS gas, would be released by trip wires, so while they weaved they had to keep looking down to search for the wires. Unfortunately, they couldn't always avoid them and the snapping reports of rifle shots emanated from inside the big house, the guns firing from the windows. 'Faster!' Billy Boy bawled.

Obeying, his men advanced much faster – or, at least, as fast as they could in the bulky CRW outfits – and managed to reach the low stone wall of the grounds without suffering casualties. Pleased, Billy Boy scrambled over the wall, slid down the other side, then raced on, still weaving at the half crouch, until he reached the front door of the house. He tried the door. It was locked. Turning away from it, he pressed his back to the wall, his sub-machine gun at the ready, while Leonard 'Len' Young, unrecognizable in his mask, blasted the lock off with his Remington 870 pump-action shotgun. He dropped to one knee as the lock blew apart, pieces of wood and metal flying out in all directions. Then he cocked the Browning High Power in his free hand and bawled, 'Entrance cleared!'

Billy Boy rushed inside, crouched low, swinging the Ingram

sub-machine gun from left to right to ensure an arc of fire that would cover the large rectangular hallway. Seeing that it was empty, he raced across to the inner doorway, followed by the others, and then entered the first corridor in what was a virtual maze of specially built 'killing' rooms.

As Billy Boy moved along the first corridor, dummy figures in painted anoraks and balaclavas, bearing painted weapons, popped out from behind open doors or up from the bottom of window frames to be peppered by a fusillade of real bullets from his sub-machine gun. This would have been brilliant fun had it not been for the knowledge that he was using live ammunition and that other trainees were doing the same as him in the very same building. If he killed or wounded one of them by accident, he would be severely punished; if, on the other hand, he did not move quickly enough – or failed to differentiate quickly enough between a moving dummy and a real person – he was liable to be shot himself and either wounded or killed. Already more than one trainee had been killed and buried out in the mountains.

Billy Boy and his men had been ordered to 'clear' the whole house by bursting into each room in turn and instantly firing two pistol rounds or short, controlled bursts of automatic fire into each of the two or three dummies that popped out from behind walls or up from window frames, aiming their painted guns at the intruders. This task was complicated by the fact that the house had deliberately been filled with smoke and CS gas; this made it doubly difficult for the men to see if they were shooting at a dummy or at one of the other trainees. Also, if a man made the wrong move, he could dislodge his respirator mask, in which case he would choke in the CS gas and possibly have to vomit his way out of the building, under threat all the time from the gunfire of other trainees who might have entered behind him.

Nevertheless, Billy Boy and his team made it the whole way through the building, using the technique they had practised repeatedly over the past few weeks. At each room, Len Young would burst in ahead of Billy Boy, hurling an instantaneous safety electric fuse before him as he went. Invariably, the thunderous flash of the ISFE exploded around both men as they rushed in and made their choice between a number of dummy targets representing paramilitaries, all standing, and hostages sitting in chairs. Their task was to take out the former without hitting the latter, delivering accurate 'double taps' – an old SAS killing method – to the head. They were practising, Billy Boy knew, for the day when they might have to rescue one or more of their own kind from RUC or British Army cells or prisons. That was now on the cards.

Originally, Billy Boy had enjoyed this new experience, but by now, having done it so many times, he was beginning to weary of it and wanted the real thing instead. Even though he was firing real weapons and using real bullets, exploding ISFEs and hurling stun grenades, he was starting to feel jaded as he 'fought' his way through the various rooms of the Killing House, named after the CQB house constructed by the SAS for training in Close Quarter Battle. The SAS, who had been the paramilitaries' bitter enemy during the Troubles, had incidentally taught them a lot.

We should send a thank-you card to Hereford, Billy Boy thought, as he and Len cleared the final room by firing bursts into the dummies that had popped out from behind a false wall, aiming painted weapons. *We owe those bastards a lot.*

By now, with the last room cleared, the Killing House was filled with clouds of acrid smoke and lead fumes so dense that they were starting to seep through the respirator masks. Billy Boy was therefore glad to make his escape from the rear door of the building and remove his mask to breathe the crisp mountain air.

Blinking in the sudden exposure to normal light which, though actually dim, temporarily seemed bright, he saw his instructors, dressed in army tunics and trousers, standing at the stone wall of the back garden, some with arms folded, others writing notes on clipboards. They were jotting down the names of those emerging from the house. In a few minutes, when the Killing House had been cleared, one of them would enter it to count the number of individual 'kills' by checking the bullet holes in the dummies. Billy Boy's team would be assessed on those counts and either praised or damned for them. As for those who had already dropped out in the forest, defeated by the CS gas or by panic, they would not be returned to Belfast to blab about it, but given a head job and buried somewhere out there in the mountains. The terminal fate of the failures was a clear indication of just how important the forthcoming 'big one' was considered to be.

However, as cocky as always, Billy Boy walked up to his team's instructors, Alf Green and Jack Peel, and said, 'So how did we do, then?'

Green checked his wristwatch and looked up. 'Not bad at all,' he said. 'You were pretty fast, actually. Getting better each day.'

'It was better than not bad,' Billy Boy responded. 'It was fuckin' good, if you ask me.'

'We're not asking,' Jack Peel said. 'And I'll tell ya how good or bad ya were when I count up the kills.'

That wee fucker, Billy Boy thought. *He's never forgiven me for bullying him at school and he'll do all he can to have me thrown out. I ought to fix his wagon for good. Slit his throat when he's sleeping.*

'What do we have to do,' he asked, 'how much have we got to prove, before we're told what the fuck's goin' on?'

'We'll tell ya when we're good an' fuckin' ready,' Peel replied. 'Now get back to yer barracks, clean up, have a rest, and wait for Alf or me to come an' see ya.'

'There's nothin' to do in the fuckin' barracks,' Billy Boy retorted, wanting to strangle the arrogant little bastard.

'Have a wank,' Peel said, then he marched off to enter the Killing House and count up the kills.

Alf Green, who rarely smiled, grinned thinly, then nodded in the direction of the east wing of the big, rambling house. 'Do as he says,' he told Billy Boy. 'Your patience might be rewarded.'

'When?'

'Today,' Green said, then he followed Jack Peel into the Killing House.

'Let's go,' Billy Boy said to his mate, Len Young. 'I can't stand the smell here.'

'You mean the smoke?'

'No, I mean those two bastards.'

'Those two can make or break us,' Len said.

'That's why they stink.'

As he walked back to the east wing, Billy Boy glanced across the land, at the magnificent splendour of the mountains of Mourne, and saw only a vast desolation. This was all to the good. The big house could not be seen until you were practically at its gate and from the air it would look perfectly normal. Nevertheless, it was not remotely normal and Billy Boy was reminded of this fact when he entered the east wing, which was a good distance away from the main building, and made his way down concrete steps to the basement. Though originally vast in its own right, it had been extended over the past years into a web of underground bunkers that housed a canteen, an armoury, stores, an indoor shooting range, a gymnasium, ablutions and accommodations for over a hundred men. Those men were all dedicated paramilitaries and they were here for extensive training in the kind of warfare normally practised by special forces such as the SAS. Indeed, according to rumour, some renegade SAS men had been recruited to devise and implement the training programmes that were, as Billy Boy now knew from personal experience, extremely demanding. Men could be dropped from the course at any time and the failure rate was high. What he still didn't know, and what tormented him daily, was just what this extraordinary set-up was for.

After wending his way through a maze of corridors, passing the armoury and stores, hearing the muffled staccato gunfire from the firing range farther on, Billy Boy, followed by Len Young, came to the barrack-like room where he had been living ever since his arrival here. There were six steel-framed beds in the room, each with its own metal locker, but right now they were unoccupied, the other men being elsewhere in the basement complex undergoing rigorous training in the gymnasium, on the firing range or at the Killing House. Billy Boy placed his sub-machine gun in his locker, stripped off his heavy CRW outfit, put everything away, then flopped down on his bed, wearing only his underpants. He clasped his hands behind his head and gazed up at the ceiling. Len Young, having taken off and stowed his combat gear too, sat on the edge of the adjoining bed and lit up a fag. Though Billy Boy thought smoking was disgusting, he didn't complain – at least not about Len.

'I don't think I can take much more of this,' he complained. 'I mean, I enjoyed it at first – thought it was real excitin', like – but we've done it so many times now, I think I'm losin' m'marbles.'

'We've learnt a lot, though,' Len replied solemnly, exhaling a thin stream of smoke. 'I mean, we're real soldiers now.'

'For what?' Billy Boy responded. 'That's what *I'd* like to know.'

'Sure they'll tell us when they're ready, Billy Boy, an' I think that time's comin'.'

'It fuckin' better be, I tell ya,' Billy Boy said, thinking of all the training he had done in the past few weeks: practice on the firing range with a wide variety of weapons, throwing hand grenades, mock assaults in the Killing House, though using live ammunition (more than one poor bastard had copped it in there), and brutally hard exercise in the gymnasium. It had been pretty amazing, almost unbelievable, really – like being in a real army – and Billy Boy still sometimes felt that he was dreaming and needed waking up.

Here they were, over a hundred hard men, living and training together in a sprawling mansion that was hidden in the mountains and, according to what he had been told, presumed by the authorities to be derelict. No doubt some in authority knew better, but they were keeping their mouths shut. So up here, high in the mountains, professional killers were being trained to be even more professional and obviously to do something on a large scale. But what the hell was it?

'I tell you somethin',' Billy Boy said, just airing his thoughts, like, 'the fuckers runnin' this place are hard, *really* hard, and we're lucky to be still in the runnin'. I mean, how many have been failed so far? An awful lot of us, right? Not to mention those poor fuckers who bought it in the Killing House from that live ammunition an' now lie buried somewhere out there in the mountains. I mean, *those* poor bastards have *really* disappeared – and for good – and their relatives will never find out what happened to them or where they've been buried. Now you've got to be really hard to do that to yer own kind an' you've got to have a really good reason – it's gotta be somethin' exceptional. Ya know what I mean, Len?'

'Ackay, sure I do. It's gotta be somethin' really big. I mean, all these things we're doin', they're things the SAS do – the Killing House an' trainin' with live ammunition an' all that – so we'll soon be as sharp as those bastards an' that must mean somethin'. This is big, Billy Boy, really big, and we should be proud to be part of it.'

'Fuck bein' proud. I wanna know what's going on. I wanna know who's behind all this and what it's all for.'

'You soon will,' Jack Leek said.

Startled, Billy Boy looked up and saw his old enemy standing in the doorway of the room. He had a face like cut granite.

'I hate to say it, Billy Boy, but your team did a brilliant job in the Killing House and that means yer in. Now get off yer arse and come with me. Ya have to meet a few people.'

'What about me?' Len asked as Billy Boy, galvanized by excitement, rolled off his bed and started putting on his clothes.

'Stay here and keep wanking,' Leek said. 'Hurry it up, Billy Boy.'

Once dressed, Billy Boy followed Leek back through the east wing, past the armoury and stores and gymnasium, past other rooms where weary men lolled on steel-framed beds, to the big room used by the top dogs as their HQ. Leek opened the door and stepped aside to let Billy Boy walk in.

Entering, he found Alf Green and some other Red Hand paramilitaries seated behind a long table. Behind them, pinned to the wall, was an immense map of the whole of Ireland, north and south. Billy Boy walked up to the table, then stopped, held his breath and just stared, not believing his eyes.

The six men behind the table were not all Loyalist hard men. Seated beside Alf Green, his gaze steady and unafraid, his formerly handsome features ruined by a livid burn mark on his right cheek, was Sean Farrell, the former head of the Provos.

CHAPTER NINETEEN

'You've got a bloody nerve,' was her opening comment as Pete pulled up a chair and sat facing her. Up close, he was struck by the brightness of her green eyes, her angular, slightly drawn features framed by shoulder-length blonde hair, her air of oddly distracted intensity. Nevertheless, she was smiling, simultaneously amused and slightly mocking. Clearly she was no wilting violet and was, indeed, in an unspectacular way, extremely attractive.

'Have I?' He shrugged and grinned. 'It comes from my many years in Australia where the folks are less formal about certain things than they are here in Protestant Belfast. I'm Pete Thompson.'

'Patricia Monaghan. I guessed you weren't a local lad from the way you approached me. They're not that way around here. All the Irish are mother's boys at heart. It's the curse of the country.'

'Well, I *was* born here,' Pete corrected her. 'In Donegall Avenue, though I left when still a boy, when my parents went to live in Birkenhead. I grew up there, then went to Australia and lived there a long time. I came back four years ago.'

'To Belfast?'

'No, to London. I only came here a few months back, about October last year. Now I live right here in the Shankill.'

'Married?'

'I was. My wife, an Australian, died in Melbourne a few years before I came back here. I guess that's why I came back.'

'I'm sorry,' she said.

'And you?'

'You're not going to believe it.' She stubbed her cigarette out and immediately lit another one. 'My husband was killed about five months ago. Blown up in his car, right outside our home in Stranmillis. We don't know who did it or why they did it, though that's no surprise.'

'He wasn't involved with the paramilitaries?'

'No. He was just a schoolteacher. Another innocent victim.'

'I'm sorry to hear that.'

'So,' she said, 'we've both lost our partners and we're sorry all round. What else can we talk about?'

She had said it with an edge of sarcasm that surprised and baffled him. Watching her smoking, he noticed the edginess of her movements and recalled what Cooney had said about her chosen method of burying her grief over her husband's death: brief liaisons with a wide variety of men. This didn't strike him as logical and her appearance only strengthened his doubts. He knew his women . . . and this one struck him as being a sensual creature who was, behind her veneer of cynicism, perhaps too romantic for her own good. If that was true, he could use it.

'You live around here?' he asked.

'No,' she said. 'I'm still in Stranmillis.'

'A nice mixed area to be in. Better than the Shankill.'

'You don't seem the type for the Shankill yourself,' she said. 'I mean, this is a solidly working-class area and you don't look like a working man.'

'I am,' Pete said. 'Though I work for myself, repairing television and video sets. Nothing fancy, I fear.'

'Some men at the bar keep looking at us,' she told him, 'with big grins on their faces. They must have seen you in here before, picking up other women.'

'Not in here,' he said. 'I certainly know a couple of them from other bars and they're the ones that are grinning.'

'You have a reputation with the ladies, do you?'

Pete grinned and shrugged. 'They've probably seen me with one or two women and, being Irish, they like to talk.'

'Men in Belfast don't normally approach women as casually as you do. If you've done it often and if those bastards have seen you doing it, that would explain why they're grinning. They must think you're a ladies' man. *Are* you?'

'I'm not sure what that means.'

'You know damned well what it means and that's just what you are.'

'Does that bother you?'

'Not particularly.'

'So what about you?' Pete asked.

'I don't have any children, I live alone, and I do what I want.'

'So what *do* you want?'

'It's what I *don't* want . . . and what I don't want is any form of serious attachment for the foreseeable future. On the other hand, I don't like sleeping alone too much and, yes, I like a certain kind of man. I'm not saying I play the field, but I don't lead a celibate life. I bet it thrills you to hear that.'

'It amuses me,' Pete said.

She studied him thoughtfully, inhaled on her cigarette, turned her head slightly to blow the smoke away from his face, then looked at him again.

'You just don't seem the type,' she said. 'I mean the type who fixes TVs and lives in the Shankill. You seem too sophisticated for that. Why on earth did you pick the Shankill to live in? I mean, people don't *choose* to live here if they can go somewhere else. So why are you here?'

Pete shrugged again. 'It just seemed like a good place to pick up business. Middle-class people don't *repair* their TVs – they buy new ones. But here, in the Shankill, which is poor, they can't afford to do that. That's why I'm doing good business. I also picked here, I suspect, because I come from the working classes – Donegall Avenue – and while I didn't want to go back to exactly where I'd come from, I *did* want to return to my roots. I don't think I rationalized it then, but I think that's what I did.'

'You weren't worried about the Loyalist paramilitaries? All the violence hereabouts?'

'I didn't worry and I still don't. I mean, I've been here for about four months now and I've never been bothered. I'm not involved and they all know that. Also, I haven't lived in Ireland for nearly thirty years, which makes me virtually a foreigner. They're not bothered by foreigners.'

'And you're not bothered by them?'

'No,' Pete said.

'Does the situation in Ulster bother you at all?'

'I'd rather the situation didn't exist, but it doesn't touch me personally. Maybe I've been too long in Australia, seeing it from the perspective of a foreigner. I mean, it strikes me as being a kind of tribalism beyond reason or sense. As for the actual fighting, from what I've picked up around here, it's evolved largely – I'm sure there are exceptions – into gangsterism, with each side fighting for control of the other's rackets. That isn't patriotism – it's crime – and now Belfast is pretty much a gangsters' city run by two gangs: the Loyalists and the so-called Republicans or nationalists. Am I being too cynical?'

Patricia smiled and let streams of cigarette smoke drift out of her nostrils. 'No,' she said. 'Not really. I'm inclined to take that view myself. Naturally, being a Catholic, I have certain sympathies for the Republicans or nationalists – take your pick – but gangsterism is certainly the growing factor that makes me, and others like me, doubt that we should support them at all. A lot of psychopaths are on the loose in this city, masquerading as so-called freedom fighters. Every day it becomes harder to ignore that awful fact; but this is still an Orange State and as long as the Loyalists stampede over Catholic rights the fight will continue and, ironically, the gangsters will prosper. It's pretty sick, really.'

Pete noticed that she did not speak with a broad Belfast accent and that she had a kind of natural sophistication, or worldliness, which indicated that she had not spent all her life in Belfast. This, too, could be useful.

'Am I allowed to ask what you do for a living?'

'You've just asked,' Patricia said, grinning.

'So?'

'I'm a reporter for a radio station in the south. I do various kinds of programme, but mostly I cover the present conflict, which is why I'm based in Belfast.'

'You don't come from here?'

'No. I was born and bred in Dublin and educated at Trinity College. Went to work as a junior reporter for a Dublin rag, then moved on to radio. I was sent here about five years ago by the radio station and I've been here ever since. I met my husband here – he *was* Belfast born and bred – and that, of course, became another reason for staying on.'

'And now . . . ?' He didn't want to mention the death of her husband, but she knew what he meant.

'Now that he's gone?' she asked rhetorically, then shrugged. 'I don't know. Right now, I don't know what else to do, so I suppose

I'll stay on. Besides, I like it here. Apart from the conflict – or the violence of the so-called peace – this is really a very lively, friendly city and I feel it's my home now. So, yes, I'll probably stay on – at least for the time being.'

Given her chain-smoking and the edginess of her movements, Pete was willing to concede that she was not a relaxed woman. On the other hand, though possibly troubled on some count, she was surprisingly calm, almost offhand, when talking about her late husband. As he had died only five months previously, this struck Pete as odd. He assumed that being a reporter, particularly one specializing in the conflict, would have toughened her up considerably; but even so, her seeming acceptance of the recent death of her husband did not appear quite normal.

'You have Republican sympathies,' Pete said, 'and you broadcast them down south, yet you aren't frightened to come into the Shankill. How come?'

'They're not concerned with me here because they know I'm a reporter and I have a reputation for objectivity. I've interviewed a lot of paramilitaries in the Shankill, as well as in the Falls, and though they know I'm a Catholic with Republican sympathies, they still want to get the Loyalist view across, particularly in the south. I don't edit their views into something else – I broadcast what they say – so these men . . .' she nodded to indicate the paramilitaries along the bar '. . . these men are happy to have me come here to hear what they have to say. A lot of them also like to fuck a Catholic and a few have fucked me.'

She was staring directly at him when she made that statement, perhaps trying to shock him.

'Lucky them,' he said, grinning.

'You fancy your chances, do you?'

'You said I'd got a nerve inviting myself to sit at your table. I think *you*'ve got the nerve.'

'I'm not shy, if that's what you mean, but you haven't answered my question.'

'I'm not as bad as you think. You looked like an interesting lady and clearly you weren't waiting for anyone. I don't assume I'm going to bed with every woman I talk to, but if I see a woman who looks interesting, I'll certainly try to talk to her. Not all of them are willing to go to bed with me and in that case we can still have a good evening, just drinking and talking, with no bad will on either side. I've never forced myself on a woman and I've never had my face slapped.'

This was a lie. In fact, he'd had his face slapped by many of his women, though certainly not for forcing himself upon them. Quite the opposite, actually. They had usually slapped his face when he was neglecting them, as he always did when involved with another woman. It was the curse of his life.

'It's a relief to know you're so pragmatic about it,' Patricia said, smiling and blowing a few smoke rings. 'It gives me time to think, like.'

'That word "like" is a nice touch of Belfast. It makes you more Irish, like.'

Patricia chuckled. 'Yeah, right . . .' She glanced at her empty glass. 'Am I going to be offered another drink or what?'

'Of course,' Pete said. 'What was it?'

'Bushmill's on the rocks. A double.'

Pete nodded. 'You've got it.' He went to the bar and ordered the drinks, which included another pint of Guinness for himself. While he was waiting for the drinks to arrive, Jimmy Robertson, a five-foot-four Loyalist with a scarred face, pugnacious personality and dubious reputation, known to Pete from another Shankill pub, leaned sideways to say, 'On the game again, are ya? Lettin' yer dick rule yer head again. Well, ya better be careful with that one.'

'Why's that, Jimmy?'

'She's gotta be a hard one. Sure her husband's only bin dead these past few months an' already she's fuckin' everythin' in sight.'

'An exaggeration, surely.'

'Maybe. But what's for fuckin' sure is that she plays around a bit, isn't shy about it, and isn't averse to a bit of Prod cock. I mean, a lot of 'em are like that, aren't they? Not satisfied with their own kind. Like to have a taste of the opposition for the wee thrill that's in it. Like them wimmen in the American south, fantasizin' about a bit of black cock. These Catholic whores aren't much different, like.'

'You're the one who's doing the fantasizing,' Pete said. 'Jealous that she hasn't picked you, are you?'

'Don't shite me, boyo. Just because ya've bin to Arsestralia and think yer all worldly, like. Take my word for it. Any Catholic bitch who likes to fuck Prods has got to be trouble. So you be careful, boyo.'

'Thanks for the advice,' Pete said as he received the drinks and paid the barman. 'I'll try to bear it in mind.'

'You do that,' Jimmy said.

Bearing in mind what Jimmy had said only insofar as it told him something of sectarian paranoia, Pete took the drinks back to the table. No sooner had he sat down, however, and was facing Patricia again, than he was wondering if there wasn't at least a shred of truth in what Jimmy had said. This woman *did* appear to have a taste for Prods and he wanted to know why.

'So what are you working on at the moment?' he asked her as casually as possible.

'Another programme for down south.'

'About the conflict?'

'Naturally.'

'So what's this one about?'

'The so-called peace plan and why the Loyalists and Republicans take turns at fucking it up.'

'How do you go about a thing like that?'

'I interview people on both sides of the divide and broadcast what they say. It's as simple as that.'

'What kind of people? Famous people?'

'Not necessarily famous, but certainly well known and representative of their respective communities.'

Be careful now, Pete thought. *Don't ask direct questions. Let her bring up Dawson.*

'Who, for example? I mean, people like the Reverend Ian Paisley?'

'That's right. Though Paisley's not top of my list right now, since he's on the way out.'

'You really think so?'

'Well, he's not out with his Prods, but he's pretty well out of it with the media who now view him as being ancient history. The new man is the Reverend William Dawson and *he*'s certainly on my list.'

'Not quite Paisley,' Pete said. 'From what I gather, he's really pretty conservative when it comes to discussing the Catholics.'

'Oh, yes,' Patricia said sarcastically. 'The voice of reason, for sure. But that's the face he shows to the media to make himself more acceptable. The real Dawson can be found in his church when he's preaching his sermons. He's not so reasonable then, that's for sure. In church he's as much a demagogue as Paisley and only marginally more subtle. Paisley rants and roars – he's not a diplomatic man – but Dawson is the consummate politician and can tread that fine line with great dexterity. He's one thing to the media and quite another to his flock of adoring Prods. For that reason, he's probably more dangerous than Paisley. He just shouts a lot less.'

'*Dangerous* is an extreme word to use. I'm sure Dawson's not that bad.'

'He's bad enough to have connections with some of the most vicious Loyalist paramilitaries. That connection's a pretty difficult one to prove, but I'm damned sure it exists.'

'I find that hard to believe,' Pete said, still being careful about what he said.

'Why? Religion and politics have always been intertwined in this country, which is why we get men like the Reverend Ian Paisley. Dawson's the same. His East Belfast Unionist Party once funded a Protestant youth movement that became the present-day Ulster Defenders – the most vehemently anti-Catholic of all the Loyalist paramilitary groups. That group, in turn, has spawned the new Red Hand, also known for its virulent anti-Catholic stance and, indeed, for the actual murder of an awful lot of Catholics. So Dawson, despite his public utterances, has blood on his hands, even if indirectly.'

'You've interviewed him?' Pete asked.

'Yes.'

'So what does he have to say about it?'

'He denies that he's still connected to the Ulster Defenders, but a lot of those bastards attend his church, so they must still be friends. Also, I've actually seen Dawson's trusted secretary, Robert Lilly, entering the headquarters of the Ulster Defenders and leaving the building with some of its members. So don't try defending him just because you're a Prod. The Reverend Dawson, at the very least, still offers a friendly hand to the most rabidly anti-Catholic paramilitaries – and that means he supports them . . . But why are we talking about this shit? Let's discuss something else.'

'Such as?'

'Hell, I don't know.'

'What about this?' Pete said. 'Where are we going to sleep tonight? Your place or mine?'

'I fuck Prods, but I never fuck in the Shankill, so let's make it my place.'

'Do we leave now or later?' Pete asked.

'I can't stand the leering of those bastards at the bar,' Patricia said, 'so let's get up and go.'

They finished their drinks and walked to the door, not without noticing that some of the men along the counter, the ones who knew Pete, were watching with big grins on their faces. Ignoring them, Pete left with Patricia, stepping into the freezing January night. The shops in the Shankill Road were long closed by now, but the street lights illuminated the ugly steel grids covering most windows and fell on the melting sludge on the road. Pete managed to flag down a passing taxi in a matter of minutes and Patricia gave the driver her Stranmillis address. She did not, Pete noticed, sit close by him in the rear seat, instead keeping a respectable distance between them as she lit up yet another cigarette.

'You smoke a lot,' Pete commented as the taxi moved off down the lower Shankill, heading for Royal Avenue and the centre of town.

'Is that a complaint?'

'No, it's merely an observation. Have you always smoked that much?'

'I started smoking shortly after I got married, but don't ask me why.'

'Okay, I won't.'

They fell silent after that, but Pete contented himself with looking out of the window of the taxi as it cruised along Royal Avenue, all modernized these days with large stores and shopping arcades, then around the floodlit City Hall and down Dublin Road. It was a small, intimate city, lively enough in this area, and soon the taxi was taking him along the Golden Mile, its pubs and restaurants neon-lit, and then on to the Stranmillis Road. Once there, it turned into an attractive, leafy side street and came to a halt outside an imposing redbrick house. Pete clambered out first. He took Patricia's hand to help her out (she smiled fleetingly when he did so), then paid the driver and followed her up the garden path to the front door. He saw immediately, from the half-dozen or so names listed beside the door, that the big house had been converted into apartments. Patricia opened the door with her key and led him inside.

'It's the second floor,' she said, closing the door behind him. He followed her up, noting that the hallway and stairs were well maintained, and waited behind her on the landing of the second floor until she had opened the door of her flat. She walked in ahead of him, switched the light on, then waved him inside.

Entering, he found himself in a fairly large living room with french windows at one end overlooking the front garden, a renovated marble fireplace, black-leather sofas and chairs, a twenty-three-inch television set with an expensive video player, a music centre with a lot of CDs on the tall rack beside it, and a large black desk with a computer and printer on it. Clearly, Patricia Monaghan was well paid and had good taste when spending it.

'Very nice,' Pete said.

Patricia did not reply. Instead, she disappeared through a side door, which he presumed was the bedroom, and emerged mere seconds later minus her overcoat and shoulder bag. She was wearing tight blue denims – obviously the expensive kind – and an open-necked shirt which, being tucked tightly into the denims, revealed her slim, shapely, seductive figure. She had kicked her shoes off.

'Do you like what you see?' she asked him.

'Yes,' Pete said, meaning it.

'You'll see more if you take my clothes off and stretch me out on the floor.'

Pete did not hesitate.

CHAPTER TWENTY

They came for Patricia at nine o'clock in the evening, honking the car horn three times to let her know they were waiting outside. Unusually nervous, though not too sure of the reason, she went to the french windows and pulled the curtains apart to look down on the street.

The familiar red Ford Cortina was parked by the pavement, just a few metres away from the garden gate, just outside the circle of yellow light thrown down by a street lamp. The sludge had disappeared from the road but the pavements were icy.

Satisfied, Patricia released the curtain, turned away from the window, picked up her shoulder bag, then left the flat, leaving all the lights on but carefully locking the door behind her. She went down the two flights of stairs, then walked out into the bitterly cold night.

Shivering, she made her way to the parked Ford Cortina. Just before she reached it, Seamus O'Leary, a Republican hard man, slipped out of the nearside front door and hastily opened the rear door for her.

'Evenin',' he said curtly by way of greeting.

Patricia just nodded and slipped into the rear seat, settling in as Seamus closed the door behind her and again took his seat beside the driver. The latter neither turned his head to look at her nor spoke a word in greeting; he merely turned the ignition on, released the handbrake and drove off down the street. After turning into the Stranmillis Road, he headed for the centre of town.

Patricia didn't know exactly where they were taking her, but Sean had said that it was well outside Belfast and might take some time.

Tired and nervous, confused by this new arrangement, she lit a cigarette, sank back into her seat and smoked with her weary eyes closed. Instantly, she saw Sean's face, the livid scar on his cheek, the ruination of his handsome features; then Pete Thompson's face was superimposed upon it to make her heart race. When her face burned and her throat went dry, she realized it was panic.

Dear God, give me peace, she thought.

Breathing deeply, she tried to still her racing heart as the Cortina carried her across Shaftesbury Square and on to the bright lights of town. By the time it had passed through the town centre and was taking the slip road onto the motorway, her racing heart had settled down, though she still felt uneasy.

The realization that Sean was no longer in the south, that he had returned to Northern Ireland without letting her know and, worse, had still not told her where he was, had given her due cause for concern. Now, though she was on her way to see him, destination unknown, she realized that she was starting to resent him, despite her love for him. This thought came as a shock to her.

Lighting another cigarette, thinking *Cancer could be a blessing*, she gazed out over the darkly glittering waters of Belfast Lough. The Cortina was racing along the motorway, taking her out of the city, but she felt that she was in a foreign country with no landmarks to help her.

Sean was exploiting her and she couldn't say 'No' to him, but she felt degraded by what he was making her do and she resented him for it. God knows, she had loved him, surrendering to him without reserve, losing all commonsense in the need to please him and be pleasured by him; but that was all before the assassination attempt, before the blood and the burning.

She had been home when it had happened, preparing to join him in the car, and when she had heard the explosion and rushed outside, she had almost died just to see it. The rear of the car had been blown off and the exposed wheels were on fire, the flames leaping up over the front seat as Sean, obscured in the smoke, fell sideways out of the driver's seat. When she had raced to the burning car, not concerned for her own safety, too dazed to think about it, Sean had been stretched out on the ground, the back of his shirt smouldering, one arm a bloody mess, his right cheek scorched and suppurating, looking like the inside of a pomegranate.

She had thought that he was a goner, but he'd survived because the bomb had been badly made and also placed in the wrong place, near the back of the car.

Oh, yes, she thought, as the Cortina left Belfast well behind and raced through the dark, moonlit night, obviously heading for Antrim. *He survived, but he was never the same after that and now I don't know how to deal with him. I'm not sure of him any more.*

She wasn't sure what she meant by that but she knew it was a fact and it made her increasingly uncomfortable as the journey continued, the Cortina eventually taking her off the motorway and deep into Antrim, destination still unknown.

Sean had changed since the explosion, since his face had been scarred, and each time she had visited him in the south, in that safe house, that big house with its top floor given over to the Provies, those in need of medical care or just on the run, she had sensed the change in him, a distance, a new hardness, and gradually realized that although she still loved him, he was not any longer the man she had known. That man had been an idealist, a freedom fighter from the old school, but the new Sean, the one with the scarred face and flat gaze, inward looking, concealing, was someone she was starting to mistrust and feel frightened by.

It was him, this new Sean, whom she dreaded seeing – and this knowledge shamed her.

Then, of course, there was Pete Thompson. He certainly had something to do with it. She had pulled him in just like the others, simply doing Sean's bidding, unable to refuse as usual, sniffing the air by bedding Prods and dropping them if they had nothing to tell her; but Pete Thompson, who appeared to know nothing, was still sharing her bed. This was a breaking of rules, her own rules, and she kept wondering why she had done it and, of course, she knew why. She felt that Sean no longer loved her and, worse, was exploiting her; and even though her secret fears still kept her in his orbit, pulled in by his gravity, she sensed that she was struggling for her freedom by looking elsewhere.

Pete Thompson was meant to be just another job, a potential source of information, but something had happened that night to make her see him as something else. He had set her on fire, making her burn with sexual heat, and although she still felt that he was more than he seemed, had his own secrets to conceal, she had kept seeing him, not because of that, but because he had gauged the depths of her masochism and made her face up to it. She could have hated him for that – and perhaps she really did – but right now she only knew that she wanted to keep seeing him without eventually causing him harm.

She could harm him so easily.

Opening her eyes again as the car travelled on through Antrim, heading, she now realized, for the mountains of Mourne, rising gradually in the distance, immense, feminine, darker than the night sky, she thought of that first extraordinary night with Pete Thompson, of the seducer being seduced, the tormentor being tormented, and realized that they had both fallen into something that could lead to damnation. That night had been touched with madness, with revelations of nightmare, the release of buried pain, the cauterizing of old wounds, and to this day she could not understand how he had drawn all that out of her. Nevertheless, whether intentional or not, he had managed to do so and now she needed him for that, if for nothing else.

She had seen him a lot since then, feeling more confused each time, increasingly frightened by the knowledge that this was supposed to be just a job, but that she was seeing him for reasons of her own, despite her own reservations. Now, on her way to see Sean, she felt even more frightened.

She didn't know what to tell him.

God, just play it by ear, she thought.

Breathing in nervous spasms, she looked out of the side window and saw the great breasts of the mountains of Mourne rising and falling darkly on all sides, under a vast canopy of stars, in the light of a pale moon. The road they were travelling was high in the hills, desolate, windblown, and below there was only a pit of darkness that appeared to have no end. Shivering, Patricia looked to the front and saw lights in the distance.

The car was slowing down, approaching two beams of light that fell obliquely upon the road – more of a track, really – and beyond those lights, far back from the track, were more lights, obviously shining out from many windows, some above the others. Gradually, as the car approached the beams of light falling over the track, Patricia saw that the other lights were indeed illuminating the many windows of a very large house, possibly a mansion, that was partly hidden by rows of silhouetted chestnut trees and dominated by a horseshoe of high hills whose dim night-time outlines rose high around it. She returned her gaze to the front as the Cortina moved into the lights beaming over the track and gradually came to a halt in front of what looked like the gatehouse to the big house farther back. The lights shone from the front windows of the gatehouse.

'This is it,' Seamus O'Leary said. 'He's waitin' for you inside. We'll wait here and drive ya home when he's finished with ya. Just go an' knock on the door.'

Noting the distinct lack of warmth in his voice, she decided not to reply and instead simply slipped out of the car, felt the shock of the icy wind, heard its desolate moaning, and hurried across to the gatehouse. She used the brass knocker on the door to announce her arrival.

'Yes?' she heard Sean query, though his voice sounded muffled.

'It's me . . . Pat.'

'The door's not locked. Come in.'

Patricia opened the door and stepped tentatively inside. The lights beaming out onto the road came from lamps on the window sills. Sean was sitting on a sofa near an old stone fireplace in which a wood fire was burning warmly. He was wearing a thick navy-blue sweater over an open-necked shirt, a pair of faded blue jeans and scuffed brown suede boots. There was a cigarette in his left hand and a glass of whisky in the other hand. The flames cast flickering shadows and light across his pale face . . . pale except for the hideously livid wrinkled skin that now covered most of the right side of his face and gave him a frightening appearance.

Trying not to notice that or, at least, attempting to accept it, Patricia closed the door behind her and crossed the room to stop directly in front of him. She had once approached him in a completely natural way, but now knew that she could no longer do that. Faking it, she leaned down to place her hands on his shoulders and kiss him on his undamaged cheek. He flinched as if he had been insulted as she straightened up and stared down at him.

'You can't kiss the other side, can you?' he said.

'I didn't think . . . I mean, I just . . .' She floundered, not knowing what to say, aware that he was right. 'Please, Sean, I just . . .'

But he waved the hand holding the cigarette, indicating that she should take the chair facing him. 'Sit down,' he said. 'Drink?'

'Yes,' she said. 'I could do with it.'

There was a bottle of whisky on the table between them and he leaned forward to push it towards her. 'Help yourself, Pat.'

She poured herself a drink and noticed that her hand was shaking. Having a cigarette would not help the shaking, but she lit one anyway. Sean watched all the time, saying nothing. His brown gaze, once so romantic, was now fathomless and fixed steadily upon her. She could not meet his eyes.

'So what are you doing here?' Patricia asked eventually, unable to stand the lengthy silence. 'I mean, I thought you were still in the south. You didn't tell me you were coming back across the border. How long have you been here?'

'A month,' he replied. 'I couldn't tell you because things were uncertain, but it's permanent now.'

'I've gone to see you once a month in that place down south,' she said. 'I could have gone again and not found you there.'

'You always visited me on the last day of the month,' Sean reminded her, 'and tomorrow's the last day of February. That's why we picked you up tonight . . . to save you from going down south and not finding me there.'

'That was thoughtful,' she said with soft sarcasm.

'It was practical,' Sean said.

Patricia glanced around the small gatehouse and saw that it was done out like a country cottage, not large but comfortable. Through a window at the back she could see the lights of the big house farther on, almost lost in the surrounding high hills, black and brooding in darkness. The wind was moaning outside.

'So why did we meet here?' she asked him.

'I'm staying here,' he replied.

'Where are we?'

'The mountains of Mourne.'

'But *where* in the mountains of Mourne?'

'You don't need to know that.'

'When are you coming back to Belfast?'

'Not for the foreseeable future. I can't risk going back there.'

'And this is it? This is where you're staying?'

'This is it, Pat.'

He sank back into the sofa, letting most of his face disappear into the shadows, hiding his scarred cheek. She could scarcely see his brown eyes in that darkness, but light fell on his lips. She noticed, for the first time, that they were thin and now displaying no humour. He had once been good-humoured.

'What's that up there?' Patricia asked, turning her head and nodding in the direction of the lights she could see through the back window. 'It looks like a big house.'

'That's exactly what it is,' he replied. 'A big country mansion.'

'You can hardly see it tucked in there between the hills . . . and this is really high up.'

'You can't see it from the road below,' he replied. 'You can't see it from the air. The nearest village is about fifteen miles from here and the locals think the house is still unused. It was locked up long ago, when its owner died, so we've quietly taken it over and no one knows we're in there.'

'It's a safe house?'

'You might say that, Pat. Let's leave it at that.' He inhaled on his cigarette, then exhaled with a sigh. The smoke drifted out of the shadows around his face to dissolve in the light. 'So what's happening in Belfast?' he asked. 'What's happening with you?'

It was the question she had dreaded and she hesitated before replying. 'Not much,' she said. 'I haven't really picked up anything that couldn't be picked up from local gossip. All they give me is gossip.'

'So what *is* the local gossip?'

Patricia inhaled deeply on her cigarette, wishing it was something a lot more soothing – say, a good dose of Valium. She released the smoke with a nervous sigh. 'Mostly about the disappearances of so many paramilitaries, Prods and Provies alike.'

'So what's the general feeling?' Sean asked her in his recently developed, curiously flat tone of voice.

'Growing unease,' Patricia said. 'At first people thought it was just Provie assassinations, but as the number of disappearances grew, the general belief was that those men weren't being killed by the Provies, but were simply going underground in preparation for some kind of unusually big Loyalist operation. Then, when Provies started disappearing as well, people became confused, not knowing what to think, and now there's talk that the Brits might be involved, though no one knows how or why. Whatever's happening, the general feeling is that it's big, *really* big, but no one has a clue who's behind it or what it's all for and that makes people, Catholics and Prods alike, even more nervous . . . *You* know who's behind it, don't you, Sean? You know what it's about.'

'What makes you think that? Did I say that?'

'Well, no, but . . .'

'Ask no questions and I'll tell you no lies. Is that all you've got for me? What about these men of yours?'

Patricia shrugged in a casual manner, but her stomach was churning. 'I wanted to talk to you about that, Sean. I really wish you wouldn't . . .'

'Make you do it?' He shook his head wearily. 'Unfortunately, Pat, you *do* have to do it, no matter how distasteful it seems to you. We need someone like you on the ground, picking up what you can, so don't complain and just tell me what they've told you.'

'That's the whole point, Sean. I get so little from them. You make me pick up these Prods, I have to fuck them in our bed, and then I've got to get them talking a lot because you want information. You make me degrade myself, Sean, and what's it all for? A few scraps of information here and there, none of it special. I'm a whore for a pittance.'

'Let me be the judge of that,' Sean said, indifferent to the shame she had expressed, thinking only of the cause that now seemed to obsess him: revenge for the Loyalist attack that had left him scarred for life. The uniting of Ireland had little to do with it. It was purely personal now. At least that was what Patricia felt. 'What about this Prod you're presently with? What has *he* got to say?'

Patricia shrugged, trying to feign indifference. 'Not much at all.'

'Really?'

'Really.'

'Normally, if the men have nothing to offer, you dump them after a day or two. But you've been seeing this man for a fortnight. Why is that, Pat?'

The question shocked her. 'How do you know I've been seeing him for a fortnight? Are you having me watched?'

'Of course.'

'*Of course!* What the fuck does that mean?'

'For your own protection,' Sean said.

She knew it was a lie and her rage threatened to erupt, but her fear – the knowledge of why she was still seeing Pete Thompson – overwhelmed the rage and helped her stay calm . . . at least, outwardly so.

'It's nice to know I'm being protected,' she said, unable to hold back the softly spoken sarcasm.

'So why have you been seeing this man so long when he has nothing to offer?'

Patricia knew that she had to be careful now. On the one hand, she still felt committed to Sean – or, perhaps more accurately, was unable to refuse him; on the other, she was drawn to Pete Thompson and felt the need to protect *him*. She wanted to lie to Sean, to protect Pete, but she couldn't quite do it . . . at least, not all the way.

'Well . . .' she began, hesitating, then bought time by pouring more whisky and having a good, soothing mouthful. 'I'm not really sure,' she said eventually. 'I mean, he's given me nothing so far, but he asks a lot of questions and I find myself wondering why. I mean, he hasn't lived in Ireland for years – nearly thirty years, in fact – he was out in Australia – and he doesn't seem to be remotely involved, but he keeps coming up with these questions. I'm trying to find out why he asks so many when, as he insists, he's not involved in the conflict and doesn't want to be.'

'Questions about what?' Sean asked.

'Well . . .'

'It may not sound like anything to you, but it could be important. So what the fuck is it? Has he been asking about the disappearances?'

'Yes. But then, everyone's been talking about those, so that isn't unusual.'

'So what *is* unusual about him?'

'He seems particularly interested in the Reverend William Dawson. He knows I've been interviewing him and he keeps asking me just what he's like . . . how he operates and so on . . . It all started casually, almost accidentally. We started talking about Ian Paisley and comparing Dawson to him – but he kept coming back to the Reverend Dawson and, given his stated lack of interest, I found that unsettling.'

'Anything else?'

'Yes. He was particularly interested when I told him that Dawson was involved in a lot of welfare projects involving young people, including the recent setting-up of that government-sponsored establishment in Antrim where troubled kids are receiving computer training. He definitely asked an awful lot about that and I was wondering why. Then, when I happened to mention that Dawson was your modern, up-to-date kind of preacher, into the Internet and e-mail and so on, he seemed to find that particularly intriguing . . . so, you know, I'm wondering why.'

'Just who is this particular Prod who hasn't been in the country for thirty years?'

'Name of Pete Thompson. Born and bred in Donegall Avenue. Left home when still a kid and ended up living in Australia, only coming back here when his Aussie wife died. Lives and works in the Shankill, repairing TVs and videos . . . and doing well at it. A bit of a ladies' man.'

'Which is how you managed to pick him up.'

'Right.'

'In your regular Shankill Road pub?'

'Yes.'

'That's the pub of Loyalist hard men. Does he go there regularly?'

'Not until he met me. That was his first night there. I picked him up the first evening I saw him there and, of course, he's been back since.'

'Did he say what he was doing there that particular evening?'

'I got the impression he liked his drink, enjoyed drifting from pub to pub, picking his women up in them, and had just finally gotten around to that one. That would certainly make sense.'

'It might and it might not. He might have gone there deliberately to meet you; maybe sent there by someone who knows you. Did he seem comfortable there?'

'He seemed right at home. He'd met some of the hard men present in other pubs and was friendly with them. He'd also gotten to know a lot of them when he went to their homes to fix their tellies or videos. He's well known in the area.'

'He's well known in the area, he gets invited to the homes of paramilitaries, he claims not to be interested in the conflict, yet he seems to have an unusual amount of interest in that Loyalist preacher, the Reverend William Dawson. Small wonder you're wondering.'

'Yes,' Patricia said, realizing that she should have kept her mouth shut, feeling stupid and guilty. 'I suppose so.'

'Stick with him,' Sean said. 'I want to know a lot more about this newcomer who claims to have no interest but asks a lot of pertinent questions. Don't let me down, Pat.'

'I won't,' Patricia said, though she felt sick to her soul and wondered why she always surrendered to Sean, despite her own reservations. She was in very deep now . . . too deep . . . and fear was growing inside her.

'Thanks for coming,' Sean said, even though he hadn't given her any choice. 'I think you'd better leave now. It's a pretty long drive back.'

'Are you all right? Is there anything I can . . . ?' She was thinking about sex, but she could not complete the sentence and Sean was aware of that fact.

'Yes,' he said levelly, 'I'm all right. Just get on home, Pat.'

Her hesitation and his response told her a lot about the changing relationship between them. They had once been so natural together, but now they were strangers. This was because *he* had changed, becoming more bitter and fanatical, distant to her, coldly using her; but it was also to do with her and Pete Thompson, with what had occurred between them that first night. Even now, even given that she had seen him often since, when she recollected that first night together she burned with excitement and shame, her heart racing in panic. She prayed that Sean could not see it in her face as she stood up to leave.

'When will I see you again?' she asked him.

'When I call you,' he said.

This time, when she leaned down to kiss him, she deliberately chose his scarred cheek, but he quickly turned his head away to let her kiss his good side. Relieved even in her shame, she kissed that cheek and then straightened up again. Because he hadn't moved from where he was sitting, his face remained in the shadows. She could not see his eyes.

'Well,' she said, 'see you soon.'

'I want to know more about that man,' he responded.

'I'll do my best, Sean.'

With her heart still racing, she turned away and walked out, closing the door quietly behind her as she stepped into the freezing, dark, windy night. The Ford Cortina was still parked near the gatehouse, but now facing back the way it had come, preparing to leave. Seamus O'Leary, who had been waiting outside the car, opened the rear door when he saw her. She clambered in and he closed the door behind her, then again took the seat beside the driver.

As the car moved off, heading along the winding track that led down the mountainside, Patricia glanced over her shoulder, through the rear window, and saw the lights of the big house beaming out into the night. She wondered just what it was being used for. It was big enough to hold an awful lot of men, that was for sure. Big enough to hold . . . Dear God . . . all those men who had recently disappeared.

Yes, big enough to hold all of them and isolated enough to let them stay there in absolute secrecy.

Hardly able to credit what she was thinking, Patricia looked to the front again and saw stars above the mountains of Mourne. She lit a cigarette and inhaled the smoke as if it might be her last breath.

'Jesus Christ,' she said softly.

CHAPTER TWENTY-ONE

For the Reverend William Dawson, this was always the glory moment of his week. Taking his position behind the pulpit, gazing down silently upon that mass of upward-gazing expectant faces in the church – the grieving mothers of bloody Belfast and the men who, often unbeknownst to their women, caused the blood to flow – he could feel the power of the Lord surging through him, to energize him and turn his thoughts into spine-tingling, inspirational words. Straightening his own spine, he raised his hands on high, took a deep breath, then commenced his sermon.

'The Lord be praised, we are gathered together this day to pray for the souls of our two unfortunate brethren, Councillors William Leek and Ken Bruce, who were so brutally cut down in their prime by butchers steeped in blood and poisoned by Popery. I come to you, friends, direct from a meeting of my Orange Lodge where, as is customary, the meeting was opened with a prayer, conducted with an open Bible on the table and concluded with another prayer. This is the Protestant way. It is not the way of those who would destroy our heritage and our culture and our religion, those who so readily ended the lives of two decent men who would, had they lived, been at that meeting with me, practising what they openly, proudly preached. And what did they preach, my friends, and how did they lead their lives? Not with the damnable heresies of the Church of Rome's confessional, not with bombs and bullets, not with hatred for their neighbours, but with the precepts of all good Orangemen and Protestants. For indeed, they followed the Golden Rule of professing Christians in all their personal and business affairs; they upheld the great Protestant principle of freedom of conscience for all people; they showed unswerving allegiance to Her Majesty the Queen, regarding the throne as the centre of all secular power, justice and law. They were therefore law-abiding.

They were also good neighbours – and councillors – concerned with the welfare of their fellow citizens. They were generous and charitable not only with their worldly goods, but also with their time, their thoughts and their deeds. They took unto themselves the responsibilities of leadership in troubled times. They were loving and responsible parents. They were respectful of the honours and glories of their Protestant heritage, viewing themselves as an extension of their Orange forefathers. They were gentlemen who respected the sanctity of women and defended women's rights; and, last but not least, they were brothers who practised the highest level of fraternalism in the tradition of their Lodge. In short, they were upstanding Protestants and Orangemen, savagely cut down in their prime because of what they believed in.'

The good Reverend paused, letting his opening words sink in, cognisant of the importance of the histrionic double-take, the dramatic silence, the brief peace before the storm of rhetoric that would transfix the listener. He had learnt this in the mission halls of his childhood and would never forget it.

'Yes, my friends, we are gathered here today to pay our respects to the dearly departed. Our brothers, our concerned councillors, William Leek and Ken Bruce, were savagely murdered by the very people to whom they had offered the olive branch of peace. Yes, friends, though not forgetting King William's crossing of the Boyne, the Battle of the Diamond, the Siege of Londonderry – not Derry, as some would have it, but *London*derry as we would have it – without forgetting, in general, our great and glorious Loyalist heritage, they offered the hand of peace to those who would destroy that heritage and, in their righteousness, they were brutally murdered by the very people to whom they were talking. Like you and I, they were Christians, saved by the blood of Jesus Christ, shed on the cross at Calvary, but their Christian goodness was repaid with a bloody barbarism that could only have taken root in the soil of sectarianism as practised by the enemies of Christ. Those enemies – the disciples of the Church of Rome and its heretical Pope – are even now plotting to destroy us. They believe that by destroying the best of us, they can destroy what we stand for. But they cannot and will not, because Jesus will lead us on, from victory to victory, opening us to the glory of God, to the revelations of the saints, to the salvation of lost souls, to the punishment of the sinner, to the defeat of soul-damning Popish heresy and its viperish bedmate, communism. So what do we do? We make war on the battlements of hell, sin and apostasy, crying "Glory be to God!" and "Hallelujah!" Let me hear it right now!'

Cries of 'Glory be to God!' and 'Hallelujah!' came back to him like a soothing benediction. Women sobbed and buried their faces in their prayer books or looked up with wide, glistening eyes, reminding him of the women who must surely have been on their knees at Calvary, looking up at the cross. The spiritual side of him was uncomfortable with such slavish devotion; alas, his more human side could scarcely resist it, though he managed to carry on.

'Our dearly departed Councillors Leek and Bruce,' he continued, 'were callously murdered because they were singular individuals who denounced sectarian violence and were taking steps to put an end to it. For this very reason, they were put to death, shot down like animals, assassinated by brutes, and those who killed them clearly hope that they have hammered two more nails into what they imagine is the coffin of Protestant Ulster. But they're wrong! *They are wrong!*'

A woman in the congregation let out a shriek and then burst into tears. It was the late Councillor William Leek's wife.

'The cause of Northern Ireland,' Reverend Dawson continued regardless, 'is greater than the individual and Protestantism in Ulster is neither dead nor buried, but marching on to the greater glory of God Almighty. We will not give up our heritage, our beliefs, our religion, to the heresies of Rome, to the Popish barbarians who shout their vile insults at our proud Orange Lodge marchers, at those decent Protestants attempting to enter their places of worship, at Her Majesty's representatives in Ulster, here to protect us. We will, instead, ensure that the dark and sinister shadow of our neighbouring Roman Catholic state, which encourages the advance of the heathen hordes at our gates, does not deprive us of our political and religious liberty. Nor will we let them drive us against our will into the damnable confessional to which the unfortunate Roman Catholic, in his ignorance and fear, entrusts his wife and daughters, thus unwittingly placing them on that moral rack which must, by its very nature, reduce them to the shame and despair engendered by blasphemy. To those heretics and to their victims, their wives and innocent children, we will proudly cry out: "*No Popery!*" '

His words came back to him, cried out by his congregation, now wracked by emotion, and he felt the satisfaction of the disciple being repaid for his servitude. The unfortunate wife of the late Councillor Leek was still sobbing, being comforted by her friends, and Reverend Dawson, in his political wisdom, took advantage of this fact.

'Councillors Leek and Bruce died – were brutally murdered, their blood shed – because they believed, sincerely, though wrongly in my view, that they could reconcile two warring sides. Let us trust that they did not die in vain. For indeed, there can be no reconciliation between us and our Popish neighbours, no marriage between Christ and the devil. Not, at least, until the heretics of Roman Catholicism fall to their knees, beg forgiveness for their sins, renounce their evil ways, and accept the one true church, the *Protestant* church, as the guiding light and living heart of Ulster. Until then we can have no truck with the vipers of Rome, with Popish deviltry and subversion; nor with that new Sodom and Gomorrah, the so-called Republic of Ireland. No! And "No" again! For so long as we are surrounded by the enemies of the true Christ, the despisers of Ulster and its proud Protestant history, we must continue to protest against the iniquities of Rome, to repudiate all Popish lies, and to brand as traitors all those who would attempt to convert us to the blasphemous fables and dangerous deceits of Popery, Republicanism and communism. We must and . . . *we will*!'

Realizing that there were, as always, members of the media in the congregation and that they would, if they could, misinterpret what he was saying for their own dubious purposes, the good Reverend took a step back from the brink and tried sounding more moderate, though this was not, for a man of his temperament, all that easy to do. He was bound to fail . . . and he did.

'I do not speak this day in order to incite you to violence or hatred for your neighbour, even if he be Roman Catholic. Nevertheless, I say fully and frankly that in order to heal we first have to wound, in order to save we must first destroy, and that for every evil and wicked slander propagated by the Fenians, we must repay them in kind. So – I put it to you – if that means entering the dark and foul lair of the Popish vipers, rooting them out from where they commit their sins against God and Ulster, then, friends, in the name of God Almighty, so it must be. We must go to the very temples of the heretics and bring their walls, like the very walls of Jericho, tumbling down. Praise the Lord! Hallelujah!'

His fervent cries came back to him, rising up from his congregation, as he bathed in the glory of God's light which, on this unusually sunny day, was beaming down through the stained-glass windows of his church to form a magical radiance around him. He felt the presence of God in that light and it helped him take wing.

'We *know* why Councillors Leek and Bruce died!,' he bellowed magisterially. 'They were killed, they were brutally murdered, they were callously shot down by Roman Catholic thugs because Rome has never given up its attempt to win back what it lost at the Reformation . . .' A deep breath at this point, released even as he continued . . . 'And because we here in Ulster, with our proud, our glorious history of evangelical Protestantism, are an affront which it wishes to destroy. And why would it wish to do so? Because as Protestants we encourage temperance, diligence, loyalty, democracy; whereas those who stand against us, tainted by the Roman Church, besotted by its Pope, insist upon subservience, authoritarianism, intemperance, and even, through the unnatural institution of bachelor priests, *sexual perversion*! So I say to you here and now – and I do so with pride and feeling – God save Ulster from Popery, from apostasy, from the demoniac Republic of Ireland, from being sold down the river by the betraying politicians in Westminster and the vile religious traitors in our own midst. Praise the Lord! Hallelujah! Now let us pray.'

Reverend Dawson lowered his head and his congregation followed suit. The Reverend let the silence linger for a lengthy period and then, paraphrasing instinctively, he let his noble voice ring out once more, though this time with humility.

'I, Thine unworthy servant, humbly do intercede with Thee, the God and Father of all, to have compassion upon the blindness and ignorance of our enemies and upon their gross errors and wicked practices. Send forth, I beseech Thee, Thy light and Thy truth, to scatter that great darkness which covers beloved Ulster and overspreads the whole land, that Thy way may be known to the heretics of Rome and to the heathen amongst us.

'Bless and preserve Thine own Protestant Church whilst removing from the Church of Rome, from the heretical temples of Roman Catholicism, all its errors and corruptions, its offences and scandals, its divisions and dissensions, its tyranny and usurpation over the minds and consciences of its Fenian brethren, that they who profess the same faith may no longer persecute and destroy us, but may, instead, be tolerant and decent towards us, as heirs to our same common salvation.

'And I beseech Thee, O Lord, to bless all our relations and friends, particularly our dearest consort, the Queen, to preserve and continue the love and affection between us; and to bless all of our allies who love righteousness and hate falsehood, standing by us in the maintenance of that just cause in which we are, in our humility and love, ceaselessly and righteously engaged. O Lord, bless us with union!

'And in Thy good time, O Lord, restore peace to this troubled province, putting an end to these bloody wars and desolations with which we have for so long been most miserably harassed. In Thine own good time, O Lord, manifest Thy glorious justice in giving check to that Popish ambition which has caused so many calamities in our formerly blessed Protestant state of Ulster. O God, Lord Almighty, to whom vengeance belongs, show Thyself to the Popish heretics; lift up Thyself, Thou Judge of the earth, and render a reward to the Protestant righteous while scattering to the four winds those Popish heretics who delight in this vicious war. Let the wickedness of the Roman Catholic, the heretic, the heathen, come to an end and establish the just. Let Ulster rise like a phoenix from the ashes as Your Kingdom on Earth.

'Finally, O Lord, our most merciful Father, we beseech Thee to forgive our enemies for all their malice and ill will, to give them repentance, to cleanse them of evil thoughts, that they might see the error of their ways and lay down their arms. We beg this for our enemies, for the heretics of Rome and its unholy dominions, even as we beg for mercy and forgiveness for ourselves – at Thy hands, O Lord! – through the merits and mediations of Jesus Christ, our most merciful God and Saviour. Amen.'

'Amen!' the congregation echoed him, their voices rising on high.

Reverend Dawson opened his eyes and smiled. Glory day. Hallelujah.

The Lord's will be done, he thought.

CHAPTER TWENTY-TWO

‘It was a clear incitement to civil war,’ Pete told Sergeant Major Walter Bannerman as they sat side by side in the hired Ford Escort, in a deeply shadowed stretch of the road between two lamp-posts, about fifty yards along from the Reverend William Dawson’s offices. It was seven in the evening and they were waiting for Dawson’s secretary, Robert Lilly, to leave. Dawson had left over an hour ago, but Lilly, that dedicated worker, was still inside the building. ‘I mean, it was couched in religious language, delivered just like a normal sermon, but the meaning, no matter how he qualified it, was as clear as daylight . . . “Go, my brethren, and burn out the Catholics before they do it to us.” That’s what that bastard was saying.’

‘So what were you doing at one of his church services in the first place?’ Bannerman asked. ‘I know you’re a wee Prod, Pete, but I didn’t realize you were actually religious.’

‘I was taken there by that reporter, Patricia Monaghan, who’s been investigating Dawson. I’ve been trying to pump her about him, pretending I thought he was on the level – at least, more moderate than Paisley – and she said that if I wanted to see the real Reverend Dawson I had to attend one of his services. So I did . . . and I couldn’t believe what I was hearing. That particular preacher may be moderate with the media, but he’s something else again when it comes to his Protestant congregation. He may be more subtle than Paisley, but he’s up to the same tricks.’

‘He may not be as bad as you think,’ Bannerman said. ‘I mean, he *is* a Protestant fundamentalist and that’s how they carry on. It doesn’t mean he’s engaged in anything that would warrant us coming here tonight.’

‘It’s more than that,’ Pete said. ‘After the service, Dawson went to the front door of the church to shake hands with a lot of those coming out. He recognized Patricia Monaghan, who'd interviewed him a couple of times, and naturally he had a few words with her. She introduced me and Dawson pretended not to know me – very pleasant, he was, delighted to see a new face and so on – but something in the way he looked at me convinced me that he knew who I was. I've had the feeling that I was being followed for the past month or so – my instincts are usually sound in this – and the way Dawson spoke to me, the way he studied me with those searching eyes of his, a kind of knowing smile, convinced me that *he* was the one having me followed. Also, he wasn't the least bit surprised that I was with Patricia, so I'm convinced that he had been told I was seeing her. He could, of course, have seen me with her when he was having *her* followed, because she told me that he'd done that very thing. Now why would a straightforward preacher put a reporter – or a TV engineer from the Shankill, for that matter – under observation? There's more to him than meets the eye.'

The very thought of Patricia Monaghan made him burn with the recollection of their first traumatic night together and all the nights they'd had together since then. Pete had known a lot of women and took pride in his knowledge of them, but nothing in his experience had prepared him for Patricia Monaghan. Even now, when he recollected what they had done together that first night – or rather, what she had compelled him to do – he could scarcely believe it, though he knew that he hadn't just dreamed the whole affair. Since then, he had seen her a lot, on the one hand obsessed with her, burning with the need for her, addicted to her as he had never been with any woman before; on the other, still shamelessly trying to pump her about Reverend Dawson. He was still trying to do his job, to keep his thoughts in focus, but his relationship with Patricia Monaghan was giving him sleepless nights.

'This is Belfast,' Bannerman said as he gazed across the dark street at Dawson's red-brick office building, shadowed under the trees lining the street, illuminated by lamplight. 'It's a very strange city. A man like Dawson has good reason to be concerned about a Catholic reporter who may not be quite what *she* seems. This is dirty-tricks time and reporters have been known to be used as a front for other business. If Dawson's as paranoid as a lot of prominent Prods are, he might think that Monaghan's interest in him has a relevance beyond a simple radio programme. He could think, for instance, that she's being used by Sinn Fein or the IRA to set him up for a fall; and if that's what he thinks, then he might indeed have her followed. If you were then seen with her on a regular basis, as you have been, he'd have good cause to wonder about you as well. You might be keeping dangerous company, Pete. Have you had this woman checked out?'

'Well, no,' Pete said, shocked by the question, yet realizing that he could have made a mistake, even with Patricia Monaghan who had, in a very different way, turned out to be not as she had seemed. 'I mean, she's so well known for what she does that it never entered my head she'd need checking. Also, she came with a strong recommendation from a friend who's completely trustworthy.'

'Can I ask who this friend is?'

'Frank Cooney. Another reporter, but Protestant. He's done a lot of work for you guys in the past.'

'Yes, I know Frank. A good man. His recommendations are usually sound. On the other hand, even Frank could be wrong in this particular city. Just what *do* you know about Patricia Monaghan?'

Feeling even more shocked and uneasy, Pete confessed, 'Not much, come to think of it. Born and bred in Dublin, she works for a radio station down south and, though generally sympathetic to the Republicans, she has an admirable reputation for objectivity.'

'Married?'

'Was. Her husband, a Belfast Catholic, was a history teacher in a local school. I say "was" because he was assassinated by a Loyalist hit team about five or six months ago.'

'He was involved?'

'Apparently not. She swears not. It was generally believed to have been a random killing. Or, if not that, they just picked him because he taught Irish history and that was enough to make him a worthy target for the more fanatical Loyalists. Not quite random, but random enough to make everyone in the Catholic community feel pretty scared.'

'I think you should let me check this out.'

'Okay, you do that.'

But he felt terrible saying it. Still shaken by what Patricia had presented him with – using her own nightmares to make him face up to himself – he was also stunned by how deeply involved he had become, wanting her too much for comfort, no longer able to run away as he had run from the rest, his three wives and the many other women, even his children, and wondering constantly how it had come to be and if he could deal with it. He had never really believed in love – he still tried not to accept it – but love, or something similar, was what he now felt for Patricia Monaghan. Yet even though he felt it, he realized that he couldn't trust her because this was not the place for such emotions. This was Belfast, a city at war, and everyone in it was a victim, which meant that everyone was also potentially dangerous. Even the innocent could harm you in this city and he should have borne that in mind.

'So what was it you wanted to tell me,' Bannerman said, 'that brought me to this place? You said it had to be done – it would be worth it – but you're going to have to convince me. If we get caught in there, all hell will break loose, so you'd better make it good. What was it, Pete?'

Pete could scarcely believe it himself, but it was happening all right. He was in so deep, he might never get out and so he had to resolve it. He wanted out of this job, out of Belfast, so things had to move quickly now.

'You're not going to believe it,' he said, giving voice to his thoughts.

'In Belfast, I'd believe anything,' Bannerman retorted. 'So just spit it out.'

'I think I'm working for Red Hand,' Pete said.

'*What?*'

Pete explained how he had gone to the home of Joe Douglas and been invited to do some work for the Loyalist paramilitaries. As Joe Douglas was known to be one of Red Hand's top men, it seemed logical that the work would be for Red Hand. Any doubts that Pete might have had about this were laid to rest when he had a couple of Friday-evening meetings with the other top two honchos of the organization, Alf Green and Jack Peel. All they needed him for, they had explained, was to set up perfectly legal surveillance systems in various of their establishments and service the computer systems of other establishments which, though not necessarily their own, were run by sympathetic Loyalists and used for the collecting of potentially useful information.

'So, naturally, I said yes. It was a dream situation. I was doing work that on the surface was perfectly legal but which let me swim under the surface to find out what was going on. Most of it was routine: everyday surveillance systems for companies known to be legitimate, though sympathetic to the Loyalists; and routine maintenance of computer systems for similar companies. However, one of these places was a computer-training establishment for troubled Protestant teenagers, based out in Antrim and, as I soon learnt, set up as a government-sponsored concern by the New Presbyterian Church and the East Belfast Unionist Party.'

'Which gets us back to Reverend Dawson,' Bannerman noted.

'Exactly,' Pete said. 'Anyway, the first time I went out there, to that industrial estate in Antrim, I saw that it was being run like a regular training college, with all these kids – mostly in their late teens or early twenties, some with damaged legs and arms, obviously caused by old kneecappings – as busy as bees on IBM clones with hundred-meg hard disks – the Internet, e-mail, CD-ROMs and so on – so they were certainly financed to the hilt. Those kids were working on bulletin board systems that enabled them to receive information and pass on messages by dialling up over the telephone lines through the use of modems. Working there, doing simple maintenance shit, it didn't take me long to understand why Red Hand wasn't worried about what I saw because most of the info on the screens seemed, on the surface, to be fairly harmless stuff: statistics on this, that and the other, mostly picked up on the Internet. Then, during my third or fourth visit, I found what I was looking for . . .'

'Here it comes,' Bannerman said, almost wearily.

'What I found,' Pete said, 'were computer printouts of the personal details of hundreds of Belfast citizens, Protestant *and* Catholic. Those details had been collated from the data banks of a great variety of perfectly legitimate sources: credit-card companies, insurance companies, private health organizations, banks, universities, and even schools. The details on each individual included names and addresses, telephone and fax numbers, e-mail codes, family histories, places of work, names of friends, male and female, and, of course, financial status with particular emphasis on debts – always useful for blackmail.'

'As are friends, male and female,' Bannerman said, no longer sounding weary.

'Right. But more importantly, when I carefully perused those printouts, I recognized a lot of the subjects – clearly potential victims of blackmail or assassination – as being the same as those on the computer diskettes passed on from the RUC to British Intelligence. There were a hell of a lot more names than I'd previously seen, but that only means that the list of names has been growing steadily since those first diskettes were found by the RUC.'

'Good God,' Bannerman whispered. 'Did you steal the printout?'

'No. I didn't want them to find anything missing. But I was working on my own, during the kids' lunch break, so I used the code words on the printouts to call up the relevant files on the computer I was checking and I copied the files onto blank diskettes. These things are hot, Walter.' He passed his two diskettes to Bannerman, who received them with a look of disbelief. 'I daren't mail them to Edmondson,' Pete explained. 'My mail might be intercepted or the diskettes might get wiped accidentally. Can you transfer them electronically from HQ Lisburn to MI5?'

Bannerman nodded and slipped the diskettes into his jacket pocket. 'Damned right I can.' Now clearly more excited, he gazed across the road to Reverend Dawson's red-brick offices. 'So what's this business with Dawson?'

'Dawson was instrumental in setting up that computer training school, right?'

'Right.'

'And Dawson's own office is computerized, right?'

'Right.'

'Well, given that those diskettes – all that hacker's information – includes details of just about every major Protestant and Catholic in Belfast, one prominent name is notable for its absence.'

'Dawson's name.'

'Correct. The good Reverend Dawson, head of the New Presbyterian Church and the East Belfast Unionist Party, both with past and possibly present connections to the Ulster Defenders, therefore to Red Hand, is one prominent Protestant who *should* be on that list. My feeling, therefore, is that Dawson is the man behind it all and that his own computer system could contain the same details and possibly even more information. So do we go in or not?'

'We could hack into the system from our mainframe computer in HQ Lisburn,' Bannerman said. 'There could be an entry code in these diskettes – an anagram of Dawson's name, his date of birth, the length of his Christian dick, or something else relating to him. Our computer could bring up every possible permutation and eventually find the correct entry code. Once we have it, we could hack into Dawson's system and see what he has on it. We don't have to go in there.'

'To hell with that,' Pete said. 'Those so-called troubled kids, those fucking hackers out in Antrim, have information on members of the RUC and even you lot. You try to hack into Dawson's system and they'll probably sit there and watch you do it. No, Walt, I say we use the old-fashioned way and go in there and just turn on Dawson's computer and see what it reveals. So I ask again: Do we go in or not?'

'Let's do it,' Bannerman said.

It was another thirty minutes or so before Robert Lilly emerged from Dawson's offices. They watched him walk along the whole length of the tree-lined street, his thin body spectral in the lamplight. Only when he had turned the corner at the far end did they get out of the car.

Bannerman, an old pro from 14th Intelligence Company, was carrying a small tool bag in his right hand. After looking in both directions to check that the street was clear, they crossed the road and hurried along the opposite pavement to Reverend Dawson's neatly built red-brick building. Pete kept watch on the shadowy lamplit pavement while Bannerman went to the front door, opened his tool kit and did whatever the fuck he had to do to get into the building. Having done it a lot of times before, he completed the job in no time. When Pete heard Bannerman's snapping fingers, he turned around and hurried up the path to follow his friend through the opened front door. Bannerman closed the door carefully behind him, then they stood still for a moment, letting their eyes adjust to the darkness. Eventually they saw that they were in an outer office with chairs lined along one wall and a desk located near another door.

'This is Robert Lilly's office,' Pete said, 'and that's his computer on the desk. According to Patricia Monaghan, Lilly is the one with the computer. Can we turn it on without fucking up?'

'Let's find out,' Bannerman said, boldly walking to the desk and turning on the reading lamp a few feet from the computer. When the lamp came on, he turned the beam downwards, keeping the light away from the windows. He sat in Lilly's chair, studied the cables on the computer, then eventually nodded and smiled.

'It's okay,' he said. 'The Reverend truly believes in God. There's no burglar lock and no trick switches. We just turn it on.'

And he turned the computer on.

Pete was fascinated. They were both fascinated. At first they couldn't enter the system, which asked them for a password, but Bannerman used his own software to run through all the possibilities – everything that might conceivably be related to Reverend Dawson: his names, his date of birth, the names of his wife and children, his home and office door numbers, his church and political party – and eventually came up with EBUP: the East Belfast Unionist Party. Once the letters were keyed in, the list of files came up and scrolling down them they came up with what they were really looking for: RHUD.

'Red Hand, Ulster Defenders!' Pete said excitedly. 'It can't be anything else.'

'I never bet on a loser,' Bannerman said as he accessed the file.

There it was . . . Every name on the original diskettes was there in the file, but many more names – the names seen on the printouts in the home for troubled youths – had since been added, their personal details meticulously itemized. The names included Loyalist and Republican politicians, prominent businessmen from both sides of the divide, Protestant ministers and Catholic priests, judges, civil rights workers, RUC officers and Belfast-based members of the British Army and British Intelligence. Also listed was a file named APOCALYPSE.

'Go for it,' Pete said.

Bannerman accessed the file and found a lengthy document entitled OPERATION APOCALYPSE: A SUMMARY OF INTENT. He scrolled down through the text with widening eyes and Pete, leaning over his shoulder, felt as stunned as his friend looked.

'Jesus Christ!' Bannerman whispered when they had come to the end of the text.

'He won't help us,' Pete said.

CHAPTER TWENTY-THREE

It's big, Billy Boy thought. *It's really fucking big. It's so fucking big it's unbelievable and I'm gonna be part of it. Not just part of it, but right there at the top if I have my way – and I* will *have my way. It all starts here and now.*

He was just leaving Divis Street, crossing the road to Castle Street, carrying his Sainsbury's shopping bag in his right hand and feeling excited. He had been with Apocalypse for two months now, training rigorously in that big house in the mountains of Mourne and daily trying to adjust to the fact that his personal Public Enemy Number 1, that Provo bastard Sean Farrell, was a partner to the whole operation – at least, a partner in the sense that he seemed to be sharing responsibility for it with the Red Hand leader, Alf Green.

Even now, Billy Boy found it hard to believe that the Loyalists and the Provos were working together, but this certainly was the case in that big house in the mountains and so far they had managed to do it without killing each other. They might have managed it, he realized, by keeping the Loyalist and Provo hardmen apart during training, by keeping them in separate billets, by letting them eat at separate tables; and he assumed that when the time came, when the 'big one' was launched, they would be given completely separate targets in different areas. They were working together, but they were still separated and, Billy Boy thought, only God knew what was going to happen when the 'big one' was over. Not ongoing cooperation – that was for fucking sure. But for now, the Loyalists and Provos were working together and it still seemed incredible.

In fact, Billy Boy bristled with indignation at the very thought of it, but Alf Green had drilled into him, as he had done with all the others, that it was vitally necessary and that he had to accept it or get out. Knowing that 'getting out', once in, entailed a head job and anonymous burial somewhere in the mountains – because no one who had trained there was allowed to go back to Belfast to talk about it – Billy Boy had played along; but he had also done so, he had to admit, because the operation, the audacity of it, the sheer size of it, had excited him beyond belief and, more importantly, showed him the way to even greater things for himself.

Which was why he was now walking this pavement with his Sainsbury's shopping bag. He was taking his first tentative steps on the route to the top. A man had to be ruthless, like.

During his two months of rigorous, dangerous training, Billy Boy had not only kept his trap shut about working with the Provos but had, in fact, worked overtime to prove himself, in particular to Alf Green, the unsmiling head of Red Hand. He had done it not only because he wanted to avoid a head job – the fate of those who failed the course – but also because he was determined to get to the very top of the organization, right there beside Alf Green.

Already, he was halfway home. Once their ruthless training in the big house had been completed, the trainees had been sent out into Fermanagh and Armagh – the old 'bandit country' of the Troubles – to be tested with some dangerous operations: armed robbery of banks and post offices, doorstep assassinations of prominent locals, both Protestant and Catholic, and ASU attacks, using mortars and machine-guns, on RUC and British Army troop trucks. In all of these activities Billy Boy had excelled, showing uncommon skill and daring, and at the end of his first month out in the field, he had been placed in overall charge of the various active service units and, more importantly, had been invited to the strategy meetings for the 'big one'.

Unfortunately, they had placed him at the extreme far end of the long committee table at which that Provo bastard Sean Farrell (beautifully scarred, Billy Boy had noted with satisfaction, after a botched bombing by Billy Boy's splinter group), Farrell's second-in-command, Neely McCarthy, Alf Green, Joe Douglas and that resentful little shite Jack Peel also sat. Yes, Billy Boy had been included in those meetings . . . but compelled to sit right beside Jack Peel, and he deeply resented it.

Billy Boy now knew exactly what the 'big one' was and that it depended on unprecedented cooperation between the Loyalists and the Provos. However, it was his personal belief that once the 'big one' was over, even if it succeeded, those cooperating right now would again turn against each other, even as they were carving most of Belfast up between them. When that happened, Billy Boy wanted to be on top of the shit-heap, the fattest fly of them all, and to do that he had to get in a strong position before the 'big one' commenced. His plan, therefore, was to get rid of Douglas and Peel, thus automatically becoming Alf Green's second-in-command. Loathing Peel, he had picked him to be the first victim. Thus, his walk into town.

Making his way towards Chichester Street, he was fully aware of the fact that he was taking a chance on being stopped by a British Army foot patrol, but he assumed that the shopping bag, with its supermarket logo, would make him look like an ordinary shopper and ensure that he passed unmolested. This was particularly necessary in this case as the shopping bag contained a crude but highly effective home-made bomb: Semtex plastic explosive, an electric initiator, a blasting cap with bridge wire and a preset timer, all fixed to a rectangular block of wood and wrapped in plain brown paper. Billy Boy was taking a second chance, even bigger than the first, in that he had already set the timer on the bomb and it was ticking away like a metronome even as he was carrying it to its ultimate destination. If he'd made a mistake with the setting – BOOM! – he'd be as good as a goner.

He had set the bomb to go off at exactly 1:30 p.m., which was halfway through Jack Peel's lunch hour and forty-five minutes from now. That would give Billy Boy approximately five more minutes to reach the café, five minutes to get into the bog and hide the bomb behind the cistern – approximately ten minutes before Peel's customary 1:05 p.m. arrival – and another five minutes to get to the pub across the road, order his pint and take a pew by the front windows where, if all went well, he would have a spectacular view of the explosion thirty minutes later.

About a quarter of the way along Chichester Street, Billy Boy saw the café he wanted – located at the other side of the road, directly facing the pub. Jack Peel, he knew, worked in a bookie shop nearby and, being teetotal and an unimaginative fucker, lunched in that café at the exact same time every day – when he wasn't out in that big house in the mountains of

Mourne, of course. Which he wasn't, unfortunately for him, this particular day.

Checking his wristwatch, Billy Boy saw that it was just turning 12:45 p.m. With not a nerve in his body, he scurried across the road, weaving expertly between the fast-flowing traffic until he reached the far side. Still wasting no time, still feeling no fear at all, he entered the café and was gratified to see that it was, as usual, packed with a lunchtime crowd of men and women, the latter being of the youngish, smartly dressed variety, mostly secretaries for the pinstripes. Some were ordering takeaways from the counter, but the rest were at the packed tables, and most of them were having a good bit of crack, talking nineteen to the dozen.

Knowing that, in a crowd of this density, he was not likely to be noticed, Billy Boy pushed his way past the ones crowding the counter for their takeaways, then made his way between the equally crowded tables to the gents' toilet at the far end of the room. It was a typical café bog with only one toilet bowl in a narrow, shallow room, so he carefully locked the door behind him and placed his shopping bag on the floor. After lowering the lid of the toilet bowl, he removed his small, compact, block-shaped bomb from the shopping bag, stood on the lid of the toilet bowl and carefully placed the bomb, still wrapped in its brown paper, well behind the cistern. It was ticking away there and that made him feel good. After ensuring that it was steady, he secured it to the wall and cistern with black masking tape, then stepped backwards off the toilet bowl, deliberately flushed the toilet in case someone was waiting to get in, then opened the door and walked back between the tables. With no one giving him a second glance, he left the café, checked his wristwatch, saw that it was 12:55 p.m. – ten minutes before the ever-punctual Peel was due to arrive – and strolled leisurely across the road to enter the pub located directly opposite.

He ordered a pint of Guinness and a plate of Irish stew, then carried both to a pew by the front window. Checking his wristwatch again, he saw that 1:00 p.m. had come and gone, which meant that Peel would be arriving any minute now. Pleased with his own efficiency, he tucked into his stew and had swallowed a few spoonfuls when Peel came walking along the pavement, lean and hard in his jeans and windcheater jacket, not soft and flabby like he used to be at school. He strode unhesitatingly into the café, disappearing inside.

'Fucking beautiful,' Billy Boy whispered before shoving another spoonful of stew into his gob and slugging down another mouthful of Guinness.

He enjoyed his lunch, though a few thoughts distracted him. After attempting to imagine what Peel would be doing in the café right now – rubbing himself slyly against a few of the pretty secretaries as he made his way to the table, offering a lecherous grin and a few witless jokes to the big-boobed, warm-hearted waitress whom he had long wanted to fuck, and trading a bit of crack with his mates at the other tables – Billy Boy found his thoughts wandering to his grubby little two-up, two-down terraced house just off the Shankill Road, where he still lived with his Mum and Dad and two sisters. Though Billy Boy, like most Irish lads, loved and revered his mother, completely ignoring the fact that she drank and smoke too much and had seriously neglected him, he couldn't stand his sisters, both overfed and overweight – a right pair of slags, really – and he fought night and day with his Dad.

Billy Boy's Dad was a practising Christian, a stout Loyalist and a devoted Orange Lodge member who revered the Royal Family, could tell a Taig from a mile off, and used to beat his missus with his fists every time he got drunk, which was, before wee Billy Boy became big and brutish, just about every Saturday night. Billy Boy's Dad had stopped beating up on his missus when his only son grew big enough to beat him. Now, though he no longer beat up on his missus, he fought constantly with his only son and was forever trying to put him down.

Billy Boy had spent most of his formative years listening to his Dad yammering on about the glories of the Royal Family, the benefits of British rule in Northern Ireland, the proud heritage of the Orange Lodge, the moral superiority of the Protestant religion, and the vileness and treachery of his Fenian neighbours – but none of that had prevented him from drinking too much and having a tongue so foul in an argument you could breed maggots on it. In fact, he had used that foul tongue this very morning when they'd had yet another argument over what Billy Boy was getting up to with what his Dad still fondly imagined was a splinter gang of hooligans out for all they could grab. Billy Boy had, in fact,

been quite amused to be standing there with his shopping bag in
his hand, a home-made bomb in that bag, while his Dad railed
against his hooligan friends who were, his Dad insisted, bringing
decent Loyalist 'freedom fighters' into disrepute. Billy Boy had
wanted to laugh in his Dad's face, but instead he had simply said
'Fuck off!' and walked out of the house, slamming the front door
behind him. Now, however, filling his face with Irish stew and
washing it down with Guinness while keeping his hard gaze fixed
on the café across the road, he did not feel amused and thought,
as he had done so often, that his Dad, like so many Loyalists – like
that bastard Jack Peel over there, about to get his comeuppance
– was a mentally deficient, typical Belfast hypocrite. At least he,
Billy Boy, though he hated the Fenians as well, was openly in it
for what he could get. He was no fucking hypocrite.

Feeling slightly better after his session of self-analysis, he finished
off his stew, checked his wristwatch, and saw that it was almost
1:30 p.m. Fondly imagining what Jack Peel was doing right now
in the café – having a smoke after his meal, eyeing the big tits of
the waitress, scratching his balls under the table – Billy Boy lit a
fag, exhaled smoke and again checked his wristwatch.

The bomb went off before he saw precisely what time it was
but he knew he was right on the button.

It was like a movie in slow-motion on a video player. He saw
the explosion before he heard it or felt it, though the sound and
the impact came soon enough. What Billy Boy saw was a sudden,
dazzling flash of light inside the café, a jagged, expanding sheet
of searing, silvery flame, then the windows of the café exploded
outwards into the street and the roaring of the explosion erupted
even as the window of the pub was rattled by the blast – the pub's
lights vibrated and tinkled like Christmas bells – and black smoke
billowed out of the café to swirl around an expanding ball of fire
in a fountain of flying glass.

Dreadful screaming could he heard. At first, Billy Boy thought
it was coming from inside the café; then he saw that it was the
screaming of passers-by, male and female, young and old, being
slashed by the flying glass or thrown off their feet by the blast.
Shouts of panic and some shrieking came from right behind Billy
Boy, from the customers in the bar, and some of those on either
side of him, at the window, dropped in panic to the floor.

Billy Boy stayed where he was, still looking across the road, and saw cars and buses swerving away from the blast, some of them crashing noisily into others.

There was different screaming now – it was coming from inside the café – and then customers staggered out of the smoke and flames, some of them on fire. They shrieked dreadfully as they collapsed. Some ran in frantic circles. Blood was gushing like water from a pump, from lacerations, cut throats and the stumps of severed limbs. Some of the victims were almost naked, their remaining clothing in smouldering tatters; others emerged with their hair on fire, their skin black and blistered. The screaming was something to hear – it was not remotely human – and passers-by, the courageous, the foolhardy, were rushing in to the rescue.

Jack Peel stumbled out, swaying, emerging from a cloud of black smoke, still alive though only just about, one arm severed at the shoulder, the other arm a bloody mess, more blood gushing from a jagged wound in his throat which glinted strangely in the bright sunlight. He had been struck by flying glass and a shard was buried in his throat. He was staggering forward, his remaining arm hanging limp, his blackened head turning this way and that, like the head of a puppet being pulled by invisible wires. Falling onto his knees, he went into a violent spasm, his whole body quivering like a bowstring, though he still didn't collapse. A siren wailed in the distance and was followed by another. The ruined café was on fire and more black smoke billowed out to cover the whole road. Jack Peel quivered and finally collapsed, falling onto his face, and a teenage girl, covered in blood, screaming dementedly, tripped on his still-smouldering body and also fell to the pavement. The dead and dying were everywhere.

Billy Boy slipped off his stool. He could hear the sirens approaching. Other customers were hurrying out of the side door of the pub, escaping down the side street, not wanting to see any more, and Billy Boy was able to follow them without fear of being seen or stopped.

He walked all the way home, feeling great, really proud of himself. Now he only had Joe Douglas to deal with and that bastard would be a cinch.

A man did what a man had to do: this was Billy Boy's way.

CHAPTER TWENTY-FOUR

Pete had already booked his flight back to London when he
spoke to Sergeant Major Walter Bannerman at British Army
HQ Lisburn, calling from a public phone box in the city centre
because he felt that his phone at home might be tapped. Already
shocked by the sheer magnitude of what the paramilitaries were
planning, he was even more deeply shocked when he heard what
Bannerman had to say about Patricia Monaghan.

'I don't know what it means in relation to you,' Bannerman
said. 'It may not mean anything. But naturally I have to warn
you to be more careful than ever between now and when you get
to the airport. Frankly, I'm glad you're leaving today.'

'So am I,' Pete said.

Putting the phone back on the hook, he left the graffiti-covered
booth, which had been freezing cold because of its broken window
panes, and walked along to the Crown Liquor Saloon for a
soothing drink. Night had fallen, but here, near the Europa, the
most frequently bombed hotel in the world, the lights of the street
lamps, shop windows and dense traffic formed a dazzling mosaic
that made the city seem less dangerous than it was. Entering the
pub, he was comforted by its Victorian charms: mahogany doors,
stained-glass windows, tiled floors, stacked barrels and baroque
ornamentation. The private booths were already packed and most
of the stools along the serving counter were taken.

Listening to the voluble crack and frequent laughter, seeing
the flushed, good-natured faces of the other customers, male
and female, it was hard to imagine any of them engaged in
the barbaric violence so endemic to this city. Nevertheless,
the violence continued, Pete thought, as he ordered a pint of
Guinness and recalled the bombing of a city-centre café the day
before yesterday. Another charnel house, of course, with lots of

innocents either mutilated or killed, but most notable for the fact that one of its victims, now dead, was Jack Peel, one of the three leaders of Red Hand. It was believed by the authorities that the bomb had been planted with the sole purpose of killing Peel – the other casualties were incidental – and Pete was intrigued by this unexpected turn of events, knowing what he now did about the astounding Operation Apocalypse. Possibly someone was trying to cause suspicion and dissension within the ranks of those planning Apocalypse, but if so . . . who? And why? Either way, the assassination would certainly harm the operation and for that Pete was grateful.

Nevertheless, he was still feeling nervous at the thought of his farewell drink with Patricia Monaghan, which was why he was having a drink right now. Though he did not normally require alcoholic fortification in his dealings with women, with whom he'd always had sexually successful albeit emotionally traumatic relationships, he certainly needed it before this particular meeting.

What Bannerman had told him about Patricia had shocked him deeply, more so given what he had already learnt about her . . . and, through her, about himself. Their first night together had been nearly two months ago, but it seemed longer than that, perhaps because he had never before experienced such an intense relationship nor felt such fear at where it might lead him. She had opened the door to his hidden self and he wanted to run from it.

Finishing his Guinness, aware of what had to be done, he left the bar and headed down Great Victoria Street, having decided to walk to where he was meeting her. Looking to his right, beyond Hope Street leading into the rough Loyalist stronghold of Sandy Row, he saw lights glittering in what appeared to be the night sky and realized that they were in fact burning inside the new houses now desecrating the once virgin slopes of the Black Mountain. As a kid, growing up in Donegall Avenue, another Loyalist stronghold, he had often explored that mountain, bravely marching up the Whiterock Road between the Fenian enclaves of Ballymurphy and Turf Lodge. A lot of the Prod kids had done it – they had dared each other to do it – and few of them had come to any grief. Now, however, only the most foolhardy or dumb Prod kids would dare to do the same, since sectarian hatreds had become a way of life and the Catholic kids up there would be on the lookout for any strange faces. A Protestant boy on the Whiterock Road would stick out as surely as a Catholic in the so-called Village, the hardline Loyalist area located between Donegall Avenue and the Broadway, where Pete had once happily played. The times had certainly changed.

After crossing Shaftesbury Square, windblown, bright with lights, damp pavements glistening around criss-crossing streams of noisy traffic and silvery fountains of glistening spray, he glanced right at the Donegall Road and recalled his childhood in that area. His father had been a welder in the Harland & Wolff's shipyard, an amiable drunk, apolitical; his mother had been bright-eyed and opinionated – you name it, she talked about it – though disappointed, as she had actually told her only son, that she hadn't had other children. She had fought a lot with his father. They had fought night and day. Yet Pete had still had a pretty decent childhood, mainly lived in the streets in a time when it was natural for kids to play there without too much to fear. He hadn't worried about the Fenians. His mother had told him not to do so. They had Catholic neighbours in Donegall Avenue and they were very close friends . . . at least until the Troubles came.

When the Troubles exploded in 1969, Pete was only eight years old and too young to understand why his Catholic neighbours were being moved out of their homes and being jeered at by their former Protestant friends as they did so. What he *did* understand, since all the kids in the street were talking excitedly about it, was that a war had broken out in the streets of the city and that a lot of Catholic houses had been set on fire. Pete could see the smoke rising to the sky in what then had seemed a faraway area, but which was in fact the nearby Falls Road.

When it became clear that the war was between the Protestants and Catholics – the street gossip was voluble – Pete asked his mother about it and was told that it was being caused by a bunch of Protestant hooligans and that he must not say bad things about the Catholics. His mother had always defended the Catholics and was in tears when their own Catholic neighbours, the McMullins, were turfed out of their house and forced to leave to a chorus of abuse.

During the next two years, life changed considerably for Pete and the other kids, most notably in the fact that they were no longer allowed to play in the streets, which, practically overnight, had become 'not safe'. Life also changed in that he was suddenly made aware of a new attitude towards the Catholics . . . they were Fenians, Taigs and fucking Provos and they weren't to be trusted. So life changed – and it did not change for the better.

Fortunately, two years later, when Pete was ten years old, his father decided to get out of Belfast altogether and subsequently moved the family to Birkenhead, Merseyside. Pete had worked there as an assistant to a television repairman, covering the Liverpool area, until he turned twenty. During that time, the Troubles in Belfast were as remote to him as they were to most of those on the mainland. Pete was young and healthy, with money in his pocket, and he had no interest in anything other than having a good time. Raised as a British citizen, not as an 'Irishman', he felt that he *was* British, by which he meant English, and so he deliberately dropped his Belfast accent and felt more genuinely 'English' with each passing year. By the time he had enlisted in the army, eventually transferring to the SAS, he was thinking of himself as an Englishman and viewing the Troubles in Northern Ireland as the aberration of a bunch of warring hooligans in a foreign country.

Even now, much older and wiser, he still believed that most of the paramilitaries were no more than hooligans, hypocritically using British rule in the province as an excuse for their criminal activities. However, since returning here, his false 'Englishness' had slipped away from him and now he felt uncomfortably Irish. Like it or not, when he walked the streets of Belfast, he felt, at last, that he was home.

Walking up Bradbury Place, heading for the lively university area, he recalled that he had come here as an apolitical mercenary, with no interest at all in the rights or wrongs of the conflict, merely seeking to find some excitement while putting a healthy distance between himself and the divorce proceedings initiated by Monica and being dealt with, in his absence, by his solicitor. Nevertheless, as he walked to his meeting with Patricia Monaghan, he was forced to accept that his relationship with her, intense beyond measure and potentially dangerous, had made him look at his past promiscuities in a different, less benign light. Patricia had, in fact, compelled him to acknowledge that his constant lust for adventure had left a trail of damage in its wake – damage to a great many women as well as to his children. That same avoidance of responsibility, he also understood at last, had made him bury his head in the sand with regard to Ulster. Patricia Monaghan had told him all about Northern Ireland – and in no uncertain terms. What she had told him had burned its way into his brain and even now haunted him. For the first time in his life, possibly the last, he felt impelled by moral outrage and wanted to take cleansing action. He owed her for that, at least.

Finally reaching the pub where he was due to meet her, located in the lively upper end of University Road, just past Queen's University, he hesitated before going in. He was still thinking about what Walter Bannerman had told him, still feeling shocked by it, and he wondered how he would deal with it when he faced her across that table inside the bar. Standing there on the wet pavement, whipped by a cold wind, his face soaked by drizzle, he felt a tremor pass through him, a ripple of dread at what they had already done together and at where it might lead to in the near future, given what he had just learnt about her. She had lied to him and he had to find out why before he went back to London.

There was that and something else ... Her revelation of nightmare ... As he stood outside the pub, trying to will himself to enter, he recalled that first night in her apartment and was again shaken by it. It was a night to shock and shame him in equal measure, still burning bright in his mind ... A night to remember.

CHAPTER TWENTY-FIVE

A night to remember . . . When Patricia walked towards him, minus her shoulder bag and overcoat, wearing her tight blue denims and that open-necked shirt tucked tightly into the waistband to reveal her slim, shapely figure, and kicked off her shoes, saying, 'You'll see more if you take my clothes off and stretch me out on the floor . . .' Yes, well . . . What could any healthy male do except follow the suggestion to its obvious, inescapable conclusion?

Except that nothing with Patricia Monaghan was remotely obvious.

'Fuck,' she said – not the first and certainly not the last obscenity of the evening – 'you're hard already. What a thrill to have a lively Calvinist Protestant. So how does the wee Prod laddie want it? Like this?' Rubbing her denim-covered belly against him. 'Or like this?' Rubbing her breasts against him, reaching down to stroke his swollen member – a gesture so lacking in Protestant restraint that it sent his mind reeling. 'Or this?' she added, parting his lips with her tongue and running it over the bridge of his mouth until his thoughts were tumbling like dice in the hands of a crazed, sweating gambler. 'Can you live without it?' she said finally, as she was unbuckling his belt and, using her own hand, guiding his trembling fingers inside her open-necked shirt to the smooth and yielding warmth of her breast. 'Can you say no and walk out?'

'No,' he gasped.

'Fucking right,' she said. 'Let's fuck.'

Pete had thought that he knew his women – it was his vanity, his vice – but nothing had prepared him for the extraordinary boldness, the brazen carnality of this particular woman, and it devastated him even before they began.

'Oh, how smooth,' she said wickedly as, still standing, he unbuttoned her shirt and peeled it off her exquisitely formed bare shoulders. 'How very fucking smooth and experienced for a poor wee working-class Prod . . . Who taught you such wickedness? Those evil women in Australia? Those unsophisticated migrants from the slums of the great British Empire? First my shirt, now my jeans. God, you're slick. You're real fast. So unrestrained for a Prod. Slipped them off like they'd never been there in the first place and now look at the state of me . . . That's it . . . Put me here where I belong. Right here, on the floor, in my underwear . . . put on just for you to take off. Sparse and scarlet and frilly like a whore's. Isn't this what you want?'

They sank together to the floor, she already practically naked, he desperately trying to wriggle out of his clothes. 'It excites you, doesn't it? Doesn't it always, for all of you? Christ, I'm dying to have it, I'm seriously *dying*, so stop wriggling like a fish and put it into me. Take it out of your pants – I'm too distracted to do *everything* – so take it out and put it in like a real man. Do I shock you? Oh, *great!*'

He *was* shocked – and resentful, normally being in command, but now feeling that he was being orchestrated and, worse, quietly mocked. He wanted to slap her face, wipe away that mocking smile, but instead he was drawn into the glittering green sea of her eyes, that drowning pool, that deep lake, and saw in it a frightening intensity that he had not seen before. She sucked him in and washed over him.

'Like your women, do you?' she whispered. 'Like to fuck them? Then fuck me. Let me see what you can do. Here, let me help you. No confession for sinning Protestants, is there? So let me do the dirty deed. Let me rub it against me . . . Oh, yes, it feels nice, it really does. I can't tell if it's Protestant or Catholic and that has to be good . . . Yes, yes, sure that's grand. That's a real bit of Irish . . . Oh, shit, yes, let's start moving. Isn't this the real works? Isn't it? Yes, it is. It's the works and you're doing it. Don't you feel real good doing it? Fuck me good, fuck you, do it, Jesus Christ. Sure what else are you good for?'

He could have killed her, but he didn't. He was lost in her flesh and bone. He was flesh and bone himself, though melting, vaporizing, and he knew instantly, despite all his experience, that he had finally met his match. They were lying together on the floor, like teenagers, without dignity, and he was wresting her scarlet brassière and panties off her as if he had never done it before and couldn't wait to experience it. He managed it somehow and then she did the same to him, though she did it with an ease that surprised and shocked him, making him feel as inexperienced as that callow youth he had been many years ago. She stripped him naked in more ways than one and left him feeling defenceless. She took his measure and flayed him.

'Oh, I know all about you,' she crooned sensually, mockingly, as he toiled rigorously, helplessly, upon her. 'The talk's up and down the whole fucking Shankill. You and all your women, your big dick, your big ego, your absolutely invincible ability to charm the knickers off any woman, young or old, smart or stupid . . . Oh, yes, don't I know it? But tell me, mister, as you do it . . . Oh, yes, yes, that's it, keep it in there, don't stop, keep moving . . . Tell me exactly what it is you want of me. Yes, me, your warm, wet piece of cunt – warm and wet just for you . . . Tell me what it is that you – my take-it-or-leave-it, Calvinist-repressed, Protestant one-night stand – tell me what it is you really want. Is it me or the fucking of every Catholic woman you can get your Prod hands on?'

'Just shut up,' he gasped.

'Shut up? No, I can't. It's the crack that makes or breaks it. I have to talk to make it real for me and let me have some control . . . Oh, Christ, yes, that's it, the in-and-out of it, the real hard, masculine thrust, the let's-shove-it-into-the-bitch, the real macho McCoy, the fuck-a-Catholic-for-Ulster Prod cock in Catholic cunt, the sweat and the smell of it. Stick it to me. Fuck me black and blue – do it! – and make me lose myself in it.'

They wrestled across the floor of her immaculate apartment, on the soft pile of the carpet, belly slapping on belly, arms and legs entangled, and the more she mocked him, the more he strove to lay her waste and make her surrender. He was enraged by her mockery, excited by her obscenity, and when she whispered into his ear, biting his earlobe, licking his neck, he was aroused to a pitch beyond all reasoning and lost himself in her. A seducer, he was now being seduced and it made him feel helpless.

'Oh, fuck,' she whispered into his ear as she licked his earlobe. 'Oh, fuck, but that's so good. It's so hard and so hot, flesh and bone, heat and friction. Sure I'm melting like a snowflake in sunlight and that's just what I want . . . Yes, that's it, go down there . . . Here, let me hold your head . . . Oh, Christ, yes, put it in and lick me clean and . . . Shit, yes, that's the business! Aren't you the smart one? Mister Thompson of the Donegall Avenue and Australia, known up and down the length of the Shankill Road for his talent with women. Now I know why. Yes, I do! Don't I ever? That's enough now . . . My turn.'

He knew a compliment when he heard one and this wasn't a compliment, but he obliged by rolling onto his back and letting her have dominion. Raised above him, she was exquisite, a heavenly vision, belly taut, breasts upthrust, before her blonde hair tumbled down to brush his stomach as she bent to her new task. She took him into her mouth, her roving tongue like ice and fire, and he closed his eyes and saw the moon and stars in a void without end. When he opened his eyes, feeling dazed, dissolving into pure feeling, she had released him and was sitting astride him to come down upon him. She sank onto him, ingesting him, taking him into her swimming depths, and he felt his thoughts draining down to his centre and dissolving inside her. They had battled their way across to the bedroom door and he glimpsed a fat, lime-green bedspread.

'Do I feel good?' she asked rhetorically, raising and lowering herself upon him, riding him like a jockey, looking down at him, smiling with mockery, green eyes glittering and too wide. 'Am I what you expected? Is Catholic cunt as good as Prod cunt or is that a rude question? We're engaged in battle, right? No surrender on either side. You want me to come, to spill my insides, but I can't do that easily. It's not something that I've done easily for a long time and that cracks all you macho men. You work so hard – you have so much pride to feed – but you still can't make me come. There's only one way – one way. It's the way the Prods taught me, my perversion, and you just can't imagine it . . . Ah, God, yes, that's good! You're hard and as hot as hell and I'm randy, I'm on fire, I'm aflame, but it still isn't enough. Dear God, what can we do?'

'We can fuck on the fucking bed,' he gasped.

'That's a long way away,' she said.

He pushed her the whole distance, letting her ride him, being her saddle, and when her shoulders, white marble, were pressed against the lime-green bedspread, he tugged her down and filled her mouth with his tongue and rolled her onto her back. Now on top, he felt less trapped, more in command, briefly sane, and he stood up, looking down past his erection at those glittering green eyes. He saw something unnatural there – the pirouetting flights of fear – and it baffled him and cast him adrift from his former self-confidence. Grabbing her wrist, he tugged her upright, pulled her against him, breast and belly, his erection between her thighs, then he pushed her, almost hurled her, onto the bed and stretched himself out upon her. She was smiling and he saw that it was mockery, though it verged on hysteria. He had plumbed the depths of many a woman in his time – that was his pride – but he could not take the measure of this creature now stretched out beneath him. He could put himself into her, which he did, but he could not really touch her. At least, not the way he had wanted to touch her. Not that way at all. There was only one way – so she had said – and he didn't yet know what it was. The possibilities tormented him.

'You take your pride from this, don't you?'

'Stop talking,' he said.

'You think you know your women, take your pride from that illusion, yet now here you are, labouring valiantly, like a trooper, like a stud, and yet I still haven't come . . . Try this . . . Oh, dear God! And this . . . Jesus Christ! Oh, it feels good, it's grand, it's the business, but I'm still nowhere near coming. Oh, fuck! Yes! Yes! Yes!'

He thought that he had her then, but this, too, was an illusion and she went from cries of ecstasy, gasps of pleasure, to groans of frustration. He tried everything he knew, turning her this way, then that, but each turn only increased his frustration and raised the dire threat of impotence. The sweat dripped from his forehead onto her eyelids as he laboured upon her.

'Are *you* coming?' she asked rhetorically. 'No, you're not. I can't feel it. You're determined to keep going until I come and if I don't you'll be shattered. Poor man with all his pride. Poor wee Prod foiled by a Taig. God, you're good – you're the best that I've had – but you're not good enough . . . Yes! Yes! That's it! Try harder. Keep pumping. Oh, Christ, am I driving you crazy because I can't come? God, yes, that's good. That's a feeling to remember. You're an animal, a real fucking machine, but even that's no help to me . . . Oh, dear God, let me show you.'

They had been at it for hours. At least, it seemed to have been for hours. She talked and kept talking, winding him up, teasing, as he tried to beat her down into silence with every trick he had learned in his long history of women loved and then cast off. But he failed and failed again, knowing the bite of humiliation, and kept failing until she revealed what it was that she needed. His flesh was a river of sweat and his mind was an empty well when she arched her spine, belly taut, nipples hard, limbs spreadeagled, skin as white as marble but softer to the touch, to grope in the drawer of her bedside cabinet and pull out a handgun.

He froze when he saw it a Swiss SIG-Sauer pistol – and she shuddered as she pressed it into his hand, whispering eerily, 'It's empty, but it wasn't always that way and I won't ever forget that fact. Now put it where I need it. Put it where you'd normally put yourself and see what it does to me.'

Initially he refused, thinking her sick, perhaps demented, but then she slipped her delicate fingers around his wrist and guided his hand to the right place.

'Not hot and hard,' she whispered, her eyes filling up with tears. 'It's hard but it's cold and repulsive and it fills me with fear. Do you know what fear is? Have you ever felt it truly? It's a river of darkness that invades you and sweeps you away. I never knew it until I felt this – the cold hardness of steel – and when it's in me, as it will be in a moment, the fear sweeps me away.'

'I can't.'

'Yes, you can. Push it in. Do it slowly, with care . . . Ah, God, yes, that's it! It's not as hot as you, but it's harder and that's what the Prods taught me . . . That's it – I can see you're horrified – but that excites me as well . . .'

He was trembling with shame, with disbelief and dread, scarcely able to accept that he was doing it and wondering why. He felt sick and perverted and slightly mad, but he did what she asked of him. In doing it, he lost the pride he had always taken from his dealings with women. He lost belief in himself.

'It excites you, too, doesn't it? I can see that – let me feel. God, yes, you're hot and hard and pulsating and ready to come. Come in me. Take it out. Put yourself in there instead. Hold the barrel of that fucking thing to my temple and keep it there while you fuck me. Do it now! *Fuck you, do it!*'

He did as he was told. It was less shocking than what he had already done. He withdrew the cold, hard barrel and held the pistol to her temple and entered her while holding the pistol there and feeling the spasms sweep through her. She was his victim, his slave, coming alive at the thought of death, and he felt sick with shame and was excited and deranged all at once. She cried out as she came, spasm piled upon spasm, and he orgasmed and automatically squeezed the trigger and was shocked when he heard the hollow clicking and realized what he had done. Nothing had happened because the pistol was empty and thank God for that. He dropped the pistol as he spent himself inside her and groaned like a dying man.

'A night to remember,' she whispered.

He would never forget it.

CHAPTER TWENTY-SIX

Pete had always been punctual, but Patricia had beaten him to the pub and was already seated behind one of the tables, nursing her customary gin and tonic. Pete approached the table, feeling unusually nervous, and said, without a smile, 'Hi. Can I get you another?'

'Why not?' she replied, looking confused, knowing instantly that something was wrong. A fringe of blonde hair was tumbling over those sea-green eyes and their increasingly troubled intensity.

'I'll be back in a minute.' Pete went to the bar and ordered two drinks: a gin and tonic for Patricia, a Bushmill's for himself. He could see Patricia reflected in the mirror above the bar, glancing in his direction as she lit a cigarette. Even from here, she stood out from the women seated around her, some of whom were only half her age. This was a fashionable pub, drawing the university crowd, and Patricia, though older than the other women, was still more attractive – not youthful, not conventionally pretty, not vibrant, but more sensual somehow. The thought of losing her did not make him happy, but now he knew that it had to end.

After paying the barmaid, he carried the drinks to Patricia's table, then took the chair facing her. He raised his glass in a toast.

'Cheers.'

'Cheers,' she echoed him.

Watching her put the glass to her moist lips, he thought again of that first, shocking night they had spent together and of the many nights they'd had together since then. He thought of the unloaded pistol that she kept in her bedside cabinet and of the sick, despairing games she had made him play with it. He had asked her many times to explain it, but she had always refused, merely smiling mysteriously, and although he wanted to ask her again, he had more pressing matters, particularly regarding what he had been told about her by Sergeant Major Bannerman. In fact, he wanted to get into that subject straightaway, but didn't quite know how to go about it.

'You look a bit grim,' she said, placing her glass back on the table and blowing a thin stream of cigarette smoke. 'You also sounded pretty tense on the phone. So what is it, Pete?'

'I'm going to London for a few days,' he told her. 'Some business to sort out.'

'What kind of business, may I ask?'

'Personal business,' he said, thinking, *The business of divorce. The business of Operation Apocalypse. The business of why you lied to me and just who you really are. Not good business on any count* . . . 'Nothing very important. Just some hangovers from when I lived there. I'll be back in a few days.'

'What kind of hangovers? The female kind? From what I've learnt about you, that would seem to be the only hangovers you might have – and in that context, you probably have more than one.'

'I'm not as bad as gossip has it,' he said. 'The Irish like their gossip and what they can't find they invent. I'm a widower and I've come here from foreign shores, so that makes me fair game for wagging tongues.'

Patricia managed a smile, but it was slight and not remotely good-humoured. 'I don't think they have to invent much in your case. You've been seen with a lot of women along the Shankill. I'm just the latest, though not the last, I'm sure, in a pretty long line. You have secrets to conceal, Mister Thompson, and that's what makes you attractive.'

'And you? What about *your* secrets?'

'What secrets?'

'Secrets and lies, Patricia. Like the fact that your late husband was something more than a mere history teacher at a Catholic school. What about him?'

She twitched visibly, as if struck by a whip, and he saw a flush brightening her pale cheeks as she puffed on her cigarette.

'Oh,' she said. 'That.'

'Yes, that. You told me your husband was just a schoolteacher when in fact he was one of the top dogs of the Provos. Why did you lie to me?'

'I didn't lie,' she responded immediately. 'He *was* a schoolteacher. I simply didn't mention the fact that he was in the Provos because I didn't see what business it was of yours and, also, it's a part of his life that I prefer to forget. It's as simple as that.'

'Is it, indeed?'

'Yes, damn it, it is. I mean, what does it matter to you what he did in his spare time? The man's dead and buried.'

'It fucking matters to me that I'm involved with a woman who was married to a leading Provo – in his spare time, for God's sake! Well, let me tell you this . . . I live in the Shankill Road and it matters a great deal who I'm seen with. You should have told me, Patricia.'

'You think you could get in trouble being seen with me? Is that it?'

'That's certainly part of it, yes. And how come that none of the Prods who saw me with you thought to mention your husband?'

'Very few people knew we were married,' she explained. 'We kept the marriage secret and didn't even live together. When we married, I kept my flat in Stranmillis and Sean remained in the lower Falls. I kept using my maiden name – my professional name, my media name, as it were – and we only ever met at my place. Sean was paranoid about security, about my safety, and his work with the Provos, while important, was absolutely covert. He was never openly connected to the organization and did all of his work behind the scenes. Don't bother asking me what that work was. He never told me and I made a point of never asking. He was an invisible man and our marriage was the same. Now he's dead, so let's drop it.'

But Pete couldn't drop it. He knew that nothing in this city could be deemed to be unusual – the unusual was commonplace – but that sick little stunt she pulled in bed had become his obsession. He still couldn't believe that he had acquiesced in the matter, not just once but every night, always with dread and shame, and now he had to know how she had acquired the habit and what it meant to her.

'What was he like in bed, this husband of yours? Did you have the same problem with him or was he the one who created it in the first place?'

Her cheeks turned red again and her hand tightened around her glass. he thought she was going to throw her drink in his face, but she merely glared at him.

'Those are fucking sick questions,' she said, 'and you've no right to ask them.'

'It's a sick thing you do when we're in bed and I have to know why you do it. *I* do it – I'm the one who has to do it – and it shames me and sickens me, so I need to know what it means. What kind of man was he?'

She lowered her gaze to study the table, then covered her eyes with her left hand. She was holding her cigarette in that hand and the smoke veiled her bowed head.

'It wasn't him,' she said, now almost whispering, breathing heavily. 'It was some Prods who found out about us just before he was killed – maybe the ones who killed him a few days after they broke into my flat to give me a warning. They just knocked on the door. I shouldn't have opened it. When I did, they shoved me back into the room and one forced a rag into my mouth even before another had closed the door again. There were four of the bastards. They all wore balaclavas. They gagged me to stop me screaming, then punched the shit out of me, then tied my hands behind my back and threw me onto my bed.They called me a Catholic whore, a Taig cunt, a Fenian slag, and they said they were going to take turns in giving me what I really required – four Prod cocks in a row. I thought they were going to rape me – though normally that's not their thing – and in the event, being mother-loving Prods, that was *not* what they did. They were all hard, you see, but they weren't hard enough, so when they tore my clothes open and ripped off my knickers, they gave me something harder than they could manage . . . the barrel of a handgun. They just slipped it in there – at least one of them did, the one I think was the leader. "That's it, Billy," I heard one of them say. "Fuck her the way she needs fucking. Let her know we mean business." Dear God, the fear was dreadful. I thought they were going to kill me. They wouldn't rape me – they respected their mothers too much for that – so I thought they'd kill me that way instead. It was a terrible thought.'

She inhaled on her cigarette, as if hoping it might kill her. When she exhaled, it sounded like the sighing of the winds of eternity.

'The fear was unimaginable. I was also humiliated. It was fear and humiliation combined, but the growing fear wiped the other out. I felt that thing inside me, cold and hard, being poked in and out, and the fear was so deep, so complete, it made me think I was going mad . . . And even then, in that madness, in my hysteria, I had only one thought: *Please God, let me live!'*

Pete tried to imagine it, but without great success. Instead, he filled up with shame and felt flayed by her soft voice.

'That thought was burned into my mind. It became my whole being. I'd never wanted to live so much before and the feeling was startling, all consuming, a kind of heightened awareness. "Just imagine what it would feel like if I squeezed this fucking trigger," the leader, the one they'd called Billy, whispered into my ear. And when I sobbed, which, God help me, I did, he removed the pistol from there and placed the barrel against my temple and said, "I know you'd love it if I did, but I don't fuck Catholic whores, Fenian cunt. I'm just here to advise you." He then told me that he knew that Sean Farrell and I were married and that he wanted me to give him a message. "Tell him we've been here," he said. "Tell him we'll come back if we have to. Tell him he's got to retire from the Provos or we'll come back for both of you. Tell him what we did to you." Then he laughed and untied my hands and cut the telephone wires and walked out, leaving me there on the bed with the flat door open. I heard them laughing all the way down the stairs and then I broke down completely.'

She stubbed her cigarette out, though it was only half-finished. In a trance of horror, perhaps continuing disbelief, she lit up another one.

'I sobbed hysterically all night – I lost my bottle – but I never told Sean what had happened. I didn't want him to know about it. A few days later, he was blown up in his car, so it didn't make any difference. With him gone, I knew that I was safe, that they wouldn't come back for me, but my intense feeling of relief at the thought that I would actually live only made me despise myself. Those fuckers, those animals, had made me want to live so much that the need even overwhelmed the grief I was feeling for Sean. God, I hated them for that.'

She raised her eyes to stare at him and he realized that the glittering he had seen before was the fire of her hatred.

'I never forgot what they had done. I never forgot the feeling of it. That piece of steel, so very cold and hard, moving up there, inside me. I felt it for months after. I kept thinking it was still inside me. I started picking up men and they couldn't do a thing for me because they couldn't make me want to live as much as I'd wanted to live that night. That's what it became for me . . . the need to get back that feeling of heightened awareness; that extraordinary lust for life that I had never felt before . . . and so, mad as it seems and, perhaps, even is, I bought that pistol – though I never actually loaded it – and I kept it in the drawer beside my bed when I started picking up Prods. They had to be Prods, you see, all those soft mothers' boys, and what they couldn't do for me, I made them do with the empty pistol, shocking them out of their tiny minds and letting them know I despised them . . . As for you, Pete, you were better than the rest but I still needed that.'

'Jesus!' Pete whispered, so confused by his own feelings that he wanted to reach out to console her, even as he was racked by a mixture of shame, dread and revulsion. This was not just for her, but also for himself. He had used her, or tried to, and been taken to the edge, at least as close to it as he ever wanted to go. He wanted out of this job, out of Belfast, out of her, but he was trapped by the job, by quietly spoken official blackmail, by his past, which was why he could be blackmailed, and by his need for her body. He was paying his dues for the first time and did not like the cost.

'You hate me, don't you?' she said. She was smiling, but it was chilling. 'You hate me because you can't satisfy me without doing that dirty thing. But it isn't moral outrage, is it? It's no more than wounded pride. The man who's had so many women he can't count them can't satisfy this one – not without that harder, colder weapon that gives most grown men the feeling of strength that they normally lack. You hate me because you feel humiliated and faced with your failure. Now isn't that the truth, big boy?'

'What the fuck are you talking about?' he responded, burning hot and then cold. 'I only did what you asked.'

'You could have walked,' she said. 'Men more decent than you have done so. But you, with all that fucking male pride, that rampaging sexual ego, the Casanova of West Belfast – you couldn't leave, no matter the cost, until you could tell yourself you'd left me satisfied. But you didn't, did you, Pete? It wasn't your cock alone that did it. What did it was what had to come before and that made your stomach churn. You were shocked, but you kept coming back for more because you just couldn't let me go. In fact, you can't let any willing woman go until you feel that you've beaten her. It's adolescent in the extreme, a bad boy's dream, and you still can't live without it. That's why you hate me, Pete. It's because of what I showed you in the mirror during those long, sweaty nights. You could never quite touch me – not really. Not just you and you alone – you and your cock – and you can't stand that failure.'

'Fuck this,' Pete said. He was livid and started pushing his chair away, about to storm out, but she waved him back down and held him there with the intensity of her gaze as she leaned across the table, her fine breasts pressed against it.

'What's the real story, Pete? Just who the fuck are you, really? What's a man like you doing in the Shankill when you could be in Stranmillis or the upper Malone Road or anywhere else where Prods not involved in the conflict would obviously congregate? You're a fucking liar, Pete. *I'm* not the liar – *you* are. You come all the way from Australia, you return to your home town, and you deliberately pick the worst place you could live in if you don't want involvement. But you're involved somehow, aren't you? You have your reasons for being here. I mean, considering you're not supposed to be interested in the conflict, you seem to ask an awful lot of questions of the kind best avoided. Like the Reverend William Dawson. Non-stop questions about that bastard. Like, is he really connected to the paramilitaries and who does he know? You think he's up to his neck in it. That thought keeps you awake at nights. Now why would it do that, Mister Thompson, if you've really no interest? No, Pete, I'm not dumb. I know when I'm being used. I used you even as you were using me because I never quite trusted you. Now I'm going to look into you – just like I looked into Dawson – and I'm going to find out just why you want to know all about that Prod bastard. So you go to London, Pete, but you'd best stay there for good, because I'm going to find out just who you are and where you really come from. Come back here and I'll tell you.'

Pete finished his drink, pushed his chair back and stood up. He was flushed and he didn't like the feeling because he wasn't used to it. He saw the brilliance of her green gaze, her rage, and his heart went out to her. When he felt that – his shock and concern and deep need – he understood what love was and why he had always felt the need to deny it. He courted danger, he had the urge to flirt with death, because he feared the greater pain of true involvement. He would run from her, as he had run from all the others, because finally, though he had courage in certain areas, he was a coward where it mattered. She had held up the mirror to this weakness and he could have killed her for it.

'Fuck this,' he said, 'and fuck you. Let's just call it a day.'

'Who are you, Pete? Who are you, really?'

'Goodnight, Pat.'

'Goodbye.'

He walked away from the table and went out into the cold night, blinking against the lights that beamed through the rainswept darkness – street lights and the headlights of passing cars, neon lights and the lights beaming out of the restaurants below the neon – and he realized that he was burning hot and cold, with shock, rage and pain. He tried flagging down a taxi, cursing as each one passed, but eventually, when he was slumped in the back of one, he tried to calm himself down. This was not easy. He had never felt so confused. He couldn't quite work out what he felt for Patricia Monaghan – Mrs Farrell – it was possibly love and fear, revulsion and addiction – but he knew, beyond a shadow of doubt, that he could be in danger. She had sussed him – not entirely, but too close for comfort – and he had judged from the passionate intensity of her green gaze that she, too, while being suspicious of him, had her own unknown side. Like himself, she was more than she seemed to be and that was the danger. Also, if she investigated him – as clearly she intended doing – she would do so with all the expertise at her command and the facts behind his fiction would come out. He could have killed her for that as well – he really could – and yet his heart, formerly healthy and steady, was now racing too quickly. This confused him even more.

Through the window of the cab, rain-soaked and misted over, he saw the centre of the city as a distorting kaleidoscope of bright lights. It seemed lively out there, a busy, friendly town, but he knew that what went on beneath the surface did not bear examining. It was a city ruled by fear, by sectarian madness, by violence, and

what was about to come down was even worse than what had
gone before . . . an apocalypse, truly. He was part of it, trapped
by it, now possibly endangered by it, and he was glad, despite his
pained feelings for Patricia Monaghan, that prismatic, blinding
creature, that he was getting out of it this very night, taking wing,
flying off. He wanted away from this city and from her with an
equal intensity.

When the taxi dropped him off at his terraced house just off the
Shankill (*Why indeed*, he thought, *would I pick this place to live in*?),
he said to the driver, 'Wait here. I have to go to the airport and I'll
be coming right out again.' The taxi driver nodded. 'Sure, I'm yer
man,' he said. Pete entered the house and climbed the stairs to pick
up his suitcase. He had packed it that morning, being organized,
in control, but even as he was carrying it out of the bedroom he
heard the squealing of tyres turning too fast on a wet road.

The taxi had taken off.

What the hell? Pete thought.

The driver must have seen something. Pete was damned sure of
that. He set the suitcase on the floor and was about to go down the
stairs when he heard the unmistakable sound of a sledgehammer
slamming into the front door.

'Fuck!' he said automatically.

The door was tearing off its hinges as he rushed back into the
bedroom, fell to his knees and pulled his toolbox out from under the
bed. He heard male bawling from below, breaking glass, crashing
furniture, as he opened the toolbox, hastily removed the top part
and grabbed the Five-seveN pistol hidden in the false bottom.
It was loaded already – he had always kept it loaded – and he
jumped up and ran to the landing when he heard the clatter of
booted feet coming up the stairs.

He turned sideways on the landing, pressing his back to the wall,
keeping himself out of sight, then glanced down and glimpsed a
balaclava helmet with two slits for eyeholes. As the man advanced
up the stairs, Pete saw a pistol in his raised hand, his chest coming
into view, and he leaned out, took aim and fired – two shots into
that chest. The man almost somersaulted, punched hard by the
high-velocity bullets, and tumbled backwards as another man
cried, 'Fuck! The bastard's upstairs!' The tumbling man came
to a halt, his body angled across the stairwell, then a burst of

automatic gunfire made a deafening row. The wall facing Pete exploded, showering plaster and wood splinters, and he reached out to fire his pistol blind and then, without checking the damage done, he slipped back into the bedroom.

He was about to slam the door when he heard another man coming up the stairs. The man had to be stupid – very stupid indeed – and he proved it by bounding onto the landing, unprotected, exposed. Like the first one, he was wearing a balaclava with slitted eyeholes, but instead of a pistol he was holding a Sterling sub-machine gun and preparing to use it.

Pete fired a double-tap and the man's chest exploded, splinters of bone in spouting blood, and then he, too, tumbled back down the stairs as his friends below bawled outraged obscenities.

Pete kicked the door shut and locked it from inside, then he ran to the window, which overlooked the back entry, opened it and scrambled over the window-ledge, still holding the pistol in his right hand and ignoring his suitcase. A small backyard was below him, enclosed in four brick walls, and he was about to step onto the left-hand wall when the bedroom door was smashed off its hinges – the sledgehammer again.

Pete turned back as far as possible, looking over his left shoulder, resting the pistol upon it, and opened fire as another masked man rushed into the bedroom even as the door was falling to the floor. The bullets blew the man's head away, turning it into a bloody mess, and he fell back into the arms of the man behind him as Pete turned to the front again.

He stepped onto the left-hand wall, tightroped his way along it, then jumped off it without even looking out for what was below. In fact, he knew what was down there – a litter-filled entry where people fucked at the midnight hour – and he landed on both feet in a pile of rubbish, then turned right and ran away.

That other bastard wouldn't follow him. Three dead men were enough. Pete ran like a gazelle, excited, alive again, and did not feel ashamed of his feelings until he was well clear.

He took a taxi to the airport, where he gladly boarded his plane and let it fly him to London. He had time for only one drink on the plane, but that was enough. Arriving home, in the safe confines of Belsize Park, he found a pile of mail waiting for him. Most of it was from Monica's solicitor and that made him feel safe. Patricia Monaghan, good or bad, sane or mad, would at least understand that.

Pete poured himself a drink then sat down and stared at the wall. He sat there the whole night.

CHAPTER TWENTY-SEVEN

It was a fine sunny day – the first real sunny day of the year – when Joe Douglas sat down to breakfast with his wife Susan and his two children, Roy and Margaret, ten and eleven years old respectively. They were all dressed in their Sunday best, with Joe sporting a natty suit with shirt and tie. The breakfast consisted of eggs, bacon, sausage, tomatoes, soda bread and potato bread, all fried and washed down with liberally sugared hot tea. Joe was a big man and his wife and children were similarly hefty. God knows what the Fenians looked like since clearly, according to Joe, they received all the state benefits denied the poor Prods. The meal was, however, being taken on the living-room table by the front window of Joe's spanking new housing executive home, located in the lower Shankill Road, not far from the centre of the city. It was a convenient location and not one that the average man could have afforded without state assistance. Joe was not, however, the average man. He was, in fact, pretty wealthy from his diverse criminal activities – his so-called 'freedom fighter' work – but he had a tendency to forget that he had that healthy income and so still relied on unemployment benefits and anything else he could claim by simply filling in the requisite form. If Gerry Adams could pick up unemployment benefits for years, why couldn't Joe Douglas?

'Majorca,' Joe was saying, speaking with his mouth full and not reprimanding his heavy children for doing the same. 'I think a coupla weeks there would do us all good. We'll go after the twelfth of July parades, when I've carried the banner, like. I think two weeks should do it.'

'Where's Majorca?' young Roy asked.

'The Mediterranean,' Margaret informed him.

'Where's that?' Roy asked.

'Near Spain,' Margaret said, now showing some impatience as well as her imperfect education. 'It's a tropical island.'

'They have beaches and palm trees,' Joe ventured, 'an' you can swim all day long.'

'I can't swim,' Roy said.

Joe smiled patiently at him. He was his father's boy, after all. A bit thick, but he made up for it with spirit, though that wore down his mother. Susan wasn't at the table, though her plate was clearly there. As usual, she was on her feet all the time, running back and forth between the table and the kitchen, looking harassed and weary. Now she came back in, wiping sweat from her brow, carrying another plate piled high with potato bread, nicely fried and still greasy. She dished the portions out one by one and then lit up a fag, taking a long, desperate drag and blowing the smoke all over the table. No one seemed to notice.

'Better hurry up,' she said, 'or we'll be late. The Reverend's always real punctual.'

'Don't worry, we'll make it,' Joe said. 'We always do, love.'

Though not as religious as Margaret, who worshipped the Reverend William Dawson and God in that order, Joe felt it incumbent on him to set a good example to his children by attending church every Sunday and dragging them with him. He also liked the ritual of it, being himself a ritualistic type. This explained his devotion to the Orange Lodge, with its quasi-secret, Masonic-styled ceremonies, and to his Loyalist paramilitary group, with its strict rules and dire punishments, the latter being ceremonially administered. Like all men with a mission, Joe saw no contradiction between his religious beliefs, the stated ideals of his beloved Orange Lodge (belief in God, Queen and Country, the manly virtues, and so forth) and his involvement in murder, organized crime and general mayhem. He had an enemy, after all, to take the blame for it all: the Fenians who got more benefits than the Prods and were insisting on even more. They were even trying to stop the Orange Lodge parades and that just about said it all.

'Okay, kids,' Joe said, wiping his lips with the back of his hand and pushing his chair back. 'Let's get up an' go.'

'I don't want to,' Roy said. His pimpled face was sullen. 'Why are *we* the only kids who have to go to church? All my mates are allowed to stay at home and do their home-work.'

'Watch TV, you mean,' his mother said, jerking his chair from under him to make him stand up. 'Now go put yer coat on. You, too, Margaret.'

'Yes, Mum,' Margaret said, being admirably obedient.

'It's so boring,' Roy said, though he went off to put his coat on. 'Reverend Dawson just talks and talks and only stops when we're singin'. I hate singin' hymns as well. I feel like a right eejit.'

'Keep talkin',' his mother said, 'an I'll wash yer mouth out with disinfectant. Now, come on, let's get goin'.' She flicked her half-finished ciggie into the fireplace and then put her coat on. 'All out,' she said. '*Now!*'

With Joe in the lead, they all piled out of the house and into his car, a standard Ford Cortina that marked him as a common man devoid of pretensions, despite what was secretly stacked up in his ever-fattening bank account. Driving with care, always mindful of Sunday drivers, the bloody eejits, he headed across town, a town now gravely resplendent in sunshine. Looking out at the imposing City Hall and the Victorian splendour of the buildings around it, he practically swelled with pride, thinking what a grand place Belfast would be if only the Fenians were all out of it. That day would come eventually, shortly after the Apocalypse (that's how he thought of Operation Apocalypse these days: it was just 'the Apocalypse') when every peace-loving bastard, Prod and Catholic alike, was put whole or in pieces into a pine box and buried well out of sight. After that, he and his mates would return to the real war and ensure that no Taig was left standing. It was a superhuman task – a religious task – but Joe thought he was up to it.

About fifteen minutes later, after a pleasant drive across this splendid city, soon to be ethnically cleansed, they arrived at Reverend Dawson's New Presbyterian Church which was, indeed, almost as new as Joe's spanking new housing executive home and every bit as functional and uninspiring. Entering the church with their two reluctant children, Joe and Susan found it already packed, but managed to find a pew near the back.

Joe liked the ritual of church. Thus, he enjoyed the hymn-singing, the praying, the passing of the collection box, but most of all, like the rest of those present, kids excluded, he was thrilled by the Reverend William Dawson's vibrant anti-Catholic sermonizing.

He was not disappointed this particular day and was given something to take with him to the grave. The Reverend stood on his toes, raised his hands above his head, closed his eyes, put his head back and let rip with all the fervour of Elmer Gantry – Burt Lancaster-style. He praised the Lord and the Holy Ghost, spoke of love and redemption, reminded all those present of Protestant rectitude and tolerance, then went on to metaphorically flay the skin off the Fenians and their heretical leader, the Pope of the vile Church of Rome. He spoke at length about the violence that was ruining his great city, of evil Republican gunmen, of the threat to Protestant freedoms from that pestilent land across the border, and of holy Ulster which, backed by Crown and Throne, was all that stood between Heaven and Hell in this dangerous age. He ranted and raved, beseeched and cajoled, and when he had finished, exhausted but unbowed, even Joe was in awe of him.

More prayers were spoken, more hymns were sung, then the congregation, at once humbled and exalted, filed out of the church.

Having made his customary bolt around the side of the church, Reverend Dawson was already standing at the front door when the first of his faithful flock emerged. He engaged them in jovial conversation and a lot of hand-shaking. Having been seated near the back of the church, Joe and his family were among the first out and were pleased to be so greeted by the honourable Reverend. The eyes of Joe's wife were glazed. Joe himself was still excited. He wasn't normally a talkative man – just the occasional, usually threatening word here and there – but he always had a few words for the Reverend, who could make him feel virtuous.

'Sure, that sermon was great, Reverend,' Joe said. 'It picked me up like a tonic.'

'I'm glad to hear that, Mister Douglas,' the Reverend replied smoothly, 'and pleased to see that you and your fine family are regular attenders.'

'Oh, yes!' Susan exclaimed.

'Quite,' the Reverend said.

'Sure, it does us good to come here,' Joe said. 'Not to mention the children.'

Roy and Margaret were both staring at the ground as they restlessly kicked up the grass and kept their mouths shut.

'Suffer the little children . . .' the Reverend murmured vaguely, his brilliant blue eyes slipping sideways to catch the glances of those still coming out and clearly desirous of his fleeting attention.

'Right,' Joe said, noting the Reverend's shifting gaze and wondering what kind of man he really was and where his loyalties truly lay. There were lots of rumours about the Reverend, but you could never pin him down. He was supportive of the Loyalists, at least verbally, politically, but no one knew just how active he was when it got down to brass tacks. Joe had tried to find out at the Ulster Defenders' meetings, but those bastards, those controlling Red Hand, always responded by turning a bit vague. So if the Reverend was tuned in, which he might be, they were keeping quiet about it.

'Well, thanks again, Reverend,' Joe said with a big grin, respectful of the preacher's wandering gaze. 'We'll all see you next week, then.'

'Absolutely,' the Reverend replied, shaking their hands and stepping backwards to let his assistant, Robert Lilly, gently usher them to the open gates of the churchyard. 'Why, hello, Missus . . .'

'A lovely sermon, Reverend Dawson!' a middle-aged female interjected excitedly, gushing like Niagara Falls. 'Sure, it was just what the doctor ordered and, of course . . .'

But Joe was back in his car by now, all set to drive his family home and then take himself off to his Orange Lodge for some more soothing rituals.

'All tucked in safe and sound?' he asked, before releasing the handbrake and slipping into first gear.

'Yes!' the kids chorused happily.

'Here we go, then.' Joe drove off, again appreciating the sunlight, the first hint of spring, thinking of how good it always made him feel to go to church, even though he did (yes, he had to admit it) appreciate why the kids would be bored. It was, however, important to him that his beloved offspring received a religious education, a sound knowledge of right and wrong – the differences, as it were, between the Protestants and the Fenians – in order that they might follow in his footsteps and grow up to be good Catholic-hating

Loyalists. He didn't want any wishy-washy liberal ideas – the Queen's University syndrome – to corrupt them into believing that Holy Ulster should treat its born enemies, the Fenians, as equals. Joe wanted only true believers in his house and that's all there was to it.

As he approached the street where he lived, running parallel to the street in which he had been born and bred, his thoughts drifted to the unexpected killing of Jack Peel, one of the three Red Hand leaders, and he wondered, as he had done so often, just who might have done it. He felt little sympathy for Peel, who'd always got up his nose, but like Alf Green, whom he trusted, he was concerned about why someone would want to assassinate a Red Hand leader at this particularly sensitive time. Operation Apocalypse was just about to be launched and neither the top dogs of the Loyalists nor those of the Provos would want it endangered. That assassination had endangered it, causing suspicion and dissension between the Prods and Fenians involved, and now a hunt was on to find the killer before the bastard caused any more damage. So far, however, the search had proved to be fruitless and it wasn't known if a Prod or Catholic was responsible. The general feeling was that it wasn't anyone involved in the 'big one' – Operation Apocalypse – but that it had to be some dumb fucker from a splinter group located in Belfast. Whether that eejit was a Loyalist or a Republican remained to be seen.

Meanwhile, Operation Apocalypse had been put on hold.

When we catch the fucker, Joe thought as he drove his wife and children home, *we'll nail his hands and feet to a fucking wall and take a blowtorch to him. We'll fry him until he cooks and croaks, then we'll bury him deep.*

Heartened by this healing prospect on the Day of the Lord, Joe parked the Ford Cortina by the kerb outside his front door. A gentleman to the end – a good example to his kids – he clambered out to walk around to the other side and open the door for his wife.

He was just crossing the front of the car when he saw movement across the road.

A man wearing a balaclava helmet with slitted holes for eyepieces had emerged from a parked silver-grey Volvo and was raising a sub-machine gun to his shoulder, to take aim and fire.

'No!' Joe screamed.

A gentleman to the end, he was thinking of his wife and kids, of the damage that might be done accidentally to them, but he only had a second to think of that before his chest exploded through his shirt and the sky swirled above him. Fading out on that terrified screaming, he found darkness and silence.

There were church bells ringing out as he died, but Joe didn't hear them.

CHAPTER TWENTY-EIGHT

They met in a suite in the Savoy Hotel, London, because it was felt that Pete could not be seen entering COBR – the Cabinet Office Briefing Room in Whitehall – and that his own apartment in Belsize Park would not be much better as it was – given the assassination attempt in Belfast – possibly under surveillance. The men gathered together here had all come at different times, some entering by the front of the building, some by the back through the restaurant overlooking the Thames, as all of them had good reason to be careful about who they were seen with: this way they would pass either as residents or men visiting residents. Indeed, so careful were these men that the head of the pack was introduced to Pete only as 'the Secretary' and at no point did anyone use his real name. Silvery-haired and patrician, wearing an immaculate pinstripe suit with his old school tie – Cambridge, Pete deduced – he had eyes of the coldest, clearest blue, set deep in civilized but absolutely humourless features. The others, all introduced, were: Police Commissioner William Hargreaves; senior Foreign Affairs minister Anthony Courtland-Smith; commander of Special Forces Brigadier Wesley Moorland; and the man who made the introductions, Pete's old friend, MI5 representative Daniel Edmondson. All of the men, burdened with grave responsibilities, were enjoying Courvoisier brandy and Havana cigars at the taxpayers' expense.

'So, gentlemen,' the Secretary said, glancing down at the folder on the long table they were sharing, 'we have all read Mr Moore's report and are, as it were, cognisant of the situation. But how do we interpret it?'

'As it reads, Mr Secretary,' Daniel Edmondson said. 'There can be no doubt about it. Unbelievable as it seems, the Loyalist and Republican hard men are joining together – at least temporarily – to mount a mass assassination attack on every well-known Protestant and Catholic who presently supports the peace plan. They plan to complete this task in one unforgettable day in order to strike terror into the hearts of the population and, more importantly, to place the British government in an extremely delicate, not to say hopeless, situation with regard to future talks with the doves on both sides. Once they've succeeded – if we don't stop them first – they'll carve the city of Belfast up between them, running it as a criminal empire, with the Loyalists and the Republicans . . .'

'For want of a better word,' the Secretary interjected acidulously.

'With the Loyalists and the Republicans,' Edmondson continued doggedly, 'each taking over previously agreed territories and interacting only when it's mutually profitable. In this way they can keep their paramilitaries at work – men, as we all know, who'd have no place in a peaceful Belfast – whilst making it almost impossible for the peace plan to make any progress. If they succeed, there'll be an unholy mess and we'll carry the can for it.'

The Secretary stared at him, not saying a word, and since no one else knew what to say the silence lingered uneasily. More brandy was poured, cigars were relit, then the conversation picked up again.

'I gather from this report,' the Secretary said at last, 'that the personal details required for this mass assassination attempt were obtained from a wide variety of data banks by computer hacks working for the paramilitaries.'

'That's correct,' Pete said. 'Though the hackers, mostly formerly troubled kids, had no idea what they were gathering that info for. They seriously believed that they were just being computer-trained on what was, after all, a government-sponsored training programme.'

The Secretary raised his bushy eyebrows and stared sceptically at him. 'Yet the report is a little vague on exactly who's behind this astonishing business. I note that the Reverend William Dawson is mentioned as a strong possibility. If he is, we would have very serious problems, so naturally . . .'

'We have no real proof,' Pete said. 'Okay, I'll admit that. But we now know that Reverend Dawson, despite his public protestations, continues to have strong links with the Ulster Defenders – presently the most powerful Loyalist group in Northern Ireland – and that they, in turn, control the Red Hand paramilitaries. While no direct link can be traced between Dawson and those groups, we now know for certain that his office computer system is linked into the network out in Antrim where the hackers are collecting the data required for Operation Apocalypse.'

'This is dreadful news to hear,' the Secretary said. 'However, I still find it hard to believe that Dawson's involved. If any major figure can be called moderate in Northern Ireland, Reverend Dawson is certainly a moderate – at least in the sense that he's willing to discuss the peace plan as if it actually has prospects.'

'He does that with the media,' Pete said, 'but not in his church. Believe me, Mr Secretary, he's a different man there and he doesn't view the Catholics with favour. He's not quite as loud as Ian Paisley, but he shares the same views.'

'And another point,' Daniel Edmondson put in helpfully. 'A study of the computer data taken from Antrim by Mr Moore indicates that every major political and religious figure in Ireland who has, whether seriously or diplomatically, supported the peace plan is entered on that assassination list . . . All except one.'

'The Reverend William Dawson,' the Police Commissioner, William Hargreaves, said, speaking for the first time.

'Exactly,' Edmondson said.

'Which suggests,' Brigadier Moorland said, also speaking for the first time, 'that the good Reverend is supportive – if not actually in charge – of Operation Apocalypse.'

'Damned right,' Pete said.

He was feeling more positive than he should be and still wondering why. Part of it, he knew, was yesterday's lunch with his wife Monica, deliberately arranged by himself because, after his affair with Patricia Monaghan, he could no longer live with himself. Patricia Monaghan – Mrs Farrell – had taught him a lot about himself, none of it nice to know, and he now knew that he had spent most of his manhood running away from real manhood. He had hurt his wives and his women and his children, never committing to anything or anyone, and he had travelled and fought wars and never put real roots down because commitment – any kind of lasting bond – was frightening to him. That had not been the case with Belfast – his parents had taken him out of there – but he now knew that he had put that city out of his mind because he had wanted it buried. Belfast was too complex, too filled with moral dilemmas, and those were the very dilemmas that he had always avoided. Now, because of Patricia Monaghan – Mrs Farrell – he was being forced to face up to them. Maybe that was why, before he could stop himself, he had asked Monica if he could come back home and try again when this job had ended. She had agreed, but this job hadn't ended and so here he sat – a benign fool in a house of wise men whose cynicism knew no bounds. At least they made him feel human by contrast.

'Mr Moore,' the Secretary said.

'Yes, sir!' Pete responded, startled out of his reverie.

'If we're to assume from this report that the Reverend Dawson is involved, then what, may I ask, are his motives? I mean, the man, though undoubtedly anti-Catholic, is certainly not going to benefit from a Belfast carved up between two criminal gangs masquerading as true Loyalists and Republicans. What would he hope to gain?'

Pete shrugged. 'I'll admit, I'm baffled. My only suggestion is that he's now even bigger than Ian Paisley—'

'Though less corpulent,' Daniel Edmondson interjected sardonically.

'—and if the peace plan falls through, no matter the consequences, he'll become even more important than he is now when it comes to dealing with us.'

'You mean the British government?' Brigadier Moorland asked.

'Yes, sir,' Pete replied. 'Just as Paisley lost ground when the first peace plan was introduced, so Dawson would lose if his particular brand of anti-Catholicism was given no ground in which to flourish.'

'Neatly put,' the Secretary said. 'You should write books, Mr Moore.'

'Fuck you,' Pete said.

The silence – and the cliché was apt – seemed to stretch out forever. Eventually, when everyone had shuffled their papers, poured another brandy or relit their fat cigars, the Secretary, whose spine had visibly stiffened, relaxed enough to say, 'Well, I'm sorry to have offended you, Mr Moore, but we must tread with care here.'

'Yes, Mr Secretary,' Pete said, 'I'm sorry, too. I didn't mean to offend you.'

'It's criminal,' the Police Commissioner suddenly said. He was a large man with a flushed, decent face, trying to smooth troubled waters. 'What we're talking about, Mr Secretary, is a very audacious, ruthless plan to take over a whole city – a *British* city, I might add – for purely criminal purposes, a plan disguised as political warfare. It is, in my experience, completely unprecedented and no matter who's in charge – or who suffers – it has to be stopped.'

Another silence ensued – the silence of indecision. Pete sat back in his chair and thought of Patricia Monaghan, of all the love and despair he felt for her, and realized that she had, willy nilly, brought him back to his wife. It had been a brutal education, humiliating, even shameful, but it had also led him back into his own history and the knowledge that he had, without even realizing it, quietly rewritten it. Now he had to return to Belfast, no matter how these men decided, because some jobs were made to be finished and certain truths had to be faced. He would face himself in the city of his birth and, perhaps, find renewal.

Dear God, he thought, *you're so damned romantic and you never suspected that of yourself. You might pay the price for this.*

'So how do we stop it?' the Brigadier asked, letting his flinty grey gaze light on each face as if etching into it.

The Secretary sighed. 'I still feel we need to know a bit more. We can't attack the wrong people. This Reverend Dawson, for instance . . .' He flipped through the papers in the thick file before him . . . 'Most of the information we have here – gleaned by Mr Moore, for which we thank him – comes from the Northern Ireland stringer of a Dublin radio station. This woman, though reportedly objective, has Republican sympathies. As I'm concerned about misinformation regarding Reverend Dawson – a not inconsiderable figure when it comes to representing our interests in the province – I have to say that I have certain doubts here. How did you get this information, Mr Moore? Was there a personal involvement?'

'Yes,' Pete said without hesitation.

'And was this personal involvement strictly professional?'

'Yes,' Pete said, lying, since, of course, though it had started as strictly professional, it had ended up as something very personal.

'So what was your assessment of this woman?'

'She was open about her Republican sympathies, but apart from that, she was pretty objective.'

'And her interest in Reverend Dawson?'

'Motivated by her conviction that he had ties with certain paramilitary groups. This turned out to be true.'

'What did *she* find out about *you*?' the Police Commissioner, formerly so supportive, asked in an ominous manner.

'Not much,' Pete said, though he felt distinctly uneasy. 'During our last meeting – early in the evening of the day I left there – she challenged me in a way that made me think she had developed doubts about my background. I'm convinced that she had nothing positive on me, but she'd certainly started to wonder about my interest in the Reverend Dawson.'

'She had suspicions that you weren't quite what you seemed?'

'Yes, Commissioner,' Pete confessed to his former ally. 'I suppose you could say that.'

'And later that evening,' the Police Commissioner said, staring down at his report, 'an attempt was made on your life by men who were clearly paramilitaries.'

'Yes,' Pete replied, his heart sinking 'That's true.'

'So someone had obviously found out who you were,' Pete's other former ally, his supposed friend Daniel Edmondson, said.

Pete sighed and shrugged. 'Yes, that's certain.'

'Who?' the Secretary asked with admirable brevity.

'Dawson,' Pete said. 'It had to be him. He was having me followed – as he had Patricia Monaghan followed – so clearly he's not as innocent as he seems. And if he was observing me, then he might have done some more research and found out who I really am. He's tied to the paramilitaries – namely the Ulster Defenders, which links him to Red Hand – and he must have known that I was being used by the latter to work out in Antrim, where all that computer hacking was going on. Add the two together – the Reverend Dawson and Red Hand – and it seems certain that they looked into my real background and decided to take me out.'

The Secretary and the Police Commissioner glanced at one another, then the former returned his gaze to Pete, his blue eyes unblinking. 'Anything else to tell us about Miss Monaghan?'

Pete knew what he was getting at. 'I assume you mean the

fact that she was married to the former Provo leader, Sean Farrell?'

'Indeed, I do,' the Secretary said.

'Yes, I knew that,' Pete confessed, 'but I didn't think it had relevance. She told me about it,' he continued, avoiding the truth of the matter: that he'd had to force it out of her. 'And she convinced me that although she knew her husband was in the Provos, she didn't approve of it and didn't know what he did. And, of course, he was, as I'm sure you know, killed by a Loyalist bomb, so that seemed to me to leave him out of the picture.'

The Secretary just stared at him, his blue eyes like lasers. Then he said, speaking quietly, with contempt, 'You're a bloody fool, Mr Moore.'

Pete turned hot and cold – just as he had done with Patricia Monaghan – and knew, from the shifting eyes of the other men present, that he had made a mistake. It was a big mistake – their eyes told him that as well – and his ego had caused it.

'Mr Moore,' the Police Commissioner said, his decent face flushed with embarrassment. 'Just how carefully did you check the names of the various paramilitaries listed in the documentation you kindly sent us on Operation Apocalypse?'

'Well, I didn't really . . .' Pete found himself floundering and despised himself for it. 'I mean, I'm not really familiar with the individuals involved in the conflict, so it's not something I thought to check in detail. I mean, I thought the names would mean more to you than they would to me . . . So I just passed on the intelligence, trusting you to deal with it.'

'Fair enough,' Daniel Edmondson said helpfully.

'Yes,' the Police Commissioner kindly agreed. 'Fair enough. Unfortunately, one of the names listed as a strategic planner for Operation Apocalypse is that of Patricia Monaghan's former husband . . . the supposedly deceased Sean Farrell . . . And that gentleman, as we all know, was one of the most brilliant strategists the IRA ever had.'

Pete burned up inside, humiliated by his own stupidity, and suddenly felt that he was back in that bar in the Shankill, looking straight into Patricia Monaghan's green gaze. He saw that gaze again, magnified, and her rage now seemed obvious. What it meant

. . . Well, damn it, he *knew* what it meant . . . And it would now be confirmed.

'He was killed in a car-bomb explosion,' Pete said, though his voice seemed to come from somewhere else. 'Damn it, he . . .'

But the Police Commissioner shook his head, as if weary of all this nonsense, then said, 'Sorry, Mr Moore. I say sorry, though I thank you. It was, of course, widely reported that Sean Farrell had been killed in that explosion, but such, alas, was not the case. According to the reported story, within minutes of the explosion, some locals dragged the mortally wounded Sean Farrell out of the blazing vehicle and transported him to the Royal Victoria Hospital. There, at least according to the reports submitted to MI5, he was found to be so badly burnt that he was barely recognizable and he died in that sorry condition an hour or two later. He was buried a few days after that, supposedly still unrecognizable, in the now renowned Milltown Cemetery – another Republican martyr. But no doubt you know all this.'

'Yes,' Pete said as he felt his heart sinking.

'I thanked you, Mr Moore,' the Police Commissioner continued, 'because you've confirmed what we here have long suspected, though couldn't actually prove. According to our subsequent investigations of that incident, there were in fact two people in that car when it exploded. Sean Farrell was the passenger. The bombers thought he would be the driver. The actual driver took most of the blast and was burnt beyond recognition while Sean Farrell, though certainly burnt and badly wounded, managed to survive. The locals who took the supposed Sean Farrell's body to the Royal Victoria Hospital were actually paramilitaries belonging to his gang and the body they transported – a man burnt beyond recognition – was actually that of the driver. Sean Farrell's belongings, including everything identifying him, had been deliberately transferred to that man's clothing. Meanwhile, the real Sean Farrell, badly hurt though still alive, was quickly removed from the scene of the incident and hidden in a safe house in West Belfast. There he received emergency treatment. When, eventually, he was deemed fit enough to be moved, he was transported covertly to another safe house across the border and there – or so we mistakenly thought – he was being kept undercover. Thanks to you, inadvertent though the discovery may be, we now know that he's returned to Northern Ireland to take part in what we now know to be Operation Apocalypse.'

The Police Commissioner rubbed his forehead, as if erasing a headache, then offered Pete the kindest smile he could muster.

'She fooled you, Mr Moore. Just like her husband fooled us. Sean Farrell, if not too healthy, is certainly still alive and presently hiding out in the mountains of Mourne – in that big house described in detail on the data you picked up for us – and he's there as the leader of the Catholics chosen to take part, alongside the Loyalists, in Operation Apocalypse.'

Pete felt that he was dying, though he wasn't – he was alive. He was more alive than he had been for a long time and his new feelings were based on his rage. She had fooled him – Patricia Monaghan had fooled him – but she had also transformed him. She had seen him for what he was, a user to be used, and she had used him even as he was using her and shown him up as a fake. Now he had no choice but to go back and finish the job. He had to do it to compensate for his past and prepare himself for the future. He had to do it, not because it was exciting, but because it needed to be done. He was involved in duplicity, but that was something he had lived by. Now he had the need to redeem himself and return to his family. This was not a big thing for common men, but for him it was frightening – and that was why he would do it.

'I fucked up,' he said.

'We were compensated, Mr Moore.' The Police Commissioner smiled at him. 'We now know where they are, who they are, and what they're up to. We just have to stop them.'

'With extreme care,' the Secretary added, not smiling at all. 'We can't target Reverend Dawson, since he might well be innocent, and we can't send in an army to do the job. In fact, we can't do a damned thing.'

'We can't?' Edmondson queried.

The Secretary shook his head. 'What do we do?' he asked. 'We have no evidence against a single individual and that keeps our hands tied. Alas, we have to abide by the law and in this case we can't act. We could, of course, target that big house in the mountains of Mourne, but . . .'

He raised his hands above his head, as if signalling his despair, though this was merely his way of saying that he could not make any statement that could be misinterpreted as a positive sanction. It was his way of saying 'Yes'.

'We can't send in an army,' the Brigadier said, carefully echoing the Secretary's previous statement.

'Of course not,' the Secretary said, having planted the seed.

'But we could,' Brigadier Moorland said, 'send in a few men.'

'Not officially,' the Secretary was quick to respond.

'But unofficially,' the Brigadier said. 'A few men, not connected in any way to this government – not regular soldiers, say; not traceable back to us – a few men willing to go in without back-up or any kind of protection.'

'You mean men who, if caught, will be dumped,' Daniel Edmondson said bluntly.

'Correct,' the Brigadier said.

Edmondson looked directly at Pete. 'Well, my friend, what do you say?'

'I say that house, given the details we have, is a pretty big place.'

'Could a few men take it out?'

'I wouldn't guarantee it.'

'We're not looking for guarantees in this instance, since our choices are few.'

'What does "a few men" mean?'

'I'd say no more than two.' Edmondson smiled. 'Plus yourself, of course. Two and one makes three – that's a lucky number – but they must be invisible.'

'Can I pick them?'

'We don't even want to know them.'

'Will you pay them?'

'A lot.'

'You've made an offer I simply can't refuse.'

'You have one month, no more.'

'A month is a long time,' Pete said, 'but I guess I'll see you around.'

'I wouldn't bank on it,' Edmondson retorted.

Pete smiled and walked out.

CHAPTER TWENTY-NINE

'Terrible, terrible,' the Reverend William Dawson said, shaking his shaggy head from side to side where he sat behind his large desk with its 'In' and 'Out' trays – no computers for him. 'I was just speaking to him yesterday, after the church service, and then I turn on the radio to learn that he was shot outside his own house. Terrible. Just *terrible*.'

He and Robert Lilly, the latter white-faced and dressed in black as usual, were discussing the assassination of Joe Douglas, shot outside his own home the previous day, just after driving his family home from church.

'And, of course,' Dawson said, 'it was the brutality of it, as usual. Not satisfied with shooting him down in front of his wife and children, reportedly the assassin deliberately walked across the road to empty his sub-machine gun into the dead man's body. Just stood there, in front of his wife and children, and kept firing his weapon. Then he sauntered back to his own car and drove off as casually as if going shopping. Wearing a balaclava helmet, of course, identity unknown.'

'He had to be a Provo,' Lilly said. 'That's how they dress. That's their style.'

'Yes, I'm sure it *was* a Provo, Robert, but that doesn't console me.'

Robert sighed consolingly. 'Don't feel too bad about it, Reverend. Better men than Douglas have died and in truth he had something of a reputation, so we could be well rid of him.'

The Reverend nodded affirmatively, agreeing reluctantly. 'God works in mysterious ways,' he said, 'and you may be right. God knows, this town could do without men like Douglas . . . But his wife and children . . . How tragic.'

'I'm sure a visit from you would be a help, Reverend.'

'Yes, of course. I'll go and see them.' The Reverend leaned back in his chair and studied the ceiling, his normally keen gaze distracted. 'So what about those people asking questions?' he said. 'That radio reporter, Patricia Monaghan, and the newcomer, Pete Thompson. The ones we'd placed under observation. Anything new to report?'

'Yes,' Robert said. 'With regard to Mr Thompson, our suspicions were correct. Our observation showed that he was seeing Miss Monaghan a lot. Also, conversations overheard between her and him revealed that he was asking a lot of questions about you. Of course, you've nothing to hide – that's not the point I'm making – but it was clear that Mr Thompson, supposedly not involved in the conflict, was taking a surprising amount of interest in those who he felt *were* involved. Eventually, when I learnt that the supposedly uninvolved Mr Thompson had started working part-time for the Loyalist group, Red Hand, and that his work included regular visits to our home for troubled youths out in Antrim, I felt that this man could present a danger to you and so I had him checked out.'

'Why would he be a danger to me?' Reverend Dawson asked, his face a picture of rectitude.

'I think you underestimate your importance to the Loyalist community. You are, in fact, a major inspiration to the Loyalists and as such you represent a clear threat to certain parties, both Catholic and Protestant. This is a dangerous city and your life is in constant danger from those who would prefer it that you didn't exist. That's why I've always insisted that any newcomer to the Loyalist community – at least in the hardline areas, such as the Shankill – and anyone taking a particular interest in you, should be checked out. That's why I had Patricia Monaghan and Pete Thompson placed under observation – and I'm glad that I did so.'

'So what did you find out about Mr Thompson?'

'That his background was false. He was certainly born and bred here, in Donegall Avenue, and he certainly left at a young age to go and live with his family in Birkenhead. However, he never went to Australia and he never had that Australian wife who was supposed to have died a few years back. Pete Thompson is, in fact, Pete Moore. After serving an electrical apprenticeship in Birkenhead, he moved to London and joined the British Army, ending up, would you believe, in the SAS. Shortly after being transferred out of that regiment, he left the army and set up his own business, selling surveillance equipment. That business, also, is based in London. Moore acts, on occasion, as a freelance bodyguard as well, so between that and the SAS, I think we can take it that he's no stranger to trouble. As for his marital status, he's been married three times and is widely known to be shamelessly promiscuous. All in all, then, I think it's safe to say that Pete Moore – aka Thompson – *could* have been a danger to you, though probably we'll never find out just what his interest was.'

'Why not?'

'Because he left the Shankill Road a few days back – reportedly fleeing from an assassination attempt against him. We know that he took a plane back to London. Given that assassination attempt, I doubt that he'll return.'

'The Provos must have found out about his work for Red Hand,' Reverend Dawson said.

'Yes,' Robert said, 'I would think so . . . And now that he's on their hit list, he won't be able to return to Belfast.'

'And Patricia Monaghan?'

'I now think her interest in you was strictly professional; though clearly she would have enjoyed finding dirt on you – which, of course, she did not. Just to be safe, however, I kept her under observation. Interestingly enough, I received a phone call a couple of hours ago, telling me that she had just been observed leaving her flat in Stranmillis, accompanied by a couple of men. They all got into a red Ford Cortina and were driven away. We don't know who those men were.'

'Could have been anyone,' Reverend Dawson said.

'Quite,' Robert said.

The Reverend nodded and smiled, then clasped his hands behind his shaggy head and stared up at the ceiling . . . perhaps at the heavens.

'Well, Robert,' he said eventually, with satisfaction, 'it would seem that at least for the moment our troubles are over.'

'I think so,' Robert said.

'Thank you, Robert.'

'My pleasure,' Robert said. 'Now I have to leave to attend to some urgent business.'

Robert walked out.

CHAPTER THIRTY

As Billy Boy opened the rear door of the red Ford Cortina to let Patricia Monaghan out, he could hardly credit what was going on. For a start, he had been sent back to Belfast to collect this Catholic bitch by the very man he had tried to assassinate the previous year, when he'd planted a bomb under his vehicle – unfortunately on the wrong side, killing only the driver. A few days before that, he had forced his way into the Stranmillis apartment of the woman now walking beside him, to terrorize her with the cold steel of his pistol – after giving her a good hammering, of course. Luckily, he had been wearing his balaclava at the time, so the bitch, now passing the gatehouse with him, heading for the big house nestled between green hills in the mountains of Mourne, did not recognize him.

Hardly able to credit this fact, Billy Boy also had a problem in accepting that he was now, at least temporarily, doing work for a hated Provo commander – one widely reported in Belfast to be dead, killed outright in that car-bomb explosion. Sean Farrell, however, was alive, if not well, and now in charge of the Catholic contingent up in the big house. He had not, of course, personally ordered Billy Boy to collect Patricia Monaghan, Mrs Farrell, from her flat – Alf Green had done that – but Billy Boy still felt that he was doing a job for Sean Farrell and he deeply resented it.

He was, however, amused by the thought that Farrell did not know that it was he, Billy Boy, who had terrorized Farrell's wife, this so-called Patricia Monaghan, and also tried to assassinate Farrell.

Innocence is bliss, Billy Boy thought sardonically as he led an anxious Patricia Monaghan up the steps to the door of the big house, then opened the door to let her in. Before she stepped inside, she turned around to gaze back over the soaring mountains, now wreathed in mist, as if she was seeing them for the last time and wanted to remember them. *She must be fucking anxious*, Billy Boy thought. *She must be wondering what's going on.* Pleased, he gently pushed her into the house, then closed the door behind both of them.

'This way,' Billy Boy said.

As he led her up the stairs, still amused by the thought that she didn't know who he was – her former evil tormentor – he amused himself further by recalling the expression on Joe Douglas's face before the first bullet felled him. Joe had looked as startled as a rabbit in a headlight, his eyes growing as big as two spoons, his mouth open to protest. In fact, he *had* protested. 'No!' he had shouted pitifully, before the first shell blew his chest apart and slammed him backwards onto the road in front of his car. His wife and kids had started screaming as he fell to the ground and Billy Boy had then advanced across the road to finish them all off. He couldn't do it, of course. It was *a mother* in that car. Billy Boy, being a good Protestant lad, could not shoot down the mother of two kids. Instead, feeling frustrated, he had emptied the magazine of his sub-machine gun into the already dead Joe Douglas, making his body virtually leap off the road before subsiding again. Billy Boy had walked away from shredded meat, feeling highly satisfied.

Now, as he led Patricia Monaghan – Mrs Toffee-Nosed Farrell – into an upstairs room where Alf Green and Sean Farrell were seated behind an oakwood desk, he realized that he had taken a hell of a risk and that the risk had paid off. Jack Peel and Joe Douglas were both dead and Alf Green, assuming some Provos had done it, had elected Billy Boy as his right-hand man. Once the 'big one' was over, when Belfast city was secured and carved up between the Prods and the Fenians, Billy Boy would turn his weapon on Alf Green and take over the whole show. He would then turn his army against the Provos – against Sean Farrell – and eventually take over the whole city. It was as easy as pie, like.

'Hello, Sean,' Patricia Farrell said as she stopped in front of the desk and cast a startled look at Alf Green. Returning her gaze to the scarred face of her husband, she said, 'I must be hallucinating. What the hell's going on, Sean?'

Farrell nodded to the chair in front of the desk. 'Take a seat, Pat.'

Mrs Farrell sat in the chair in front of the desk, her head moving slightly left and right as her eyes went from one man – a Loyalist Red Hand leader – to the other – formerly, before his assumed death, a top dog in the Provos. Billy Boy, amused by her consternation, remained by the door, listening intently.

'We have a temporary arrangement,' Sean Farrell said, referring to himself and Alf Green, 'and that's all you need to know for now. We want to ask you some questions.'

'*We?*'

Farrell smiled, but his eyes remained dead, even as his gaze remained steady. 'I repeat, we want to ask you some questions. That's why we brought you here.'

'So ask,' Patricia replied, showing little warmth for her husband. 'I can't go anywhere, can I?'

Farrell nodded, clearly agreeing with her, and her spine stiffened visibly.

'You were involved with one Pete Thompson,' he said.

'Yes,' Patricia said. 'At your request.'

'Yes, you were involved as you were involved with all the others . . . to pick up information. So what did you learn from him?'

'Not much. I've already told you all I learnt. He seemed obsessed with knowing about the Reverend William Dawson and, given his stated non-involvement, I thought that was odd. However, apart from his background, which you know already, I didn't find out any more about him.'

'Are you still seeing him?'

'No.'

'Why not?'

'Because as usual I was using my professional name – not my married name – and then he found out that I was married to you. Of course, like many he thought that you were dead, killed by the Loyalists, and though I didn't disillusion him, he was outraged that I hadn't told him that my supposedly late husband had been a leading light in the Provos.'

'Since supposedly he wasn't involved,' Sean said, 'didn't you wonder why that concerned him?'

'Yes, I did. In fact, that's what caused the break. I was suspicious and I raised the subject with him, but I didn't get anywhere. He only said that I should have told him because it mattered a great deal who he was seen with along the Shankill. He was really outraged by that.'

'And did this concern you, Pat?'

'Of course it concerned me. I reminded him of all the questions he'd asked me about Reverend Dawson, about his growing obsession with Dawson's supposed connection to the Loyalist paramilitaries, and then – since I was convinced of it myself – I accused him of being more than he seemed.'

'And that's when you broke up?'

'Yes. He didn't answer the questions in any way, shape or form. He simply lost his temper, told me to get fucked, then kicked his chair back and stormed out of the pub. He'd previously told me that he was returning to London for a few days – and certainly I haven't seen him since.'

'And probably won't again,' Sean Farrell said, though he looked, according to Billy Boy's reckoning, to be relieved by the answers his wife had given. 'Pete Thompson has definitely returned to London and isn't likely to come back.'

'What makes you think that?'

'Because we know who he is and he's not what he seems. That fucker's never been to Australia in his life – he's lived most of his life in England – and, even worse, he was once a member of the SAS.'

'Jesus!' Mrs Farrell exclaimed softly.

'We believe he was here on a mission,' Sean continued. 'On behalf of the fucking Brits. We believe he came here to pick up some intelligence on a matter that's of vital importance to us. Unfortunately, one of our men – that bloody eejit, Joe Douglas – invited him to do some work for him, including the maintenance of computers that contained our own intelligence . . . almost certainly the intelligence he was after. Whether or not he found anything we still can't say for sure, but we're convinced that his return to England signals that he did.'

'Jesus!' Mrs Farrell exclaimed again. 'So how did you find out about him?'

'We can't say,' Alf Green said, speaking for the first time.

So it's a Protestant source, Billy Boy thought. *It came from one of our own. That's one up for us.*

'We tried to stop him from going back,' Alf Green added, 'but the bastard eluded us. Now he's back in London, safe and sound, but at least he's out of the picture.'

At that moment, the door behind Billy Boy opened and a man resembling an undertaker entered the room. Billy Boy did a double take. He could hardly believe his fucking eyes. The man entering was the Reverend William Dawson's assistant, the white-faced, black-suited Robert Lilly. He walked across the room as if he owned it, glanced at Farrell's wife, then turned to face the men behind the table, his gaze focused on Farrell.

'Well, is she clean?' he asked.

'Yes,' Farrell said. 'We think so.'

'Good,' Lilly said. 'For your sake, I'm glad to hear that. But she still can't go back until the big one's over. She has to remain here.'

'What big one?' Mrs Farrell asked.

'That's not your concern.'

'Do you mean I'm going to remain here as a prisoner?'

'Temporarily,' Lilly said. He turned back to Farrell. 'Because of Pete Thompson – sorry, Pete Moore – we're going to have to bring the operation forward. If he's found out about it, which we assume he has, we have to move before he can stop it.'

'How soon?' Farrell asked.

'The day after tomorrow,' Lilly replied.

'We'll be ready,' Alf Green said.

It was him, Billy Boy thought. *He's the one who found out about Moore and he's the bastard in charge. Well, I'll be damned! What a turn-up . . .*

'So this was your source?' Mrs Farrell asked, nodding in the direction of Robert Lilly. 'The Reverend Dawson's assistant?'

'Yes,' Lilly said.

'And does Dawson know about this?' Mrs Farrell asked, looking directly at Lilly.

'No,' Lilly said. 'We do all our work on computer networks these days and the good Reverend, while being bright otherwise, isn't into computers. Our computer, as you know, is in my office and the Reverend trusts me completely. Now please stand up, Mrs Farrell.'

Mrs Farrell stood up, looking shocked beyond measure, as Robert Lilly turned to Billy Boy.

'Take her along the corridor to the next room. You'll find the door open and the key's in the lock. When she's in the room, lock the door securely and bring the key back to me.' He turned back to his prisoner. 'I'm sorry, Mrs Farrell, but this has to be done. The room has an en suite bathroom and food and drink will be delivered to you on a regular basis. When this job's over, when we're satisfied that we've succeeded, you can return to Belfast. Now please follow that gentleman.'

'What kind of Christian are you?' Mrs Farrell asked.

'A Christian with a vision,' Lilly replied. 'Now please go to your room.'

The woman cast a despairing, pleading look at her husband and then, seeing his impassive, scarred face, she turned away in disgust. Billy Boy opened the door and bowed mockingly as she walked out. He followed her the few yards along the corridor until they came to the open door. Mrs Farrell walked in. Billy Boy locked the door. He removed the key from the lock, pressed it tenderly to his lips, then hurried back to the other room, dead keen to take part in the forthcoming strategy discussion about Operation Apocalypse.

Billy Boy felt like a big boy at last and the feeling was good.

CHAPTER THIRTY-ONE

The observation post was located high on a hill overlooking the big house in the mountains of Mourne. It was hidden under a hessian screen, with a camouflage net, supported on stakes, looped over one end of a hedgerow and held down with iron pickets and rope. It was a rectangular, long-term, top-to-tail OP with one end running under the hedgerow. Dug out of the ground with spades and pickaxes, it had four shallow 'scrapes', one for the observer, one for the sentry, and two as 'rest bays'. Of the two 'rest bays', one was for the man having a proper sleep in a sleeping bag and the other was for the man resting from guard or observation duties while remaining awake as a second observer and guard. A fifth shallow 'scrape' had been dug out of the middle of the OP as a 'kit well' for their equipment and weapons, including the water and food. The soil from the scrapes had been scattered around the ground a good distance away to ensure that no observer would see any difference in the landscape. A camouflaged entry/exit hole had been made in the hessian hanging to the ground near the rear end of the OP and a camouflaged, rectangular viewing hole had been shaped from the hessian and hedgerow covering the side overlooking the big house below. The view was clear and wide.

The three men in the OP were wearing DPM windproof clothing and Danner boots with Gore-Tex lining. They were not wearing hats of any kind. However, the exposed parts of their faces, necks and hands were smeared with stick camouflage, which blended in with the local foliage.

They had brought with them one general-purpose machine-gun (GPMG), a couple of M16 assault rifles with M203 grenade launchers, three 5.56 Colt Commando semi-automatics with thirty-round box magazines, a variety of hand grenades, ammunition for all the weapons, and Semtex explosive and firing devices. These had been

supplied covertly by the British Army HQ in Lisburn. Known as
the 'groceries', they had come from a secret dump that could not
be traced back to the army. For good measure, the groceries
included a Davin Optical Modulux image intensifier connected to a
Nikon 35 mm SLR camera with interchangeable long-distance and
binocular lenses. This could take photographs of those entering the
big house below, whether by day or by night. Also in the OP was
a plentiful supply of high-calorie rations and water, the latter to
be used for hygiene as well as for drinking.

The three men had driven here, carrying all their equipment,
in a green-painted van that was now covered with camouflage
netting liberally sprinkled with local foliage. Therefore, just like
the OP itself, it could not be seen from the air.

The three men were Pete Moore and his two SAS buddies, Stan
Remington and Mike Bentine. Like Pete, Stan was no longer with
the regiment and Mike, who was, had come along unofficially,
taking two weeks of his annual leave days and not telling his
superiors what he was up to. Like Stan, he was along for the
ride because he needed excitement. So there they were, Mike and
Stan, both in their mid-thirties, the former with thick brown hair
and a face slightly scarred from old shrapnel wounds, the latter
golden-haired and still smooth-skinned, an eternal schoolboy. They
both knew that if they needed help with this mission, it would not
be forthcoming. They both knew that it could end in their deaths
and that thought excited them.

They had been here for three days and nights, observing the
house below, photographing those who came in and out, taking
notes on their movements, gradually working out how the place
was run, who came and went when. Even more dangerously, they
had gone out every night, always after midnight, to make their way
down the hill and reconnoitre the whole building, both sides, front
and rear, checking the best way to get in and, more importantly,
the best way to get out. Now, in the moonlit darkness of the third
night, they were all set to go.

The idea was not to kill everyone inside – since, given their
numbers, that would have been impossible – but to cause havoc
and mayhem, making most of the men inside scatter, then to
demolish the building with explosives. They also intended killing
the leaders of the operation and for this purpose they had been

well briefed, with full descriptions and identifying photos of each individual.

Even now, after studying the photo of Sean Farrell for three whole days, Pete could not look at that scarred face without thinking of Farrell's wife, Patricia Monaghan. The photograph disturbed him, being a threat to his vanity, but he forced himself to burn that scarred face into his mind for the time when he and that man might meet for what would be a deadly confrontation. The other leader was Alf Green, whom Pete had already met during his few encounters with Red Hand leaders. The third, at least according to MI5, courtesy of the RUC, was a young man named William 'Billy Boy' Beattie. This young man who, in his photo, had wild eyes and a snarling grin, was responsible for some of the worst Red Hand atrocities and, according to the most recent intelligence report, had been next in line in the Red Hand hierarchy to the late Jack Peel and Joe Douglas. With those two dead, he was now high on the shit-heap and needed to be terminated. With those three men gone, with the other men scattered and leaderless, and, finally, with the building destroyed, it was hoped that Operation Apocalypse would be terminated.

'Okay,' Pete said, during their final meeting in the OP at ten in the evening. 'Let's go over it once more.' He glanced at each man in turn, searching for bored resentment, but both of them, disciplined in the SAS, just nodded agreement. 'There are guards front and rear, so they have to be silently dispatched before we can do anything else. You, Stan, will advance down the hill and set up the GPMG to cover the front of the building. You'll also have your M16 and grenade launcher at the ready. Mike and I will leave you there and then advance all the way to the front grounds, where we'll dispatch any guards in our path. With those men silenced, we'll make our way round the back of the building and dispatch the guards we find there. According to our intelligence most of the other men are in the basement and, as we've already seen from our reconnaissance, there are windows on all four walls of the basement, all the way around the building. Mike and I will fix bombs with timers to each of those windows, each with enough explosive to cause considerable damage inside and force those not wounded or killed by the blast to flee the premises. Once the bombs go off, Mike and I will enter the building from the rear, taking advantage of the confusion inside. Most of the men in the basement – those not wounded or killed – will attempt to escape by the front door or the smashed side windows of the basement, which will bring them all out onto the front lawn. You, Stan, will decimate them with broad-arc fire from your GPMG and then alternate between that and the grenade launcher. Since you'll be on the hill, and in total darkness, they'll have difficulty in seeing you and, once they do, they'll probably not guess that it's one man alone and, imagining it's a full-scale siege, will almost certainly scatter into the hills. Meanwhile, Mike and I will attempt to clear the building, with particular emphasis on the leaders of the pack. Our time limit will be exactly twenty minutes from the first explosions, so at that point you, Stan, will stop firing your GPMG and grenade launcher, enabling us to leave the building by the front exit without you scoring an own goal by firing accidentally at us. Once we've left the building, you'll give us covering fire until we get back to your position. By that time, we'll have placed more timed bombs inside the building and they should go off approximately ten minutes after we reach you. With the building ablaze – and, hopefully, the leaders of the pack dispatched – we'll make our way back to the OP, hurriedly dismantle it and cover up all traces of it, then get the hell out of here in that van . . . Any questions?'

'Yeah,' Mike said, rising up slightly to get a better view over Pete's shoulder. 'Who the hell's that down there, just getting out of that car?'

Turning around to look through the rectangular viewing hole of the OP, Pete saw a black-suited man emerging from a silvery-grey Volvo. Unable to see him clearly from this distance, in the moonlit darkness, he picked up his binoculars to study him more closely. Just before the man turned his back to walk towards the building, Pete saw, with a shock, that it was the Reverend Dawson's assistant, Robert Lilly.

'Well, I'll be damned,' Pete whispered. 'So *that*'s who's responsible!'

'What's that?' Stan asked.

Pete watched Robert Lilly enter the building, then he lowered the binoculars to his lap. 'That's a man with a computer,' he said. 'That's all I can tell you . . . Except that I want him taken out. He's as thin as a reed, as pale as a corpse, and wears a black

suit with shirt and tie. He's an undertaker – you'll recognize him
when you see him – and I want him dispatched.'

'So let's go do it,' Mike said.

It took them another fifteen minutes to pack their bergen
rucksacks, check their weapons and reapply their stick makeup,
darkening their faces until they merged with the night. They were
just humping the rucksacks onto their backs when they heard
another car approaching along the road below. Looking back
down through the viewing hole, again using his binoculars, Pete
saw two more people getting out of a red Ford Cortina. One of
them was Patricia Monaghan, or Farrell, and the other was the
young man known as William 'Billy Boy' Beattie.

'Shit!' Pete whispered, genuinely shocked.

'What is it *this* time?' Stan asked.

'Fuck,' Pete said, lowering the binoculars to the ground and
turning round to face his two friends. 'One of them is that Red
Hand psychopath, Billy Boy Beattie – the one whose photo you've
seen – and I want that little bastard taken out. Unfortunately, the
other's a woman and I want her alive.'

'Why?' Stan asked pragmatically.

'Because we don't kill women,' Pete said.

'That's your excuse,' Stan said. 'You know her, is that it?'

'That's it,' Pete said. 'Is that enough?'

'If you say so, boss.'

'I say so. Now let's go.'

Stan moved out first, crouched low to make his way through
the entry-exit hole with his packed bergen rucksack on his back,
his heavy GPMG and tripod strapped across the rucksack, a
5.56 mm Colt Commando semi-automatic rifle in one hand and
his M16 with M203 grenade launcher in the other. Pete and Mike
followed in that order, each also heavily burdened with a packed
rucksack and carrying a 5.56 Colt Commando semi-automatic. All
three men had a holstered Browning 9 mm High Power handgun,
a fighting knife and incendiary hand grenades, or 'flash bangs',
attached to the webbed belts around their waist.

Once outside the OP, they made their way down the hill, advancing crouched low, carefully avoiding the patches of moonlight. Stan
was out front with the other two at either side of him, their Colt
Commandos at the ready, prepared to give Stan covering fire if

necessary. They stopped at a point about three-quarters of the way down the hill, in the dip of a slight hollow that would give Stan some protection and with a perfect view of the grounds of the big house, its gatehouse about fifty metres away, at the other side of the country track that ran across the front of the property. From here they had a clear view of the lights beaming out of the gatehouse onto the lane, and of the many lights of the big house farther back, illuminating the front grounds, though the two men guarding the front door were obscured in deep shadow.

While Pete and Mike kept watch, Stan released the webbing holding the GPMG onto the rucksack, then lowered the heavy weapon to the ground and slipped the rucksack off his shoulders. He opened his tripod, fixed it securely to the ground, then attached the GPMG to it. Opening the rucksack, he withdrew several 200-round belts of 7.62 mm cartridges, piled them up beside him, then inserted the top one into the GPMG. This task completed, he checked his lightweight breech-loading M203 grenade launcher, placed it on the ground beside him, then spread a dozen buckshot grenades around it. Now ready, he took up his firing position behind the GPMG and raised his right thumb in the air.

Pete returned the gesture, then he and Mike made their way down the rest of the hill, still at the crouch, and advanced across the track with extreme care until they were at the front wall of the gatehouse. While Mike pressed his back to the wall beside the door, preparing to rush in if necessary, Pete glanced through the front window and saw a single man inside, wearing dark-blue coveralls, slumped in a chair, his feet, in soft-felt boots, crossed lazily on the desk beside a telephone, his chin on his chest as he slept.

Using his right hand, Pete silently indicated to Mike that he should make his way up the left-hand side of the grounds of the big house to dispatch the guard on that side. Mike nodded and then moved past the closed door of the gatehouse to disappear around the side of the building.

After glancing through the gatehouse window again, to check that the guard was still sleeping, Pete made his way along the front wall of the expansive grounds until he reached the closed front gate. Once there, he peeked around the gatepost, saw that the guards at the front door were conversing with each other, so dropped onto his belly to crawl from one side of the gate to the other. Once safely on the far side, he stood up and advanced at the half-crouch along the rest of the wall, then turned left and made his way up that side, hidden by the hedgerow, until he was a few metres down from the front wall of the building. He stopped there, listening intently, hearing nothing but the murmuring of the guards.

Satisfied, he dropped onto his knees, lowered his Colt Commando to the ground, then used his fighting knife to quietly hack a hole near the base of the hedgerow. When the hole was big enough to crawl through, he sheathed the dagger, picked up his Colt Commando and crawled through to the other side. Standing upright, he inched along to the side of the front wall and peered around the edge.

The two guards had stopped talking and were now smoking cigarettes, both facing the front gate.

Mike was peering around the far side of the front wall, beyond the two guards.

Pete carefully lowered his Colt Commando and rucksack to the ground. Straightening up again, he removed his fighting knife from its sheath and then used a hand signal, indicating that Mike should advance on the guard at his side of the doorway. When Mike did so, slipping around the corner (he, too, had shucked off his rucksack) and advancing at the half-crouch along the front wall and ducking lower to avoid the windows, Pete did exactly the same, at exactly the same pace, hugging the shadows just as Mike was doing. They reached the guards at the same time, unseen, unheard, and then moved with dreadful speed and precision.

Each threw an armlock around his unsuspecting victim, choking off his breath and preventing him from screaming, then jerked his head back and raised the locking arm just enough to enable the blade of the dagger to cut the exposed throat with one quick slash. The guards shuddered simultaneously, as if having a fit, and were lowered gently, silently, to the ground as their throats gushed blood. They were then dragged away from the front door, in opposite directions, and rolled into the shadows of the high wall, where they could not be seen.

Pete's victim was lying beside one of the two front basement windows. Glancing down through that window, which was long and narrow at ground level, Pete saw a dormitory filled with men stretched out on steel-framed beds and either sleeping, smoking, reading or cleaning their weapons. Using another hand signal, Pete indicated to Mike that he should start placing his bombs all around the window on his side. When Mike nodded in response, indicating that he understood, Pete commenced to do the same thing on his own side of the building.

He hurried along to the corner of the building, picked up his rucksack and Colt Commando, then returned to the side of the basement window. Opening the rucksack, he withdrew one of the half-dozen small bombs he was carrying – Semtex explosive attached to a wooden block and wired to a timed detonator. Being careful to make no noise, and not exposing his body to the view of the men in the basement, he set the timer for fifteen minutes, then taped the bomb to the nine-inch-deep concrete window frame. After checking that it was secure, he glanced along the front of the building and saw that Mike was holding his thumb up, indicating that he had just done the same thing and was ready to move off. Pete raised his thumb in turn, indicating 'Okay', then he made his way back to the end of the front wall, turned the corner and went to the next window. There were three basement windows along that wall and he attached a bomb to every one of them, reducing the timing on each by one minute to ensure that they would all go off more or less simultaneously.

At the end of the side wall, he turned left again and was relieved that there were no guards at the back wall. Instead, he saw Mike advancing towards him. They kept advancing towards each other, attaching a bomb to each window they passed, until they met up at the back door. Pete attached two more bombs to the door and then they both turned and hurried across the back garden, all the way to the far end, where they took up protective positions behind the trees and waited for the explosions.

Pete checked his luminous wristwatch. The bombs would go off in two minutes.

Exactly two minutes later they exploded and all hell was let loose.

CHAPTER THIRTY-TWO

Patricia lay on the bed in an upstairs room in the big house and felt the weight of the world pressing upon her. She was, in fact, deeply shocked . . . Shocked that she was being kept prisoner here. Shocked that she had been wrong about the Reverend William Dawson and that his undertaker assistant, Robert Lilly, so reticent, so seemingly weak, was the brains behind this whole sordid business. Shocked that Sean had changed so much and that she, despite her reservations, could not cast him aside. She was deeply shocked by all of this.

Closing her eyes, she cast her mind back to how it had been when she and Sean were both younger. She saw him clearly in her mind, his face unscarred and handsome, his liquid brown eyes filled with love, his features moulded by decency. They had met through mutual friends and the attraction was immediate; when they first went to bed together, which they did quickly, without embarrassment, he satisfied her as no other man ever had and, probably, never again would. She had loved him desperately after that, could hardly breathe in his absence, and when finally he confessed that he was in the Provies, she accepted even that, despite her normal reservations. He was a believer, after all, not a hooligan with a gun; he was a man who took the long-term view and was searching for peace. So she had accepted it, convincing herself of his sincerity, and only when she found out that he was also on the Provies' war council, a leading strategist, did she realize that he was more than he had said and that he might well be dangerous.

Nevertheless, she still loved him and could not let him go and, aware of this, he soon started using her in ways that made her uncomfortable. At first it was simple spying, passing on information that she picked up during interviews, and she

managed it by throwing commone sense out the window and
fooling herself. It was harmless, she told herself, just bits and
pieces of information, but when some of those whose details she
had passed on were assassinated, she started putting two and two
together and wondering about it.

She raised the subject with Sean, asking if there was a connection,
but he always vehemently denied it. She knew that he was lying –
she really did – but she kidded herself that he wasn't. When he
saw that – the depths of her love for him – he started demanding
more of her.

Before long, she was not only passing on information picked up
from her interviewees, but specifically making contact with certain
men, practically making dates with them, in order to loosen their
tongues and pass on what they said to Sean. It was a kind of
prostitution and, although no sex was involved, it always made
her feel dirty.

Still she kidded herself, pretending that Sean wasn't using her,
that he genuinely loved her and was just including her in his life.
But then, when his car was bombed, when his face was scarred
and he turned bitter, he had asked her to start bedding certain
Prods to loosen their tongues even more.

She was shocked when he first suggested it, deeply wounded
that he could do so, but she loved him so much, she was so
frightened of losing him, that eventually she found no reason
to resist and she did what he had asked of her. It was another
kind of prostitution, this time involving actual sex, and it made
her feel as degraded as a whore forced into the business. She felt
that, but she still couldn't refuse him and it went on and on . . .
until the day she ran into Pete Thompson and found herself in a
quandary.

Pete Thompson . . . Peter Moore . . . Had she loved him? Not
really. She had stopped having sex with Sean – or, to be more
precise, he had stopped having sex with her – when she had
started taking Protestants to bed to screw gossip out of them.
She had started that way with Pete, doing her job, despising
herself, but very soon, to her surprise, she was depending
upon him to release her, at least temporarily, through sex,
from her helpless dependence upon Sean. Pete was good with
her, doing everything she demanded, despite his distaste for it,

and he helped her dissolve into herself to find the truth at her centre.

That truth was that although she still loved Sean, she had become frightened of him. Compared to him, Pete seemed harmless.

Yet duplicity was everywhere. It was in her and in Sean and in Pete Moore and they were all tainted by it. The duplicity was in this country, in its people, in the conflict, and she had shamed herself to make a contribution dictated by love – the love for a husband who was no longer a husband but a pimp, using her as his whore. When she came to this realization through her involvement with Pete Moore, her love for Sean became tainted by loathing and the fear he instilled in her.

Now, lying on this strange bed in this strange room in this strange house, imprisoned by her own husband after interrogation, she wondered what Sean would have done had her answers to his coldly uttered questions not been satisfactory.

She was convinced, by the urgent beating of her heart, that if Robert Lilly had ordered her execution, Sean would have complied.

The pain was excruciating. The knowledge seared her like a flame. Yet she knew that despite her fear and loathing, she still loved Sean Farrell.

She was thinking this when she heard a dreadful roaring from the level below, then felt the floor rock beneath her, shaking the bed.

Shocked once more, she jerked upright, opening her eyes, realizing that bombs were exploding all around the building.

CHAPTER THIRTY-THREE

The exploding bombs made a catastrophic din, coming one after the other in rapid succession to illuminate the night with jagged, silvery flashes and fill the air with flying debris, dust and billowing smoke. Instantly, even as the fading noise of the explosions gave way to the screaming and bawling of the men inside the big house, Pete and Mike burst out from behind the shelter of the trees and ran towards the irregular smoking space where the back door had been, releasing the safety catches of their Colt Commando semi-automatics while on the move.

As they advanced, they heard the distant, savage roar of the GPMG being fired by Stan, indicating that some of the men inside the building were already trying to make their escape by the front door and side windows.

Reaching the back door, which lay in smouldering pieces on the ground, Mike dropped onto his belly, aiming his weapon at the door space, prepared to give covering fire, while Pete entered the building crouched low, swinging his weapon from left to right. He saw two human-shaped shadows in the depths of the billowing smoke, both moving quickly, and he fired two rapid, short bursts, aiming at each man in turn. Both men were hit, shuddering convulsively, screaming, and Pete ran forward as they fell out of sight, hitting the floor with a dull thud. The men were dead when he reached them, both wearing bloodstained white smocks, and he realized that he was in the kitchen and had just killed the chefs.

'All clear!' he bawled.

Mike jumped back to his feet and followed Pete through the kitchen, through the dense, choking smoke. They escaped together through the door, into a corridor where the smoke was less dense. The corridor, which was empty, was located on the ground floor and Pete knew, from the intelligence report he had studied, that while most of the terrorists were housed down in the basement, where the armoury and stores were also located, the important people were on the upper floor and, judging from the recent entrance of Robert Lilly and Patricia Monaghan, were almost certainly up there right now.

Mike's task was to enter the basement to plant as many timed bombs as possible, with emphasis on the armoury, which if blown up would destroy most of the basement. Pete's task was to clear the upper floor before the important people could make their escape and before the armoury exploded. They had twenty minutes to do this.

Advancing steadily and surely along the corridor, still crouched low and repeatedly swinging his weapon from left to right to cover the doors on both sides, Pete came eventually to a set of concrete steps leading down to the basement. He could hear the chaos down there, men bawling, the wounded screaming. Smoke was drifting up the stairs from the fires ignited by the explosions.

Pete jabbed at the air with his index finger, indicating the stairs, and when Mike, with a nod, went down into the smoke, Pete continued his advance along the corridor, heading towards the front of the building where more chaos reigned. He opened each door as he passed it, kicking it open, dropping low, swinging his weapon from left to right, and though all of the rooms were unoccupied he threw an incendiary grenade into each of them, noisily blowing furniture apart and setting curtains on fire. Those flames, he knew, would spread rapidly to turn each room into a furnace.

There was, however, another flight of concrete stairs near the far end of the corridor, where it bled into the hallway, and as Pete reached it, two men rushed up the stairs, one in coveralls, the other in his underpants, both holding semi-automatic weapons and coughing smoke from their lungs. Pete fired in a broad arc, cutting both men down at once. They convulsed and practically jackknifed, then were punched back by the force of the bullets and tumbled back down the stairs. Pete unclipped a hand grenade, released the pin and threw the grenade down the stairwell. Then he pressed his back to the wall, slid down onto his haunches, his weapon angled across his chest, and waited for the deafening roar of the explosion before running on.

A man entered the corridor ahead, trying to escape from the smoky hallway, and Pete fired a short burst at his body and watched him falling away, his arms flailing wildly over his head as he slammed back to the floor. A second man, also trying to escape from the hallway, suffered the same fate. Then Pete stood up and hurried forward again.

He stopped when he reached the hallway. Though long and wide, it was filled with the smoke coming up from the basement. A lot of men were in that smoke, some in coveralls, others almost naked, some carrying weapons, others not, and most of them were in a state of deep confusion as they made for the front door. Stan's GPMG was roaring outside, obviously cutting down the men already on the front lawn, and some of those in the hallway had smashed the windows and were desperately, blindly firing back at their unseen assailant.

In the dense smoke and confusion, Pete went unnoticed as he turned right out of the corridor, into the hallway, and made his way, hugging the back wall, to the foot of the main stairs. Men were hurrying down the stairs, a few bawling incoherently, others carrying weapons and papers. Some saw Pete as he started upwards and they realized instantly, from the rucksack on his back, that he was not one of them. A pistol and a Sten gun were aimed at him, but he managed to fire first. Both men collapsed and went rolling down the stairs as Pete continued to make his way upwards.

Other men, seeing the rolling men, bawled warnings and turned towards him, but Pete unclipped another incendiary grenade and threw it over his shoulder. He heard the roar of the explosion, felt the blast across his back, then heard screams of pain, more bawled warnings, as he reached the top of the stairs.

A white-faced man stared at him, looking very surprised. Pete smashed the butt of his weapon into the side of the man's head, grabbed his shoulder and hurled him bodily down the stairs, then turned right on the landing. Some men were hurrying in his direction, not looking at him, carrying piles of papers and files, obviously important documents, so he fired a sustained burst, swinging the barrel from left to right, and saw them spinning away like skittles in a bowling alley as he moved on again.

Turning the corner of the short landing, he found himself in another corridor with windows on the left side overlooking a courtyard, and half a dozen closed doors on the right-hand side. Two men were blocking the corridor, down on one knee, aiming Sterling sub-machine guns at him. He spun backwards around the corner, back onto the landing, pressing his spine against the wall as the two weapons roared simultaneously, spraying the corridor with gunfire, peppering the walls with bullets that exploded the plaster and filled the air with flying debris and swirling dust. Pete unclipped a hand grenade, leaned forward and threw it blindly, letting it arc into the corridor. It exploded with the sound of clapping thunder, producing an even greater cloud of dust and a high, lacerating, inhuman scream. Pete stepped out and fired a burst from his Colt Commando, aiming at the two men already writhing on the floor, obscured in swirling dust and billowing smoke. They spasmed like epileptics having a fit and then sank into stillness.

Pete rushed into the corridor and kicked the first door open. He fell to one knee and took aim with his semi-automatic, preparing to fire at any man who moved, but taking just enough time to ensure that it wasn't a woman. There was only one woman in the building and her name was Patricia.

The first room was empty, but he threw in an incendiary grenade, instantly following it with another, hurling them in opposite directions to ensure maximum damage. He pressed his back to the outer wall as the two grenades exploded, one after the other, then, when the double blast had subsided, he glanced into the room. He saw curtains burning beyond billowing smoke and smouldering furniture, set to ignite.

Satisfied, he turned away, heading for the next door, but then he heard a muffled explosion from the basement, followed by another, much louder . . . then another . . . and another, until it became a whole series of explosions, a staccato roaring. It was the armoury going up (Mike had clearly made it that far), the ammunition exploding, each explosion starting another, and that dreadful clamour, which signalled the end of the building, was obviously heard by those upstairs.

Before Pete could advance along the corridor to the next door, that door was opened and two men came out. The first man, the youngest, was wearing an open-necked shirt under a bomber jacket, with blue jeans held high by braces to show off his badly smudged trainers. He had a Nike baseball cap on his head and his eyes were as blue and wild as a stormy sea. He emerged with great speed, spinning towards Pete, spreading his legs and holding a pistol in the firing position, his left hand holding his right wrist, keeping the firing hand steady. The man behind him was an undertaker – black suit, shirt and tie, his face white and gaunt – and he was sticking close behind the first man who, Pete knew instantly, was William 'Billy Boy' Beattie.

Billy Boy fired the first shot.

The corridor was filled with smoke and Pete had dropped to one knee, so the bullet went whistling above his head to hit the wall of the landing.

'Fuck!' Billy Boy said, lowering his pistol to get off another shot.

Pete fired his Colt Commando, aiming for Billy Boy's body, and the bullets shattered his target's chest, practically lifting him off the floor and pummelling him backwards, his whole body convulsing, into the arms of the undertaker behind him. The undertaker – Robert Lilly – stepped backwards, letting Billy Boy fall to the floor, still suddering violently, his legs kicking. Then the undertaker looked wide-eyed at Pete and said, 'You can't do this. I'm a man of God, my son. I don't think you quite understand . . .'

But his voice trailed off. He knew that death was unavoidable. He took another step backwards, opening his mouth to scream his protest, then Pete put a short burst into his chest, making him dance like a puppet on a string, turning this way and that, splashed in blood, his eyes agog, before he finally gave up the ghost and fell onto his back. He did not move again.

Pete walked up to Billy Boy, who was still alive, though clearly dying. He stared up at Pete, his eyes blue and wild, blood dribbling from his lips, and he choked and coughed and managed to say 'You fucker!' and then he went to his Maker.

'Fuck *you*,' Pete said.

He spun around to face the doorway, looked into the room, and saw Alf Green jumping up from behind a desk, aiming a handgun at him. Pete spun away as the shot was fired. That shot was followed by three others. Pete unclipped a hand grenade and

threw it into the room and then pressed his back to the outer wall
to avoid the explosion. The grenade exploded and Pete thought he
heard Green screaming, but as the flash receded and smoke poured
out of the room, he dropped to one knee. Edging his head around
the doorframe while preparing to fire his weapon, he saw Green
spreadeagled in front of a badly shredded smouldering desk, his
body bloody and torn. Pete saw no one else in the room, so he
jumped up and ran on.

He came to the next door and found that it was locked. He
blew the lock off with a short burst from his semi-automatic, then
kicked the door open, dropped to one knee, and prepared to fire
his weapon.

Patricia Monaghan was sitting upright on a bed and aiming a
handgun at him.

'Oh, my God!' she exclaimed softly.

'Yes,' Pete said, 'it's me.' He stood up slowly, holding his
Colt Commando across his chest and suddenly feeling unreal.
'I recognize that pistol,' he continued. 'It's the one you kept in
your bedroom.'

'But always unloaded,' she responded. 'This time it's loaded.'

'You won't need it,' Pete said. 'We're getting out of here. Now
get off the bed.'

'She won't do that until I tell her to,' someone said directly
behind him. 'Now turn around, you fucker, and let me see you.
I want to know what she sees in you.'

Pete turned around slowly, still holding the Colt Commando
across his chest, but otherwise being careful. He saw the scarred
face of Sean Farrell and then looked into his eyes. They were
brown eyes that would have been beautiful had they not been
so cold. They were the eyes of an idealist who had lost his faith
and become the creature he had formerly despised. They were the
eyes of a man holding a killing weapon and preparing to use it.

'Lower your weapon,' Farrell said. Pete lowered his Colt
Commando. 'Look straight into the barrel of my pistol,' Farrell
said, 'and get a foretaste of infinity before you actually experience
it. You're a traitor to your own kind, a Prod lackey to the Brits,
and you've come here to cause mayhem and destruction and you're
going to die. Goodbye, Mister Moore.'

Pete closed his eyes and heard the shot. The sound exploded

through his head. The real world was blotted out, he saw infinity, and then he opened his eyes again. Another noise had made him do that – a grunt of pain, a crashing sound – and he looked down and saw Farrell falling to the floor with half of his head torn off. His scarred cheek was now covered in blood and the other side was still perfect.

Pete turned back towards the bed where Patricia was still sitting upright, still carefully aiming the handgun at him. He saw smoke coming out of it.

'You fucking men,' she said. 'You fucking lovers of violence. You have your big dicks, your big egos, your schoolboy pride, your childish dreams, and you think you own the whole fucking world and can take over from God. But this is God's domain, Pete. It's His vale of sweat and tears. It's where He plays His grand games, using men and women alike, but it's the women He makes suffer the most and it's the men that He uses. You men use us the same way. You fuck us, then fuck us up. You make us whore for security, for the kids we need and love – though, God knows, I had none – and you create your damned wars and then fight them and let us pay the price. I paid the price, Pete. I loved that bastard and he used me. I met you and I thought you were different, but then you used me, too. You could have got me killed, you bastard. You knew that, but you still used me. But by that time I was used to being used and so I used you as well. I made you use this pistol, Pete. It was this before your cock. Without this, you couldn't have given me satisfaction and that knowledge destroyed you. You made mistakes because of me. You let your cock rule your head. When you did that, when you made your first mistakes, your love for me turned to hatred. Oh, yes, Pete, it was love! What you felt for me was love. It was never true love, not the love of a decent man, but it was the only kind of love that a man like you could ever hope to aspire to. You told me all about it, Pete – about all the women in your life, the ones you never could cleave to, the ones you loved and then left – and then, when I found out who you really were, I knew the lay of the land. A Prod who left home early and tried to cut off his roots. An Irishman who pretended to be English and denied his own history. A poor fucker who hardly knew who he was and tried to compensate for it. The Army, Pete. The SAS. Large adventures for a small man. You denied your wives and children, lived for adventure, for the instant, and then you came back here and used me, as you'd used all your women, and then discovered, to your horror and despair, that the exploited could use you. You loathed me for that, didn't you? You still wanted me, but you loathed me. So let me tell you that the man I've just killed is the man I've loved most. I loved him as a woman does – with total commitment, in all innocence – and he knew that and used me as you all do and so I put an end to it. That only leaves you, Pete – the catalyst; the one who brought all the threads together and tied us in knots – and when I've put a bullet through your fucking head, I'll turn this gun on myself. Fuck you, Pete. Fuck you all. Close your eyes, take a deep breath and think of England. It all ends right now.'

'You won't do this,' Pete said.

Patricia didn't do a thing. She was torn apart in a hail of bullets. She exploded into gushing blood, flying bone splinters, spilling entrails, her body convulsing as if jolted by a burst of electricity, her head flopping sideways. Pete saw it before he heard it – the dreadful roar of a Colt Commando – then he turned around and saw Mike standing behind him, still holding his weapon level with his waist, in the firing position.

'There's no time left for small talk,' Mike said. 'We have five minutes left. The basement's been devastated, the whole building's ablaze, and the fuckers who managed to escape are fleeing into the hills. Come on, Pete, let's go.'

Pete went for his throat. He dropped his weapon and tried to strangle him. Mike pushed him away, stared thoughtfully at him and then slapped his face.

'Fuck it, Pete,' he said, 'I don't care who she is. Get a grip on yourself. You brought me here to do a job and I've done it, so let's get the hell out.'

'Right,' Pete said. 'Of course.'

He picked his weapon up and followed Mike out of the room, deliberately not looking back for fear of falling apart. The pain he felt was overwhelming, the shame led to infinity, but he managed to follow his friend along the corridor and back down the stairs. Mike planted bombs as he went, determined to bring the building down, and then he led Pete across the smoke-filled hallway and out of the big house. The lawn was littered with dead bodies.

The GPMG had fallen silent. Pete glanced left and right at the surrounding hills, and saw men scattering through them. The big house burned behind him, the smoke black, the flames yellow, and the light of the conflagration, which looked beautiful, illuminated the night sky. Then the last of the bombs went off, bringing down most of the building, and they saw the smoke thickening with boiling dust as the roof caved in to make the walls collapse, sending sparks showering skyward.

They made their way across the lawn, passed through the gate, crossed the track, and then clambered up the lower slopes of the hill until they reached Stan's position. He was smoking a cigarette, his smile beatific, his weapon already dismantled.

'Fucking good show, boss,' he said proudly to Pete. 'Are we good boys or aren't we?'

Pete could muster no reply. Stan's words merely laid waste to him. He thought of Patricia Monaghan, of what she had said, and he understood, finally, beyond all shadow of doubt, that what she had said about men was all that needed to be said.

'Fuck it,' he said. 'Let's get out of here. Let's put an end to this mess.'

They dismantled the OP, hid all traces of its existence, then removed the camouflage from the van, climbed in and drove back to Belfast like commonplace men.

The big house, Pete knew, would keep burning and eventually turn into ash. That ash, which included the ashes of Patricia Monaghan, would be dispersed by the cold winds of Ulster and rise to the sky where, according to Christian people, God had dominion. Patricia Monaghan, torn by love and despair, might find relief there.

Thinking this, Pete closed his eyes and smiled. He was still alive, with a future.

Not too many had that.

CHAPTER THIRTY-FOUR

D ressed in a blue denim shirt belted at the waist and tucked into tight blue jeans that showed off her long legs, Monica was looking quietly beautiful. Her raven-black hair was tumbling down around her shoulders, framing her pale-skinned fine features, her large, almost childish brown eyes and those lips that could be either caustic or loving, depending upon her mood at the time. Her moods, as she had often told Pete, were entirely dictated by him and, therefore, were his concern. He was now willing to accept this responsibility.

It was the middle of summer and they were having a barbecue in the back garden of their house in Hampstead, just up the hill from the flat that Pete had given up a few months back, shortly after his return from Belfast. Friends had come for the occasion. Pete's kids were present. The air was filled with the smoke and smell of grilled sausages and baked potatoes and flowers that only grew in England – that small and insular, too powerful island.

Monica, an English rose, middle-class and proud of it, said, 'Good Lord, it's been a long time since we've done this and isn't it nice?'

'More than nice,' Pete replied.

He didn't talk much these days. He had nothing much to say. He felt at peace for the first time in a long time and that said it all. He and Monica were back together, he had nothing to prove, and he had lived the past six months like an astronaut returning to fresh air. It was a very nice feeling, redemptive in its small way, and he knew that he was not what he had been and now preferred to be what he had since become . . . A married man with children, growing older, calming down, not concerned because he had no war to win and with no yearning for flight. He would remain here, an immigrant, a stranger in a strange land, but this time not disguising the fact and, instead, taking nourishment from the knowledge of his strangeness and becoming healthy because of it. There were benefits to being middle-aged and constant, and at last he could see them.

'How does it feel?' Monica asked him.

'How does what feel?' he replied.

'Being here in an English garden, forking sausages, drinking beer, making small talk.'

'It feels pretty good,' he said. 'It doesn't seem like small talk. It seems like a very nice afternoon in the Lord's warming sunshine.'

'Do you mean that?'

'I do.'

'I worry about it, Pete.'

'Stop worrying about it, Monica. Just enjoy. Look at your kids and feel proud and drink your beer and get drunk and that's it. Have a sausage. Be happy.'

'You Irish . . . You're so fucking verbal. Do I sound crude when I swear?'

'You couldn't sound crude if you tried. But keep trying, I like it.'

'Do you like being back with me? You say you do, but I'm not sure. We're so different, you and I – different backgrounds and so forth. I talk up and you talk down. I'm prim and proper, you're common as muck. I like a sound, secure life, you like adventure and change. I come from a well-off happy family and you come from Belfast. We don't have a damned thing in common, but we're good for each other. I believe that, but I'm not sure that you do and the thought makes me restless.'

'Being restless isn't such a bad thing, so I'm not too concerned.'

'You'll run off again,' she said.

'No, I won't,' Pete insisted. 'I've kicked off my running shoes and cracked my toes and the feeling is good. We're different? Yes, we certainly are, but that's not such a bad thing. Trying to live with your opposite, trying to reconcile differences, can lead to good things. What the fuck? We're surviving.'

'That's my deepest hope,' Monica said earnestly. 'Oh, oh, look who's coming!'

The new arrival was Daniel Edmondson, Pete's old MI5 friend, and he entered the garden, having come through the kitchen, with all the aplomb of an ageing matinée idol who still knows his audience. He was wearing a neat grey suit, his old school tie, and black shoes polished to an immaculate glassy sheen. Grey-haired and disgracefully handsome for his age, he offered the kind of smile that most women would kill for and more than one woman smiled back as he walked through the garden. Still smiling, blue eyes twinkling, he took hold of Monica's hand and turned it over to kiss the back of her wrist.

'Charmed as always,' he said, letting his lips linger, then raising his head as if with great reluctance. 'It's been such a long time, dear. I'm so glad to see you both back together. Life seems normal again.'

'You smooth bastard,' Monica responded brightly. 'Here, have a sausage.'

'Not quite my style,' Edmondson replied smoothly. 'But I *will* have a drink.'

'We have beer and white wine,' Pete told him.

'I'll have the latter, dear boy.'

Pete poured him a drink, then walked him away from the glowing barbecue. He had observed Edmondson staring at the sausages as if he was seeing maggots. They stood together at the far end of the garden, gazing out over Hampstead Heath which, in the summer's silvery light, looked like heaven on earth.

'A lovely view,' Edmondson said.

'Yes,' Pete said, 'it is.'

'A far cry from Belfast,' Edmondson said. 'You must be glad to be back.'

'I suppose so,' Pete said.

Edmondson stared at him. 'Is that doubt I hear, old son?'

'I don't think so,' Pete said. 'I'm glad to be back. I feel better for living a normal life and waking up in a safe bed. I have no doubts about that.'

'So what is it, dear boy?'

Pete wasn't too sure. It all seemed so long ago. That big house in the mountains of Mourne had burned down, all the conspiracy's leaders had been killed, Operation Apocalypse, minus real leadership, had collapsed, and Patricia Monaghan had died

with all the others, turned to ash in the ruins. Pete had succeeded
in doing what he had been sent out there to do, but the memory
of Patricia Monaghan would haunt him forever and he would
live for the rest of his life with a lot of unanswered questions.
Right now, though, he didn't know what to ask and so he asked
nothing, making instead the only statement that made any kind
of sense to him.

'It's just confusion,' he said, 'because of things left unresolved.'

'Oh, really?'

'Yes, really.'

'So what's unresolved?'

'The Reverend William Dawson. I never worked out if he was
involved or not and you never told me.'

'He wasn't involved,' Edmondson said. 'His hands were clean
in that regard. A good Christian, indeed. A stout Loyalist – ah,
yes! He incited, and continues to incite, the Protestants against the
Catholics, but he had no direct connection to the paramilitaries
since, as he's often stated – correctly, as it turns out – he wiped
his hands of them a good many years ago. Also, he knew nothing
about his own computer system nor, more importantly, about
how his troubled youths were being used, or misused, in that
government-sponsored computer-training school he helped to set
up. The mastermind behind that was his assistant, Robert Lilly,
and Dawson, whilst certainly dubious in other areas, knew nothing
about it. I fear you had him all wrong, Pete.'

'I'll never make that kind of mistake again,' Pete said, 'because
I'll never go back there.'

'Don't bank on it,' Edmondson said.

Pete caught the sly mockery and was not offended by it. He
knew that Edmondson could not believe that he had changed
and probably thought that he never would. Smiling, he glanced
back across the crowded garden, at his family and old friends, his
children, the cats and dogs, the smoke rising up from the barbecue
to obscure – and romantically enhance – his wife's very English,
gradually ageing beauty and the hope in her dark eyes. She was
his hold on this country he had adopted and he loved her for
that, at least. He would never really, truly, belong here, but she
could help him to live here. He had come a long way for this.

'Another drink?' he asked of Edmondson.

'I think not,' his old friend said. 'I only came to be sociable. I hate sausages and baked potatoes and lettuce and holding plates in my hand. I'm a snob, I suppose – an English snob – though I have common friends. Are you one of those, Pete?'

'I guess so,' Pete said. 'Let me walk you out.'

'You're too kind, dear boy.'

Edmondson said goodbye to Monica, waved to some friends, then let Pete walk him back through the house, all the way to the front door. When Pete opened the door, he started out, but Pete called him back.

'So given all we learnt over there,' Pete said on an impulse, not really understanding what he was asking but compelled to ask anyway, 'who's now the most dangerous man in Belfast?'

Edmondson turned back to face him, looking thoughtfully at him, as if wondering where the question had come from and if he really should answer it. He studied Pete for what seemed like an eternity, though it only took seconds. Finally, with a judicious nod of his head, he gave Pete his answer.

'The Reverend William Dawson,' he said. 'But the Lord protects him . . . And the Lord is a Loyalist.'

Then he smiled and walked out.